Unconditional

Always Book 1

LEXXIE COUPER

The characters and events portrayed in this book are fictitious. Any similarity to real persons, living or dead, is purely coincidental and not intended by the author.

UNCONDITIONAL
Copyright © 2014 by Lexxie Couper

All rights reserved. No part of this book may be reproduced in any form by any electronic or mechanical means—except in the case of brief quotations embodied in critical articles or reviews—without written permission of the authors.

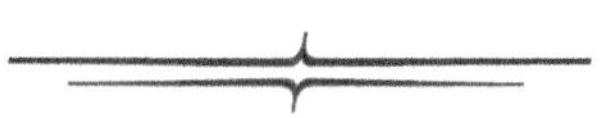

DEDICATION

For my dad and my brother, who both have Parkinson's disease and refuse to let it get them down. And for my mum and sister-in-law. Who love and support my dad and brother unconditionally through the good times and the bad.

CHAPTER 1

The Arrival

Australia was not what I was expecting. Sure, I hadn't even made it out of the airport, but still, where were the kangaroos? The koalas? Where were the hot guys walking around in Speedos? Where were the Tim Tams? Didn't those delicious chocolate cookies fall from the sky over here? I'm sure I'd read that somewhere? Or maybe I'd dreamt it.

I must admit, the second I'd learned I'd won my college's scholarship to study Environment Studies abroad—and by abroad, I mean a gazillion miles away from Plenty, Ohio, my hometown and the only world I'd ever known—I'd been experiencing weird dreams about Australia.

In one, I was dating a kangaroo that sounded like Chris Hemsworth. I remember waking in the morning stroking my pillow with the words "You had me at g'day," whispering through my head. In another dream, a shark called Bruce kept trying to take a bath with me.

See what I mean? Weird dreams. I chalked them up to

nerves. Winning the scholarship, partly funded by Plenty's only college, partly funded by the University of Sydney, was a double-edged sword.

On one razor-sharp side there was the awesomeness of winning the scholarship in the first place. Mind you, winning makes it sound like luck had something to do with it, which it didn't. Hard work, long hours studying, zero time socializing, movies missed, days and days researching, so many days I sometimes forgot what the sun looked like. *That's* what earned me the scholarship. That, and my passion for the environment.

I'm what my folks call a tree-hugging greenie. Well, my *mom* calls me that. My dad—who had grown up in Australia and moved to the US when he met Mom during a vacation in LA—has been dead for over three years now. Killed when a drunk driver ran off the road and struck him and our dog as they were jogging.

I was a tree-hugging greenie wrapped up in the unassuming guise of a twenty-two-year-old hometown girl who still had bangs and wore pigtails on the weekend. Who still ate peanut butter straight from the jar and loved watching *Sleepy Hollow* and *Glee* when she wasn't studying environmental degradation and its impact on wildlife the world over.

On the other even sharper side of the damn blade was the fact I had to fly a whole day to get to Australia. Did I mention I'd never been outside of Plenty? I *did* mention a drunk driver killed my dad and my dog only a few years ago, right? Leaving my mom a widow?

Did I mention my mom suffers from Parkinson's disease?

Did I mention I do as well?

No on the last two, huh? Sorry about that.

Yeah, I'm a shaker. But I've got it under control. Good meds, meditation, tai chi, and did I mention good meds? Add them together and I'm okay. Mom, however, isn't. And with me being on the other side of the world, who's going to help her up when she falls down? Which she does. Often.

She told me to go, that's why I'm here. She *demanded* I go. But being this far away from her ... God, I don't even ...

Sorry. Didn't mean to get maudlin. Long and short of it, Mom has Parkinson's. She's alone and I'm here because I've never seen her so proud as when I won that scholarship. How could I not go?

But now that I was here—and I was excited to be, I really was—where were the kangaroos? Even a stuffed one on a pedestal or something. And more to the point, where was my passport?

Oh my God, where was my passport? I was about to go through Australian customs in about twenty seconds and I couldn't find my passport. It was in my bag on the plane. So where was it now?

"Next."

I started at the deep, authoritarian command, and shot the man behind the counter a harried look.

I shook my head.

He raised his eyebrows and beckoned for me to approach.

I swallowed. Suddenly aware my fingers were shaking, I clenched my fist. Was it nerves? Or—

"Miss?"

The customs official was now frowning at me. A prickling pressure at the back of my neck told me my fellow travelers were probably glaring. Why wouldn't they be? I'd be glaring too at the idiot who was rooted to the spot and holding up the line that allowed you to enter the country you'd just flown over nineteen hours to get to.

I swallowed again. Cleared my throat. Squeezed my fist— crap, I really *was* shaking—and stepped forward.

The man behind the counter gave me an expectant look. "Passport?"

During the nineteen-hour flight over, I'd passed the time by imagining my first few moments in Australia. In my admittedly sleep-deprived fantasy, the customs official who granted me access would sound like the kangaroo I dated in my dreams. Yes, I will admit now, I have a thing for Chris Hemsworth. But how could I not? Have you looked at him? Is there a sexier, hotter guy on the planet? No, I don't think so. Anyway, the customs official of my dreams would smile at me and tell me I looked amazing after such a long flight.

I didn't, by the way. My hair was flat and greasy, my eyes were scratchy and puffy, and I'd managed to spill most of the coffee the flight attendant had given me somewhere over the Pacific Ocean, somewhere around three am, all over my shirt. Or maybe it had been two pm? Who the hell knew? Helpful tip if you're planning on any long-haul flights—don't wear a white T-shirt, no matter how cute you think you look in it. It's a bad idea.

So, going back to my mid-flight fantasy ... I'm greeted by a super-hot customs official who tells me I look amazing, just as a camera crew from one of those travel shows runs over and asks me if I mind being interviewed about being an American college student in Australia. Added to that, they also inform me Chris Hemsworth is in the airport and wonder if I'd like to meet him. He's researching a role in a movie about the plight of the dingo in the outback and has read my paper about the environment and native animals online and wants to talk about it with me.

In *that* fantasy, I had my passport.

In reality, I had no idea where it was. God, how could I lose it between the plane and—

"Passport, miss?"

I gave the official—who didn't appear inclined to say anything that sounded like "You look amazing"—a weak smile.

Would they arrest you in Australia for trying to enter the country without a passport? I suspect so. I opened my mouth. A sound that may or may not have been a strangled squeak emitted from my throat.

The official's frown deepened. I couldn't help but notice his right hand slipped under the counter.

"I've lost my passport," I said, although I think I may have mouthed it. For some reason, my voice had disappeared. Maybe it was with my errant passport? Perhaps both were on their way to Paris?

The man behind the glass leaned forward. "Please repeat that, miss."

"I've lost my passport," I said again. Louder this time. With less silent asphyxiation.

His eyebrows shot up. "Since you boarded?"

I nodded.

"What flight?"

My mind went blank. Oh God, I was doing an appalling job of representing the USA at this point in time. "Err," I said. "Big plane. Had a ... a kangaroo on the tail."

The man's forehead furrowed. "A Qantas plane?"

Relief flooded through me and I nodded, looking, I'm sure, like an unhinged bobble-head. "That's it. Qantas."

"So you've just disembarked a Qantas flight from ..."

His silence told me I was meant to supply the answer. "Plenty," I gushed. "I mean Dallas."

Tears prickled at the backs of my eyes. I ached for Mom so badly my heart felt like it was being torn out of my chest. What the hell was I doing here? Where was my brain?

"I'm sorry." I rubbed at my eyes with the backs of my

hands. My vision went that special kind of blurry that happens when you put too much pressure on your eyeballs, and I blinked. I needed to get a grip. Or a passport. A passport would be nice.

I wondered for a stupidly surreal moment if the traveler behind me would let me borrow hers. Only until I actually got *into* Australia. Then she could have it—

"Are you Maci Rowling?"

A deep male voice with an obvious Australian accent caressed my tired, overwrought mind, and I jerked my head around, my heart pounding fast.

An elderly gent, who had to be at least ninety in the shade, was standing at my elbow, holding what looked to be an American passport in one hand. In his other, he held a cane. Truth be told, it was the cane doing most of the holding, keeping the gentleman vertical.

"I found it on the floor in the line a second ago," he said, a friendly smile on his wrinkled face. "Think it might be yours."

He was old and feeble and holding a passport.

And if he knew my name, it meant it was *my* passport.

What else could I do? I threw myself against his frail body in a massive hug.

Knocking him to the ground.

Three hours later, I was allowed into Australia.

It's insane how long it takes to apologize sufficiently to an elderly gentleman you've just injured in your enthusiasm to thank him for finding your passport. Who knew it would be so easy to knock an eighty-two year old to the floor with a hug? I didn't help that my hug was pretty ... enthusiastic. Of course, *after* the poor old guy was taken away in a wheelchair, I received a rather stern lecture about my "enthusiasm" from the airport police. One of whom seriously looked like Russell Crowe. If Russell Crowe was fat. And older. And a woman.

And after *that* I received an even sterner lecture about passport security from the same humorless officials.

Finally, with the public humiliation over and done with, I was allowed into the country.

Only to wait at the luggage carousel, watching it go round and round until I was the only person left, with no sign of my luggage on the conveyor belt.

Thirty minutes later, I accepted the fact that my luggage —with all my clothes, including my Victoria's Secret bra and panties I'd saved for freaking months to buy just for this trip— wasn't going to appear through the clear flappy-plastic opening in the wall.

Yay.

I made my way to the service counter only to be informed the airline had no clue as to the current whereabouts of my suitcase.

"I'm very sorry," the cheery attendant behind the counter said, beaming up at me. "We shall contact you as soon as we locate it. Welcome to Australia."

Welcome to Australia? Yeah, right.

Suffice to say, I wanted to go home.

There and then.

Badly.

So badly I actually pivoted on my heel to head back toward the customs counters. And then I stopped when I realized I was being silly.

Okay, confession time. I'm not exactly emotionally … stable. I mean, I'm not insane or anything. In fact, I'm quite intelligent and at times grounded—Mom's word, not mine. But more often than not, I'm impulsive. I'm also sensitive, self-conscious, uncertain and … well, to put it bluntly—broken.

It happens. When you spend almost ten years of your life watching your mother slowly being devoured by a disease with no known cure, a disease that was robbing her of her ability to smile, her ability to cut her own food, button her own buttons, talk at a normal volume, have normal bowel movements—hell, have *any* kind of normal movement, even something as simple as blinking and swallowing—and you know one day that disease is going to do all those things to you, you get a little screwed up.

That's what Parkinson's disease does. It screws you. Messes with you. That's what it'd done to *my* family, at least.

I had to tell people Mom wasn't drunk at my father's funeral, that it was just her muscles refusing to allow her to walk without staggering about because her brain was betraying her. That messed with *me*.

I'd sit opposite her nightly at the dinner table, on edge—terrified even—that her throat muscles would stop working halfway through her eating, causing her to almost choke to death, an event that had happened at least three times.

It was bad enough for me to learn my mom had Parkinson's when I was twelve. Try being told when you're twenty-one that you have the same disease.

I'd been living with early-onset Parkinson's disease for a year now, and it wasn't getting easier. Twenty-two was not meant to be like this, it was meant to be lived large, partying, meeting new people ... not new doctors and specialists and medical-insurance representatives.

Jesus, I sound miserable, don't I?

I'm not. Honest. I try to laugh about it. I tell Mom I'm racing her to complete neural shut-down. Whoever gets there first wins. And what does the winner get?

A complete loss of dignity and—

Holy shit, sorry. I truly didn't mean to go there. It's a bleak place, my self-pity, and I hate it. Let's try not to go there again, okay?

I forced myself to turn back around, hitch my carry-on bag—containing a spare pair of panties, thank freaking God—farther up my shoulder, stride through the last stage of customs. I had no food to declare. No insects, reptiles, items made of wood or animal body parts. I passed over my declarations card to the smiling lady collecting them, and stepped through the gates and into the Sydney International Arrivals terminal, surrounded by excited people waiting for their loved ones.

It was then I realized I needed to pee. I hadn't peed since somewhere over Hawaii.

Oh boy, did I need to pee.

And the second I acknowledged I needed to pee, the more I needed to go.

Searching frantically for the restroom sign, I spied what I thought was the ladies' room and ran for it, head down, fist gripping the strap of my bag as if it were a lifeline to bladder relief.

So of course, when I slammed into something rock-solid but warm and firm as well, the first thing I thought was I was going to pee myself. Not, argh, I've just run into someone and I need to apologize.

I stumbled back a step, flinging the poor woman in my way a harried glance. And froze when that harried glance found not a poor woman, but a tall, broad-shouldered, stunningly hot—no, change that—stupefyingly hot, gorgeous guy with shaggy dark-brown hair hanging over equally dark-brown eyes so intense and beautiful and sexy and—

He wrapped strong fingers around my upper arms and steadied me before I could fall completely on my ass.

"Hey, I think you're heading into the wrong loo."

I gazed up at him and didn't say a word. I'd've liked to

have blamed sleep deprivation and jet lag for my ridiculous silence, but they weren't the culprits.

The guy holding my arms, keeping me upright, was stunning. Gorgeous. Hot. Like a brown-haired, brown-eyed version of Chris Hemsworth. Only sexier.

I didn't think that was even possible, but there you go. Tall, with a crooked grin that made my heart skip a beat and a goddamn divine body, all muscular and sculpted and perfectly proportioned with the broadest of shoulders, all wrapped up tight in a snug white T-shirt and snugger faded jeans.

And he had an Australian accent.

Oh boy.

I gaped at him, my heart thumping in my throat.

"Can you speak?" he asked.

I caught my bottom lip with my teeth and shook my head.

His eyebrows shot up. "You can't?"

"I can," I blurted, nodding this time. Talk about being a mess of contradictions. "I'm just ..." I paused, stopping myself from telling him I was falling in lust with him. Yeah, not exactly cool behavior. Gushing all over a complete stranger on the way to the bathroom? Welcome to Australia.

"I'm just ... desperate," I finished, ducking my head. I sounded like an idiot.

He gave a warm, friendly laugh. "To go to the loo?"

I peered up at him through my bangs. "Yeah."

That crooked grin returned to his face. As before, it made my body do things I wasn't entirely used to.

"You better go then." He stepped aside and held an arm out, directing me deeper into the men's restroom.

Oh my God, was I blushing? I shuffled my feet, frowning.

Devilment danced in his dark-brown eyes. "Something else you're desperate for?"

Something else? Was he serious? A guy that looked like him, asking me what I wanted? If I were the brave, take-no-prisoners kind of girl, I'd tell him straight up. *Something else I'm desperate for? Hell yeah, a kiss from you would be a start.* But I wasn't that kind of girl. I was a sleep deprived, jet lagged student with poor social skills and a disease that wasn't exactly high on the sexy list. Of course, I wasn't going to ask him for a kiss.

No matter how much the thought made my tummy flutter.

He studied me with a playful grin. "Going to tell me what it is?"

"A kiss." The word fell past my lips before I could stop it.

My face went cold as the blood drained from it. And then hot as all that blood rushed back into my cheeks just as fast. Holy shit, had I really said that aloud?

"A kiss?" he repeated, lifting an eyebrow.

Oh God, I *had* said it aloud. I stared at him, once again dumbstruck. What was I doing? Was I really *that* tired? Had to be. Why else would I say something so ... so ... *embarrassing?* I couldn't be flirting with him. I wasn't any good at it. I was an environmentalist dork with Parkinson's. As if I knew how to flirt.

Was I delusional? Was my brain finally betraying me compl—

Warm lips brushed over mine in a lingering caress of skin on skin. I would have melted on the spot ... if it wasn't for the fact I yelped in shocked disbelief and stumbled back a step.

Mr. Broad Shoulders laughed. "Sorry. Didn't mean to freak you out."

Just to make it clear before I continue, I'm not a virgin. I lost my virginity four nights after my sixteenth birthday, to my high school boyfriend—the quarterback, no less. How's that for both an achievement and a cliché? But since I found out I have Parkinson's, I've pretty much shut down any and all notion of romance. Who wants to get romantic with someone who's going to be a shaky mess in a few years? I can't imagine there are many guys out there willing to roll with that kind of burden, so I stopped putting myself out there. Which *might* explain my very active fantasy obsession with a married Australian actor, now that I think about it. Hmmm. Desire the impossible to substitute the denied. Makes sense, right?

I gaped up at my mysterious kisser—again. Heart beating way too fast, I pressed my fingers to my lips. "Why did you do that?"

"You asked." His grin turned wickedly playful, hinting at a dimple in his right cheek, and he leaned a little closer to me, his brown eyes holding mine. "And you looked so damn sexy with your mussed-up hair and coffee-stained shirt."

A wave of embarrassment flooded my face. I slapped my hand to my left boob, hurting myself in a rather ridiculous attempt to hide the stain he'd already pointed out. Why do we do that, by the way? Try to conceal something once it's been pointed out? Like the way mining corporations plant rows of trees around the boundaries of their open-cut mines, as if some greenery will conceal the massive gaping wound gouged into the planet by their machinery.

His low chuckle drew a frown from me. "Are you mocking me?" I asked, a distant part of my mind telling me I still needed to use the bathroom.

"No. Honest. The second you ran into me, I wanted to kiss you."

It was my turn to cock an eyebrow. I *love* that I can do that —it speaks volumes. Attitude from your waiter? Cock an eyebrow. Lip from your study partner? Cock an eyebrow.

Absurd claim from a stranger in a public restroom? Cock an eyebrow.

"The second?" I echoed.

His lips twitched. Christ, he was hot. "Okay, maybe the second after the second. When you realized who you'd run into."

Who I'd run into? Didn't he mean *where* I'd run into? The men's toilet rather than the ladies'?

I frowned.

He frowned in return. "You *do* know who I am, right?" he asked, curious conviction in his deep voice. Have I mentioned the sexy Australian accent? "That's why you asked for the kiss. Because of the way my sister met the prince?"

My eyebrows shot up my forehead. I'd like to say I had a hand in their journey, but my brain was too busy being stunned by what I'd just heard for any conscious direction to body parts or facial features. What did he just say?

"Prince?" I echoed.

It was obvious I had no freaking clue what he was talking about. Clear enough for him to pull a grimace. A sexy grimace, if that's possible to visualize.

"You don't know who I am?"

I shook my head. Deep in the pit of my stomach, a twisting tension curled tighter. A sexual tension. Or maybe it was bladder tension, due to the fact I still hadn't peed.

He let out an amused sigh, dragging his hands through his dark hair as he did so. "Fuck, 'eh? So you just asked for a kiss because ..."

The question hung on the air between us, looking for an answer. One I couldn't provide. What was I going to say? 'Cause you're really, really hot? Instead, I said, "Who *are* you?"

He flashed me that lopsided grin again, let out another laugh and ducked his head. "No one important," he said.

And then, before I could stop him, he closed the small distance between us, lowered his head to mine and kissed me again.

Longer this time.

Holy fuck, did he know how to kiss. He parted his lips, dipped his tongue into my mouth—when had *my* lips parted, I wonder?—and found mine with wicked ease, teasing it with a slow, lingering stroke.

The heat in the junction of my thighs fluttered and pulsed and throbbed in a way it never had before, and a soft little moan vibrated deep in my chest. Whoa.

And then someone cleared his throat behind us and I let out another yelp of surprise, this one a violent, full-body yelp involving jumping and spinning about.

A massive man wearing a dark blue suit and dark sunglasses was standing a few feet into the bathroom's entryway looking at Mr. Broad Shoulders. "It's time, Mr. Jones."

Behind me, Mr. Broad Shoulders—correct that, Mr. Jones —uttered an almost inaudible "Fuck".

He slid warm fingers up my arm, making me flinch, and I turned back to face him, completely mystified as to what the hell was going on.

"I have to go," he said, a grin playing on his lips. Lips that only a second ago had been on mine. "I'll make sure no one comes into the loo while you're in there, okay?"

And without another word, he strode past me, past the man in the dark blue suit, and out into the airport terminal.

Leaving me standing in a public restroom that obviously wasn't the ladies', with the moisture of his kiss a cool memory on my lips.

I gaped at the man in the suit, waiting for an explanation. It didn't come.

The man pivoted on his heel and stood with his back to me, muttering something into his shirt cuff.

If that wasn't a WTF moment, I don't know what was.

I blinked. Took a step to follow the now-absent Mr. Jones —could that really be his name?—and was suddenly hit with the need to empty my bladder. Again. With all the force of a wrecking ball hitting an outhouse made of paper.

I let out a little cry, doubled over, rammed my thighs together and did that ridiculous sprint you do when you need to go to the bathroom in a hurry. The one where your knees are stuck together, your jaw is clenched shut and your hands are balled into fists.

I hit the door running, spun 180 degrees, slammed the door shut, locked it, dropped my bag, yanked down my jeans and panties in one go and made it without a second to lose.

If it weren't for the man in the suit only a few feet away, I would have let out an *ahhhh* of relief.

But there *was* a man in a suit only a few feet away. A mysterious man who seemed to be connected to an even more mysterious man who'd kissed me because I'd asked him to.

What the hell was up with that?

A few minutes later, with the sound of the toilet flush a loud roar in the surreal silence, I emerged from the cubicle only to discover I was completely alone.

"Huh. Weird."

By the time I finished washing my hands, a string of men was pouring into the bathroom. They all balked at the sight of me just as they were about to approach the urinal, hands on flies. No one said anything.

With heat flooding my face yet again, I hightailed it out of there as quickly as I could. I tried not to look around for the mysterious Mr. Jones and the man in the blue suit, but how could I not? There was no sign of them anywhere.

That was probably a good thing. My first few hours in Australia hadn't exactly gone to plan, and truth be told, if I *did* see Mr. Jones again, I'd probably make a fool of myself and ask him to kiss me again. It had been that good. I still had the tingles and a fluttering belly to prove it. But whoever he was, he was gone.

Life back to normal for me. Well, as normal as it could be given I was on the other side of the world from everything I knew and loved, in the country of my father's birth without a single person I could call a friend and—

Okay, let's stop right there and get off the self-pity bus. I was here, in Australia, about to start the most amazing experience of my student life. No need for dramatics.

Hitching up my bag, I took a deep breath, scanned the crowd one more time for any sight of Mr. Broad Shoulders and then headed out the exit. I had to catch a taxi to Sydney University, my home for the first half of my adventure.

Two steps outside, I was almost knocked over by a man running with a camera in his hand.

"Hey!" I protested, staggering to regain my footing. It was never fun to lose your balance, especially when the disease fighting to control your body liked to throw you *off* it just for shits and giggles.

The running man didn't slow down. Nor did the one following him. Or the one after that.

Suddenly, it dawned on me there were lots of hurrying, rushing, sprinting men with cameras, all heading toward a stretch black limousine parked at the curb a few feet away. A limo that Mr. Broad Shoulders, AKA Mr. Jones, AKA my mysterious kisser, was now climbing into, the man in the blue suit guiding his head as he glared at the approaching wave of frenzied photographers.

Confused by it all, I frowned. Who the hell *was* this guy to deserve so much manic attention?

Camera flashes detonated around the limo. The photographers shouted. Most of the calls sounded like, "Oi, Raphael." Which couldn't be right. Who had a name like Raphael these days? The crowd around me surged forward, sirens wailed from somewhere nearby and then, in a moment of surreal calm amongst it all, a gap in the madness formed between me and the limo, and Mr. Broad Shoulders' stare met mine.

Met.

Melded with.

Fixed on.

Pinned.

Our gazes held, and in that gaze, an entire conversation took place:

I liked kissing you.

I liked being kissed by you.

Shame it had to end.

Ditto.

And then the man in the dark blue suit shoved the photographers backward and slammed the limo door shut, ending my ocular correspondence with Mr. Broad Shoulders, just like that.

I blinked.

The limo engine roared, the man in the blue suit hurled some rather unpleasant words at the horde and then pulled open the front passenger door and disappeared into the cabin.

A chorus of boos rose from the paparazzi—it's safe to assume that's what they were—although I still didn't know who they were photographing. Someone famous, obviously.

Someone famous who'd kissed me. In the men's restroom, no less.

I tracked the limo's path as it sped past me and everyone else on the sidewalk, my tummy twisting and knotting and fluttering and generally being all manner of unsettled. It wasn't until the limousine vanished around the sweeping bend a few yards away that I finally found my brain and grabbed the photographer nearest to me.

"Who was that?" I asked the sneering man trying to disengage my grip on his wrist.

"In the limo?"

"Yes," I answered, trying not to sound agitated. Who else would I be talking about?

"You don't know?"

I shook my head.

"That was Raphael Jones." The man smirked.

"Who—"

But before I could finish asking who Raphael Jones was, the photographer had shaken off my hold and was hurrying away, studying the small screen on the back of his camera.

I stood and watched the dispersing photographers and crowd, racking my brain to find any clue as to why the name should mean anything worthy of such frenzied excitement.

Nothing.

I shrugged. "Must be an Australian celebrity."

Deciding to google the guy when I finally made it to my campus accommodation (my iPhone wasn't talking to the Australian network yet, damn it), I headed for the first available cab, climbed into the back and gave the driver the address I'd be staying at while I was a student of the University of Sydney.

The memory of Raphael Jones's kiss sent a delicious little thrill through me and I wriggled deeper into my seat. So I'd been kissed by an Australian celebrity not even a few hours in the country. Not bad for a college dork from Plenty, Ohio, even if I do say so myself. It kind of made up for the otherwise dismal start to my adventure. Pity I was never going to see him again or I'd show him how an American girl did things.

Okay, maybe not, given how much of a twitchy, emotional wreck I was, but a girl can kick ass in her fantasies, can't she? It's not like I *was* going to see him again. Australia's a big country, after all.

Right?

CHAPTER 2

On Campus

The first surprise was I had a room to myself. I'm not sure why, but I thought I was going to be sharing. When I arrived at Mackellar House, one of the campus dorms at the University of Sydney and my home for the first half of my time in Australia, the very perky, chirpy and all-round friendly Foreign Student Liaison Officer, Heather Renner, met me at the bottom of the front steps. Heather was taller than me—I'm only five foot four—with long red hair that fell about her face in a mass of tight curls and made her look like a Pixar heroine. She grinned and hugged me and talked at five miles a minute. To be honest, I had trouble keeping up.

Our conversation went something like this.

Heather: "Are you Maci Rowling?"

Me: (opens mouth)

Heather: "You are, aren't you? Welcome to Australia. What do you think so far? No, don't tell me, you've only been in the country for a few hours, as if you've made up your mind yet. Bet it's different from Plenty though. I googled Plenty this morning when I was assigned to greet you. It's a small place, isn't it?"

Me: (mouth still open)

Heather: "Looks lovely. You'll find Sydney lovely as well. Well, certain parts of Sydney. The part you'll spend most of your time at. Have you seen much of the uni yet? Oh, when I say 'uni', I mean the university. Did you know that? I have a friend in the States and she keeps telling me she can hardly understand a word I say. Can you understand me?"

Me: (shuts mouth)

Heather: "Am I talking too fast? I talk fast, I know. Can you understand my accent? Anyways, I'm going to show you to your room and let you settle in. You've arrived during O Week, so be ready to party. Oh, I should tell you what O Week is, shouldn't I? O Week is basically a party for all the new students. O for Orientation. Get it?"

Me: (opens mouth again)

Heather: "Mackellar House has its own O Week party tonight, so be prepared. Maybe you should get some sleep beforehand. Are you jet lagged? You look jet lagged. C'mon, I'll take you to your room. I arranged a welcome basket for you, filled with Aussie stuff. Watch out for the Vegemite. And the toaster in your room will set off the smoke detectors if you're not careful. Maybe better to have pale toast. Do you like toast?"

Me: (mouth still open)

Heather: "God, listen to me. Carrying on when all you probably want to do is have a shower. The communal amenities here are really good. But be warned, they really mean communal. It's a progressive thing Mackellar House is trying out. Boys and girls. No one's complained so far but, boy, did it freak me out the first time a guy came in for a shower while I was cleaning my teeth. But then, I grew up with sisters. No boys in my family except my dad. Hey, your hand is trembling. Are you okay?"

Me: (shuts mouth)

Damn. It was time to crash in my room. I was shaking. I could feel it deep in my body. A quaking beyond my control. It happened when I was tired. Or stressed. Of which I was both. Excited, but tired and stressed. And still slightly obsessing over my kiss in the bathroom from the mysterious, hotter-than-hot Australian celebrity.

So while I really wanted a shower, what I needed was the chance to sit and be calm and still and take my meds (I may have missed one or two mid-flight, now that I thought about it).

I smiled at Heather, thanked her for the lovely welcome, passed off my trembling as jet lag and asked to be shown to my new digs.

"Absolutely," gushed Heather, obviously not worried that I was—in the nicest way possible—shutting her down. "Follow me."

She damn near pirouetted on the spot and then skipped up the stairs of Mackellar House.

I followed. It occurred to me Heather hadn't asked about my luggage, or lack thereof. Curious. Or maybe college students in Australia—or uni students, as they were called over here—were the same as college students back home: free of common sense in the face of impending responsibility.

The life of a graduate student was a strange mix of adult accountability and teenage angst and irresponsibility. On one hand, you were in your twenties—legally an adult. You had to decide all on your lonesome what classes to take, what time to eat breakfast, what time to go to bed. On the other hand, you still had to answer to teachers, still needed to justify why you hadn't handed in your homework, ('My computer crashed' really didn't cut it in high school, so it sure as shit wasn't going to pass at college) and you were still under the merciless control of hormones way more powerful than your brain.

Weird, huh?

Chatting the whole way, Heather led me through Mackellar House. She introduced me to everyone we passed. "Hey, this is Maci Rowling. She's the environmental student from the US. Be nice to her, 'kay?" And then she'd whisper tidbits about them as we moved farther away. "She's failing English Lit. He's spent the last five nights drunk. She's trying to seduce her History professor."

By the time we made it to my room on the third floor at the end of the hallway, my head was spinning. But in a good way. Apart from the accents, I could have been back home in Plenty. Uni life seemed very similar to college life—young adults flexing their independence after years of living under their parents' thumbs. In other words, chaos.

With a flourish, Heather pulled a key from her pocket and handed it to me. "Your key. Now remember, wonky toaster, communal showers and loos. Your uni info is on the bed, along with your welcome basket. Vegemite should only be smeared on lightly, not slathered on thickly. *Smear*, not slather. There's milk in the fridge if you want a cuppa. That's a cup of tea, if you didn't know. Do you drink tea? Oh, and don't forget that party tonight I mentioned earlier. Nine pm in the common room downstairs. The theme is underwear, which means you're going to be prancing around in your undies and bra for the night. How cool does that sound?"

And with that, Heather skipped away. Seriously. She skipped. Wow.

I watched her go, having a strange Dorothy in Oz moment, and then turned back to my room.

My room. Not mine and so-and-so's room. My room. Alone. I had a room all to myself.

It was nice. Small and uncluttered with a single bed on one side, and a desk, mini fridge, flat-screen television and armchair on the other. In between was a large window framed by a sheer blue curtain currently dancing on the warm summer breeze.

As I said, nice.

I took a step in, dropped my carry-on at my feet and drew a deep, slow breath. I backed up that step when I heard someone behind me shout, "Oi, Jones! You going tonight?"

A guy—a rather hot-looking guy, I had to admit—was leaning halfway out of the room three doors down from mine, hanging from the doorjamb by his fingers, staring at the closed door opposite me.

I frowned. For some reason, my heart beat faster.

The rather hot-looking guy grinned at me. "G'day. You the Yank?"

Before I could answer, the sound of the door opposite me being opened snagged my attention.

I watched as it swung wide. Watched as a tall guy with dark hair and dark eyes stepped to the threshold. Watched as he leaned an elbow against the doorjamb and nodded at the guy three doors down. "Yep."

I gasped.

The guy was Mr. Broad Shoulders, my mysterious restroom kisser. Raphael Jones.

My belly flipped and flopped. My breath caught in my throat. My heart punched away at my stuck breath, trying to take its place. My nipples ... Well, okay, you probably don't want to know about them. All in all, I was having a whole-body reaction to the sight of my bathroom kisser right there in front of me.

Holy crap, how could he be right there *in front* of me?

Just like in a movie—except maybe in even slower slo-mo —Raphael Jones swung his gaze to where I stood just inside my room. Surprise registered in his dark-brown eyes. Followed by confusion.

And then suspicion. The open friendliness that had been in his face vanished at the sight of me. Just like that. His jaw bunched. His eyes narrowed. His nostrils flared.

One second he was a relaxed guy with a hint of a dimple in his right cheek, the next he was glaring at me as if I was the anti-Christ come to cancel spring break. Except Australians don't have spring break and I wasn't the anti-Christ. The only thing I was truly *anti* was Fox News.

I swallowed, struck dumb.

This was the same guy that had kissed me, seriously kissed me, less than an hour ago. And now he was glaring at me?

"What are you doing here?" His voice was just as deep and sexy as it had been before.

"She's the Yank, Jones," my neighbor three doors down offered, laughter in his voice. "The one here on scholarship to study the impact of global warming on native wildlife."

Raphael Jones glared some more. Remember when I said earlier he'd somehow managed to make grimacing look sexy? Well, he was doing the same thing with his glare. There was a potent smolder to his expression now, an arrogant haughtiness that awoke a throbbing sensation in the very apex of my thighs.

The effect, however, was somewhat dampened by the suspicion *behind* the glare.

What had I done?

The thought maybe *he* thought I was a stalker popped into my head. He *had* been chased by paparazzi, after all. And

I *did* slam into him in the men's room. And ask for a kiss. I *still* can't believe I did that. Maybe he thought I was some kind of crazy fan?

"I'm not a stalker," I blurted. "Honest."

His hand—initially relaxed beside his head—curled into a tight fist.

What had I said?

He looked me up and down and then, with a low sound that may have been a growl, turned his attention back to Mr. Info Dump down the corridor. "I'll let you know later about tonight, Macca. May have to go to a function."

His accent made my tummy do weird things, like twist and knot and clench. It dawned on me no other Australian accent affected me the same way, not even Chris Hemsworth's. There was something about the way Raphael Jones spoke that messed with my head.

Which was stupid. I had enough things messing with my head, what with the Parkinson's and its inconvenient goal of turning me into a walking, talking tremor machine.

"Later?" Mr. Info Dump flicked me a curious look as if I'd grown an extra head. Maybe because Raphael had changed his mind about attending the party tonight after seeing me? Maybe because the tremors had hit me? Hard. My left hand was shaking pretty bad. I could feel it working through me, a bone-deep quaking I couldn't control.

God, I hate it.

Hate it.

Having Parkinson's sucks. Big time.

An itching sensation on the side of my head jerked my rather unfocused attention away from the guy three doors down and back to Raphael. He was staring at me. The glare was gone. Replaced by hesitant uncertainty.

My heart kicked up a notch or two. Our eyes met. The hint of a dimple flashed at me.

I swallowed, the memory of his kiss making my breath shallow. My head swam a little and, like it always does when my body and brain are under some kind of stress, the tremors intensified. At my side, my hand slapped lightly against my hip. Over and over again.

And then it happened. The thing I hated more than having Parkinson's disease. The thing I hated the most.

Someone becoming *aware* I had Parkinson's.

Raphael's gaze dropped to my stupid shaking left hand and his dark eyebrows instantly knitted in curiosity. "Hey," he said, his voice low. Worried. "Are you—"

I turned and hurried into my room.

Okay, it wasn't quite that perfect. I spun on my heel, banged my hip on the doorframe, collided with the damn door and almost fell into my room.

The last thing I heard before I slammed the door was Raphael Jones calling out to me. "Hey, American girl? Are you—"

I slumped against the door and rammed my left hand to my left thigh in a furious attempt to stop the tremors. It didn't work. No matter how hard I pressed my palm to my leg, my hand kept shaking. I'd like to say I didn't cry at that point in time. I'd like to say that almost a year of suffering Parkinson's, as well as ten years of living with it, had hardened me to the emotional devastation it wrought upon me.

I'd like to say that, but I couldn't.

Squeezing my eyes shut, I gripped my fucking thigh with trembling fingers and wept. Great, silent sobs of self-pity and loathing and homesickness.

Christ, what the fuck was I doing here? At least back in the States my friends knew what I had. They knew how to

deal with it, which was—by my request—to ignore it. Here
...

I slid to the floor, hugged my shins and buried my face
between my knees, my tears hot as they soaked through the
denim of my jeans. I stayed that way for a long time. Long
enough to finally get a cramp in my lower back and for my
butt to go numb.

My first few hours in Australia had been far from
auspicious.

If it wasn't for a knock on my door I may have stayed there
for the night. What better place to have an existential crisis
than on the floor? But someone *did* knock on my door. I felt
the three sharp raps vibrate through the wood and into my
back.

Swiping at my eyes with the back of my hands—my left
one still shaking—I pushed myself to my feet and opened the
door. I had no idea who would be on the other side, but I
doubted it would be Raphael Jones. If he were truly interested or concerned in this here American girl's emotional
state, he would have knocked earlier, right?

It wasn't Jones. Unfortunately, there was a part of me
disappointed by that fact.

Instead of Raphael Jones, a short man with no hair, a
paunch and a porn-star moustache covering his upper lip,
stood on my threshold. To his right was a grinning Heather.

"Maci," Heather gushed, wrapping her fingers around my
right wrist in what I assume was meant to be a friendly form
of contact. "You didn't tell me your luggage got lost by
Qantas. So I almost told Mr. Reuben here—is that right?" She
cast the bald man beside her a dubious look. "Is it 'Mr.
Reuben'? I thought that's what you said." With a smile at the
nodding man, she turned her kilowatt enthusiasm back to me.
"Anyway, I almost told him to go away. We get all sorts of

weirdos trying to get into the campus houses. Not that you're a weirdo, Mr. Reuben. You're *not* a weirdo, are you?"

For a frozen moment, silence reigned. I waited for Mr. Reuben to say something. Mr. Reuben didn't say *anything*. He appeared too shell-shocked by Heather to utter a word. For her part, Heather studied him with what may have been suspicious anticipation or enthusiastic joy. Honestly, she looked like a Beagle puppy that couldn't decide if it wanted to play, bay or grab the hem of your pants and shake it about.

Silence stretched on.

And then Heather laughed. "Of course you're not. You work for Qantas."

At the word Qantas, something clicked inside my jet lagged, med-deprived, sleep-deprived, dignity-deprived brain.

Qantas. Luggage.

I looked down at Mr. Reuben's feet and sure enough, there was my suitcase in the same condition as the last time I'd seen it. No broken zipper, no clothes or Victoria's Secret undergarments poking out the sides. Just my suitcase—a shiny silver super-light hard-shell thing Mom had bought for me as a celebratory gift when I'd won the scholarship. Undamaged. Intact. Here.

"We located your luggage," Mr. Reuben said gruffly. "It had been incorrectly placed with the luggage from First Class."

I lifted my gaze from my shiny suitcase to the balding man beside Heather.

His responding smile was contrite. "On behalf of Qantas Australia, may I extend my sincere apologies for any inconvenience this error has caused you."

Before I could say a word, he shot Heather a fearful sideways look. "Can I leave now? Alone, I mean? Without you walking me out?"

Heather gave him a toothy smirk, and for the first time since meeting her, I suspected there was something else altogether behind the perky, almost ditzy front. Hmmm. Color me intrigued.

"Of course you can go, Mr. Reuben," she said, patting him on the forearm. "But don't you think you should get Maci to sign that clipboard in your hand first?"

I suppressed a laugh. She had the poor guy completely frazzled.

With a grimace—one nowhere near as sexy as Raphael Jones's earlier grimace, I can tell you that—Mr. Reuben held said clipboard out to me, withdrawing a blue pen from his shirt pocket as he did so. "Just sign at the cross," he mumbled.

Giving Heather a small smile, I took the offered pen with my right hand—the one not shaking, thank God—and signed my name in the appropriate place.

"Thanks, Miss Rowling." Mr. Reuben retrieved his pen and tucked the clipboard under his arm. "Miss Renner," he said with a harried nod at Heather.

Then he was gone, damn near scurrying along the corridor away from us both.

I gave up trying to hold back my giggle.

Heather grinned at me. "Did he seem scared to you? Why do you think he was scared?" Devilish delight danced in her eyes. "Maybe he's never met an American before?"

I laughed. Perhaps it was the joy of something finally going right for me since touching down, maybe it was the fact Heather was proving to be lots of fun. Whatever it was, I allowed myself to relax.

Unfortunately, occasionally when I laugh, I snort. Nothing too loud or animalistic, but a snort all the same. Of course, that was the *exact* moment Raphael Jones opened his door and stepped into the space behind Heather.

Great.

Awesome.

Fan-freaking-tastic.

Once again, our eyes met. Once again, the thoroughly disturbing memory of our kiss played with my head. I stopped laughing and just stared at him.

He stared back.

"Raph!" Heather's exuberant cry filled the corridor. "Have you met Maci Rowling yet? She's from America. Do you remember the American student I mentioned last month? This is her. Maci, this is Raphael Jones. Have you heard of him?"

Raphael Jones regarded me with an expression they should put in the dictionary as a perfect example of *ambiguous.* "We've met."

Heather damn near gave herself whiplash looking at me. "You have?"

Raphael nodded. A single nod that spoke volumes.

I bristled. No, more than bristled. I got angry. I don't normally do angry, but Raphael Jones, *Raph* Jones, had pissed me off. What the fuck was this guy's problem? One minute he's sticking his tongue down my throat, smiling at me like we're best friends, eye-flirting with me through a crowd of paparazzi, and the next he's regarding me like I was some kind of serial killer.

Jutting my hip at a snarky angle, I crossed my arms over my breasts and, gaze holding his, said, "We have met. In the men's restroom at the airport." I cocked an eyebrow. "Where he kissed me."

An unexpected glower fell over Raph's face.

I refused to look away, clenching my left hand into a hard ball. I'd be damned if I was going to let anyone see I had the shakes.

"Kissed?" Heather squeaked. Just that one word. If I wasn't so furious at Raph's peculiar attitude, I'd be impressed I'd managed to curb her constant stream of chatter.

But I was irritated. I didn't care who the fuck Raph was, he didn't have the right to be so goddamn—

"Kissed," he echoed, his voice a low purr as indecipherable as his scowl. "One of the best I've had, I have to admit."

My heart smashed up into my throat. An insane horde of maniacal butterflies threw a dance party in my belly. *One of the best he's had?*

Heather gaped at us both. Silent. Lost for words. Who would have thought?

I arched another eyebrow at Raph. "One of the best you've had?" I repeated. "Really? I thought it was quite average."

And with that, I reached down, wrapped my fingers around the handle of my suitcase, and straightened again. "Now if you'll excuse me, I'm going to take a shower."

I turned back to my room and entered it, this time without colliding with the door. Yay me.

Heather followed. I knew she would. I'd just dropped what I guessed was a monumental bombshell. And really, I wanted her to come in. As much as he infuriated me, I needed to know *who* Raph Jones was, so I could be ready the next time I encountered him.

Refusing to let myself look over my shoulder—would he be watching my awesome display of indifference?—I crossed to my bed and deposited my suitcase onto the mattress.

The sound of the door closing told me Heather had decided we needed some privacy. I was okay with that. If I did turn back and discover Raph still looking at me, I wasn't sure what I would do. Maybe poke my tongue out at him.

Yeah, I'm a real grown-up. Twenty-two going on four, that's me.

"Okay." My new Australian bestie flopped onto the bed beside my suitcase. "Cough up. You and Raph Jones *kissed*? In the men's loo at the *airport*?"

I nodded, undoing the zipper on my suitcase and flipping the lid open. My clothes were a jumbled mess inside, but they were all there. "We did."

"How?"

I pulled a face at Heather. "With our lips."

She rolled her eyes and whacked my arm with the back of her hand. "That's not what I mean. How did you and Raph Jones end up kissing in the loo? Where was his bodyguard?"

"Who *is* Raphael Jones?" I asked, ignoring her question. The unsettled sensation in my tummy had calmed down somewhat, but I was still flustered. I really needed to take my meds. And some serious yoga was in order. Or maybe a session at a gym. Something to burn off the stress playing havoc with my brain and muscles.

"You don't know?"

I shook my head, making a half-hearted attempt to organize the chaos in my suitcase. "I gather he's some kind of celebrity, given all the paparazzi photographing him at the airport. Is he a TV actor or something?"

Heather laughed. "No. His older sister married the Crown Prince of Delvania a few months ago. One of those rare commoner-meets-royalty-and-they-fall-in-love stories. It seems to be a trend with Australian women. The same thing happened a few years ago with Mary Donaldson from Tasmania. She met a guy at a pub during the Sydney Olympics who turned out to be the Crown Prince of Denmark. Four years later they were married, and still are to this day."

I frowned. "So Raph isn't royalty? What's with the body-guard then?"

"Since the wedding he's become a reluctant celebrity, very much like Pippa Middleton since Kate married William. Of course, her *butt* is more famous than she is."

I must have looked confused, because Heather gave me another one of those looks that told me she thought I was a clueless American.

"Pippa Middleton is the older sister of the woman who married Prince William. You know, the British royals? Australia is still a member of the colonies, as much as I wish we weren't. So of course *all* the media talked about for months before the wedding ceremony was what the bride was going to wear, what the vows were going to be. Then when the wedding took place, all everyone talked about was Pippa's arse and how good it looked in her bridesmaid dress." She sniggered. "So when Raph's sister married the prince and he was photographed at the wedding looking very yummy in his tux, the media went into an absolute frenzy. There are Facebook fan groups out there dedicated to him. I'm pretty certain there are also groups dedicated to *his* butt as well. *Cosmopolitan* magazine named him one of Australia's sexiest men last month. I've heard he can't leave campus without being mobbed by screaming girls who want to touch him, and the royal family wants him protected. There's a rumor there's a nutjob stalker obsessed with him. There's also a rumor that the prince's sister wants him for herself. They've been photographed enough together at royal events for the media to already start talking engagement and marriage.

"Plus, just about every girl who's ever been near him, even just sat beside him in a class, sells her story to *Woman's Day*, or *New Idea*—they're trashy magazines, by the way. Oh, I've even heard he's been hit on by one of the professors here. And apparently women keep sending him their undies. How gross is that?"

"So," I said, trying like hell to keep up with her machine-gun-fire answers. "Raph Jones is famous because his sister married a royal, a princess may have the hots for him, and he looks good in a tux? Is that it?"

"And he has a reputation for being arrogant and standoff-ish." Heather plucked my Victoria's Secret bra from the tangle of clothes in my suitcase and inspected it. "Even the girls he dated before the whole famous-for-being-famous thing say he rarely showed that much affection and wasn't big on kissing." She eyed me with curious contemplation. "Except he kissed *you*."

I looked at her, unsure what to say. Unsure what to *think*, to be honest. Now that I knew who my mysterious restroom kisser was, I was completely clueless why he'd kissed me. What had been going through Raph's head at the time?

I dropped onto the mattress beside my suitcase and gave Heather a frown. "Maybe he secretly wants the fame and attention? Maybe that's why he kissed me? Maybe he thought I'd post it on Facebook or tweet about it or something?"

"Yeah, right. The guy spends most of his day snarling at anyone who even *looks* like they're thinking of taking a photo of him with their mobile phones. Trust me, attention and fame are not what he wants." She held my bra up to her chest, studying the way the lacy cups covered her T-shirt-covered boobs. "Maybe it was chemistry. A spark between you both? They say his sister asked the crown prince for a kiss before she knew who he was. They ran into each other in a Starbucks in the city. He spilt coffee all over her, and when he asked if he could do anything to make it up, she jokingly said he could kiss her." Raising her atten-tion from my bra and her boobs, Heather shrugged. "Perhaps it's a family thing— to kiss complete strangers in weird places?"

I let out a wry grunt. "Yeah, that's it."

Inside, I was a trembling mess of confused uncertainty. I tried to remember the words Raph had said to me after the first time he'd kissed me. Something about the way his sister had met the prince. Now I knew about his sister, it made sense that he'd thought I was making a reference to the kiss between her and the prince in Starbucks. The thing was, even if that had been the case—which it wasn't, we both knew that the second he mentioned it—that still didn't explain why he'd granted my request. Nor why he'd kissed me a second time.

The memory of his lips on mine played with my sanity. There truly wasn't anything *average* about his kiss at all. It was incredible and amazing and even now, I wanted him to kiss me again. Despite the fact he was a grade-A jerk, I really wanted to feel his lips on mine. Feel him slide his tongue over mine. Feel his body pressed to mine.

At the thought of Raph Jones holding me in his arms so our bodies touched, a wickedly delicious throb began deep between my thighs.

The second we'd looked at each other I'd forgotten everything else. I'd stood there in the bathroom, completely neglecting the need to pee, and done something I never ever do—flirted. And he'd flirted back and flashed his dimple at me and kissed me. Twice. Instant sexual connection.

A spark.

It was the silence from Heather that made me realize I was staring at the door. I blanched, heat flooding my cheeks. Damn it. Busted.

"Don't tell anyone about the kissing thing, okay?" I asked.

Heather studied me. "Okay. On one condition."

I narrowed my eyes at her. "What's that?"

"When he kisses you again, you text me immediately."

"Err, no."

"No to the texting?"

I shook my head. "No to the kissing again. Not happening. I don't do kissing."

Heather threw back her head and laughed. And laughed. "Maci, by the way you were looking at Raph earlier, you don't only want to *do* kissing with him. You want to *do* all sorts of other things as well, like f—"

"Okay." I leapt to my feet, snared Heather's elbow and pulled her up. "Shower time."

She laughed at my pathetic attempt to silence her. "You'll see. You're here in a foreign country with a guy notorious for not kissing already laying one on you. A guy, I might add, who was practically making love to you with his eyes only a moment ago. Of course you're going to—"

I shoved her to the door, singing, "La la la". My cheeks weren't just hot, they were on fire.

By the time I got Heather to the door and flung it open, she was describing in euphoric detail what Raphael Jones was going to do to me. I've got to say, it was the most unorthodox way of making a new friend I can possibly think of. I liked it, even if I did think she was a deluded motor-mouthed lunatic. At least she was happy about it.

And she hadn't made any mention of my stupid shaking left hand. Even though she couldn't have missed it, she hadn't said a word. For that alone, she was lovely.

"Oh," she said, a second after I propelled her from my room into the corridor. "Do you wanna come to the gym with me tomorrow morning? Of course you do. I'll come get you at eight, okay?"

Raph's door was shut and he was nowhere to be seen. I

checked. I opened my mouth to tell her working out would be a great idea and closed it when Raph's door opened.

Without looking at me, he walked out of his room, closed the door behind him and made his way along the corridor, stopping at the room three down from mine. He knocked on the door once with a short, sharp rap.

Heather shot him a look and then turned back to me. "Enjoy your shower, Maci," she damn near shouted at me, grinning. "And I'll see you tonight at the party."

I tried not to look at Raph. Unfortunately, I failed. Before I knew it, my gaze was on him.

And before I could look away, his gaze was on me.

"Oh," Heather called, now striding past Raph, her grin wide. "Don't forget the theme. Underwear. Make sure you wear that sexy bra and knickers you packed. I reckon the guys will be lining up to meet you."

Raph scowled, banged on the door again with furious force and barged in.

My face on fire, I retreated into my own room. Heather might be wonderful, but this would be the shortest friendship in history. I was going to kill her.

Letting out a dramatic sigh, I crossed to the bed and stared at the mess of clothes in my suitcase. I needed a plan of attack. Stress was trying to take charge of my brain and I couldn't let it.

I could call Mom, but she would instantly hear it in my voice and freak out. I did not want her freaking out while I was on the other side of the world. When a Parkinson's sufferer freaks out, their brain takes them to a very dark emotional place. Depression decides to muscle in on the situation and then you're left with a stumbling, trembling, stuttering bag of glum misery, entertaining ideas best not entertained. Ideas like how the world would be better off without you in it.

I knew this not only from watching my mom go through it.

Chewing on my lip, I dug my toiletry bag out of my suitcase, along with a pair of shorts and my college T-shirt (Go Plenty Woodchucks!).

Plan of attack: Take my long-overdue meds, have a shower, wash my hair, brush my teeth, put on fresh clothes—although not my Victoria's Secret combo, given I'd be wearing it tonight in front of a horde of complete strangers. Well, complete strangers and Heather and Raph.

After that, and only after that, I'd call Mom, tell her I was awesome, tell her I'd met a bonafide Australian celebrity already—omitting the part about it being in the men's public bathroom *and* about the kiss—and then have a nap.

Fuck, I was tired. Hopefully, when I woke the trembles would have subsided enough that I could spend the Mackellar House party walking about in my Victoria's Secret underwear without my left hand shoved under my right armpit.

When I finally found the communal bathroom I had to swallow a little gasp of surprise at the sight of three guys washing their hands.

They all stopped talking to each other and regarded me in the long mirror that covered the entire wall above the basins.

I offered them a smile that was meant to be cool, calm and confident, but probably looked like I had gas. "Hi."

The one closest to me, who looked like he could bench-press a semi-trailer, grinned. "Ah, you're the American?" He nudged the guy beside him with his elbow. "Ando said she was a looker."

The one on the end, the leanest of the three and wearing a

Walking Dead T-shirt, smiled at me in the mirror. "What do you think of Australia so far?"

"So far, so good," I answered, hugging my clothes and toiletry bag to my chest. "Strangely enough, I've spent a lot of my time in bathrooms."

All three guys laughed. The semi-trailer bench-presser chuckled. "Well, when you gotta go, you gotta go, I guess."

For an awkward moment, no one moved. They stood at the basins, looking at me in the mirror's reflection. I stood inside the doorway, looking back at them.

"All right," Walking Dead finally spoke. "We'll let you shower in peace. Have fun." And with that, he hustled his friends past me.

Just as they were about to leave the bathroom, the biggest of them swung back to me. "You going t'night? To the undies shindig?"

I blinked. God, his accent was thick. "The what?"

He grinned. "The party tonight. Only wear your under-wear. You going?"

I nodded, feeling my cheeks heat. That was another thing I wasn't going to tell Mom—first night in Australia and I was planning on wearing nothing but panties and a bra in public. God, she would kill me.

"Excellent." His grin stretched wider. It was cute. In fact, so was he. In a geeky kind of way. "See you then."

And then I was alone.

Turning from the door, I let out another dramatic breath and studied the four empty shower cubicles before me. There were two bathrooms in Mackellar House. This one on the top floor—my floor—and one on the second floor. Heather told me the showers in this one had hotter water. She'd also told me there was a strict ten-minute shower limit, thanks to Mackellar House's "ridiculously small" hot water tanks.

Ten minutes to wash and condition my hair, clean all my … areas … that required cleaning and shave my legs. I could do that. Knowing a guy could walk into the bathroom to go to the toilet or use one of the other showers at any time would make it easier to be quick.

Picking the shower bay next to the far wall, I hurried in, deposited my clothes and toiletry bag on the small bench, locked the door, checked I'd locked it, checked again, stripped off my dirty clothes, checked once more on the door—yep, locked—and then turned on the water and stepped under the spray.

It wasn't until I'd de-stubbled my legs and was in the process of sudsing up my hair with apple-scented shampoo, that an important thought dawned on me.

I hadn't brought a towel into the bathroom.

Come to think of it, I hadn't brought a towel with me from home.

Was there a towel in my room?

Holy shit, I didn't have a towel.

I was having a shower in a strange bathroom on the other side of the world in a three-story dorm full of complete strangers and Heather and Raph (natch), and I had no idea how I was going to dry myself after.

Great.

Excellent.

Awesome.

Perfect.

Rinsing my hair as quickly as possible, I shut off the taps and stared hard at the back of the quadruple-checked locked door as if my eyes had the power to magically produce a cotton rectangle from thin air.

No towel appeared.

I chewed my bottom lip, flicked some water from my

hands, and then squeegeed off my thighs and butt with my palms.

The way I saw it, I had three options: One, while dripping wet, I could sprint for my room, which was just down the corridor, using my dirty clothes as a kind of shield to cover the appropriate bits.

Two, I could dry myself with my discarded long-haul flight attire and then casually walk to my room like there was nothing wrong, my damp clothes clinging to me like a stinky, coffee-stained second skin.

Or three, I could wait in the cubicle until someone entered the bathroom, introduce myself through the door, play up the jet lagged American damsel in distress angle—my accent had to come in handy somehow, right?—and ask them to get me a towel.

The second option was the easiest, but the latter was the least gross. I really did *not* want to put my dirty clothes back on. I'd been wearing them for almost twenty-four hours. If I put them on again, I'd feel like I'd need *another* shower.

As stupid as it sounded, I decided to go with the third option.

If I was lucky, Heather would realize she'd forgotten to tell me about the towel situation in Mackellar House, come back to fill me in on this vital piece of information and discover my absence in my room.

Up until this point in my life, I hadn't given much thought to towels and their presence in the universe. There were always just there, in the bathroom at home or in my dorm room at college, ready to be used and abused by me. Of course, now I realized, in a moment of guilt—the kind only those who think they've been independent grown-ups for years and years, ever since they turned fifteen and got their ears pierced without asking permission—that Mom had been the bearer of dry, clean towels in my life for my entire twenty-two years.

It took standing and waiting for someone to come rescue me from my own ignorance before I accepted getting my ears pierced in a moment of rebellious teenage-ness didn't make me a self-sufficient adult at all. It made me a twenty-two year old who still assumed clean, dry towels magically grew in the bathroom of my home. A home I was a long, long way from.

Hot tears prickled the backs of my eyes.

I sucked in a sharp breath, balled my stupid trembling left hand into a fist, rammed it under my armpit—my *wet* armpit, *urgh*—and prayed for someone to enter the bathroom. There were close to eighty people residing in Mackellar House. One of them had to need to pee at some—

The sound of the main door opening, followed by footsteps on the tiled floor, filled me with glorious relief. And sickening dread.

"Err, hello?" I called, refusing to step closer to the locked door of my cubicle. I knew they couldn't see me, but I still felt really exposed. "I'm Maci Rowling, the student from America." I didn't pause or wait for an answer. I figured something like this was better approached the Band-Aid way—quickly. "I've only just arrived today and I stupidly forgot to bring a towel with me and I remembered in the middle of my shower and I'm wondering if you could help me out by finding Heather ... Heather ..." Crap, what was Heather's last name again? "Renner!" Yay, well done, brain! "Could you find Heather Renner for me and ask her to bring me a towel? Please?"

Silence answered my plea.

"Umm," I called, suddenly aware my wet skin was making me feel a little chilly. "I can make it worth your while. I've got a whole bag of Hershey's Kisses in my suitcase I'm willing to give you."

Silence again. Followed by the sound of footsteps moving closer to my cubicle door.

Closer. Closer.

And then a deep, male voice with a sinfully sexy Australian accent I knew all too well, said, "I'm not remotely interested in Hershey's Kisses, American girl."

Raphael Jones was my savior? You've got to be fucking kidding me.

CHAPTER 3

The Argument about Copulating Koalas

Walking among close to a hundred strangers in just a skimpy lace bra and an equally skimpy pair of lace panties was strangely liberating. It helped when said hundred people were similarly attired. It also helped that my mom was on the other side of the world. God, what would she say if she knew what I was up to?

Taking a sip of my drink—some potent concoction I'd been handed on arrival that included vodka and coconut rum, going by the kick—I weaved through the crowd. I didn't normally do alcohol, mainly because it fucked with my Parkinson's medication. But better to be seen with a glass in hand than not. In this case, the glass was a plastic stein with the words *I Love a Sunburnt Country As Well, Dorothy* printed on the side. No idea what that meant. I *really* needed to do some googling. After the party I was definitely opening my laptop *and* getting my cell phone to connect to the Australian network.

Beside me, Heather did what Heather seemed to do best —talk, gossip and talk. She had me giggling into my barely consumed drink more than once, mainly at her acerbic commentary on the state of one guy or another. I was learning quickly that despite the accents and adoration of flip-flops—called thongs over here, thongs, of all things—Australian college guys were the same as American ones. Party animals itching to get laid. Or at least feel up as many college girls as they could.

Four times in the last hour, I'd had to shrug off an overly enthusiastic greeting. I wasn't pissed. I had come to the party in my underwear, after all. But there was only so many times you could feel strange fingers on the top of your boob before you had to take a stand. Especially when most of those fingers were attached to inebriated bodies.

Hey, it was a college party, after all. I mean, *uni* party.

"Maci, Maci, Maci." Heather clamped her hand around my wrist, bringing me to a halt. "Look who's just arrived. Your knight in shining armor."

Frowning at my Australian BFF, I tried to tug my wrist free. "My what?"

She threw a nod over my shoulder.

Twisting to see who she was talking about, a strange sensation telling me I already knew, I bit back a curse.

Raph Jones was descending the stairs to the main party area dressed only in a pair of black satin boxer shorts and a loose black satin robe left open, both of which revealed a body that made Chris Hemsworth's look wimpy by comparison. I know, how is that even possible, right? It was. Raph Jones, arrogant son-of-a-bitch douchebag, was proving that unques-tionably.

Christ, he was sexy hot.

My pulse slammed hard and fast in my throat.

Dammit, and I'd been having so much fun.

Grinding my teeth, I looked away. But not before Raph's arrogant son-of-a-bitch gaze clashed with mine. For a split second. Long enough for my breath to catch. Long enough for him to check me out—from head to toe and back to head again.

Long enough for my nipples to harden at that inspection.

Fuck.

Grabbing Heather's hand, I began to walk, dodging the laughing, giggling, dancing, drinking crowd. Heading in the opposite direction of Raph.

"We're in a rush, are we?" Heather chuckled. "Where we going?"

"Somewhere away," I answered.

"Out of the party?" Heather's grin was knowing. What she *thought* she knew, I had no idea. If she thought I was flustered by Raph Jones, she was wrong.

Shut up.

"Just out," I said through gritted teeth. "Not here."

"Do I need to remind you we're in our undies?"

I stopped. Damn it, she was right. Strutting about in my underwear was all well and good inside at a party, but outside of Mackellar House was Sydney. Not just the University of Sydney, but Sydney. Mackellar House was situated in a residential suburb, which meant beyond the door and down the sidewalk to the left were homes. With families living in them.

I guess I could turn right and go storming through the university grounds, but did I really want to do that at nine pm at night? In my Victoria's Secret?

No.

I was staying at the party.

With Raph.

Yay.

I should probably point out why I was so ... flustered by him. He *did* go get Heather when we were in the bathroom together that afternoon—Australians call afternoons "arvos", by the way—and Heather *did* deliver me a towel, but when I finally emerged from my shower cubicle, I found Raph waiting for me, his butt perched on one of the basins, his arms crossed over his chest, one ankle crossed over the other.

I hadn't been expecting that.

He'd studied me, that enigmatic light in his eyes again. The one I couldn't decide was friendly or suspicious.

I'd jutted out my chin in response to his silent scrutiny, held out my arms a little and curtsied. "Do I meet with your approval, Mr. Jones?"

Why I'd provoked him, I'm still not sure. I think it had something to do with the whole hot-cold thing he had going with me.

He'd pushed himself away from the basin and strode forward. "We have a habit of bumping into each other in bathrooms, don't we, American girl?"

I'd stood my ground. Jutted my chin out some more—I was in serious danger of dislocating my neck at that point. "No bumping this time. You were the one who came in here. Twice. Perhaps *you're* stalking *me*?"

My jibe hadn't stop him closing the distance between us. I'd hoped it would. Smug bastard or not, he was still causing my body to do strange things when he was close to me. Or looking at me. There in the bathroom, both were taking place. "I'm not a fan of stalkers."

I'd swallowed. Caught my bottom lip with my teeth. Caught myself catching my bottom lip with my teeth and stopped myself. What kind of twenty-two-year-old still chewed her bottom lip when facing down a hotter-than-hot guy?

"What *are* you a fan of?" I'd asked. I wasn't one-hundred-percent certain, but I suspected we were flirting with each other. In an edgy kind of way.

He'd drawn to a halt directly in front of me, so close that the toes of his shoes brushed my bare feet. "Do you want me to say 'you'?"

I'd licked my lips. "I don't know what I want you to say."

"If I say I want you to kiss me, will you?"

I'd stared up at him, my pulse thumping a mile a minute. "I—"

"Are you in here, Jones?" a male voice had shouted, just as the bathroom door swung open with a slam. "Ah, there you are. You playing pool with us or—ah, the Yank! Heya, how you going?"

I've never seen anyone move away as quickly as Raph had then. When Mr. Info Dump came barreling into the communal bathroom, Raph had damn near leapt backward like a cat who'd just realized its tail was burning.

I'd frowned at the sudden change, at the disparagement on his face. At the way he'd hurried across to Info Dump—what was his name again? Heather had told me. Umm, McDonald? McNamara? Something like that? Macca for short?—without another glance.

"C'mon," he'd said, pushing past Macca. "Double or nothing on this game."

Macca had given him a curious look, then shrugged and grinned at me. "You coming to the party tonight? We'll see you there, 'eh?"

And before I could say anything, both guys left the bathroom and I was alone.

Now do you understand why I was so flustered seeing Raph at the party? The bastard son-of-a-bitch douche bag was quite happy to flirt with me, stick his tongue down my throat when we were alone, but whoa, if there was anyone actually around, witnessing it, *no*, I was a leper. A shaky one.

Beside me, Heather chuckled. "I don't know if your plan was to get away from Raph or not, but he's following us."

I glanced over my shoulder. Sure enough, he was only a few feet behind. About a dozen girls in skimpy bras and thongs—the kind that go up your butt crack, not on your feet—were swooning over him as he walked, slipping their hands around his biceps and generally pawing at him. He scowled and shrugged them off. I'm ashamed to admit I was both jealous and happy. Talk about being a conflicted mess.

Our eyes clashed again, for another one of those brief seconds that go on forever, before I looked away and turned a sharp right, dragging Heather with me. Oh yeah, I was smooth.

"Is this some kind of weird game of Catch and Kiss I'm not aware of?" she asked, a grin in her voice. "Or are you playing Tag, You're It? Oh, is this a social experiment you're conducting about how easy it is to make Australian guys follow you around? Hey, he's still on our tail. He's trying not to look like he is, but he is. Wow, what did you two do in the bathroom after I left? He keeps looking at you.

"Oh, and now Macca's handed him a drink and he's watching you over the rim of it. Hee, he just told Shelly White to go away. That's huge. Every guy here wants to bonk Shelly White. She's a swimsuit model who's studying—oh hi, Brendon. I didn't know you were coming tonight? Maci, this is Brendon Osmond, the uni gym's fitness manager."

I jerked my attention from the crowd around me back to Heather. The tall guy standing beside her was wearing a pair of bright-red pajama pants, and was possessed of muscles so exquisite, my mouth began to water.

Hello, Brendon.

Brendon Osmond flashed a friendly smile at me, held out his hand and said, "G'day."

I gaped up at him.

His smile turning into a grin, he took my hand—which I'd apparently extended to him. "Maci. How you going?"

"Good," I said, finding my voice. What the hell was it with this country? Raphael Jones looked like a sexier Chris Hemsworth, and now this guy looked like a sexier, blond Robert Downey Jr., complete with Iron Man body and devilish glint in his blue eyes.

Brendon's eyebrows rose. "American? Or Canadian? Sorry, I can never tell the difference with the accents."

"American," I answered. Damn, his fingers felt nice wrapped around mine. Warm and firm and steady. "I'm from Plenty, Ohio. But my dad was Australian, if that counts. I can even say g'day if you like. G'day."

Brendon bent at the waist a little in a playful bow. "That wasn't too shabby, Plenty, Ohio. Welcome to Oz."

I smiled. "Thank you, Uni Fitness Manager."

He chuckled. "Call me Brendon. Not such a mouthful."

I grinned back. "Call me Maci. Not so geographically specific."

He laughed, dropping my hand. "Done. So tell me, are you studying here or just visiting?"

"Studying," I answered. Hmmm, I think I liked it better when he was holding my hand. "I'm here on a scholarship offered by my college to study the effects of global warming on native wildlife, specifically the koala population."

"Koala population? That's left of field for an American, isn't it? Even one with an Aussie for a dad?"

I laughed. "I've never been one for conventional thinking."

Brendon raised his eyebrows again. Opened his mouth and—

"There *is* no effect on the koala population," a familiar male voice with its unsettling Australian accent said behind me.

My lips tingled as if they remembered just what the owner of that voice was capable of doing to them. Damn it.

"G'day, Raph," Brendon said, offering his hand over my shoulder. "Haven't seen you in the gym for a while."

Another hand appeared beside my head, wrapped around Brendon's in a firm grip and then withdrew. "I've been in Delvania. Family thing. Just got back today."

The warm presence at my back told me Raph Jones was right there. Right behind me. So close I could feel his heat seeping into my body. So close I could feel the smooth skin of his bare chest brush the back of my shoulder.

For a giddy moment, my head swam.

Thankfully, Brendon laughed. "The curse of family, 'eh? Forcing you to skip the country and escape the madness of the media attention. Must be hell."

"You could say that," Raph's voice rumbled from behind.

Beside me, Heather watched both guys, her gaze flicking back and forth as if she was watching a tennis match. There was an almost frenzied excitement in her eyes. Something was going on in her head. Something she found thrilling. I didn't know whether to be suspicious ... or to laugh.

"So, Jones." Brendon took a drink from the bottle in his hand—mineral water. What every good, muscular gym fitness manager drank, no doubt. Did I say muscular already? "Tell us why you think there's no effect on the koala population due to global warming. You know much about copulating marsupials? I thought your major was in biology or animal husbandry."

"I'm studying a Bachelor of Animal and Veterinary Bioscience," Raph answered. "I grew up on a cattle station—what you Americans call a ranch—on which there is a very large koala colony. I can tell you firsthand, the global warming situation isn't impacting their numbers at all."

Unable to stop myself, I swung around to give him a narrowed-eyed stare. "Oh really?"

The look he gave me was steady. Condescending. "Really."

"Then what is then?" I shot back.

"Human stupidity," he answered.

"And on that note," Brendon said, a hint of amusement in his voice, "it's time to change the subject. I'm sure there's a guideline that states politics and science can't be discussed while dressed only in underwear."

At my side, Heather giggled. "I've heard of that guideline."

Raph's stare didn't leave my face. "But of course," he continued, as if Brendon hadn't uttered a word, "you, being an American, would be an expert on Australian native wildlife."

If it was possible—and until then I didn't think it was—I narrowed my eyes even more. "Me being an American?" My heart kicked up a notch. Or maybe it was my ire. Yeah, it was pretty much up there. "Because it's not remotely conceivable an *American* could have knowledge on something as precious to you Aussies as koalas? Is that what you're saying?"

"Actually—" Brendon stepped a little closer to us both, filling the right side of my peripheral vision with his towering, sculpted form, "—now that I think about it, that guideline isn't a guideline, it's a rule. Strict one."

"I'm saying—" Raph's stare turned into a frown, and once again, he acted like Brendon hadn't made a sound, "—it's typical of you Americans to think you know all the answers about the—"

"Koala facts," I said, cutting him short. I was keeping my cool. Honestly. Well, sort of. "There are fewer than eighty thousand koalas in the wild in Australia today, possibly as few as forty-three thousand, compared to the millions thought to exist before European settlement. In 2012, on advice from the Threatened Species Scientific Council, the koala was listed as a threatened species."

Raph opened his mouth.

"Since 1788," I continued without letting him say a word, counting off my second point on my finger, "when Australia was first settled by Europeans, nearly sixty-five percent of the koala forest in Australia has been cleared, over 116 million hectares. The remaining thirty-five percent, approximately forty-one million hectares, remains under threat from land clearing for agriculture, urban development and unsustainable forestry. *All* contributing factors to global warming."

Raph's expression turned black. He obviously didn't like being argued with. Or stood up to in public.

"Koala populations are also being decimated by chlamydia," I went on, counting down on my fingers, "a disease exacerbated by stress. Koalas are increasingly under stress due to habitat loss and destruction."

His face grew darker.

I rammed my index finger to my pinkie finger, refusing to blink in the face of that menacing glare. "Habitat loss is the greatest problem facing koalas today. Habitat loss caused not only by land clearing, but by the rise in bushfires due to the increasing number of electrical storms. Storms that are growing in intensity and number due to the planet-wide changing weather patterns and rising temperatures, not to mention diseases like dieback in eucalyptus, which, by the way, is on the rise due to warmer climates in Australia, a symptom of …" I raised my eyebrows, waiting for him to provide the answer.

He didn't. Heather did. "Global warming?" she offered.

"Global warming," I echoed, giving Raph a humorless smile. "And last fact of the night, but most definitely not the argument, Australia has one of the highest land-clearing rates in the world. Over eighty percent of koala habitat has already been cleared, reducing the viable mating and living areas. A forest can only have a certain number of koalas living in it, referred to as a forest's carrying capacity. Most koala populations are now in a dire state. The Australian Koala Foundation estimates that as a result of the loss of their habitat, around four thousand koalas are killed each year by dogs and cars alone."

I paused and crossed my arms over my Victoria's Secret-covered boobs, and glowered back at him. "Want to know anything else?"

"How do they mate?" Heather piped up.

Brendon snorted into his bottle of water. Raph curled his lip.

"Simple," I answered, hoping Raph could see my disdain. "When a koala is sexually mature, it leaves the safety of its home range and the protection of its social group and goes in search of a new area beyond its territory. If there are no new areas due to habitat loss, a sexually mature koala can't find a new mate, or will risk injury encroaching on an existing social group. Once again, can I point out one of the contributing factors to koala habitat loss is global warming's effect on the environment?"

"They can't bonk because it's too hot?" Heather paraphrased. "That sucks."

"It does," I agreed.

A muscle in Raph's jaw throbbed. If it wasn't for the fact I was pissed at him, I would have gladly acknowledged—to myself, at least—how wonderful that jaw had felt under my palm earlier that day.

"Thank you for the school project," he said.

Damn, his voice was steady and level and smooth and deep and ... Wait, I was pissed at him. I had to concentrate on that, not the way his voice sounded. Focus, Rowling, focus.

"Now, would you like me to offer a counter-argument to every point you just made?"

"What she'd like," Brendon's strong voice—just as deep and smooth and Australian—sounded at my side as he wrapped warm, firm fingers around my hand, "is a drink that doesn't have an umbrella in it, isn't that right, Maci?"

I swung my gaze up to him, my heart rate still as charged as my ire. What was it about these goddamn Australian guys thinking they could tell me what to do? But at the sight that greeted me, I bit back my angry tirade before it could begin.

His lips were curled in a relaxed grin, there was genuine amusement in his eyes. The expression instantly put me at ease, which surprised me. Eased surprise. How's that for a strange mix?

"Something tells me," he said, leaning a little closer, his gaze playing with mine as he plucked the alcoholic concoction from my hand, "that you're more a mineral-water kinda woman."

I laughed. I know, right? What were the odds of laughing at that point given how angry Raphael Jones had made me? But there was something about Brendon ... something calming. Warm and friendly. Nice. And it had nothing to do with his impressive body. Well, not much. "Mineral water *is* more my style," I answered.

He winked. "Thought so. C'mon, let me get you one."

Before I could say another word, before Heather could say another word—can you believe that?—and before Raph's glower finished turning his face into a Greek tragedy mask, Brendon smoothed his hand over the small of my back and steered me away.

"Was that your way of saving me from an argument?" I asked with a grin as we weaved our way through our fellow partygoers.

Blue eyes glinting, he affected an expression of mock surprise. "God, no. I just want to hear more about koalas without all this party noise."

I raised my eyebrows.

Brendon chortled. "Okay, you're right. I was doing my bit to protect the Australian-American relationship. Wouldn't want your country going to war against ours over copulating koalas."

An image of two koalas mating in the middle of a smoke-filled battlefield filled my head and I giggled.

"Besides," Brendon continued, directing me to a door leading to what looked like Mackellar House's backyard. "We'd kick your arse if we did. Go to war, that is."

Once again, I raised my eyebrows. "Really now?"

He nodded, pausing only long enough to snatch a bottle of mineral water from the large plastic pail loaded with ice and other drinks next to the open door. "Of course." He twisted the lid from the bottle and handed it to me. I couldn't help but notice the way the muscles in his arms, shoulders and chest coiled and flexed with subtle strength. I have to admit, it was rather delicious to watch. "We'd only have to let loose our wildlife and you're all screwed."

I took the offered mineral water with a chuckle. "American soldiers attacked by post-coitus koalas? Is that what you're saying?"

He raised his own bottle to his lips. "Something like that."

The cool kiss of night air on my bare skin told me we'd exited the building before my brain registered it. I stopped on the top step of a smallish deck and lifted my attention to the black sky above me.

The stars were completely different here. Completely. No Cassiopeia, no Orion. Nothing familiar at all. It was then, more than at any other moment, that I realized I was far from home.

My throat grew thick. I missed my mom. I missed the smells of Plenty. I missed the stars. *My* stars.

"It messes with your head a little, doesn't it?"

I flinched a little at Brendon's soft words. "What does?"

He glanced up at the sky. "The stars. How different the stars are. I remember the first time I went to the States. I was all, 'Hey, I'm down with all this, I'm not a tragic tourist', and then I saw the stars on my first night and kinda lost it a little. The absence of the Southern Cross ..." He drew closer to me, bending down until his head was beside mine as he pointed up to the sky at the crucifix-shaped constellation represented on the Australian flag. "That one, well ... not seeing it up there, where it always was ... my head couldn't process it. It's a weird habit of mine to find the Southern Cross in the sky every night, but those weeks I spent in San Diego ..." He chuckled. "It's stupid, I know, but I missed the stars. My stars."

His words, an echo of my own thoughts, unsettled me a little. Made me feel something. Not quite sexual desire, but ... something. A sense of connection, maybe? I wanted to move away from him in case he sensed the way I was reacting to his words. And his heat. And his relaxed, friendly presence. I also *didn't* want to move away. Not at all.

It was a seriously confusing sensation, especially on the

heels of my thoroughly carnal and emotional reaction to Raphael Jones. "When were you in San Diego?" I croaked.

If Brendon detected my fluster, he didn't show it. And let's be honest, he wouldn't have been able to miss it.

"A year ago," he answered, straightening again. "Followed a girl there."

The confession sent a funny little blip though me. Not jealousy, just … funny. Man, my descriptive skills are woeful, aren't they? Good thing I never planned on being a journalist.

"Did she follow you back?" I asked.

He smiled at the stars, his Adam's apple sliding up and down the muscular column of his throat. "No."

We stood there for a moment in silence. It was nice. Companionable. The nerves in my belly calmed and my pulse returned to its normal pace.

And then he said, "So how long have you had Parkinson's disease?"

My blood ran cold. I forced a puzzled frown on my face. "Why do you think I have Parkinson's disease?"

His smile wasn't sympathetic or pitying or repulsed, or any of the other emotions I'd grown accustomed to seeing on people's faces when they discovered my condition. No, it was understanding.

"Haven't you noticed?" He raised his arm and made a fist. "I'm all about muscles and muscle movement."

His unexpected answer pulled me out of my rattled state and I dragged my eyes from his arm up to his face with a laugh.

"Okay, I'm going to admit I just did that to show off," he said. "Sorry, but the point is, I know about muscle movement and motor-neuron function. Any personal trainer and fitness manager should, and I'm not just your average gym junkie. I'm in my last year of a Bachelor of Applied Science majoring in Exercise and Sport Science. My aunt has ALS, what you guys in the States call Lou Gehrig's disease, so I've got a personal interest in it as well."

I stared at him. "Wow."

He grinned. "Told you I wasn't your average gym junkie."

I shook my head. For some reason, I was lost for words.

"My favorite movie is *Batman Begins*," he went on. "I love peanut-butter-and-lettuce sandwiches, am partial to the color blue, have a serious thing for Emma Watson, own every Coldplay album ever released and can't stand the *Twilight* series."

I frowned. "And the reason you're telling me all this ...?"

"I'm a firm believer in transparency and getting the important facts out there straight up at the start of a new relationship."

"We have a relationship already?"

He laughed. "Hey, I *did* say start."

I smiled, raising my bottle to my lips. "You did." I took a sip of water. The fact we weren't talking about my Parkinson's was a good thing. He might be blasé about it, but that didn't mean I was ready to open up. "So what's your issue with the *Twilight* series? Is it the sparkly vampire thing?"

"That and the whole Bella-is-so-beautiful-everyone-wants-to-bone-her-even-though-she's-a-submissive-waste-of-space thing," he answered. "And don't get me started on the pubescent werewolf who's constantly strutting about without a shirt on."

"Says the shirtless man," I pointed out with a grin.

He looked down at himself, surprise pulling at his face. I *did* mention he looked like a younger, blond Robert Downey Jr., didn't I? "Hey, where the hell did my shirt go?"

I laughed. A lovely, warm, contented sensation was making itself at home in my chest, the place my mom always pressed her palm to when talking about her soul. Taking another sip of water, I turned to the yard beyond the deck railing. There were a few people out there, most getting to know each other in ways beyond the cerebral. I felt odd watching them. A tad self-conscious, seeing as I *was* standing next to a half-naked hot guy in my underwear who was, I think, flirting with me in a relaxed kind of way. I could only imagine how I'd be feeling if it were Raphael Jones I was standing beside, half-naked or not.

At the thought of Raph Jones I grimaced.

Crap, why was I thinking about *him* again?

"By the way," Brendon uttered, his voice a low conspirator's whisper. "Don't think I'm not impressed with how well you dodged answering my question about your Parkinson's."

I pulled in a swift breath, tightening my grip on my bottle. At the mention of my condition, my brain decided it was time to acknowledge my hand was shaking. Not badly, but enough to be obvious. Embarrassed dismay scraped at my happiness.

"Nor," Brendon continued with a nudge of his hip against mine, "that you chose not to mock my taste in music."

So he'd sensed my apprehension and was happy to let the subject drop. I lowered my gaze to my hand, watching the slight tremble moving it.

I thought of what Brendon had revealed, about his aunt, about his studies. I thought of the way he'd mocked himself in his efforts to make me feel at ease.

I thought of his friendly smile and relaxed humor.

And, I have to admit, a small part of me thought of his muscles.

"I was diagnosed last year," I said, watching my fingers shake. Not much, but enough. Hell, anything but steady was enough. I'd taken my meds, so what was up with the tremors? "My mom has it as well, although she was diagnosed ten years ago. It's not a hereditary disease so the fact we *both* have it is either some higher force's idea of a bad joke or just a horrible case of random bad luck. I haven't decided which yet."

Brendon didn't say anything for a while. Around us, the party continued. More than one underwear-clad couple spilled past us, laughing their way down the stairs into the shadows of the backyard. I watched them, a small smile pulling at the corners of my lips. Even though I had no idea what the Australian beside me was going to say, I felt okay fessing up to my situation. There was something about Brendon Osmond that made me feel safe. And after the turbulent emotional rollercoaster that was Raph Jones, safe was a good thing.

"Reckon daily sessions getting hot and sweaty with me might be in order for you."

Brendon's unexpected statement yanked me out of my reverie. "Huh?"

"Getting hot and sweaty," he said. "With me. In the gym. In the morning before anyone else gets there."

I kind of gaped at him. Was he suggesting what I think he was suggesting?

"Physical exercise is good for Parkinson's," he went on, a glint in his eyes "Keeping the muscles moving the way you want them to move."

"Oh," I breathed. "You mean working out. Like a cardio-and-weights type thing."

He laughed. "What else would I mean?"

A blush flooded my cheeks and he laughed again.

"Damn, Plenty, Ohio. Let me at least buy you a coffee or green tea or something before you start thinking about us having sex."

It was my turn to laugh, the heat in my cheeks creeping up into my scalp. "Hey, I'm jet lagged, okay?"

He chuckled and nudged me with his hip again. "Okay.

I'll let you off this time. But what do you think about us getting some clothes on and getting out of this place? There's a cafe around the corner that brews the best green tea ever. My—"

"There you are!" A female voice rose above Brendon's invitation.

I swung away from him as Heather wrapped her arm around my shoulder. She hugged me as if I hadn't only just left her company a few minutes ago.

"Whoa, girlfriend." I giggled into her hair. "I missed you too."

"Someone else is missing you," she whispered. "And didn't look too happy when you took off with The Biceps."

Right away, I knew who she was talking about. Before I could stop myself, I peered over her shoulder, searching for—

"He's not there," Heather muttered a second before pulling away from me. Grinning up at Brendon, she said, "I'm stealing my American friend back, Brendon. Sorry. You've monopolized her for too long tonight."

Brendon let out that relaxed laugh of his. "That's okay. I've got her tomorrow morning."

Heather pulled a wickedly intrigued face. "*Oh*, do tell."

"She's getting hot and sweaty with me."

"Is she now?" Heather cocked an eyebrow.

Brendon grinned. "Oh man, am I going to make her body move."

"*Are* you now?" Heather looked at me with awed approval. "Go you."

I rolled my eyes. "A physical therapy session, you dirty-minded woman."

The second the words popped out of my mouth, I tried to bite them back.

Sure enough, Heather asked the question I knew she

would, a frown creasing her forehead. "Physical therapy? Why do you need physical therapy? What's broken?"

"Her heart," Brendon said, stepping up beside me. "I told her I'm not available."

"Ah, that's right." Heather grinned. "You're saving yourself for Emma Watson."

Brendon gave a sage nod. "I'm saving myself for Emma Watson."

Heather threaded her fingers through mine and fixed him with an exasperated look. "You're delusional, Brendon Osmond."

He preened, obviously taking her insult as a compliment. "And a thorough optimist. You'll see, me and Emma. It's the way it's meant to be."

"All right, all right," Heather said. "Whatever you reckon. Come along, Rowling. I want to see you try Vegemite."

"Vegemite." I frowned as Heather tugged me away from Brendon and toward the door. "That's the jar of black stuff in the welcome basket in my room, right?"

"Run, Maci!" Brendon called after us. "Run now! Before it's too late!"

Heather chuckled, dragging me back inside. "Shut up, Osmond," she tossed over her shoulder with a grin. "Go bench-press a train or something."

Brendon's laugh told me he wasn't offended by her jibe. I flicked him a look just in time to see a girl in the skimpiest thong and bra set imaginable, plaster herself to his body and rub her palms up his very impressive chest.

He grinned at me over her head, and then turned his attention to her with a smile and a laugh.

A flutter of that same emotion I'd experienced earlier danced in my belly again. Not jealousy but ... who knows, maybe there *were* the makings of something between us? I already knew more about him than the other Australian who'd shown an interest in me, although *interest* really didn't describe the weird thing Raph and I had going on. And Brendon was so much more easy to be around. Maybe that weird flutter inside me needed to be fostered? Maybe I should kiss Brendon and see what—

"He's a really nice guy," Heather said in my ear as she led me back into the party. "But such a player. Serious commitment-phobe as well. He's broken more than a few hearts, and that's not including any of the poor girls who've fallen in love with him without even going out with him."

I cast her a dubious sideways glance. "Really?"

She nodded. "Seriously. I know of more than one girl who goes to the gym for no other reason than to watch him, hoping he'll notice her fumbling away on the treadmill and come to her rescue."

"Wow," I said.

"Pretty lame, isn't it?"

I narrowed my eyes. "Are you one of them?"

Heather laughed. "Hell, yeah. I spent a good month prancing about in the gym in my sexiest Lorna Janes before I realized what I was doing."

"Lorna Janes?"

"Oh my God, woman," she gasped. "We are going shopping tomorrow. If you're going to be working out with The Biceps you need to deck yourself out in Lorna Jane. It's like Nike with attitude. It'll drive him wild and make Raph utterly mental with jealousy knowing you're getting hot and sweaty in it with The Biceps."

I stumbled. "Raph utterly mental with *what*?"

Impish delight flittered across Heather's face. "Jealousy. Did you *see* the way he was looking at you tonight? When you were lecturing him about koalas? Lust. Pure and simple and open lust. Like you were an ice cream and he wanted to devour you even though he was on a diet."

I let out a low *hmpf*, aware my belly was competing with my pulse for the fastest fluttering. "I saw the utterly *disdainful* way he looked at me. Not sure about lust and the whole ice cream simile."

Heather grinned. "Hence the diet. He wants you even though he reckons he's sworn off ice cream for his health. You're like the delicacy he's craving now, the only thing that'll sate his hunger and he's grumpy about it. Furious in fact. And then, while he's devouring you with his stare, thinking about how much he wants to lick you up, along comes his antithesis, his polar opposite, his nemesis for want of a better word—"

"Nemesis?" I interrupted, eyebrows journeying up my forehead.

"—who swoops you off your feet and away from him," Heather continued, ignoring my incredulous expression. "So not only is he now craving what he's ruled unsuitable for his diet, he's watching someone else put you on his menu and tuck a napkin under his chiseled chin. It's priceless. Awesome even. Worthy of a Hollywood blockbuster starring Channing Tatum. Or Ryan Gosling. Or Liam Hemsworth. Maybe all three."

I fixed her with a skeptical stare. "Heather, what exactly *is* your major again?"

Her grin grew wider. "Mechanical engineering."

I burst out laughing.

"C'mon." She reclaimed my hand with hers. "Vegemite time. Josie Witmore's got a jar opened and a packet of Saos ready to roll."

I shook my head at her. "I have no idea what Saos are."

"Of course you don't. But you will soon. Oh and guess

who's arrived, dressed in the sexist white boxer briefs you've ever seen?"

Once again, I shook my head, caught up in her vivaciousness.

"Josh Blackthorne."

"Who's Josh Blackthorne?" I asked.

She burst out laughing. "Honey, Josh Blackthorne is Liam Hemsworth, Ryan Gosling and Channing Tatum all rolled up into one. Let's go. It's time to educate you on all things Australian."

Naked Men in Cafes

At an ungodly hour the next morning, while I was still semi-catatonic in bed with a slight hangover, a brisk knock sounded on my door. Unwisely, I had consumed more of those damn drinks with the umbrellas in them, most of them with Josh Blackthorne, a student at the Sydney Conservatorium of Music. Bad move for someone meant to be having an early start, right?

"C'mon, Plenty, Ohio," Brendon's voice came from the other side. "Time to get sweaty."

"What the hell?" I grumbled, shoving my head under my pillow. "Go away. Come back when it's later."

He laughed, and then started to knock what sounded like a frenzied rap song on the door.

Five minutes of that, plus his insistence he wasn't going anywhere until we worked up a sweat together, finally propelled me out of bed. Part of me suspected he was doing it to irritate Raph in the room opposite to mine. I may have had a few too many umbrella drinks, but I *did* remember what Heather had told me about Brendon and Raphael. And what Heather had told me about the way Raph looked at me and the way he'd looked when I left with Brendon. I didn't know

Brendon well at that stage, but I also remembered the glint in his eyes when he was talking to Raph before we departed.

They might not be enemies, but they were definitely competitors. I still hadn't decided how I felt about being the object of that possibly friendly rivalry. If indeed I *was* said object. I've never really had that big an opinion of myself, but I couldn't deny having two hot Aussie guys interested in me was a bit of a buzz.

"Okay, okay," I grumped at the door. "I'm up." I dug out the gym gear I'd packed from my suitcase—Adidas. *Tsk, tsk.* What would Heather think?—pulled it on, swished my mouth with mouthwash, realized I had nowhere to spit it, scrunched up my face and swallowed it, grimaced, yanked my hair back in a ponytail and hurried to the door.

Brendon stood grinning on the other side. "Morning."

I was about to return his greeting when movement behind him caught my attention.

Raph's door was opening.

Wide enough for someone to step out of it.

The perky little blonde who'd plastered herself all over Brendon last night, to be precise. Wearing nothing but the skimpy thong and bra set and a satisfied expression.

A hot, sour taste filled my mouth. Jealousy. Pure, undiluted, totally unjustified jealousy.

I must have pulled some kind of face, because Brendon twisted around to see what I was looking at.

The blonde smiled at us both, wiggled her fingers at Brendon, pulled the door shut without making a sound and hurried away on tiptoes, as if afraid to wake people.

I swallowed at the sudden lump in my throat, unsettled.

"Well, that was unexpected."

Jerking my stare back to Brendon, I tried to force an air of indifference to my face. "What was?"

He frowned. "I could have sworn Claudia had a tattoo."

As it had before, his relaxed sense of humor pulled me from my unsettled state. He was making a habit of it. I liked it.

With a grin, he jogged a couple of times on the spot. "Race you to the gym?"

I laughed. "Seeing as I have no idea where it is, you'd win."

"Oh well, in that case ..." He held out his right arm. "Let me escort you there instead."

Smiling, I slipped my fingers around his bulging biceps—holy smack, did he feel incredible. "With pleasure."

Ten minutes later, we arrived at the gym. Brendon unlocked the door, hit the lights, turned on the music and spun around to face me. "Ready?"

I nodded.

He slapped his hands together, eyes twinkling. "Let's do this."

Sixty minutes later, I swore I was going to kill him. My body had never worked so hard. Or sweated so much. I groaned my way through a session of cardio and weights designed—I'm sure—to make a professional athlete curl up and cry. If I wasn't so determined to show I was capable of doing it, I would have burst into tears somewhere around the twentieth burpee.

While I worked out, Brendon talked to me. Most of it was casual chatter, but every now and again he'd ask an obscure question, trying to learn more about my Parkinson's. Questions like which hand did I clean my teeth with and did I wear lace-less shoes because I didn't know how to tie shoelaces yet?

I answered both honestly. I brushed my teeth with my non-dominant hand because my dominant hand—my left one—was weaker than it used to be and I didn't like the reminder every morning and night. I wore lace-less shoes because they looked cool. I didn't tell him doing up my shoelaces was only a problem when I was really tired, stressed or behind on my meds.

Brendon might make me laugh a lot, and look absolutely delicious in his loose white tank top and black running shorts, but I wasn't quite ready to divulge all. I'd promised myself my condition was never going to be a topic of conversation, and even though Brendon was more versed on what I was going through than most, I still wasn't going to be defined by it. I refused to be.

But since I'd arrived in Australia—less than twenty-four hours ago—my Parkinson's had occupied a large part of my focus. Along with Raphael Jones and now Brendon Osmond.

That had to change. While I couldn't get rid of my damn tremors, I could at least spend less time thinking about them.

The gym started to fill up with young, lithe, tremble-free bodies. I could see what Heather meant about women in the place all doing whatever they could to make Brendon notice them. There was an amazing amount of tight Lycra and push-up sports bras on display. Along with an equal amount of lingering looks directed at the gym manager.

When he finally said we were finished, seventy-five minutes after we'd begun, I was so exhausted and physically drained I didn't know whether to laugh, cry, hug him or punch him. So I settled with collapsing to the floor in a melo-dramatic swoon.

And that's when Brendon did the unthinkable. He made a fuss.

"Hey, hey, hey," he cried, alarm in his voice as he dropped to his knees beside me. "You okay?"

I opened my eyes, finding him hovering over me, concern on his Robert Downey Jr.-handsome face. Behind him, curious onlookers watched us.

The smile died on my lips, the satisfaction of my achievement curdling.

"Maci?" Brendon frowned, pressing his fingers to the pulse point on my throat. "You should have told me I was pushing you too—"

I slapped his hand away, dismayed not just at his fussing, but at the trembles in *my* hand. Goddamn it, couldn't I even work up a sweat like a normal twenty-two year old without my body behaving like a fucking eighty year old?

"I'm fine," I muttered, rolling away from him. I pushed myself to my feet. And staggered sideways.

Fuck.

Fuck, fuck, fuck.

I think I may have mentioned one of the things with Parkinson's disease is an occasional inability to retain balance. It can hit you anytime, but especially when standing quickly from a seated or horizontal position. To be honest, at that point I don't know if it was my Parkinson's that made me stumble, or sheer physical exhaustion—I *was* still operating on Ohio time after all, jet lag was still clinging to me like goddamn seaweed—but I was too wounded to let rational thought get in the way.

Unfortunately, my feet weren't being nice to me and Brendon was by far faster at regaining his. He leapt upright and caught my elbow, halting my sideways stumble.

"Whoa, Maci," he murmured. "I gotcha."

Heat flooded my cheeks. I could feel the stares of those around us crawling over my face like frenzied ants. I shrugged my elbow out of Brendon's grip and, head down, muttered a thank you, followed by, "I've got to go."

I hurried past him, not looking back, refusing to even raise my head.

I was at the gym's entry door when he caught up with me. "Hold on there, Plenty, Ohio," he said, catching my arm.

Grinding my teeth, I turned back. "What? We're finished, aren't we?"

He studied me. I could make out in my peripheral vision the other gym attendees doing the same thing. "I stuffed up, didn't I?"

I shook my head. "I'm fine. Just want to go have a shower."

"Ahh, the dreaded word *fine*." He let out a slow sigh. "The bane of every guy's existence when uttered by a woman. The word that really means I want to break you in half and stuff your stupid face with your stupid words."

I didn't laugh. Instead, I shucked my arm from his grip and gave him a tight-lipped smile. "What do I owe you for today?"

He didn't answer and I could tell he was trying to decide how to proceed.

Here's the thing with Parkinson's disease. It's not just all shakes and trembles and falling down. It is a brain problem, after all. It can, at times, make you very surly. I watched Dad tiptoe around Mom often, especially in the last few years before he was killed. I don't know if my surliness at that moment was because of the fucked-up state my brain was in from jet lag, sleep deprivation, my goddamn pain-in-the-ass disease, or because Brendon Osmond had made me feel the very way I hated feeling—vulnerable and weak. Either way, I was happy to entrench myself in it.

"That much, huh?" I sneered.

With an ambiguous nod, he held up his hands, palms out. "On the house today."

For a second, a wave of guilty regret washed over me. He'd been so nice, he *was* so nice, and he'd only been concerned. And then I caught a glimpse of the curious onlookers, remembered they'd all seen Brendon behaving like I was an invalid, and guilty regret was strangled by annoyance and embarrassment again.

See what I mean? Surliness.

With my own ambiguous nod, I walked through the door. "Thanks."

I wasn't three steps away when I heard the door open behind me. My heart thumped faster, and given I'd just finished a massive workout, it was already freaking fast. I didn't want him coming after me. I wanted to wallow in my irritation.

"Same time tomorrow, Plenty, Ohio," Brendon called at my back.

It wasn't a question. Nor could I detect any anger or disappointment in his voice. Damn, this guy was unflappable.

I made it back to Mackellar House without stumbling or lurching once. No one looked at me like I was a debilitated freak. No one made sympathetic noises or pulled pitying faces.

Why would they? No one knew much about me. Those who were at the underwear party last night knew me as the new American student here on a ten-week scholarship to study koalas and global warming. Those who weren't there most likely didn't give a rat's ass who I was. Just another student trudging through the university grounds dressed in gym gear and looking drained.

And still, the image of the other gym-goers peering at me on the floor wouldn't leave my head. Wondering what was wrong with me, why Brendon was so alarmed ...

The concern in his eyes still mocked me.

I ground my teeth and walked faster up the stairs to my room. I needed a shower, food and my meds.

My fucking meds. Damn, I hated that I needed them.

Hated it with a passion.

There was no one in the communal bathroom when I got there, I thanked God for that. While I was in the shower, I heard people come and go, mostly other girls. At the sound of Macca's deep rumbling voice, I almost forgot to breathe. Was Raph with him?

When silence fell over the bathroom once again I let out a ragged sigh, rinsed my hair of its conditioner and killed the water. Five minutes later, dry and dressed, I opened the shower cubicle door and came face to face with Heather.

"Ready?" she asked with a grin.

I frowned. For some stupid reason, disappointment swelled in my stomach. Surely I hadn't wanted Raphael Jones to be there, had I? We'd made it a habit of bumping into each other in public bathrooms, but that didn't mean I wanted the habit to continue. Did I?

"For what?" I asked, slinging my damp towel over my shoulder. I'd remembered it this time. Maci Learn-From-Her-Mistakes Rowling, that's me.

"For all things Australian." Heather's grin grew wider. "Starting now, with Vegemite on toast and Milo."

The next two weeks—or *fortnight*, as the Aussies call it—passed in a blur. Heather did, in fact, make it her mission to educate me on all things Australian, and I spent every day when I wasn't in class trying or experiencing something only found or originating in the country. I discovered I *hated* Vegemite, loved Tim Tams, could take or leave pavlova, and would never get enough lamingtons. Oh boy, those sweet little vanilla cakes covered in chocolate syrup and dipped in coconut are addictive. If you ever get the chance to try one, don't. Not unless you plan to gain a gazillion pounds.

Thank God I was working out every day.

True to his word, Brendon Osmond turned up at my door the morning after our first session in the gym, as bright and cheery and relaxed as ever. If he'd been expecting surly Maci to greet him, he didn't show it.

By then, almost twenty-four hours after I'd crumpled to the gym floor in a melodramatic show of over-exertion, I'd calmed down somewhat. I wasn't as angry at him as I had been and I was determined to just get on with life. Getting on with life was, after all, my mantra.

However, I have to admit I was a little less open to engaging with him in conversation. It wasn't childish pettiness over the fact he'd made me feel vulnerable and weak, but rather a defense mechanism. Better to keep someone who could make me feel that way at arm's length.

It was hard, especially given Brendon's engaging nature. I kept telling myself he was just the guy with muscles helping me with the physical therapy side of my condition. It helped he didn't raise the topic of my Parkinson's again.

It also helped, in a weird way, that I didn't see Raph at all in those two weeks. Not once.

We didn't share any classes—Plenty's small college was a world apart from the University of Sydney, not just in size, but in structure. Quite often, whole days would pass in lectures where I didn't recognize anyone. Whereas college at home felt like an extension of high school, just with a few more parties and less parental involvement, university and campus life in Australia was like being thrown into the world without a map.

Suffice it to say, it made my head spin.

What also made my head spin—something that took me a

whole two weeks to identify—was that I hadn't talked to my mom every day.

I didn't realize how much of who I was hung on how much time I spent looking out for her, making sure she was taking her meds, eating well, and staying out of trouble. By trouble I mean not doing things she physically couldn't—or shouldn't—do anymore.

But in the two weeks since arriving in Australia, the only person I'd needed to think about was essentially me. Which made the morning of my fifteenth day in the country all the more ... irritating.

I had no one to blame but myself.

Thanks to my busy schedule—workout with Brendon, breakfast with Heather, morning classes, lunch with Heather, afternoon study, hitting the shops or the beach with Heather, followed by some kind of dinner somewhere that wasn't necessarily of the healthy variety—and without Mom's advanced Parkinson's to remind me of my own condition, I'd grown remiss about my meds. Or maybe careless was a better word. Negligent was probably an even better one.

Whatever the word, I missed a day's dose here or there. Nothing too disastrous, but I wasn't prepared for my body and brain's reaction.

So when Raph found me at my door the morning of my fifteenth day, sweaty and drained after my session with Brendon, unable to open the damn thing because my hand and arm were shaking so much I couldn't insert my key into the lock, I kinda ... well ... lost it.

I was banging my forehead against the door, eyes squeezed shut, one hand gripping the goddamn knob, the other gripping the goddamn key, frustrated curses falling from my lips, when I heard him.

"Working out with Osmond exhausting you, American girl?"

There was no denying the sarcasm in his voice. Nor was there any denying the way my stupid, quaking, messed-up, traitorous body reacted immediately to his presence. Fourteen days—a fortnight—without a single *glimpse* of him, and of course, here he was now, when I was at my worst. Fate was a bitch sometimes.

I pressed my forehead harder to the door and poured every ounce of will I possessed into making the key slide into the lock.

It didn't.

A choked sob escaped me. Followed by a muttered *fuck*. Yeah, I was in a bad place.

"I didn't ask what you were doing," Raph drawled beside me. There was a part of me that recognized his sarcasm was gone, replaced with something else. That part, unfortunately, was being suffocated by my increasing agitation and self-contempt.

I tried to slide the key into the lock again.

Again, my hand, my shaking, useless, worthless, weak, good-for-nothing hand, failed me.

Another sob burst past my lips, louder than the previous.

"You okay, American girl?" Concern laced his voice this time. No sarcasm, no mysterious emotion that may or may not have been jealousy. Concern. Of course, you know that only made it worse, right?

I turned my head away from where he stood at his door, hating everything, *everything*, unable to even find the strength or balance to stand up straight.

"Maci?" He drew closer. I didn't just hear that fact, I could feel it. "Is everything okay? Are you and ... did Osmond

... Jesus, why is your hand shaking so much? Are you okay? Do you need me to do anything?"

And there you have it. The moment I snapped.

I'm not proud of what happened next, but I'll own it.

I spun around as well as my body would let me, which wasn't much. My fingers slipped from the doorknob as my stare locked on his. I knew I looked a sight—sweaty from my workout, hair hanging in damp clumps over my eyes, face no doubt red from anger. I didn't care. "I don't need you or anyone else to do anything for me."

The snarled rebuff would have been infinitely more impressive if my hand wasn't shaking so much I slapped my own thigh and dropped the key to my room.

Awesome.

Raph moved so fast, he'd picked it up before I could finish biting back my curse. He straightened, his gaze on my face.

I held out my right hand. There wasn't a hope in hell I was holding out my left. "Key?"

Raph's eyes narrowed. He shook his head. "Not until you tell me what's going on."

"Nothing!" I snapped, thrusting my right hand out farther. "Except some guy who thinks he's all that won't give me my key."

"Oh, I don't think I'm all that." He shook his head, crossed his arms over his chest and leaned his shoulder against my closed door. "I *do* think you're being stubborn though. And keeping something from me."

I tried to snatch my key from where it dangled from his index finger against his biceps. Unfortunately, I was so angry I tried with my left hand.

Raph caught my wrist in gentle fingers before I could retract my arm. Which only made it worse.

"Let go," I growled. There was little point tugging against

his grip—I knew I had no strength in me at the moment—but I tugged anyway. Sure enough, the effort was laughable.

Despite my weak attempt at escape, he did let go of my wrist. And then he moved closer to me, gazing down into my face. "I really think you should tell me what's going on. I want to … If you need help, I don't mind giving—"

"I don't want your help," I repeated, terse anger cutting my words. Deep in my chest, my heart hammered. "I want my key."

Without a word, he gave it to me.

I snatched it—right hand, of course—and spun back to my door. And then fell against it when my balance deserted me.

My shoulder struck the door first and my key fell to the ground, clattering beside my foot. The fingers of my left hand splayed against the door and, without a pause for common decency, began to tap against it in that familiar, erratic way I despised so much.

I ground my teeth, balled my hand and slammed it against the wood with a pathetic thud. "Please go away, Jones," I begged, casting him a sideways glare.

He shook his head. "Not happening."

"You going to shadow me all day?"

"If I have to."

"Going to cramp your romantic style if you do that, isn't it?"

He shrugged, the corners of his lips twitching.

With a contemptuous huff, I bent down and plucked my key from beside my foot. And fucking lost my balance again. Not a lot, but enough that I hit my head on the door.

There was no stopping the tears. Hot, exasperated, furious tears of self-hate and hate for the world.

Two warm, firm hands smoothed up my back, over my shoulders and down my arms. Steady fingers found my hands and before I could stop him, Raph was gently helping me to my feet and—without a word—pulling me against his body. Not an embrace, just a solid wall of support.

I both hated it and cherished it.

"Have you had breakfast?" he asked, his chin nudging the top of my head, deep voice vibrating through me.

I croaked out a "No."

He pulled away from me a little. "Will you bite my head off if I ask you to have breakfast with me?"

I wanted to tell him where he could stick his breakfast. I really did. Of course, my stomach chose that moment to growl like a goddamn lion. And the feel of Raph's fingers threaded with mine, holding them, keeping them steady, really was lovely.

Oh boy.

"Just breakfast," he said. "No public bathroom snogging. Promise. Don't want The Biceps coming after me."

My gut flip-flopped at the implication. "Brendon and I—"

"Hey, Jones!" Macca's shout stopped me dead.

I flinched. As did Raph.

"Getting it on with the Yank, 'eh?" Macca loped up to us, grin wide. "Hey, Maci. Heard you had a thing at the gym the other morning. You okay?"

"She's fine," Raph answered. Impatience scratched at the words. "We're just about to go for breakfast."

"Cool." Macca ran a quick gaze over me, not so much sexual interest, rather a curious inspection. Talk had made it around to the small population of Mackellar House about my *collapse*, it seemed. Damn it. I'd really hoped it had been forgotten. I was also longing for the massive, almost impersonal size of college back home. In a dorm of over two hundred people, my ... quirks didn't really make for much conversation compared to what everyone else was getting up to.

"Can I come?" said Macca. "To breakfast."

"Fuck off," Raph said. He was smiling at his friend, but I couldn't help notice he drew closer to me.

I liked it. Too much.

Before I could change my mind, I ducked my head, pulled my fingers from Raph's and slipped my key into my lock. All without dropping anything or stumbling off balance. Thank freaking God.

"Actually," I said, "I think I'm just going to have a shower and get to class early. I have a paper due to Professor Firth tomorrow and I want to ask him a few questions before class starts."

I didn't wait for an answer.

With far more grace than I'd possessed a few minutes ago, I slipped into my room and closed the door behind me.

First port of call was my meds bag.

Breathing fast, hands shaking more than ever, I extracted a small orangey-yellow pill bottle from the bag's crowded innards, popped the top and shook—ha, ha, get it?—out two tiny white pills.

For a long moment, long enough for me to overhear Macca laughingly tell Raph he'd been "Burned, mate. Burned," I stared at the pills.

They sat on my palm, both my salvation and my curse.

Pills to stop my brain from betraying my body.

With a slow, deep breath, I opened my mouth and smacked my hand to my lips.

The meds struck my tongue. Instantly, a strong, bitter taste assaulted my taste buds. As it did every time I took my medication, a shudder claimed me, a visceral reaction to the tiny things keeping me normal.

Normal. What a poor excuse for a word to describe an existence with little hope for normalcy. Parkinson's disease robs a person of that. Normalcy. And if you let it, it also robs you of hope.

Hope of being able to tie your own shoelaces.

Hope of being able to apply eyeliner.

Hope of being able to reach the golden years of your life without the need for adult diapers.

Hope of living beyond the use-by-date of your ravaged brain.

Hope.

I swallowed the pills without the aid of water. A decade of watching Mom do the same had taught me the trick, as well as over twelve months of doing it myself—a quick jerk of the head and a grimace was all it took. Like swallowing mouth-wash without the minty freshness.

Ten minutes later, meds slowly dissolving in my gut, towel and fresh clothes slung over my shoulder, I opened my door.

And found Raph standing there, shoulder leaning on the doorjamb, lips curled in a smile. "Breakfast?"

"Have you been waiting there the whole time?" I asked, not sure if I was excited or angry.

"Yep."

I scowled. "Then you shouldn't have bothered. As you can see, I'm going to have a shower and go to class."

He laughed. "Shower, yes. Class, no. I know for a fact you don't have any classes this morning."

My eyebrows shot up. "How do you know that?"

He shrugged, the motion one part boyishly cute, one part ... arrogantly confused. Yes, I know that makes no sense, but it's the only way I can describe it. Like he was just as confused as I was about our chemistry.

And man, was I confused. Forcing myself to look calm, I crossed my arms over my breasts. Not because I was miffed—okay, I was a little—but because my nipples were pinching into tight little points of excited delight.

Holy crap, he'd been keeping tabs on me? What did that mean? Did it mean what I thought it meant? And how the hell did I feel about that if it did?

He laughed. "Actually, Heather walked past a second ago and mentioned you were having breakfast with her. I told her *I* was going to take you to breakfast instead."

Crap, I'd forgotten all about that. We were going to catch a bus into Paddington—an artsy inner-city suburb—and pretend we were art students at a cafe called Triptych, where naked models sat around all day, just waiting for people to draw them. Had Heather told him where we were going?

"But ..." His smile turned to that devilish grin I remembered from the airport bathroom, the one that made my body react in a very sexual way. "If you really *want* to go to Triptych, I'm happy to drive us."

Damn, she had.

Heat flooded my checks. Goddamn it, I was blushing more on this side of the planet than I ever had back home. WTF? "What about your bodyguard?" I asked, hoping to ruffle his feathers a little. I needed some kind of upper hand here.

It didn't work. All he did was grin. "I've seen his doodles. Don't think drawing is his thing."

I rolled my eyes. "That's not what I meant."

Raph laughed and held up his hand. "I know. But c'mon, you have to admit, that was funny."

I couldn't stop my lips twitching.

Raph's grin stretched wider. "Ah, there it is."

"What?"

His gaze met mine. "Your smile. I haven't seen it since the airport. So? Breakfast at Triptych? My treat?"

I opened my mouth, ready to say no even if a warm yumminess was blooming in my belly.

"Or," he went on before I could, dark eyes glinting, "we could just stick with our normal routine and I could follow you to the bathroom and we could make out there?"

"Are those my only two options?"

He nodded. "'Fraid so."

I let out a sigh. A maelstrom of butterflies whipped up a storm of nerves inside me. "Breakfast it is then. But only if I'm allowed to laugh at your drawings."

"Deal. Now hurry the hell up, will you? I'm starving."

I rushed through my shower and dressed after the fastest towel-drying ever. As a consequence, my skin was a little damp when I shoved my legs into my shorts and yanked my tank over my head. I kept squirming in my seat as we drove to Triptych, trying to inconspicuously separate my clinging clothes from my body.

Raph kept giving me curious sideways glances, but he thankfully didn't say anything. By this stage, my meds had kicked in and my tremors had subsided. I was grateful for that, at least, even if I did look like I had ants in my pants.

His car was nothing like I'd expected. For some reason, I'd placed him in a sleek, expensive number, like a Porsche, or the kind of car Iron Man drove. Instead, he walked me to a beat-up, baby pickup-looking thing with a row of massive spotlights attached to a thick metal bar in front of the grill.

Inside, on the passenger seat and floor, there were empty Red Bull cans and chip bags, and a stack of books with titles like *Statistics for Veterinary and Animal Science*, *Biofilms and Veterinary Medicine*, and *Pathologic Basis of Veterinary Disease*.

"Just some light reading," Raph said, his expression deadpan as he gathered them all up and shoved them in the narrow space behind my seat.

I thought of my *lightreading* back in my room—the latest Stephen King novel, three *Girlfriend* magazines I'd brought from home, and my copy of *The Age of Global Warming*. To my credit, there were also the required text books for my study at University of Sydney, but apart from when I'd been in class and lectures, I hadn't paid them that much attention.

Thirty minutes of casual chatting—and squirming—later, we pulled into an empty space near the cafe. I was enjoying myself already, damn it. Yes, there was a part of me that desperately wanted to discover Raph was a boring slug when we weren't making out in public bathrooms. Unfortunately, he wasn't. He was funny, with a dry sense of humor a lot like my dad's.

That wasn't helping my situation any, but I was laughing too much to really care. As we climbed out of his car—he called it a ute, which must be some unique Aussie term for pickup—I was momentarily confused when he reached behind the driver's seat, withdrew a baseball cap and pulled it low over his eyes. "Aren't we going inside?" I asked, watching him over the roof of the ute.

He looked at me with an enigmatic smile. I couldn't see what his eyes were doing; the sunglasses he wore were so damn dark it was like gazing into two fathomless black holes. "Yep."

When he didn't offer any further elaboration on the cap and sunglasses, I shrugged. "Okay."

Walking around to where I waited for him on the foot-path, he took my hand. My heart leapt into my throat so freaking fast I almost choked. Oh boy, his fingers threaded through mine felt nice. No, more than nice. Wonderful. Incredible.

Perfect.

He leaned closer to me, his dimple flashing in his right cheek. "I'm sort of famous, remember," he whispered, as if sharing an important secret. "Don't want to be swarmed."

At first I wasn't sure if he was joking or not. And then I remembered the paparazzi at the airport the day I met him. "Shall I call you Bruce?" I whispered back, unable to hide my own grin.

His dimple creased deeper. "Bruce it is. Let's go draw naked people."

We entered the cafe. And I stumbled to a halt.

There were three completely naked men and two completely naked women of various shapes and sizes perched on stools scattered around the interior. Bustling about them were waitstaff dressed in the typical uniform of black and white, delivering orders to the patrons sitting at tables circling the models. Most of those eating in the cafe were doing so while casting long gazes at the naked man or woman closest to them, a fork or sandwich in one hand, some kind of drawing implement in the other.

"Shit," Raph muttered at my side, his grip on my hand firm. "We didn't bring anything to draw with. Or on, for that matter."

I noticed the tension in his jaw as he looked about the cafe. Was he really concerned about that? Or about someone recognizing him?

Turning my attention to the diners nearest us, I walked over to one table populated by two young men who looked my age and gave them my shyest smile.

"Hi there. How are y'all?" I said, emphasizing my accent. "I forgot to bring drawing supplies. Do you think you could possibly lend us some paper and a pencil or two?" I caught my bottom lip with my teeth and turned on the coy charm. "Please?"

"Give me your phone number and I will," the guy closest to me said, smile wide.

"How about I just buy it from you?" Raph's deep voice sounded beside me as he held out his hand. I caught a glimpse of a bright golden-colored note—Australian money is very colorful, by the way—in his fingers, and the other guy snatched it away.

"Done," he said, ramming the note—fifty dollars, can you believe it?—into his pocket and nudging his friend with his elbow. "For another, you can have our table as well."

"Deal." Raph produced another golden note from his wallet and held it out.

Holy crap, he'd just paid one hundred dollars.

One hundred dollars.

The two guys jolted to their feet, scooped up their coffee mugs and sketches and vacated the table, leaving us with a collection of what looked like charcoal sticks, pencils and erasers.

"I can't believe you just did that," I said, dropping into the closest seat.

Raph lowered himself into the seat beside mine, dimple flashing again. "Me either. I must like you or something."

His quip sent tingly heat straight to the junction of my thighs. Thankfully, a waiter appeared, saving me from trying to stumble through a lame response.

We placed our orders—me, egg-white omelet with baby spinach and grilled tomato; Raph, scrambled eggs and bacon, with a side order of mushrooms—and then turned our atten-tion to the model perched on his stool a few feet away.

"Wow," I breathed before I could stop myself.

He was, umm, how shall I put this? Large. Everywhere. And I mean *everywhere*. And hairy. Really hairy. His man-boobs rested on his round gut, a gut that hung low over his groin, a groin that ... well ... I'm sure porn stars would have been envious of what hung between his legs. I couldn't stop looking at it. Damn, it was ... I don't know what it was. Part mesmerizing, part gross, part ...

"You're staring." Raph's whisper jerked my gaze upward and, God help me, I discovered the model *watching* me.

Heat flooded my cheeks again with blush number 242.

"Here." Raph thrust a charcoal stick at my hand. "Go for it."

More than a little flustered, I looked at him. I hadn't really thought sitting in a cafe studying a naked person would be so confronting, but oh boy, was it ever. Or maybe it was the fact the naked man *knew* I was looking at him that messed me up? I had grown up in Plenty, Ohio, after all. Naked people didn't just sit around waiting for people to draw them in Plenty. Not in cafes, at least.

Hand shaking—this time from nerves, I'm happy to report —I took the offered stick of charcoal and gave Raph a smile in return.

He plucked a pencil from the table and, lowering his sunglasses a little, winked at me. "Masterpiece time, American girl."

And with that, he started drawing.

A horse.

I burst out laughing.

He'd finished his first sketch of the horse—wearing stilettoes, I might add—by the time our breakfast arrived. I was halfway through my first sketch of Mr. Check Out The Size Of That Thing. I lowered my charcoal stub, studying what I'd created so far.

Can I say that as an artist, I make an awesome tree-hugging greenie.

Raph, it seemed, agreed with my self-critique. "So you're going for an abstract approach?" he asked.

"Hey." I pouted at my abysmal drawing. "It's not that bad."

He laughed.

We ate our breakfast quickly. Surprisingly, I found myself returning to my drawing often, making little adjustments to Mr. Check Out The Size Of That Thing's image. I still hadn't attempted to draw his schlong, a fact Raph pointed out with a smirk.

I wanted to tell him to concentrate on his own drawing, but when I looked at his page I discovered he'd not only sketched another horse—this one with a koala wearing sunglasses and a baseball cap riding on its back (yeah, I got the joke)—but also a really impressive drawing of our model's large, hairy hand resting on his meaty, equally hairy thigh.

"Are you sure you shouldn't be studying art?" I asked in a low voice.

Raph chuckled. "My father would kill me."

I raised my eyebrows. "Why?"

He considered his artwork. "It's a given that I follow tradition and take my place in the family business when I finish studying."

I didn't miss the taint of embittered melancholy in the declaration.

"What *is* the family business?" I asked. I couldn't help myself. Raph was such an enigma. One I wanted to know more about. The fame by marriage, the lofty arrogance at university, the concern when he'd found me unstable, the playful flirting this morning, the scorching kisses ... If I wasn't careful, I'd fall for him.

And as I've pointed out, falling for anyone is not allowed. Not in Maci Rowling's world.

Lifting his focus from his sketch, he gave me a smile that said he was done being resentful. "Farming. Remember I mentioned all the koalas on our property a fortnight ago? When we were discussing global warming and koala mating habits? Right before you left with Osmond?"

At the mention of Brendon, a finger of guilt traced up my spine. I don't know why. Because I was messed up? Confused? Conflicted? A skanky ho currently falling in lust with two hot guys?

Pretending not to be unsettled at all, I made an *ah* sound. "That's right," I said. "Maybe I should call you Farmer Bruce from now on?"

"Maybe. What have you been calling me up until now?"

"Asshole," I answered honestly.

Raph laughed. "Yeah, let's go with Farmer Bruce."

"Farmer Bruce it is." I said. "It suits you."

He grinned.

A few moments of silence later, after we picked at our food and worked on our sketches, he fixed me with a contemplative gaze. "Why koalas? I've been meaning to ask since the underwear party. I know your dad was Australian, but is that the only reason?"

Adding some extra hair to my drawing—God, our model really *was* hairy—I smiled. "When I was eight we went on a family vacation to San Diego. We spent a whole day at the zoo and almost half of that day in the Australian section. I remember Dad getting a loopy, dreamy look on his face as we walked through it, like he was home again. Mom kept giggling at him, especially when he'd tell us these long, funny stories about encounters he'd had with whatever Australian animal we were looking at. Like how he got pushed into a river by a kangaroo, or had his lunch stolen by an emu. It was awesome. But the best bit for me was when we got to the koala exhibit. They were so gorgeous. I wanted one straightaway. From that point onward, I was obsessed with them."

Raph grinned. "Define obsessed."

I laughed. "By the time I was thirteen, I had over fifty stuffed koalas in my bedroom."

"Yeah, that's obsessed. So I guess you'll go a little silly if I tell you I hand-raised a koala when I was ten?"

I gaped at him. "Are you serious?"

He nodded. "I told you one of Australia's largest koala colonies lives on our property. I found a baby koala whose mum had been killed by a feral cat and I took it home and cared for it until it was old enough to return to the wild."

"Wow."

Raph smiled at my awestruck response. "It was pretty cool. But man, do those buggers have claws on them. This scar here—" He lifted his right arm above his head and pointed at a pale white line running the length of his triceps, "—is the result of Kenny trying to get away from our dog."

"Kenny?"

He grinned again. "Nothing wrong with the name Kenny. Well, apart from the fact Kenny was a girl."

I threw back my head and laughed.

Our waiter returned a little after that and whisked our plates away, leaving us to focus on our sketches. An hour later, after Mr. Check Out The Size Of That Thing left, only to be replaced with Miss Holy Crap Could Those Boobs Be Any Bigger, Raph suggested we finish up.

Disappointment sheared through me. I was having fun. Lots of fun. But that disappointment morphed into excitement when he said, "Want to go climb the Harbour Bridge?

They run sessions every fifteen minutes. Reckon I could pull the celebrity card and get us in for an afternoon session."

"Would you do that?"

He grinned. "Probably not. But if we're lucky there might be a cancellation or no-show. Want to risk it?"

Every muscle in my body tight, I nodded.

"Excellent. I'll just go pay the bill and we can get on our way."

He rose to his feet and strode to the counter, and I'm not ashamed to say I watched him the entire time.

"Is that Raphael Jones?"

The question uttered from a soft female voice on my left, drew my attention so fast I think I got whiplash.

Our new model, the one with the huge boobs, was staring at me, a predatory gleam in her eyes.

"Err ..." I said, startled momentarily into inarticulate stupidity.

"I knew it," she whispered. "That explains all the photographers outside."

The blood drained from my face. An unpleasant tension crawled up the back of my neck and over my scalp. Photographers? How long had there been photographers outside? Had they followed us? Oh boy, this wasn't good.

"He's so hot," she went on, leaning towards me. "Can you introduce me?"

Behind her, someone muttered a less-than-quiet complaint about models who didn't know how to sit still.

"I ..." I began. "He's not—"

Before I could finish denying Raph was who he really was, he returned. Freaking perfect timing, right?

"Oh my God," our model squeed, gaping at him. "You really are Raphael Jones. Oh my God, I think you are so gorgeous. Will you sign my boobs?"

His smile froze. He stared hard at the woman before turning his dark sunglasses on me. "Did you tell her?"

I shook my head, my heart an insane trip hammer in my chest.

"Raphael Jones?" I heard someone nearby say. "Is it really Raphael Jones?"

The muscle in his jaw knotted.

"Raph," I said, rising to my feet. "She recognized you. She said there are photographers out—"

He spun away from me, digging for something in his pocket. Pulling out his cell phone, he slid his thumb over the screen before ramming it to his ear. "We're coming out," he said to whoever was on the other end of the connection, the words damn near a growl.

Around us, our fellow diners and Triptych's staff stirred at the realization they had a celebrity in their midst.

"Raph?" I repeated his name. It was such a lame thing to do, but I was so dumbstruck by what was happening, I couldn't grasp at anything like logical, rational thought. "I didn't tell her. I promise. She recognized you. She said there are photographers outside."

He turned back to me, his expression bleak. Guarded. Black sunglasses even darker due to the shadow cast by the peak of his cap. "Okay, we have to go, all right?"

I nodded, feeling a cold sense of relief that he wasn't abandoning me. I wasn't sure if he was angry at me or the situation, but at least he was including me in his planned escape. That was something, right? "O-okay."

He grabbed my hand with a strong grip, threading fingers through mine.

His name floated on the air, accompanied by more than one flash from more than one smartphone. Movement outside caught my eye. Lots of movement. And people.

My stomach dropped.

Damn it, the model hadn't lied. There were paparazzi waiting. A lot.

"Raph?" I croaked, watching the at least five guys with cameras shove and jostle for position beyond the protection of the cafe's front window.

"Fuck." His mutter was barely audible.

A massive man in a suit barged through the front door, the same massive man in the same blue suit I'd encountered at Sydney Airport.

I blinked. Where had he come from? Had he followed us as well as the paparazzi?

"Sir?" he said, fixing Raph with a level gaze, one arm extended toward us both. "Time."

Raph's fingers squeezed mine. He turned to look at me, his face a stiff mask hiding whatever he was thinking. "Damn it, this isn't what I wanted. I'm sorry but we've got to move quick, American girl. Can you do that?"

I nodded, guilt smashing through me. I hadn't blown his cover, I hadn't, but I felt responsible anyway. Like I'd somehow fucked up when our model first asked if Raph was indeed Raph. "I can."

He gave me a crooked smile. "I'll catch you if you stumble. Promise."

And with those words, he strode toward his bodyguard, tugging me along behind him.

Say Cheese

I never made it to the car. Shooting me an indifferent look, Raph's bodyguard—who went by the name Mr. Horn, I found out later—wedged his way between us and, like a hulking, glaring blanket of muscle, shielded Raph from the frenzied paparazzi and the curious public amassing on the sidewalk.

My fingers slipped from Raph's and before I knew it, I was being jostled and shoved by photographers and pedestrians alike. I think I heard Raph call my name above all the commotion. I heard him demand Mr. Horn get me. I *think* I heard Horn tell him he would. Given that the bodyguard *didn't* come back and help me, I could be wrong. There was a lot of shouting from the paparazzi. Shouting and catcalling and general frenzy as they all tried to get Raph's attention. I even heard one or two ask who the girl was. I assumed *the girl* they were referring to was me.

Raph didn't respond to any of them. Probably because by this point, Mr. Horn had shoved him into the backseat of a shiny black SUV.

The madness grew. The paparazzi turned nasty, no doubt pissed at being denied their prey. They hurled insults at Raph's bodyguard, who ignored them all as he reefed the front door open and climbed in.

I pushed through the mob, trying to get to the car. Trying to get Horn's attention. He didn't look back at me.

The paparazzi rushed the car. They slapped their hands against the back passenger window, a window tinted so dark I couldn't see through it. If Raph was looking for me in the crowd, I had no hope of knowing it.

Shocked beyond belief, I called out to Raph, to Horn, as I struggled to get to the SUV. Struggled through the melee.

Struggled in vain, it turned out.

With the roar of an engine, the black SUV took off, leaving a furious, cursing, running jumble of photographers in its wake.

I was bumped into so many times I was surprised I didn't fall over. I probably would have if there hadn't been so many people squishing around me. I bounced off more than one, muttering apologies every time even as a part of my flustered brain told me I had no damn reason to apologize. They were smashing into me, damn it. At this point, my flustered brain hadn't figured out that I'd essentially been abandoned in an area of Sydney I knew nothing about without any real means of getting back to Mackellar House save hailing a cab.

And then the paparazzi turned to me, and my brain—flustered as it was—finally registered I was alone. Alone and utterly unprepared.

Holy. Crap.

One second they were watching the shiny black SUV speed away, the next they were spinning to face me, cameras raised, flashes exploding, questions flying.

"What's your name?"

"Are you Raphael Jones's girlfriend?"

"Are you part of the royal family?"

"Who are you?"

"Are you sleeping together?"

"Tell us your name!"

"Give us a smile."

I swear to God, it was like they were a pack of ravenous hyenas and I was a ... a ... shit, a gazelle or some other delicate creature they'd devour.

I blanched and flinched at every blinding flash. I raised my arm in an attempt to shield my face from their greedy, predatory stares, noticing all too late my hand shaking like mad.

Fuck. Here we go. Stress-induced tremors. Joy.

The horde of paparazzi didn't let up. Not even when I shoved my way free of them. Apparently, I must have said something because suddenly they were demanding to know where in America I was from, still taking photos as they hurried beside me.

I walked as fast as I could one way, stopped and tried to

get my bearings. It was impossible. I had no idea where I was other than somewhere in Paddington. I didn't even know where Raph's pickup was in relation to where I was now.

The paparazzi badgered me still, a collective unit of irritating tenacity. Like some hive mind, they shadowed my every move, shouting questions at me.

It really was ridiculous. And scary.

Yeah, I was scared.

I wasn't cut out for this type of thing. My body and brain, what with its faulty design, wasn't genetically equipped to deal with it.

Biting back a sob, I yanked my phone from my bag. My hand and fingers were shaking so much it took me five fucking tries before I could get my thumb to connect with the correct place on the screen, let alone swipe it smoothly. I was walking with my head down, bumping off paparazzi and basically stressing the fuck out.

I dropped my phone, bit back a curse, bent over to pick it up before someone—most likely me the way I was going—stomped on it.

Thank freaking God, I straightened without falling over. I don't know what I would have done if I'd lost balance and fallen to the ground. Cry, no doubt. Which would not only be embarrassing, but would also be captured by the slathering photographers around me, ending up on the net where the world could witness my humiliation.

Still refusing to look anywhere else but at my phone, I powered down the sidewalk, surrounded by shouting paparazzi. They were relentless. They had the smell of blood in their noses, and no matter how much I ignored them, they weren't going to leave me alone.

I had to get away somehow.

Willing my hand to steady, I woke my cell again and,

vision blurred by the tears threatening to overwhelm me, I jabbed the phone icon on the screen.

A list of all the recent numbers I'd called and received appeared and, head roaring, body shaking and eyes filled with stinging tears, I jammed my stupid trembling thumb down on the top number.

Brendon Osmond's number.

"C'mon, tell us your name," a man jostling for position on my right cajoled, shoving a camera at my face.

"What's your relationship with Jones?"

"Is he good in bed?"

"Have you met the king?"

I pushed my way through the throng of photographers, phone pressed to my ear, praying for Brendon to pick up. Oh God, I really needed him to pick—

"Plenty, Ohio." His cheery, happy-go-lucky voice sounded in my ear. "What's up?"

"Brendon," I burst out, squeezing my eyes shut. Christ, I had the shakes worse than when Raph had found me at my door only a few hours ago. In fact, I don't think I'd ever been this bad, and I was medicated. Holy fuck, was this really what I had to look forward to?

"Who's Brendon?" a guy on my left asked, firing his camera. "Does Jones know about him?"

"Are you American?" another called, obviously new to the party.

A raw sob tore at my throat and I spun on my heel, frantic to escape them.

"Maci?" Sharp concern cut Brendon's voice, and for a second, I had an image of him standing frozen in the gym, a powerful, threatening tower of muscle. "What's going on?"

"I don't ..." I began, turning again, going nowhere,

flinching every time a camera clicked or a man shouted a question at me. "The paparazzi ..."

As one, the photographers around me let out a whooping cheer, as if ecstatic to be a part of my breakdown. And that's what it was, a breakdown. I was dangerously close to system shutdown. My brain and my body couldn't take any more.

"Maci." It wasn't just concern in Brendon's voice this time, but alarm. "Where are you? What's going—"

"Say cheese, love!" a man directly in front of me guffawed, camera lens pointed right at my head.

I let out a yelp, flung my hand up to protect my face, spun around once more and threw myself into a wobbly sprint. Head down.

Which is why I didn't see the street sign pole before I slammed into it, forehead first.

There was a sickening crack, a burst of white, searing pain, braying laughter, Brendon's voice calling my name.

And then nothing.

Nothing but blackness.

***

I really don't know how long I was out. All I know is I came to in the hospital.

Yep, the hospital. One of the paparazzi had the decency to pick up my phone when I collapsed, tell Brendon where I was and then call an ambulance.

Apparently—and I'm only going on what I was told by a nurse after I regained consciousness in the ER—all but one of the paparazzi bolted after I hit the ground. The one who didn't run stayed with me until the ambulance arrived. By that time Brendon had arrived as well. The nurse told me the paramedics told *her* Brendon had come damn near close to punching the photographer before the paramedics stopped him.

Even then, what he said he'd do to the paparazzo—did you know that's the singular noun for paparazzi? Me neither until the conversation between myself and the nurse took place—had the nurse declaring he was both heroic and scary.

Apparently—and again, this was all hearsay from the nurse—when it took too long for a doctor to see me, Brendon walked up to one, fixed him with an unwavering stare, and *demanded* I be seen to straight away.

My chatty nurse said that all the women who witnessed it swooned. I don't know how true that was. When I asked Brendon about it as I was being discharged—over four hours after finally regaining consciousness—all he did was laugh.

And yet I couldn't help but notice the way my attending ER doc flinched whenever Brendon looked his way.

Hmmm.

Anyways, getting knocked out is a bit of a deal when you've got Parkinson's. Alarm bells go off in medical-type peoples' heads. I had to endure X-rays and CAT scans and MRIs before they allowed me to leave. I had to give them a list of the medication I was on. When I confessed to missing some, I don't know who gave me the more disapproving look— the doc or Brendon.

It wasn't until we were in Brendon's car driving away from the hospital, that he decided a lecture was in order.

"Missing your meds, Plenty?" he said, disappointment in his voice as he studied the road. "Really?"

I shrugged. "I'm okay now. Honest."

I wasn't really. My head was hurting still, hot embarrassment licked through my veins, and for some reason I was feeling guilty. The last emotion confused me. I couldn't figure it out. Why was I feeling guilty? What had I done wrong?

"I don't believe that," he answered. "I know you hate talking about your condition, but you can't ignore you've—"

"I'm not ignoring it," I cut him off, watching the streets of Sydney pass by. "I just missed a few days here and there over the last two weeks. And you've seen me every goddamn morning. Have I looked like I was deteriorating? Maybe I've been so shaky of late because you've been pushing me too hard in the gym."

It was a petty, unkind thing to say. And wrong. He hadn't been pushing me too hard in our sessions, the complete opposite in fact. But that guilty sensation churning in the pit of my stomach had increased to a ball of unsettled tension.

He looked at me sideways, a question in his eyes.

"What?" I asked, surly.

He didn't say anything for a moment, his expression puzzled. Finally, he asked, "Why did Jones leave you to fend for yourself?"

And there it was—the reason for my guilt.

Sitting here, in Brendon's car, after being rescued by him, I felt guilty for going out for breakfast with Raph.

A lump formed in my throat. "He didn't mean to," I answered, aware the response sounded lame. "His bodyguard pulled him away and shoved him in the car and we got separated."

Brendon's grip on the steering wheel shifted a little. "And he didn't make his bodyguard come back for you?"

I drew in a deep breath and shook my head. "I think he tried," I said, feeling like I needed to defend Raph's actions.

"I'm sure he did."

There was no censure in his voice, or contempt. So why was I feeling even more guilty?

"Thank you for coming to get me," I said. My hands were trembling again. A lot. They shouldn't have been, the doctor at the hospital had topped up my meds with a shot. Which meant I was shaking for a wholly different reason.

I suspected the shock of the situation was finally setting in.

"No worries." Brendon threw me a smile. It wasn't as relaxed and open as usual, but it still sent a warm sense of happiness through me. "Although I think the paparazzo who waited with you did so more for the opportunity of taking photos of me rescuing you, than any concern about your health. He kept asking who I was and what my relationship was to you."

He paused for a second, giving me another one of those ambiguous glances. "He kept calling you Raphael Jones's girlfriend."

Heat prickled my cheeks, but before I could say anything —like what, I hear you ask? No freaking clue—he chuckled. "I told him I was your personal manicurist and if he took another bloody photo of you *or* me, I was going to shove a nail file up his arse."

I burst out laughing.

"Manicurist?" I ran a look over Brendon, noting his workout attire. Loose black shorts, loose black tank top that did nothing to conceal the sculpted strength in his body.

He shrugged, grinning. "It worked. He didn't take any more photos. In fact, I think he may have broken the land-speed record running away. I do, however, suspect Jones isn't going to be too happy with whatever spin the gossip sites are going to put on the shots he took before he bolted. Anyone with half a brain will work out I'm not your manicurist."

"Because of your muscles?" The question popped out before I could stop it.

Brendon shook his head. "Because of the state of your nails."

I looked down at my hands and my bitten-down, paint-chipped nails.

"Maybe you're really bad at your job and I hire you out of pity?" I offered, the unsettling tension in my tummy returning. Now I was feeling guilty about sitting in the car with Brendon. What the fuck was wrong with me?

"Makes sense."

Fifteen minutes later, we pulled into a parking lot outside a building I didn't recognize. "Here we are," he said, cutting the engine.

I studied the building, confused. It looked like a small apartment complex, surrounded by lush trees. "Here we are where?"

He grinned. "Home."

"Whose?"

"Mine. C'mon, I'm taking care of you until Heather finishes class."

"Here?" Oh boy, why was I suddenly so ... so ... nervous?

Brendon gave me a mock frown. "Would you rather I take you to Jones's room?"

With a grunt, I swung open my door and scrambled out of the car, determined to prove to Brendon he was being a jackass. On reflection, it was a silly thing to do. A wave of wishy-washy dizziness swept over me and I staggered a little to the left.

Brendon caught me before I got too off-balance. I should have been angry. To be honest, I had no freaking clue how I felt. The day had been the most confusing of my short life.

"All right, Plenty, Ohio," he murmured, sliding an arm around my back and gently supporting me with a firm hand. "Let's get you inside so I can lecture you some more about your meds."

I tried to shrug him off. I failed.

"Yeah, yeah," he chuckled. "I know. You don't need help. You're good. You're awesome. You're fine. Now shut up and let me take care of you for a bit, will you? You may be Raphael Jones's girlfriend, but I'm your knight in shining armor and I'm the one here looking after you now, got it?" He gave me a playful grin. "Well, knight in sweaty gym gear, but you get my drift."

"I'm not Raph's girlfriend," I muttered, my throat tight for some bizarre reason.

Brendon drew me a little closer to his hard body. "Good," he said with a tone I had no hope of deciphering.

Neither of us said another word until we were inside his apartment. I cast a long inspection around. An exercise bike sat in the middle of the living area next to an elliptical trainer. Beside that was a rowing machine. Attached to the far wall by a metal hook, above the television, was a set of resistance bands. On the floor in front of the television was a set of dumbbells. Hanging on a hook on the opposite wall was a mountain bike which, to my untrained eye, looked like it cost more than my car back home.

Various containers and tubs sat on the kitchen counter, all with labels like Protein-Max, Recovery Plus and Nature Bulk. I couldn't contain myself any longer, I burst out laughing.

"What?" he asked, depositing me on a sofa half covered in health magazines, more dumbbells and textbooks.

"I'm not really sure," I said, getting comfortable on what little space there was left, "but I think you might like to work out at home, yes?"

He chuckled. "Shut up, Plenty, Ohio."

Striding into the kitchen, he grabbed one of the containers and a banana before opening the fridge—stuffed full of fruit, vegetables and an obscene number of eggs—to withdraw a carton of milk and a tub of blueberries.

I watched him, curious. "What are you doing?"

"Making you a smoothie," he answered as he removed the lid from the blender. "You missed lunch and your body's energy levels need to be replenished." He paused for a second, his smile wide. "Don't worry, I make a mean smoothie."

Five minutes later, he crossed back to where I was sitting and handed me a tall glass filled to the brim with frothy blue liquid. "Get this into you."

I took it.

"Heather's on the way," he said, moving back into the kitchen. "I've got to get back to the gym, but I'm not leaving you alone. Concussions are nasty things at the best of times, but worse when you're on medication."

"I'm okay," I said, gripping my glass.

He shook his head, an uncharacteristic seriousness falling over his face as he regarded me from behind the counter. "Don't care. I know you're trying to hide it, but I can tell your hand is shaking more than normal. A part of me wants to blame it on missing your meds, but another part of me wants to beat the shit out of Jones for leaving you like he did."

Those butterflies that kept fluttering around in my belly burst into wild flight again. "He didn't—"

"No, Maci," Brendon cut me off. "He did. Doesn't he realize stress is one of the last things someone with Parkinson's should be exposed to?"

"He doesn't know I have Parkinson's," I said. "No one here does except you."

He frowned. "You mean you've been in Australia for a fortnight and not told anyone?"

I shook my head, stomach churning.

"Not even Heather?"

Again, I shook my head.

"Because you don't want anyone to know?"

"Because I don't *need* anyone to know," I corrected. "It doesn't change who I am, and all that'll happen is people will treat me differently."

"*Look after you*, you mean? Not take off and leave you to fend for yourself against a horde of paparazzi?"

"You don't understand," I said, angry. Confused. I glared down at the smoothie in my hand, the smoothie he'd made for me.

Dropping onto the sofa beside me, Brendon let out a soft chuckle. "You really are a monumentally moody pain in the arse, Plenty, Ohio. You know that, right?"

I raised my head and gave him a sullen frown.

"And if you *are* Jones's girlfriend," he went on, "or want to be Jones's girlfriend, or are thinking about becoming Jones's girlfriend, then I'm really, *really* sorry in advance for doing this."

Before I could ask what he was talking about, he kissed me.

It was nothing like the kisses Raph had given me. Raph's kisses were demanding, possessive. Those kisses reached into the very pit of what made me a woman and grabbed it with an inescapable grip. This kiss wasn't like that, but damn, it sure as hell stole any hope I had of uttering a word.

Brendon's lips, warm and firm, brushed over mine once with a feathery, almost hesitant touch before, with a little moan, he parted his lips and stroked his tongue over mine. Which of course was there waiting for him.

I whimpered. Apparently, I do that when being kissed by a hot Australian guy after just being harassed by paparazzi, knocking myself unconscious and then being released from the hospital with a possible concussion. It vibrated at the back of my throat, sounding for all the world like a confused invitation. Which it was.

Brendon, smart fellow that he is, picked up on the invitation and deepened the kiss. Whoa. His tongue stroked over mine, he combed his fingers through the hair at the back of my head and balled his hand into a fist. It was the kind of kiss you see in the movies. The kind that makes the girls watching the film get all breathless and the guys sitting beside them squirm. *That* kind of kiss.

And yet ...

Sucking in a ragged breath, I pulled away.

Brendon gazed down into my face, bewilderment in his eyes. "Okay. That was ..."

I caught my bottom lip with my teeth and stared at him. "Not what I thought it would be like."

He laughed, the sound puzzled. "Me either. I'm not going to lie, Plenty. I've thought of kissing you a lot since the night we met, even *before* I discovered you're just about everything I want in a girl, but ... yeah, that felt ..."

"Like you were kissing your sister?"

He pulled a face. "That's just gross. But yeah. Not the hot and horny and bothered event I thought it would be. Maybe we need to try again?"

Breath growing short, I nodded. It would be so much easier if Brendon *was* the one my stupid body and stupider heart got all *hot and horny and bothered* over. Brendon, who knew about my condition and didn't make a big deal about it. Well, except that one time in the gym. Brendon, who was funny and didn't make me all flustered and confused and tongue-tied and hot and bothered ... and ... and ...

Sigh. Yep. That was the problem right there.

Do you see it? I liked Brendon, a *lot*, but he didn't get under my skin. Didn't make me squirm and make that place between my thighs that never lies grow hot and achy in a very, very intense way.

Like Raph did.

Ninety percent certain I knew the outcome of the second kiss before it even happened, I leaned toward him, offering my lips. He lowered his head to mine and, fingers threaded through my hair at the back of my head again, touched his lips to mine.

Our tongues did that little dance thing that happens in a kiss. Our breath tickled each other's cheeks. Our lips slanted over each other ...

And then Brendon chuckled into my mouth and we pulled apart. "Well, fuck." He shook his head, his lips twisting into a grin. "That sucks."

It was my turn to nod. "It does."

He pulled another face. "Doomed to the friend bench by natural chemistry. Damn it."

I gave him a lopsided smile. I understood his exasperation.

With a disgruntled sigh, he dropped his fingers from the nape of my neck and rose to his feet. "Okay, I've got to go, before I totally blow my cool image and try for third time luck—"

The sound of Eminem singing "Berserk" near his thigh cut him short. He shoved his hand into his right pocket and withdrew an iPhone. "It's Heather," he said, swiping his thumb over the screen and raising the phone to his ear. "Hey, Heather, what's up?"

Feeling way too rattled, I watched an exasperated expression cross his face; there and gone just as quick. "Of course you have," he said with a chuckle. "That's an extra fifty burpees added to your program next time you're in the gym, you know that, right?"

Whatever Heather said in response made him laugh

harder. With a shake of his head, he handed me the phone. "She wants to talk to you."

"Oh God, Maci." Heather's voice cried when I pressed Brendon's phone to my ear. "Are you okay? Brendon said you were in some kind of riot and got knocked out by a photographer."

A self-conscious laugh fell from my lips. "I'm fine, Heather. Honest. And I think *riot* is exaggerating somewhat."

"Is he pissed?"

I flicked a look at Brendon, who stood beside the sofa, watching me. "I don't think so. Should he be?"

"Yeah. He didn't want you traveling any more today. I was coming to stay with you at his place until you'd recovered a bit and I ..." Heather paused a second. "Well, I was a bit stressed and flustered about what happened to you and I ... I locked my keys in my car."

I laughed and then groaned as a dull red pain shot through my head. "Why am I not surprised?" I asked with a wince. Damn, my head really did hurt.

Brendon crouched down beside me. I didn't look at him. I knew what I'd find on his face—worry. I was sick of worry. And pity. Especially when piled atop confusion and disappointment.

"I'm hopeless," Heather groaned. "Tell The Biceps I'm sorry. If it helps, I'll be out the front of Mackellar House waiting for you both when you get here. *And* I'm taking care of you for the rest of the afternoon."

I rolled my eyes. "I don't *need* taking care of. Honestly. I'm fine."

Heather laughed in my ear. "Too bad. I'm not risking any more extra burpees added to my workout. I'll see you soon, okay?"

She hung up.

Lowering the phone to my lap, I gave Brendon a small smile. "Heather. You gotta love her, right?"

He studied me, eyes narrow. "Do I need to point out you *do* need taking care of?"

"Do I need to tell you, I don't? Again?"

"Why are you being so stubborn about this?"

I glared at him. If sex and romance with Brendon was out of the question, I was giving myself permission to be churlish. "Why are *you*?"

It seemed he'd adopted the same attitude. With a growl, he threw up his hands. "This is getting us nowhere."

"I agree," I snapped back. And to think only a few moments ago we were on the verge of ... of ... well, y'know, doing *that*. "Take me back to Mackellar, please. Where I can be fine in peace."

Brendon let out a strangled groan and stomped to the door. Stomped. "Fine. God, I hate that word."

A part of me wanted to laugh. A part of me wanted to say sorry for being a bitch. A part of me wanted to fly back to Plenty, hug my mom and ask her to make me some of her famous chocolate-chip cookies so I could pretend I was six again and none of this craziness was happening.

The part of me that functioned on a basic level forced me to my feet and made me follow Brendon to the door. He looked at me, frustration on his face, and then shook his head and dropped a kiss on the top of my head, the kind a big brother gives his annoying little sister when she's got a boo-boo. Yep, that's the relationship we were in, right there.

"What am I going to do about you?" he muttered.

He didn't wait for an answer, which was a good thing, because I didn't have one. Instead, he opened the door and strode through it.

I followed. Again.

Hey, what else was I going to do at this point?

The drive back to Mackellar House was quiet. I sat in the passenger seat, alternating between confusion over the two infuriating guys occupying my mind, and festering anger at Brendon's insistence I needed to be looked after. That anger clung to me like seaweed, familiar and undeniable.

I know what you're currently thinking. You're thinking,Geez Maci, what's your deal? You've got concussion, for God's sake. And to be honest, Brendon knowing I needed help, Parkinson's-type help, hospital-type help, wasn't really the thing making me grumpy now. It was the very fact I needed *any* kind of help because of my PD. And yeah, that's my pride talking, I get that, but sometimes pride is all you've got to hold on to.

I'd seen Mom's pride erode away in the ten years before Dad died. For ten years, I watched him look after her, watched him insist he do things for her when she could still do them, solely out of fear she was going to hurt herself. Watched him take away her independence out of love—the very emotion that's meant to *give* strength, not reduce it—watched him inadvertently destroy her pride when he never, ever meant to ...

Out of his unconditional, fathomless love for her, out of his desire to care for her, to make her life easier, to take away her frustration and humiliation, he took away her ability to function as a normal person. He took away her pride and dignity.

He didn't realize he was doing it until Mom couldn't take any more and they'd argue about it. I'd hear those arguments, even when they tried to hide them from me, and for a long time I just didn't get it.

He wouldn't let Mom retrieve the new bottle of ketchup from the top cupboard shelf because it required her standing on a small two-rung stepladder and he worried she'd lose her balance and hurt herself. That kind of thing. He'd insist he get the ketchup for her, but in doing so, he inadvertently told Mom she wasn't functional anymore. I remember watching her face etch with hurt and anger during those moments and couldn't understand why she was so upset.

When they fought about it—Mom saying Dad treated her like she was handicapped, Dad saying he loved her and only wanted to help—I used to get angry, really angry, with her for being so stupid and ungrateful. I would be furious with her for throwing Dad's help and love and care back in his face. Once, when I was sixteen, I even told her she was being a stubborn, selfish bitch.

She yelled at me that I didn't understand and I had no right talking to her like that, before she burst into tears and closed herself in her bedroom.

I remember feeling guilty and at the same time right. Like I'd picked a side in a war, and it was the winning side and the other side was just being obstinate. It wasn't until years later, with my own muscles and brain attacked by Parkinson's, with my own pride and sense of being a normal, functioning human equally attacked, that I understood why Mom hated Dad doing things for her when she was still capable of so much. It had nothing to do with being insulted and everything to do with being reduced to your worst fear before your time.

And a Parkinson's disease sufferer's worst fear is losing everything that makes you a person. Not just your ability to think and move, but your pride and dignity and independence.

All that and more was running through my head on the drive back to my student accommodation, so yeah, I was being a surly pain in the ass.

Brendon, however, was being Brendon. Relaxed and casually at ease. I think if we'd been driving a longer distance, his affable, unflappable good mood would have eventually worn me down and I would have stopped being a lump of grump. But the trip from his apartment to Mackellar House wasn't that long, so by the time we pulled to a halt outside the building, I was still silent and churlish.

We sat for a moment, neither of us moving, the *tick, tick, tick* of the engine cooling the only sound in the car.

"You're too hard on yourself, Plenty," he said, finally breaking the silence.

I shot him a sideways glance.

"And too good for Jones," he finished, studying the view beyond the windshield.

"With what's in my future," I said, my chest tight, "I'm not good enough for *anyone*."

I turned away from him, opened my door and climbed out.

He met me on the footpath. I knew he would. Expression set somewhere between angry and sympathetic, he stepped up to me and took my hand. My left one. Which was trembling, of course. "That's bullshit," he whispered, gazing into my eyes. "And the sooner you realize that, the—"

"Maci!"

We both jumped at the sound of Raph calling my name. I swung my head toward his shout to find him almost running toward me from Mackellar House's front door.

"Jesus, Maci," he said, drawing closer. "I've been worried sick. Are you okay? I made Horn go back for you but we couldn't—"

Brendon's fist smashing against his jaw shut him up and sent him staggering backward.

"You took off and left her, you fucking prick!" Brendon

snarled, bearing down on Raph. "What kind of idiot moron does that?"

"What the hell, Osmond?" Raph gaped at Brendon, hand pressed to the side of his mouth. I was horrified to see a little trickle of blood oozing past his fingers. "You hit me. What's your—"

"Of course I hit you," Brendon cut him off, storming straight for him again. "You abandoned her to a pack of frenzied paparazzi. Stress like that is the *worst* thing someone with Parkinson's can be exposed to. She spent the afternoon in hospital, you privileged, arrogant fuck—"

Four things happened at once. Four horrible things. All in messed-up, terrible slow motion.

One. Raph swung around to stare at me, the stunned confusion on his face giving way to open pity.

Two. Three scruffily dressed men came running at us along the sidewalk, expensive-looking cameras in their hands, all shouting Raph's name and asking if he was going to sue.

Three. Heather ran up behind Raph, mouth open, agog with shock.

And four. Mr. Horn, still dressed in his somber blue suit, came out of nowhere and slammed shoulder first into Brendon, driving him across the footpath and to the ground.

I flinched when a warm hand wrapped around my wrist.

"What's he saying?" Raph stood in front of me, concern swimming in his dark eyes as he gazed down at me. "Parkinson's?"

"Jones!" one of the paparazzi called, shoving the lens of his camera in Raph's face. "Why'd the big guy punch you? Who is he? Are you sleeping with his girlfriend?"

Raph ignored him, his stare fixed on me.

Heart pounding, I snatched my wrist free of his grip. "I've got to go."

Heather bounded up beside me. "Maci, are you okay?"

"Maci?" the second paparazzo shouted, shoving at the crowd amassing around us in an effort to get closer. "Are you cheating on Jones?"

I turned my stupefied stare—yes, I was shocked into inactivity at this point—to where Brendon and Raph's bodyguard were trying to beat each other to bloody pulps. I don't know who was winning, but based on the fact Brendon was steady on his feet and Mr. Horn was lurching about somewhat, I was putting my money on Brendon.

"Maci?" Raph grabbed my wrist again, alarm in his voice. "Do you have Parkinson's disease? Is that why your hand shakes a lot? Are you sick?"

It was that last question that got me moving. Not the paparazzi hurling insulting questions at us as they photographed every damn second passing. Not Heather gasping at my side. Not the people—my fellow Mackellar House occupants and curious passersby—watching the ridiculous spectacle. Not the sight of Brendon and Mr. Horn punching into each other like rabid grizzlies.

But the last question Raph had asked. And the last word of the last question.

Sick.

I looked up into his worried eyes and yanked my wrist from his fingers. "Yes," I said, the word flat. Empty. "I'm sick. But don't worry. It's not catching."

And with that, I turned and ran straight for the safety of Mackellar House's open front door.

Thank freaking God, I made it without falling over.

If that had happened, I really do think I would have curled up in a shaking, trembling, vibrating ball of self-contempt, and died.

CHAPTER 4

When the Going Gets Tough, the Tough Get Shaky

Heather followed me all the way up the stairs and into my room. I ignored her. Mainly because my brain wasn't functioning properly at that point. It was taking all its neurons and synapses to keep me upright and stable. And tear-free.

I wanted to cry.

I wasn't sure if this pressing need to sob was due to my condition, or to the totally surreal events I'd just been a part of, but whatever the reason, I wasn't going to give in. There was no damn way in hell I was going to cry. Not only did I look ridiculous when I cried—what girl doesn't? Seriously? If a girl doesn't look like a snotball of misery when she's crying, she's not *really* crying, do you know what I mean?—but it would mean what was going on had defeated me.

I wasn't going to be defeated on the other side of the world by two Australian guys, some photographers, and a revelation.

A revelation.

Oh damn, Brendon had told Raph I had …

My knees crumpled beneath me.

Heather caught me before I hit the floor.

"C'mon, Maci," she murmured, wrapping her arms around my torso as she helped me straighten up. "Let's get you to the bed."

She hooked my arm around her shoulder and, with a grunt, carried me the rest of the way across my room and deposited me on the bed.

I slumped into a back-aching bow and pressed my forehead to my knees. Oh boy, I felt … messed up.

"Is it true?" Heather smoothed a hand up my back, the mattress shifting as she sat beside me. "You have Parkinson's disease?"

There was no pity in her voice. Only curiosity.

I nodded against my knees. "Yes."

"Did you only just find out?"

"No. I've known for over a year."

The hand on my back grew still. "Is it getting worse since you've been here?"

I shook my head. At some point I was going to need to lift my forehead from my knees but not yet.

Heather was quiet for a moment. "Did you want to keep it a secret?"

My forehead mashed up and down on my knees as I nodded.

"Why?"

Finally, I raised my head and looked at her. "Because it sucks. Because people treat me differently when they know. Because I feel …"

The word to describe how I felt about it all wouldn't come.

Heather watched me frown and wave my hands about in

some ridiculous effort to scoop up the word from the air around me.

"Less?" she offered.

I let out a sigh and dropped back onto the bed, staring up at the ceiling. Hot tears leaked from the corners of my eyes to dribble a path down my temples and into my ears. I sniffed, my nose well on its way to being blocked with the snot of self-disgust and self-pity. "Less is a good way to describe me. Especially when you add it to the word *functional*. Maci Rowling—less functional. That's me."

She sat beside me for a bit, silent. "Is that the only reason you're so flustered? Did the paparazzi upset you? And did The Biceps *really* punch Raph in the mouth?"

"The jaw," I corrected from my place flat on the bed. "And I think ..." Letting out a ragged sigh, I sat upright again and raked my hands through my hair. "I'm upset because I didn't want people to know I had Parkinson's and now it's just out there, and ..."

"And?" Heather prompted when I didn't finish the sentence.

"And the way Raph looked at me when he found out, and the word he used ... and Brendon beating him up and ..."

Heather did exactly what I didn't expect her to do. She burst out laughing. "Oh God, Maci. Being your friend is like being on one big American TV show. I love it."

I swiped at my nose with the back of my hand and gave her a surly glare. "I'm glad my misery is entertaining for you."

Not in the least bit contrite, she laughed again. "Maci, in case you haven't noticed, I have ADHD. I'm medicated up to the eyeballs most days, and on the days I'm not, I feel like I'm a hummingbird on crack. I know it's not going to kill me, but it's not exactly fun to live with. However, I'm not in the least bit embarrassed by it or ashamed of it. I know the people who really matter to me, my real friends, will like me, *love* me, regardless."

I shook my head. "I know what you're trying to say, Heather. Honestly, I do, but Parkinson's *will* kill me. Eventually."

"So you're going to live in what? A state of duplicitous, untrusting denial until then?"

I studied my knees, my throat tight.

"Look, I know we've only been friends for a fortnight," Heather went on, her voice kind, "and it's not really my place to say anything, but I'm going to anyway because I have zero filter and I like you a lot. Living a lie, even a lie of omission to protect yourself, is dumb. If you're not going to be honest with people, how do you ever expect them to be honest with you?"

Scrunching up my face, I balled my fists. My hands were shaking. Both of them. Badly. In fact, I could feel the ticks and tremors begin to take over my whole body. "You sound like Brendon."

"A very smart man," Heather said. "Who would have thought it under all that yummy muscle? Speaking of Brendon, has he kissed you yet?"

The unexpected question pulled me from my grumpy pout. I half grunted, half chuckled. "Today."

She grinned, wriggling like a puppy about to get a new chew toy. "*And?* Was it as hot and crazy and wild as I imagine?"

The knock on my door saved me from answering.

"So?" Raph arched an eyebrow at us from where he leaned against the doorjamb, his expression ... ambiguous. "Was it?"

My breath seized in my throat. Probably because my heart was doing its best to smash its way into it. "Was it what?"

Raph's stare didn't waver. "Was Osmond's kiss hot and crazy and ... and whatever other adjective Heather used?"

Heather took my hand. "How could it not be?" she replied.

I didn't correct her. Not because I wanted Raph to think otherwise. I was just too damn tongue-tied. And embarrassed.

And angry.

Raph's dark eyes studied me. "How could it not be ..." he echoed, the tone in his voice as unreadable as the expression on his face.

I ran my gaze over that handsome face, seeking out an answer to the mystery of his state of mind. Instead, I found the split on his lip caused by Brendon's fist mashing against it.

For some reason, the sight filled my throat with a lump. I met his stare again. Numb disappointment rolled through me. Raph had looked at me in many different ways since our first meeting in the men's restroom at the airport—with amusement, with enjoyment, with lust and confusion—but never had he looked at me with pity.

Until this wonderful, fucked-up day.

I turned my head away, not wanting to see it.

"Has the fracas outside calmed down yet?" Heather asked, her warm fingers interlaced through mine. An anchor I really needed.

"Don't know," Raph answered. As always, the dark timbre of his voice with its distinct Australian accent made the junction of my thighs throb. Damn it.

"I left Osmond and Horn having a discussion about the situation and the pap took off at the sound of a cop siren nearby."

"Someone called the cops?" Surprise filled Heather's voice.

I risked a glance at Raph. He was watching me, his

expression unreadable. Still, at least it wasn't pity anymore, right? "No idea."

"Is Brendon okay?" I asked.

Raph's jaw bunched. "If you mean did Horn break him, the answer's no. He's still in one piece." A wry grunt escaped him. "In fact, I think he may have broken Horn. Guess Osmond isn't just glamor muscles after all."

Heather chuckled. "You sound miffed, Raph. And jealous."

Despite the squirming unease trying to take a hold of me, I didn't look away from Raph. I needed to see his reaction to her jibe.

The muscle in his jaw clenched again, and then, his gaze holding mine, he pushed himself from the doorjamb and walked into my room. "Mind giving me and the American girl here a moment alone, Heather?" he asked as he crossed to where we both sat on the bed.

My heart smashed into my throat again.

Heather's hand in mine squeezed tighter. "You need me to stay?" she asked, her voice soft. Understanding shone in her eyes.

Catching my bottom lip with my teeth, I shook my head. "I'm ... I'm okay."

She studied me with a narrow-eyed inspection for a heartbeat and then let out a short sigh. "If only you really believed that, Maci," she whispered.

Before I could respond, she rose to her feet and left. Just like that. Closing the door behind her. Leaving me alone with Raph.

Dropping my stare to my legs, I brushed my palms over my thighs. Oh boy, I wished I wasn't wearing shorts.

The end of my bed shifted as Raph sat beside me. My stomach—and other areas of my body—clenched at his close proximity. I didn't move. Didn't lift my stare from my lily-white thighs.

"*Sick* wasn't a wise choice of words, was it?"

His low voice caressed my sanity. As did his statement.

I shook my head, keeping my gaze locked on my thighs. Nerves gnawed on my insides like a pack of ravenous dogs. "No."

Silence stretched between us for a moment, heavy and tense. "I'm sorry," Raph finally said. "I'm sorry about everything. I've been worried sick about you since we lost you. I didn't have your mobile number and I couldn't find Heather. And when I did she said you were in hospital, and I freaked out and rang every bloody one in Sydney. When I finally found the one you were at, they said you were gone and they didn't know where to. And that freaked me out even more."

I stared at my thighs. Inside, I was an emotional mess.

"And then I saw you with Osmond and I got jealous. I acted like a complete dick when what I should have done the whole time was look after you. Look at you, Maci, you're hurt." He touched my forehead gently, tracing the tips of his fingers over the grazed bruise just above my eye. "You're hurt and it's my fault. You'll never be able to forgive me, will you?"

I didn't answer. I couldn't. The nervous anticipation overwhelming me at the touch of his fingers on my forehead, the way he'd told me he was jealous ... those things and more stole my ability to speak.

He let out a ragged sigh. "I feel like shit and I just want ... I just ... I was just ... the whole situation ... Fuck, why do I get so messed up around you?" The last bit was muttered, frustration clear in the question.

I raised my head to glare at him. "I don't know. Maybe for the same reason you swing hot and cold with me."

He let out a sigh, raked his hands through his hair and

turned to look at me. I could see tormented confusion in his eyes, like dark storm clouds on the distant horizon. Good. I was glad I wasn't the only one feeling so wretched.

"I'm not good at trusting people," he confessed. "Or putting myself out there. *Or* being open with people."

"Wow." I fixed him with a level look. "No kidding."

He grimaced. "It's not an excuse and there's no messed-up backstory of family tragedy to justify it. Mum and Dad are still together, they still function as great parents and I don't think I've ever seen them fight."

"So what's your excuse then?" I asked. Inside, I was still nervous and agitated. I think because I didn't want Raph to give me a reason to *not* be angry with him. If I *was* angry with him, I didn't have to deal with the consequences of *not* being angry with him. God, does that makes any sense?

He sighed again. "We Joneses don't do emotional connections or sharing. We were raised to be self-sufficient and self-reliant. I think the need for a connection with *anyone* was starved out of us. Four individuals living under the one roof. That was us.

"And because we're fifth-generation cattle farmers living on a massive property out in the country, that one roof was pretty sizable. And the boundaries of our land are huge. Dad would spend the day checking the herd in one paddock or the other. Mum would spend it in the house office, door closed. And my sister and I would spend it at school, followed by working at whatever jobs had to be done when we got home, usually on the back of a horse or out in whichever paddock Dad wasn't. Which meant if you didn't need to interact with a family member in a given period, you just didn't. So while I never saw them fight, I never saw them being affectionate with each other either."

I studied him, his description of his detached family life

sending a curling wisp of sympathy through me. Damn. What would that kind of upbringing be like? Being on the other side of the world from Mom during my stay in Australia was the longest I'd gone without talking to her at least every day. And when my dad had been killed by the drunk driver ... Man, that tore me apart. Still did.

A cold shiver rippled up my back. I swallowed, casting Raph a sad frown. "It sounds lonely."

He shrugged. "It is what it is. Things exacerbated when my sister met Franz."

"Franz is the prince?"

He nodded. "Our life turned into a fishbowl. Anything we did, had done or were going to do, became fodder for the media and gossip mags, and all my walls—the ones ingrained in me thanks to my upbringing—went up. It didn't help when old girlfriends came out and sold bullshit—sorry, I mean lies, about me. And then the royal family discovered the stalker threats against me, assigned Horn as my bodyguard and ..." He shrugged again. "And I turned into a bigger bastard than I normally am."

He stopped, let out a wry grunt and turned his attention to his hands where they hung loose between his thighs, before raising his head to give me a small smile. "But when I'm with you ... those walls ... I don't want them to be there."

I stared at him, every fiber in my body tingling. Whatever my mind wanted to say, it couldn't find the words. I wanted to be furious with him for saying something so wonderful, for taking away my reason to be angry with him. All I could do was stare at him.

He stared back at me, a frown pulling at his forehead. "Can I ask you a question, American girl?"

I nodded, my throat tight.

"Are you—"

Someone knocked on the door, interrupting him. He frowned and muttered, "Jesus."

"Hey, Plenty." Brendon's relaxed voice played with the room's silence and I let out a gasp, turning to see him push the door wider and walk through it. He strode into the room, ignoring Raph completely as he crossed to where I sat. "You okay?" he asked, squatting in front of me to cup my knees with his hands.

I studied him. I could feel my eyebrows knitting. I opened my mouth but nothing came out. One attack of the guilts, coming right up.

He grinned. "Shall I take that as a yes?"

"You leave my bodyguard in one piece, Osmond?"

I started at Raph's question. There was no malice or anger in his voice. In fact, he sounded ... amused. Go figure.

Brendon waved a hand in a so-so gesture. "His skull is harder than yours. And he swings a mean haymaker."

I noticed the angry red mark on Brendon's right cheek, just under his eye. I hissed. It looked painful.

Raph grunted. "Glad he landed at least one. I think you damn near broke *my* jaw. I had to talk him out of pressing charges against you for public assault, by the way. You owe me one."

My head was spinning at the casual way they were discussing the fight.

Brendon grinned. "Thanks. Think I damn near broke my fist when I landed one on you."

I couldn't take any more. This was all too ... too ... *not* normal. "Wait, wait, wait, wait." I held up my hands, switching my gaze back and forth between them. "I'm sorry, but how can you be talking to each other like this now? After Brendon ..."

Brendon smoothed his hands over my knees again, his

laugh relaxed. "Would you like me to finish what I started, Plenty? I'll do it for you."

"Try it, Osmond," Raph said. There was a chortle in his voice, but also a threat.

I narrowed my eyes, studying them both. They might be giving the appearance of relaxed humor, but it was a facade, no doubt for my benefit.

Pulling a breath in, I shook my head and stood. Brendon's hands slipped from my knees and he straightened, towering over me. So did Raph.

Short and shaky, that's me. And stuck in the middle of two guys who seemed very capable and willing to beat on each other. Over me. Weird. And unsettling, I have to say. And ... okay, slightly good for the ego.

I looked up at them, a subtle tremor building deep in my body. "I think I need you both to leave now. It's not that I'm not enjoying the testosterone oozing from your pores, but I need to be alone for a while." I looked directly at Raph. "Parkinson's disease and all."

Raph opened his mouth, shoulders stiffening, his eyes locked on my face.

"Okay, Plenty," Brendon said with warm calm. "Jones and I will take off." He stepped closer to me and dropped a kiss on the top of my head. My heart skipped a beat. Not because he was kissing me—we'd already established the whole Brendon-Maci thing wasn't a thing—but because he was kissing me in front of Raph. Taunting him?

I heard Raph suck in a breath.

"C'mon, Jones." Brendon slapped Raph on the back of his shoulder. "Let's give the girl what she wants."

For a second, I thought Raph was going to argue. God, what would I do if he did? Call for help? Jump out of the way when he swung a punch at Brendon? Brendon *had* spilled my secret, after all. Truth be known, a part of *me* wanted to punch Brendon, even though I knew he'd done so out of worry.

But then, with a level look at Brendon, and an intense gaze at me, Raph nodded his head once, and walked from my room.

Brendon watched him leave before, with a surprised, "Huh," he turned back to me. "*Are* you okay, Maci?" he asked.

I arched an eyebrow. "What do you think?"

He ducked his head and scratched the back of his neck. "You're pissed I told him about your condition."

"Told everyone. You shouted it."

"I was angry."

"I saw that."

He let out a soft laugh. "Sure you don't want me to kiss you again? Just to be sure there's nothing—"

I rolled my eyes and gave his chest a shove. I knew the only reason he stumbled back a step was to humor me. "Get out of here, Osmond," I ordered. "I need to sulk for a while and I *am* still angry at you."

He laughed, a second before he snared my wrist in a loose grip, drew me to him and placed another kiss on the top of my head. We really had moved onto the whole brother-sister relationship, it seemed. "Call me if you need me. I'm sending Heather back in now. Don't argue. Just deal with it."

And with that, he too pivoted on his heel and strode from the room. Far less stompy than Raph, I noticed.

Heather hurried through the door a few moments later. Dropping onto the edge of the bed beside me, she grinned. "Wow. That was tense."

I frowned. "What?"

"Raph and The Biceps out there."

My breath caught in my throat. "In the hall?"

She nodded. "Raph waited until The Biceps came out. They then did that caveman-chest-thumping thing at each other with their eyes before The Biceps told Raph he's not good enough for you, and Raph told The Biceps to stick his opinion up his arse. Oh, by the way, according to Macca, The Biceps broke Raph's bodyguard's nose in the fight."

I blinked.

Heather grinned again. "So, two guys fighting over you. How's that feel? Oh, and you still have to tell me what it was like being kissed by The Biceps," she said, eyes twinkling. "And are you going to do it again? Who kisses better? Who are you going to pick?" Grinning at me, she squirmed on the edge of the bed, the excited puppy once again. "Oh, do you think they'd agree to a ménage? Oh man, imagine *both* of them making love to—"

I smacked my hand over her mouth. "Stop!"

She giggled against my palm.

Rolling my eyes, a smile playing at my lips, I lowered my hand. "I can't believe you."

She laughed. "Hey, admit it, you went there as well."

I burst out laughing. Warm happiness flowed through me and, I wasn't afraid to admit, a little bit of naughty excitement. I allowed myself a moment to imagine what it would be like to have *both* Brendon and Raph doing wicked things to my body at the same time before I pressed my hand to Heather's smirking face and shoved her away. "You're debauched," I admonished with a smile, watching her flop back on my bed.

The rest of the afternoon was spent lying around my room, chatting and relaxing. We even did clichéd things like braid each other's hair, paint our toenails—Heather had the most out-there collection of nail polish, including glow-in-the-dark yellow—and discuss celebrity crushes. When she went into great detail about what she would do to Robert Pattinson,

I covered my face with my hands, begging her to stop, laughing so much the words made zero sense.

She didn't mention my Parkinson's once. When I got up to take my meds, just before the pizza we'd ordered for dinner arrived, she didn't ask me about them, which is what most people did when they saw me swallow the collection of tiny pills. Nor did she try to help me when I struggled to open one of the bottles. I knew she noticed. It was kind of hard not to when I was having one of those moments, muttering curse after curse as the pills rattled like maracas inside their plastic container.

It was then that I realized just how much I liked her. Really liked her. In the short time I'd known Heather, she'd become one of the best friends I'd ever had. Like, *ever*.

I mean, I have friends back home in Plenty—good friends—but my best friend up and moved to New York when she was accepted into NYADA. And when I was diagnosed with Parkinson's ... well, I withdrew from most forms of interaction and focused on my studies at college. That withdrawal most likely played quite a large part in me winning the scholarship and being here now, which, when you think about it, was ironic. I'd distanced myself from friends due to my condition and ended up in Australia, where I'd made one of the best friends of my life. Freaky, huh?

Sitting back on the bed beside her, listening to her describe her last date—B-grade horror-movie marathon followed by skinny dipping at Bondi Beach—I couldn't help but smile and send up a word of thanks to whatever all-powerful force put Heather in my life. Fate had dealt me a pretty crummy hand, but this vivacious Australian who spoke a mile a minute was making it easier to deal with.

I was going to miss her so much when I had to leave. Damn, was I going to miss her.

Brendon rang three times to make sure I was okay. Every time I was torn between being angry with him for his concern and being touched by it. A part of me still wished like hell our kiss had been the explosive, melt-your-bones-and-make-you-horny kind. True, I wasn't in the market for a boyfriend, but I was still human and I still had needs and, despite the fact my hands sometimes shook with all the force of a Duracell-powered vibrator, they—or a vibrator—were no substitute for a body-to-body orgasm.

Was that too much information?

Another part of me admitted it wasn't Brendon who was making me more aware of those needs.

A third part of me wished to hell those goddamn needs would just fuck off.

Ha ha. Fuck off. Get it?

Anyway, at some point after we finished the pizza, I must have fallen asleep. I wasn't surprised. I'd had a busy day, what with the pre-breakfast workout, naked-man drawing session over breakfast with Raph, fun and games with the paparazzi, unplanned concussion and trip to the ER, followed by the events on Mackellar House's front lawn.

What I *was* surprised by, however, was the person in my room when I woke.

It wasn't Heather.

A dull, fuzzy ache throbbed in my head when I opened my dry and scratchy eyes who knew how many hours later. The sunlight streaming through my room's one and only window told me it was daytime, as did the sounds I'd grown accustomed to of my fellow Mackellar House occupants moving about on the other side of my door.

Squinting against the bright light, I levered myself up to a sitting position and froze when my sleep-blurred gaze fell on the person sitting in my uncomfortable desk chair beside my bed.

My heart slammed into my throat like a linebacker into a quarterback.

"Did you know you talk in your sleep?" Raph asked with an amused smile.

I stared at him. "What ... wh-why ... how long ..."

Oh God, talk about being articulate.

He raised an eyebrow. "Have I been here? Since eleven."

"In the morning? What time *is* it?" I swung a glance around my room, stunned enough by his presence to make my brain wonder if it was working properly. Well, as properly as it *can* work. Was it after lunch already?

"Eleven pm."

His answer sent a sudden thump into my chest. I turned back to him, mouth open. "You've been here all night?" I pulled a face. "That's a little *Twilight*-ish of you, isn't it?"

He frowned. "What?"

I raised a hand and waved off my lame attempt at flippant sarcasm. "Forget it. Why are you in my room?"

He studied me. "I bribed Heather."

"What?"

"I bribed Heather. She told me Osmond was going to stay with you through the night and I bribed her to tell him *she* would. And then I bribed her to let me stay instead."

I didn't think I could gape any more, but apparently I could. "You *what*?"

"Do you really want me to say all that again?"

I gave him a confounded stare. "Why?"

"Why did I bribe her?"

I nodded. Even in my baffled state, I could see how damn sexy he was, what with his tousled hair—hair that looked like hands had worried it all night—muscular, jeans-clad legs stretched out in front of him with relaxed ease, and broad, broad shoulders.

Between you and me, I'd never woken up with a guy that wasn't my dad in the same room as me. The fact my very first guy was Raphael Jones only made the event all the more ... daunting.

His dark eyes held mine with steady calm. "I was worried."

I don't know what I wanted him to say, but *I was worried* wasn't it. Disappointment shot through me, hot and bitter. Followed by the very familiar taint of self-contempt.

"Worried," I echoed. "Of course. Because I have—"

He moved before I could finish. Like a sexy, tousled-haired blur. He shoved himself from my desk chair to the side of my bed, his hands cupping my face with firm but gentle pressure, his lips crushing mine.

Okay, forgive me for a moment here, but I'm going to pull a Heather and get descriptive. *Really* descriptive.

It was the horniest fucking kiss I've ever had. And let's be serious, Raph's kisses had already been off-the-scale hot.

His lips ravished mine. There was no other way to explain it. Ravished. He feasted on them with his own. He swept his tongue into my mouth—already open and willing, despite my surprise—and mated with mine. He groaned, sliding his fingers up the sides of my face to tangle in my hair.

I groaned back, not from pain—remember, I'd lost a head-butting contest with a light pole only the day before—but because every fiber and nerve ending in my body was on fire with lust and desire and need.

Need. I needed him to kiss me. I needed it more than I needed medication to stay steady, more than I needed air to live.

He nibbled at my bottom lip, sucked it gently and nibbled

again. He flicked his tongue over my teeth, deeper into my mouth and back to my teeth once more. Every time our tongues slid together, he groaned, a raw sound of utter want and surrender.

Every time he groaned, the hot place between my thighs grew hotter, damper. Heavy with urgent, impatient hunger.

I met him in his passion, incapable of doing otherwise. I was burning up in the fire of his kiss. I was drowning in the hot pleasure rolling through me. I could have sat there and died in the sheer potency of Raph's kiss for the rest of eternity. It left all the restroom kisses we'd shared in its wake. It was incredible. Amazing. Consuming.

And then he pressed his knee to the bed between my thighs and eased me back to the mattress without breaking the kiss.

Holy. Fuck.

Ribbons of tight heat and searing pleasure unfurled through me. I whimpered into his mouth, smoothed my palms up his chest and scraped my nails across his shoulders.

He covered my body with his, supporting his weight with an elbow even as his groin aligned with mine. He was long and hard and so goddamn there, right *there*, his denim-trapped erection nestled against me. Rolling my hips, I fisted my hands in his hair at the back of his head.

He groaned, pushing his bulge harder to the curve of my sex. My head swam, and it had nothing to do with Parkinson's or my injury and everything to do with the molten desire flowing through me. I dragged my hands down his back, teasing his tongue with my own as I rubbed my pussy against his erection.

"Fuck, Maci," he rasped against my lips, "I've wanted to do this ..."

He didn't finish. Instead, he continued kissing me as if he

couldn't stand our lips and tongues being apart long enough to form words. I understood that notion. I couldn't get enough of kissing him either. Every nerve ending in my body sizzled with building heat. My very core, the center of what made me a woman, throbbed and ached and craved him. All of him.

Bunching my hands in his shirt at the small of his back, I tugged the material free of his waistband. I wanted to feel his skin under my palms. No, I needed to feel it. I needed more flesh-to-flesh contact.

He groaned into my mouth when my fingers touched his skin. He rammed his cock harder to my sex, our clothes separating us with infuriating resistance. I raked my nails over his back, up the line of his spine. He rolled his hips again, ravishing my mouth as he did so. The pressure of his engorged length on my pussy and his savage tongue rolling over mine sent liquid heat to my core and I broke our kiss, rolling my head to the side, desperate for air.

It was so good. So goddamn good. I'd never been kissed like it.

He took advantage of the moment by searing a line with his lips down the line of my throat, up to my ear, down to my collarbone. I writhed beneath him, alive with sensations too wicked and incredible to deny. He continued to explore my throat with his lips and teeth, tiny nips and sucks of my flesh that left me breathless. I rolled my head, wrapping my leg around his hip as I did so. I wanted him inside me. There was no denying it.

He ground against me again, levering his upper body away from mine. I cried out in protest and clawed at his back.

He growled, the sound low and wonderfully exciting, and moved his hand to the top button of my shirt.

Oh boy.

He popped the first button open, tasting the skin he'd exposed with a flick of his tongue.

I let out a gasp and tightened my legs around his hip. "Yes," I moaned, unsure if he was waiting for permission to go further.

Raph released the next button and nipped at the flesh between my breasts.

I shivered. "Oh God, Raph," I rasped, staring blindly at the ceiling of my room, digging my nails into his back through his shirt.

He shifted between my thighs a little and, lips charting a journey up to my chin, popped open the next button, the one that would allow my bra-covered breasts to be revealed.

A shudder claimed my body. Tight and primitive. Any thoughts of my condition, my future self, shattered in that moment. I was a creature born for the pleasure Raph awoke in me, that was all. His creature.

I arched my spine, offering him what he'd exposed.

He took my offering with his mouth, capturing my taut right nipple through the lace of my bra.

"Oh God," I repeated, though far less breathy and far louder. "God, that feels ..."

He sucked harder, drawing the pebble of my nipple deeper past his lips, rolling his tongue over its tip.

I scraped at his back, eyes closed, head swirling with intense colors, body thrumming with just as intense a need. The solid pole of his arousal pressed to my sex only heightened my response to his worship of my breast. Was it possible to have an orgasm without anything actually being inside me? Was it? Cause it sure as hell felt like I was about to have one.

"Raph." His name fell from me on a hitching moan. "Raph, I w-want you ... oh God, please ... so ..."

I was making no sense, and yet Raph knew exactly what I wanted.

He dragged his mouth across the expanse of skin between my breasts and captured my other nipple with his lips, sucking it hard enough to hurt. I cried out, the sensation a wicked mix of pain and pleasure.

He covered the breast he'd only just been feasting on with his hand, kneading it with increasing speed as he sucked on my nipple. I moaned and arched and writhed beneath him, working his shirt higher up his torso.

He raised his head from my breast and tore the rest of my shirt open.

I let out a shocked cry. And then a shaky moan as he moved his fingers to the bra clasp between my breasts.

I gazed up at him, knowing what he was about to do next.

He did it. Nostrils flaring, stare locked with mine, he released the little clasp and the cups of my bra slid from my breasts.

With a ragged breath, I closed my eyes.

I felt him stroke his tongue over my right nipple first. Followed by his lips encircling the puckered tip of flesh.

A soft sigh sounded at the back of my throat. I buried my fingers in his hair.

He drew deeper on his prize, the action slow and deliberate and thorough. Shards of wet tension shot through me, sinking into the pit of my belly and lower. My sex contracted, squeezing something that wasn't there.

Yet.

With equal purpose, he covered my other breast with his hand, his fingers trailing over the swell of my flesh to the very tip of my nipple in such a way I felt sure I was going to melt into a puddle of bliss.

He worshipped my breasts that way for a long time, his

mouth alternating between nipples, propelling me higher and higher to a place I'd seldom been. There were no words for the pleasure Raph awoke in me just by sucking and touching my breasts. Nor for the building tension in my core.

I knew it wasn't an orgasm about to crash over me, it couldn't be. He hadn't once touched me down there, the place Heather called her hot button when she'd been describing her fantasies about Robert Pattinson, but it sure as hell felt like an orgasm. A big one. Rushing at me. Turning my blood to molten pleasure. Turning my very soul to—

I came.

Yep. I came.

The orgasm hit me hard, powerful, taking me completely by surprise. I let out a moan, rammed my pussy harder to Raph's trapped erection and clawed at his back.

And what did he do? Did he stop? Did he gloat about his prowess? No, he continued to suck and tease and play with my nipples until I shook and trembled and pleaded for mercy. And then, only then, did he raise his head from my chest and gaze down at me.

"Tell me you're not going out with Osmond," he said, the words a choked plea. "I know I should have asked this before now, given what ... what we've just been doing, but please tell me—"

I pulled his head to mine and crushed the rest of his question with a savage kiss. I didn't want to talk or think about Brendon. I just wanted Raph. Wanted him hard. Now.

I kissed him with a ferocity I've never felt before, my hands fumbling at his clothes as I did so. I wanted him naked. I wanted him in my bed, naked, slicked in sweat and sliding in and out of me.

I found the top button of his shirt and tugged at it without success. I let out a frustrated growl and tried again.

He shifted between my thighs, holding his weight above me with his hands even as he continued to kiss me.

I fought with the top button. Growled again when my fingers didn't achieve the simple task.

"Let me," he rasped against my lips, moving his right hand to where mine were on his shirt. "I can do it."

Something cold and dark stirred in the deep recesses of my soul.

"So can I," I said, closing my fingers around his wrist. Damn, I was shaking. Badly. Was that why I couldn't undo his button? Oh God, please don't let it be because of my condition. Please. I didn't want to be shaking. Not now. Not—

Raph raised his head and gazed down at me, his eyes unreadable. "I—"

Someone knocked at my door.

CHAPTER 5

Insta-Fame Sucks

The third rap had barely sounded when the door flung open and Heather charged into the room, hand pressed flat over her eyes, her grin wide.

"Two things," she announced, stopping a few steps from the end of my bed. "One, you're on all the breakfast news programs now. And two, The Biceps is on his way here. Also now."

Raph jerked away from me. Just like that. Our eyes connected for a split second and then he was on his feet, his wrist pulling free of my weak grip. "I'm going."

What the fuck? Struggling into a sitting position, a turbulent thundercloud of frustration, I frowned up at him. "What do you mean going?"

Not exactly my smartest question, but he'd thrown me for a loop.

"Damage control," Raph replied with a grunt. "Plus, I

didn't let Horn know where I was going to be for the night and if he discovers I'm not in my room, he'll panic."

The answer made me frown more. "Is that the only reason?"

He studied me. "Should there be another?" He shook his head. "Unless you want Osmond to see you half-naked, I suggest you fix your shirt up."

And with that, he turned on his heel and left.

I confess, I had no clue what was going on. How had we gone from hot, oh-my-God-I'm-having-an-orgasm making out, to this?

I thought of his question about Brendon and the fact I didn't give him an answer. Did Raph really think I'd have done what I did with him if I was going out with Brendon? Or was his sudden departure about something else? My head filled with the last few moments before Heather had knocked on the door ... my shaking hands, his insistence on unbuttoning his shirt.

My stomach knotted. Was he taking off because he realized he was making out with someone whose hands didn't work properly? Or was he as impatient to be naked with me as I was with him? Or was it just as he'd said—damage control? With this new media attention, was he going to need to make some kind of statement? Answer to someone? Have a conversation with a royal advisor?

Who knew being involved with a celebrity could be so goddamn confusing.

"Is he gone?"

I started at Heather's question. Letting out a sigh, I turned my attention to my unbuttoned, disheveled shirt. "Yeah."

When I looked up, my shirt once again in an acceptable state, Heather was grinning at me. "Did you ask him if he wanted to have a three-way with you and The Biceps?"

I threw a pillow at her.

She laughed, caught the feather-filled projectile and threw it back at me. "Where's your remote?" she asked, dropping on the bed beside me. "How's your head, by the way? Did Raph kiss it bet— Ahh, there it is." Snatching up the remote control she pointed it at the TV and pressed the *on* button.

Two perpetually cheery breakfast show anchors in a vividly colorful studio set filled the screen, the coiffed woman waving her hands about her head as an image of a man wresting a crocodile played on the large screen behind them.

"Am I really on TV?" I crossed my legs into a Buddha position, forcing myself to focus on the television. I didn't want to think about what had sent Raph running so quickly from my room. Not at the moment. I needed to digest it alone. And after I'd taken my meds. It was smarter that way.

"You are." Heather gave me a nudge with her hip and positioned herself beside me. "You look awesome, by the way. Shocked, but—oh, look, look, there you are!"

I stared at the screen. A hot prickle of shame flooded through me.

There I was on television, captured in shaky footage— how appropriate—gaping as Brendon punched Raph on the Mackellar House sidewalk.

The footage continued long enough to show Raph stagger back a step. Long enough to show Brendon bearing down on him, angry contempt on his face. I could see the word Parkinson's form on Brendon's lips—a word I could never, ever escape—a second before Mr. Horn slammed into Brendon, driving him sideways, and then the footage started all over again from the beginning.

"... Australian brother to the future Queen of Delvania." The voice of the female anchor suddenly filled my room and I realized that Heather had turned up the volume. "But at this point in time we don't really know why the university's gym manager hit him."

"Two big young men like that?" the male anchor said as video Brendon smashed his fist against video Raph's jaw once more. "I'm betting it had something to do with the girl—"

"An American student here on scholarship, apparently," his co-anchor interjected, the tone of her voice so full of innuendo I wanted to throw up.

"With the *American* girl," the male anchor went on, his tone as suggestive as that of his female presenter. "Oh, and there's the bodyguard, taking the big guy out. Damn, that's an impressive tackle. Can we see that again in slow motion?"

"It *was* a good tackle."

At the sound of Brendon's chuckle I let out a squeal, jerking my eyes from the television to where he now stood leaning against the doorframe.

He ran a slow gaze over me, both worry and amusement in his eyes. "How you feeling, Plenty, Ohio?"

I shrugged. "Y'know," I said, my throat tight and dry. "Famous."

Heather nudged me with her shoulder. "Watch out. She'll be demanding we follow her around like an entourage soon."

Brendon laughed, pushing himself from the doorframe with a shove of his sculpted shoulder before crossing to the bed beside me. "It'd be a bloody horrible job following her around."

He reached out and, with gentle fingers, brushed my bangs away from my forehead. I sat still, watching him study the bruise left over from my fight with the light pole. "Look okay?"

His gaze moved to mine. "Looks amazing."

I knew he wasn't talking about the injury. We may have

decided on a non-sexual relationship, but I knew Brendon pretty well by now. He wasn't going to hide the fact he thought I was special. It was … nice.

It was also, I suspect, why I felt guilty about what I'd been doing with Raph only a few minutes earlier on the very bed Brendon now stood beside. And why the tremor in my hand chose that moment to become more pronounced. Damn it.

With a disgusted grunt, I climbed off the bed and hurried to where I kept my meds. I didn't look at Heather or Brendon while I took them.

"So?" Heather said behind me, a schooled indifference to her voice. "Today's plan? Normal classes? Or should we go taunt the paparazzi hanging around outside, hoping to get more action shots? You planning on beating up Raph again today, Brendon?"

"Depends," Brendon said. "Has he done something to deserve it?"

I turned back to them both before Heather could answer. I knew she was wondering if I was going to tell him about Raph being in my room for the night. She had, after all, busted Raph and me … well, let's be honest, in a rather compromising position.

"I thought we'd start with my normal session," I said, recapping the bottle of water in my hand. I really needed to tell her Brendon and I weren't anything but friends. But if I did point that out now, Brendon would question why I was making a deal of it and I wasn't ready for him to know Raph had sat beside my bed all night, had been *on* my bed this morning.

Had covered my body with his, made love to my mouth with his tongue. Had undone my shirt and bra and made me come by sucking my breasts. Holy wow, by sucking my breasts!

The pit of my belly fluttered. No, Brendon definitely didn't need to know any of that. Especially given how insistent he was Raph wasn't good enough for me.

Studying me with a contemplative gaze, Brendon shook his head. "Nope. No working out for you today."

I narrowed my eyes. "Why not?"

"Because the gym is already full of damn near every student enrolled here wanting to gawk at you." He pulled a face. "*And* me, for that matter, and I'm not used to being gawked at."

Heather threw back her head and laughed. "Oh my God, Brendon. You are so full of shit. You thrive on being gawked at."

He chuckled. "Okay, I'll give you that. But being gawked at because I'm hot and sexy and incredible is different from being gawked at because I'm one third of a scandalous love triangle every man and his dog is talking about."

Another wave of prickling guilt swept through me. I knew he wasn't a third of a love triangle just as much as Brendon did, but I still felt bad. Whether I felt bad for him, bad for not telling him what I'd done with Raph or bad for Raph, I didn't know.

To be honest, I think it was just bad, period.

And to think I'd come to Australia to study koalas. Huh. It seemed I'd come to Australia to study how to be a character in a bad soap opera.

"Maybe you need to get an agent?" Heather asked, smirking up at Brendon.

"Maybe you need to think about who decides how many burpees you do each workout?" Brendon shot back.

Heather grinned. "You don't scare me, Osmond. You might scare Raph, but you don't scare me."

He gave her a quizzical frown. "Scare Jones?"

"With the way he bolted from—"

"Heather," I burst out.

To Heather's credit, she slapped a hand over her mouth, her eyes wide as she stared at me.

Brendon turned to me, jaw tight. "Bolted from where?"

Once again, the gods of timely door knocks halted the conversation. With the number of times someone knocking on my door had interrupted my life since arriving in Australia, I was beginning to think I'd made some kind of unbeknownst sacrifice to said gods at some point.

All three of us turned to the door, where Mr. Horn regarded us with a level gaze.

"Miss Rowling? May I speak with you alone, please?"

"What's the problem, Horn?"

Raph's bodyguard glanced at Brendon, straightening his shoulders, and puffing out his chest a little. I noticed a faint purple bruise ringed his right eye, along with a red graze on his jaw.

"It's not any of your concern, Osmond," he said gruffly.

"Like hell it isn't," Brendon shot back. "Your *client* has already caused Maci enough stress, let alone you fucking off and leaving her yesterday morning when things got a little uncomfortable for the poor baby. None of this crap would be happening if you'd taken her with you instead of—"

"Brendon," I cut him off, keeping my voice calm. I could see his anger growing, turning ugly. If I didn't do something, it was very possible he'd finish what Horn had started out on the lawn yesterday. "It's okay. Honest." I gave him a reassuring smile and held up my hands. Thankfully they weren't shaking. Too much.

Turning to Heather, I jerked my head at Brendon. "Think you can control the mountain of muscle here for a while?"

She laughed. I'd be lying if I said there wasn't a hint of

apprehensive concern in the sound. "I can do that." She climbed to her feet, crossed to where Brendon stood and wrapped her fingers around his impressive biceps. A small part of me wanted to giggle. She'd been wanting to do that for a long time, I suspected. I would make sure she knew she owed me one when I saw her next.

"C'mon, Osmond." She gave his arm a tug. "Let's get your famous arse out of here."

Brendon's gaze found mine for a second over Heather's head. I nodded, needing him to see I really *was* okay.

He let out a grunt, fixed Horn with a steady glare, and then allowed Heather to lead him from the room.

Releasing a well and truly pent-up sigh, I looked at Raph's bodyguard. "Okay, we're alone."

If he was perturbed by my obvious sarcasm, it didn't show on his face. But then in the few times I'd had some interaction with Horn, he'd never shown *anything* on his face. For all I knew, he was about to decapitate me in some super-secret bodyguard move.

He adjusted the lapels of his suit. My mind—hopped up on adrenaline and meds—pictured an impressively shiny gun tucked into a holster strapped under his armpit. For a fleeting second, I wanted to call out to Brendon and Heather. Instead, I jutted out my chin and met Horn's direct stare. "Well?"

God, did I sound surly? Brave? Or petulant?

Horn adjusted his lapels again and then, with a quick glance over his shoulder up the hallway, he stepped deeper into the room and closed the door.

"Errr ..." I said, my pulse an insane thumping in my ears. Brave articulation for the win.

Horn closed the distance between us in four steps, his right hand sliding inside his jacket, his stare locked on my face.

Holy shit, *was* he going for a gun?

I staggered back a step. The back of my knees hit the end of my bed and, totally ungracefully, I dropped into a sitting position, gaping up at him. "What are you doing?" I cried.

Expression unchanging—natch—Horn withdrew his hand from inside his jacket and extended it toward me.

I'm sure you've guessed he wasn't holding a gun—okay, so my imagination *may* have gotten a bit carried away. What he was holding in his thick, slightly hairy (eww) fingers was a slip of paper.

A check, to be precise.

I frowned at it, my brain completely uncooperative at this point. It had nothing to do with my condition and everything to do with the surreal situation. "What's this?" I asked.

"Encouragement," Horn answered, his voice as flat and devoid of expression as his face.

I frowned. "Encouragement for what?"

"To cease your interaction with Mr. Jones."

You know when you read the phrase in books "the blood drained from her face", you kind of imagine said character turning a comical white? I'm pretty certain that's exactly what I looked like. A weird prickling sensation razed my cheeks and lips. My face went really hot very quickly and then really cold.

"What?" I croaked.

"On behalf of the royal family, I am to inform you that it's in everyone's best interests if the relationship you have with Raphael Jones no longer continues. This—" Horn shoved the check at me, his brown eyes like dead pools of dark mud, "—is to help you reach that decision." He had the decency to pause for a second before adding, "Promptly and silently."

My head roaring, I lowered my eyes to the check in his fingers. It protruded out at me from between his index and thumb, the bank's red-and-white logo on the top right corner far more colorful than a bribe had any right being.

I swallowed. Raised my hand—oh goodie, it was shaking—and took the check.

I read the number written on the dollar-amount line. Whatever blood remained in my face drained away completely.

The number typed on that line was more money than I could ever hope to possess. Like, ever. Enough to pay for my meds and Mom's meds for ... for ... God, probably for the rest of our trembly, wobbly, unstable lives. Enough to pay for specialist appointments and consultations. Enough to pay for a private hospital ...

I swallowed, staring at the check. My mouth tasted like dust.

Jesus.

"This is not a slur against you personally, Miss Rowling," Horn's impassive voice scraped against the room's thick silence. "But the princ—" He paused, a scowl pulling at his face for a second before his ubiquitous impassive expression returned. "But the royal family has plans for Mr. Jones that don't include an American student."

Bam.

Just like that, scalding, incensed anger flooded through me, destroying the numbing chill of my disbelief. I jerked my head up and glared at him. "What's wrong with an American student? Not good enough for some obscure royals no one outside of Europe has heard of?"

For the first time ever, I saw a flicker of something in Horn's eyes—disquiet. Huh. This wasn't what he'd expected. Good. Screw him.

I snapped to my feet. The move forced Horn to take a step backward. Also good. "And does Raph have a say in these plans?" I asked, eyes narrowed. Fury and contempt turned my blood hot.

A muscle in Horn's jaw ticked. "Mr. Jones is aware of the expectations placed upon him."

"The expectations?" I echoed. I was genuinely angry, not just about the slur against me, but for Raph. "Why the hell do his sister's in-laws have *any* say in what he does with his life? In who he has a relationship with?"

The tick in Horn's jaw grew more pronounced. "If the figure on the check is not acceptable—"

"Screw the figure," I snapped. "Screw the royal family."

Horn's dark eyes turned cold. "I have been granted the authority to double the number."

I sucked in a breath. Double the number? Holy fuck.

Horn's top lip curled into a sneer. "*Now* how do you feel about the royal family?"

I couldn't find the words to answer him. They weren't in my head.

Double the number?

Double the number?

"As I thought," he went on. He plucked the check from my fingers, folded it once and tucked it inside his jacket. "I shall have the new check drawn up this afternoon. Do I need to remind you what you are being encouraged to do?"

My chest felt like it was being crushed with a cold band of steel. I thought of all those zeroes printed on the check. Thought of the cost of being a Parkinson's sufferer. Thought of Raph's kisses. Thought of his laugh, his smile. Thought of how he'd made me orgasm, and thought of the open hunger and desire in his eyes when he looked at me.

Thought of how he'd withdrawn from me when I couldn't undo his button.

Thought of my future and how no one should be

burdened by it. *No* one. Not even a guy who made me feel so incredibly alive the way Raph did.

Thought of it all.

"I don't want your encouragement," I said in a flat voice. "You can stick your encouragement up your ass. Now if you'll excuse me, I have classes to attend."

Before Horn could utter a word, I shoved past him, snatched up my bag and strode to the door. I yanked it open—for once my shaky hand was on my side and actually gripped the doorknob without any problem—and then turned to face Raph's bodyguard. "Make sure you close this on your way out. There are some complete assholes in this place who think they can just invade a person's life whenever they want."

Horn stiffened.

Yeah. Be afraid, I thought. *Be very afraid.*

I spun on my heel and stepped from my room.

Straight into Raph.

He stumbled back. I did the same.

"Whoa, American girl." He caught my upper arms in a gentle grip. "You shouldn't be moving so—"

With a grunt, I shrugged out of his hands. "I gotta go," I muttered.

I didn't look up at him, didn't make any eye contact at all. Hitching my bag up my shoulder, I sidestepped him with all the grace of a shambling bear and hurried down the hall.

It didn't surprise me at all that he came after me.

"What's going on, Maci?" He caught my hand with his as I was about to descend the stairs, bringing me to a halt. "Why was Horn in your room?"

Around me, I heard the normal rumbles of my fellow Mackellar House inmates die off. The heavy heat crawling all over me told me we were being watched.

"Nothing's going on," I said, loudly. "Your walking gorilla

just wanted to apologize for abandoning me. I forgave him and told him to say hi to the royal family for me.”

“You what?” Raph frowned over my shoulder, no doubt at his bodyguard who naturally would have followed us. At this point, I really didn’t give a flying fart what expression Horn was wearing. “What the hell is—”

I let out a ragged sigh. “You know what? I’m done. Too much drama. I have to get to class. Believe it or not, I’m actually here in Australia to learn stuff, important stuff, not be a part of some weird ... messed up ... media circus royal family ... stuff.”

As snappy, snarky comebacks go, it was pretty lame.

Raph must have thought so as well, if his chuckle was anything to go by. “Okay, now why don’t you tell me what’s *really* going on?”

I shook my head and glared up at him. “Class. Really. And after that, lunch with Brendon.”

It was a low blow.

I regretted it the second it passed my lips. Regretted it and hated myself for saying it.

But I had to do *something*. And letting myself believe there was some kind of deluded fantasy happy-ever-after in my future with Raphael Jones was not it. That was only asking for heartache. My future wasn’t going to be fun and easy and stable. It was going to be ... bleak. And no one deserved to be a part of that.

Brendon’s name had the desired effect on Raph.

A cold tension fell over him straight away. “Osmond?”

Christ, I wanted to take it all back. Wanted to say I was sorry and kiss him. Instead, I nodded. “Osmond. He’s a great guy. Doesn’t care at all if I have Parkinson’s. *Definitely* doesn’t try to help me with his buttons.”

Yeah, I went there. Could I go any lower?

Disbelief etched Raph's face. Pain flared in his eyes.

With a sigh I hoped to God sounded bored, I shook my head and pushed past him. "I've got to get to class," I threw over my shoulder as I hurried down the stairs. "See you around, Jones."

This time, he didn't follow.

I wasn't sure how I felt about that.

Cold? Empty?

Numb. Yeah, I felt numb. And broken.

I hurried from Mackellar House. More than one person photographed me with their smartphones as I did so. I was kind of expecting that. What I wasn't expecting was the madness that occurred when I crossed the threshold to the outside.

A swarm of people ran at me. Some of them had cameras. Some of them held microphones. All of them yelled questions. A lot of them shouted my name.

Great. They knew who I was.

Seemed I was no longer just the nameless American student anymore.

I shoved through them, head down, hand up, doing a pathetic job at shielding my face.

The sound of cameras clicking peppered the air like gunshots. The questions lashed at me like whips.

"Are you sleeping with Raphael Jones?"

"How long are you in Australia?"

"Are you cheating on Jones with Osmond?"

"Have you met the royal family?"

"Who has the bigger dick?"

My head swam as I gripped the strap of my bag like a lifeline. My forehead throbbed, the injury from yesterday's encounter with the paparazzi mocking me. But it wasn't just paparazzi this time. The microphones were proof I'd been elevated to a mainstream-media level of interest.

Dodging the horde, I stared at my feet, praying I'd get to class before I made a fool of myself by falling on my face in a stumbling failure of muscles and stress.

It wasn't until I heard a siren off in the distance followed by muttered curses that I raised my head. I saw a car with red and blue flashing lights screech to a halt at the curb, got a glimpse of the words *Campus Security* on its side …

And then a firm hand grabbed my wrist, followed by a firm arm wrapping around my shoulders, pressing me to a hard body, burying my face into a chest I knew, filling my breath with a scent I'd grown addicted to.

"Fuck off," Raph snarled above my head. "The lot of you. Just fuck off and leave her alone."

The photographers and reporters went crazy. Questions and camera flashes assaulted him. Raph ignored them all.

At least I think he did. I couldn't tell. He was cupping the back of my head, holding my face to his chest, his other arm holding me tight as he walked us slowly along the footpath.

There was a shuffling of feet. I heard someone yell, "You're on Sydney University property. You will be charged with trespassing if you don't leave *now*."

Someone shoved at my back. Raph growled. He drew me closer to his body. "Back the fuck off or I'll break your fucking—"

"Raph!" Heather's voice rose above the melee.

"Jones!" Brendon's voice followed.

The crowd surrounding Raph and I grew frenzied. The questions began again.

"So who stole who, Jones?"

"You ever considered a threesome, Jones?"

"How much can you lift, Osmond? Reckon you could hit Jones again for us?"

"Osmond," Raph called, his chest vibrating against my face. "Get her out of here. Now."

And then I was being scooped up in strong arms, arms I'd admired every morning even as I sweated and groaned and complained about being exhausted, and we were moving. *Brendon* was moving, carrying me through the chaos in a powerful run.

"You lot are sick," I heard Heather shout at our side.

"Fuck, the bitch hit me!" an unfamiliar voice cried.

More sirens sounded above the madness. Growing louder by the second. Closer.

Cameras continued to flash. Questions continued to be shouted. I heard Raph's voice snarling warnings behind me. Heard Heather telling someone they were scum. And then I was suddenly shoved into a car—Brendon's car—the door was slammed shut and all I could do was stare out the passenger window, dumbstruck at the feverish reporters mashing against the car, staring in at me, shouting questions I could barely discern.

Questions about my sex life, about Raph, about Brendon.

I sat there, head reeling. Stunned.

The sound of the driver's door opening jerked me around. A rush of adrenaline flooded through me as I prepared to shove out whoever had found their way in.

"It's me," Heather gushed, eyes wild as she pulled the door closed behind her. "We gotta get out of here."

Without waiting for my answer, she shoved the key into the ignition and twisted her hand. Brendon's car roared to life.

She shot me a crazy grin. "Man, being your friend sure isn't boring," she laughed before flooring the accelerator.

The media and paparazzi scattered away from the car. I twisted in my seat, looking out the passenger window.

Looking for …

Brendon and Raph stood surrounded, flinching at camera flashes and swiping away microphones thrust in their faces.

I don't know if it really happened or not, but I swear Raph's gaze connected with mine for a split second and then Heather turned a corner and I couldn't see him or Brendon anymore.

But not before I saw Horn barreling down Mackellar House's front stairs, suit jacket open, holstered gun clear for everyone to see.

"Oh my giddy aunt!" Heather gasped beside me as we sped down the street. "That was … that was …"

Letting out a choppy breath, I turned back to the front of the car and stared through the windshield. "Insane."

"Insane. That's an apt word. You okay?"

I nodded. Surprisingly, given what had just happened, I was. Sure, my heart was beating a mile a minute. Sure, my hands were shaking like crazy and I could feel the stress-induced tics beginning to take hold of my limbs. But I was okay.

Which didn't really make sense, did it? I mean, I should have been an emotional mess. I'd just been offered money to stay away from Raph. I'd refused that money—money that would have made my and Mom's life easier. I'd hurt Raph in such a mean, nasty way I still couldn't believe I'd actually done it, and then I'd become the focus of a media frenzy determined to make me the filling in a Raphael Jones-Brendon Osmond manwich.

I should have been a blubbering, snotty, shaking mess.

But I wasn't. I was … something. What that something was, I wasn't sure. In denial, most likely.

"I'm okay," I said at Heather's worried frown. "But I really do think I need to decompress somewhere away from people."

She smiled. "Hell yeah. I've got the perfect place."

A few moments later, after we'd sped down various quiet streets and turned too many corners for me to keep track, she parked Brendon's car outside a tiny cafe situated between an empty barbershop and a pet-grooming parlor, on a street that looked like it was trapped in the nineteen-fifties.

Heather was a maniacal driver. If I hadn't *already* been shaking and trembling and twitching thanks to the media circus we'd so recently fled, I would have been by the time we pulled to a stop. Damn. Seriously scary stuff.

"My uncle owns it," she said as we climbed out of Brendon's car, indicating the cafe with a nod of her head. "To be honest, I think it's just a front for some nefarious money-laundering scheme he somehow got caught up in. Probably doesn't even know what he's doing. I think no one is meant to actually come here but bikies, but it means there's no chance of the media finding us. *And—*" she grinned wider as she took my hand and walked me to the front door of the dimly lit cafe, "—the coffee is incredible."

We went inside.

I blinked a few times as my eyesight adjusted to the shadowy interior. Heather hurried over to the man behind the counter, who looked as if he could bend a steel girder with his bare hands. He had tattoos of naked women, skulls and dragons covering his massively meaty arms, and the smiliest eyes I'd ever seen. I watched them hug over the counter, wondering what she was saying, when they both cast a look my way. I realized I was too over the whole situation to care. I shuffled over to the table farthest from the door and dropped into one of its wicker chairs.

Oh boy, what a morning.

I glanced at my watch. "So much for Environmental Sciences with Professor Grant," I muttered.

"*Pfft.*" Heather plonked into the seat opposite me. "Professor Grant is a moron. You already know more than he does."

I cocked an eyebrow at her. "You're a mechanical engineering student, Heather. How do you know Professor Grant?"

"I dated his son for a week back in first year." She dug about in her bag and withdrew her iPhone—with a zombiefied Hello Kitty cover. God, I really did like her. "Both are morons," she went on, swiping her thumb across the screen, focused on what she was doing. "But at least his son had a great arse. No conversational skills, but a great arse. But then I wasn't dating him for his conversational skills. Ahh, there we go."

She raised her head and grinned at me. "You're trending on Twitter right now."

My mouth fell open. "I'm what?"

With a laugh, she held her phone out to me. "Number three trending topic. Maci Rowling."

I gaped at the screen, heat prickling my face. There it was. On the Twitter app's trends list. *#MaciRowling*.

"Wow," I whispered.

"And look at Number one."

My stare slid up the screen at Heather's prompt.

#RaphaelJones.

"Wow," I whispered again. What else could I say?

Heather turned the phone back to her and tapped her finger on the screen. "Let's see what they're saying, shall we?"

I swallowed. Did I really want to know?

I watched her studying the small screen and chewed on my bottom lip. Beneath the table, my left leg insisted on jerking up and down, filling the silence of the cafe with a dull *thud, thud, thud, thud.* I grabbed at a small glass salt-shaker, needing something in my left hand. It wasn't much, but at least it stopped my hand whacking about on the table like a damn jackhammer. The sound of my heel constantly banging on the floor was enough, thank you very much.

"Hey, cool," Heather exclaimed, making me jump. "I'm in this photo."

She turned the phone toward me again. I got a quick glimpse of the image—Brendon carrying me through a horde of photographers, Heather beside us, obviously yelling at someone—before she turned the screen back again. "I look pretty, don't I?"

I stared at her, lost for words.

"Okay," she said, dragging her thumb down the screen, her stare fixed. "It's mainly jealous women and teenage girls saying you're not good enough for him, that he should get an Australian girlfriend. There're a few saying they'd swap places with you, *quite* a few suggesting what I've already suggested—that you should have a three-way with Raph *and* The Biceps. More than one commenting on The Biceps's biceps." She laughed. "And oh, here's one from a guy with the username @BiggusDickus asking you to ... err, actually, let's not worry about that one."

I laughed, partly from shock, partly from nervous tension.

"Let's see what they're saying about Raph." She wriggled about in her seat, red curls bouncing about her head as if sharing her thrill at the whole thing. "Oh yeah, of *course* Shelly White has to chime in. God, she's a cow. '*I happen to know Raph is an amazing kisser*'. As if Raph has ever kissed her. Oh goodie, Macca put her in her place. '*Shut up, Shelly. Go strut a catwalk*'. Man, I like Macca."

Heather's uncle arrived with two squat, round mugs of

what looked like cappuccinos, saving me from having to respond.

Heather bestowed the man a warm smile. "Thanks, Uncle Brock."

Uncle Brock nodded before giving me a level look. "If you need a bodyguard, I know a few guys."

Heather smacked his sizable gut with the back of her hand. "Oh God, Uncle Brock. She's got paparazzi after her, not the mafia." She turned her smile on me. "Besides, with both The Biceps and Raph lusting after her body, I think it's pretty well guarded."

I kicked her under the table.

She winced and then grinned. "True though."

Uncle Brock let out a grunt. "You're incorrigible, Sparrow."

"Yeah, Sparrow," I teased Heather.

"I'll own that," she said before picking up her coffee, taking a sip and letting out a dramatic *ahh*.

Uncle Brock shook his head and ambled back to the counter.

Heather returned her coffee cup to its plate and then waved her phone about. "The good news is," she said, "that tomorrow something else will be trending and this will be forgotten."

"And the bad news?" I asked.

"I probably should have told you before now you've got mascara smudged all around your eyes from falling asleep last night without washing it off."

I burst out laughing.

She slid her phone across the table to me. "Go on, see what they're saying on the interwebs about you."

A thick lump formed in my throat at her suggestion. I

looked at her phone, its Twitter app still open, *#RaphaelJones* obvious on every tweet displayed.

I could see images of us taken outside Mackellar House that morning, tiny squares of color permanently capturing the madness and shared with the world by people I didn't even know. People who thought it was completely and totally okay to judge me and speculate about me. Strangers who were now condemning me, congratulating me, propositioning me.

It was, in a word, unnerving.

With a shake of my head, I pushed Heather's phone back to her. I didn't need that kind of emotional stimulus. I had enough to deal with.

Heather's lips curled in a slow, warm smile. "Yeah, I figured you'd feel that way." She swept her phone from the table and shoved it into the deep recesses of her bag. "So? What's next? You going to tell The Biceps that Raph's beaten him to your heart or what?"

Before I could answer her—before I could tell her Brendon already knew, even if Raph didn't and could *never* know—the Beatles started singing "I Am the Walrus" in my bag. I scrambled to retrieve my phone. That ringtone only meant one thing: Mom was calling me.

Hands shaking from nerves and happiness and excitement, I swiped to answer the call and pressed the phone to my ear. "Mom!"

You know what's the weirdest thing about being an adult? The second you hear your mom's voice, no matter how independent and grown-up and self-sufficient you think you are, you instantly become the little kid who needs your mommy's hugs to make everything better.

"Hey, Bear." Mom's softly husky voice stroked my senses across the thousands of miles separating us. "I'm missing you so much. Just wanted to make sure everything is okay over there."

Throat thick, eyes prickling with hot tears, I nodded.

Heather nudged my shin with her foot. "She can't see you," she mouthed at me.

"I'm okay," I gushed. "I'm missing you too."

Mom paused. Long enough for me to know something was wrong. Mom never paused during telephone conversations. It was like she was scared the line was going to be cut and she'd never get the chance to talk to whoever was on the other end again.

My heart slammed into my throat. "What's up, Mom?"

"Your cousin Nathan just called me. You know, the one who lives in Dallas?"

I frowned. Cousin Nathan was a grade-A jerk who thought it was hilarious to follow Mom around at family get-togethers, shaking his hands like an idiot. He thought he was being funny. I thought he was asking to have his teeth smashed in by my foot. "Okay. Why did he call you?"

"He said you're on the internet."

Remember that sensation I had earlier when Horn offered me a check to never have anything to do with Raph again? Yeah, I got that again.

"Something about two Australian men fighting over you," Mom went on, her voice laced with concern, "actually punching each other over you, and one of them is from a royal family. And the other is a bodybuilder or something. He said you were in a hospital as well because the royal family guy left you behind and you got attacked by some photographers and that the bodybuilder one came and rescued you but then beat up a member of the media." She paused again, a heartbeat of silence. "Is that true, Bear?"

Something sucked all the air from the room. Must have,

because I sure as hell couldn't breathe. I gripped my cell, my chest one big, heavy weight of holy-fuck-what-was-I-going-to-do. The last thing I'd wanted when I came to Australia was my mom to be stressed. But now, being in the middle of some insane European-royalty-Australian-celebrity internet controversy was clearly doing that. It was stressing her out.

It sure as shit was stressing *me* out.

"Bear?" Mom repeated, maternal concern clear in the nickname she'd used since I was too young to remember.

I cleared my throat. "That ... that sums it up."

"You didn't want to tell me about it?"

I shook my head at Mom's question. Heather pulled an exasperated face.

"No," I said quickly into the phone. "I didn't want you to worry." I let out a weak laugh. "Remind me to beat the crap out of Nathan when I get home."

Mom, God bless her, let out her own chuckle. Hers wasn't as lame as mine though. "I can understand that. He is a bit of a douche, isn't he?"

"*Mom!*"

She laughed again, sending wonderful warm licks of happiness through me. God, I missed her, missed her stability. I know that sounds stupid, given how much time I've spent telling you how Parkinson's makes us unstable, both on our feet and emotionally. But Mom—even with her tics and shakes and emotional moodiness—was the one constant in my life.

"I want to come home."

It wasn't until I uttered the words that I realized how true they were. I wanted to go home. I wanted to be hugged by her. I wanted to shake and tremble with her, not fear, pity and sympathy. I wanted to stop hiding what I had and let her brush my hair from my face and curl up on the sofa and watch cheesy Hallmark movies with me.

I wanted to be a little girl again.

On the other side of the table, Heather regarded me with sad eyes. A lump formed in my throat. Maybe I could take her with me? Mom would love her. Mom would smother her with hugs and make her s'mores and cookies—the real kind, the American kind—and we could show her what life in Plenty was—

"I'm not going to let you do that."

The steel in Mom's response caught me by surprise. I frowned, shocked. "Why not? I should be home with you, not over here being the star in some messed-up media threesome thing. Did Nathan tell you the media is implying I'm sleeping with them both? *Both*, Mom. Did he tell you Brendon had to bodily carry me away from the reporters? That Raph has a bodyguard because he can't leave Mackellar House without people wanting to touch him?"

"Raph is the royal one, yes?"

"Not exactly. Raph's sister married the future king of Delvania."

"And Brendon is the bodybuilder?"

"He's the gym manager. He's studying applied sciences and he's been working out with me every morning. His aunt has Lou Gehrig's disease so he knows how horrible Parkinson's is."

"Do you like these boys?"

"I do. Brendon is incredible, like the brother I never had. And Raph ..." I stopped, scrunching up my face as I thought of Raph. "Raph is ... is ..."

Shaking my head, I opened my eyes and dragged my hand —yep, shaking. Booyah!—through my hair. "None of that matters though, Mom. What matters is that I'm going to be hounded by paparazzi here, harassed and talked about. I don't want to be here anymore. I want to—"

"Oh, Maci." Mom's murmur cut me off. Even though I was on the opposite side of the world, I could see her face, could see the kind disapproval on it. "This is not how we raised you. We didn't raise you to run away from tough things, did we?"

I swallowed. The lump in my throat was hot and big and miserable. "No," I mumbled.

Mom made one of those sighing noises only moms seem to be able to make. The kind that tells you they love you even if they're monumentally disappointed with you. "Honey bear," she said, "I know you think your life isn't worth sharing with anyone now. I know you think it's better to hold everyone at bay so they don't get hurt by what you have, or to stop them from hurting *you*, but by doing that, you're just robbing yourself of a life."

Tight pain shot through me. I squeezed my eyes shut, aching all over. Aching and trembling.

"You are so young and beautiful and smart, Maci. And I am so proud of you, but you're not doing yourself any favors shutting your heart off from the world. Do you think your dad would have wanted you to do this? Do you think he'd be happy?"

"No," I whispered.

A soft sigh tickled my heart through the phone. "When I was diagnosed all those years ago, I told your father to leave me. I told him to go find a new life with a new woman who wasn't broken. I wanted him to take you and start again. I hated him for not doing it."

Cold disbelief and shock chilled me. My mouth fell open. "Mom!"

"I did," she went on. "I didn't want him to stay around

to watch me become something less than what I was. I didn't want him or you to be burdened by what was happening to me. I hated that he wouldn't leave. And I loved him, oh God, did I love him for not listening to me. He refused to give up on my life, even when I had. He refused to let me give up on living. He refused to let me wallow in my misery. He was my strength and he took the future I saw for myself—a scary, horrible, humiliating future —and turned it into something wonderful. A future of love and happiness and support and togetherness. Don't rob yourself of that, Bear. Don't."

A hot tear trailed down my cheek.

"But you loved Dad," I said, the words a hoarse croak. "And he loved you. And he was *Dad*. He was, he still *is*, the best guy ever born. Ever."

"He farted in his sleep, picked his nose when he didn't think anyone was looking and never, ever put the toilet seat down," Mom countered, gentle laughter in her voice. "And he used all those weird Australian terms and insisted we watch cricket on ESPN. *Cricket*. The most boring game in the world."

"Oh, Mom." It was my turn to laugh. Shocked as I was, I laughed. I missed my dad so much every molecule in my body hurt.

She gave a soft little giggle. "It's true. And I wouldn't have changed him for anything. But if I'd pushed him away, I never would have lasted, Bear. I never would have watched you grow up to be the woman you are now. Although I'm worried the woman you are now may be a tad too stubborn. And foolish, if she doesn't see what she has now for what it is."

Throat tight, I closed my eyes. "And what is it?"

"An adventure that life—or God, if you'll permit me—has given you," she answered. "Grab it with both your hands,

Maci, and hold on to it with such force there's no way they can shake."

The lump in my throat grew thicker.

"Don't give up on life yet, Bear," she said quietly. "Life hasn't given up on you."

I chewed my bottom lip, incapable of finding words.

"You only have to look at those two Australian men to know that," she said. "Even if you want to turn your back on it, life is coming after you. And Maci, Australian men really know how to make you feel alive. Trust me," she finished with a very unmom-like snicker that made me blush.

"Mom," I protested with a smile, even as my cheeks grew warmer.

"I love you, Bear. And that's why I think you should stay in Australia and enjoy yourself as much as you can. Okay?"

I nodded. And then croaked out a husky, "Okay."

"Good girl." Love filled her response. "Now stop talking to me and get back to it."

And with that, she brought the conversation to an end.

"I hope your mum just told you to stay here and enjoy your fame," Heather said, watching me over the rim of her coffee mug.

I smiled. "She did."

Heather grinned. "I think I love her."

My cell phone burst into life in my hands before I could say I did as well. I didn't recognize the caller ID but I answered and pressed my cell to my ear. "Hello?"

"Maci Rowling?" a strange male voice rumbled through the connection. "This is Professor Watkins, Dean of Students. I think it's best you come into my office ASAP. We need to discuss your place here at the University of Sydney."

Well, fuck.

CHAPTER 6

Unexpected Changes

An hour later, I walked out of Dean Watkins's office.

Wow. In the short time I'd spent sitting in the musty room full of leatherbound science tomes, every plan I'd made for my time in Australia shifted.

Apparently, the university wasn't exactly pleased with the media attention my ... situation ... with Raphael Jones and Brendon Osmond had caused. Apparently, they'd decided it was time I moved to the field study component of my scholarship.

I could be completely wrong—and very likely a little paranoid—but I suspect the good dean may have pocketed a nice bribe to help get me out of Raphael's life. I'm only assuming this based on the way he went bright red and stammered about for a bit when I mentioned the royal family of Delvania's part in my accelerated timeframe. My imagination, possibly a tad overactive I'll admit, suggested when Horn had failed dealing directly with me, he'd moved onto the dean, who was now getting rid of me. I wondered if he'd get a knighthood in Delvania for a job well done.

It was hard *not* to be angry when he called an end to the meeting with a laborious wave of his hand at the door and a condescending, "Perhaps you will be less distracted and more focused on the *reason* for your studies in Australia once you're out on the farm."

The *farm* was a cattle property roughly the size of the town of Plenty, situated some four hundred miles northwest of Sydney on the fringe of the outback. A large koala population existed there, left alone by the owners of the property for the sake of ongoing research into the marsupials' survival and existence. My original pre-RaB schedule (that's pre-Raph and Brendon, in case you hadn't figured it out) called for me to spend the last five weeks of my studies there, tagging koalas in the wild and collecting data on their movements to support my thesis. Those last five weeks weren't meant to occur for another three weeks.

But due to the media circus—or due to a phone call from Horn, I wasn't sure which—I was being shipped off at the end of this week. In four days. According to Dean Watkins, it would have been tomorrow if not for the fact the family I was staying with had yet to return from a holiday in Fiji.

In four days, I was leaving Sydney for good.

Four days.

I felt ... cheated. After Mom's incredible pep talk, after the encouragement Heather had given me on the drive to the university to "rip off Raph's clothes and ride him silly", I was more than just a little excited about facing the rest of my adventure in Sydney.

Okay, I wasn't exactly about to confess to Raph that I thought I was falling in love with him, and golly gee wouldn't it be wonderful if we spent the rest of our lives together in splendid bliss. That *definitely* wasn't part of my plan. But I had decided I *was* going to enjoy myself for the rest of my time here.

It wasn't like Raph and I could have any kind of relationship once I returned to Plenty. For starters, he lived in Australia and I lived in America. As far as long-distance relationships went, that was freaking far. By the time the dean's secretary showed me and Heather into his office, I'd made up my mind to spend the next three weeks enjoying myself with Raph. If that meant we made out from time to time—and by *made out*, I mean ... well, you probably know what I mean—all the better.

Three weeks of living. Three weeks of not worrying about my future.

Three weeks now robbed from me.

Goddamn it.

"Man, is he a sour old sod," Heather muttered after we left the dean's office. She looped her arm through mine and nudged my hip. "Think we should invite him to the next Mackellar House Underwear Bash?"

"Probably *not* a good idea," a deep male voice uttered to our right.

Both Heather and I let out matching startled *eeps* and spun around.

Raph stood leaning against the door, arms folded over his chest, dimple creasing his right cheek in that sexy way it did when he was almost, but not quite smiling.

My heart damn near slammed out of my chest.

"Raph?" Heather's laughter echoed along the silent hallway. "You scared the bejesus out of us."

He levered himself off the wall with a grin and stepped closer. "That wasn't my intent." His dark gaze found mine, an unreadable question in their depths. "Are you okay, American girl?"

Throat tight, I nodded. Four days. I only had four days left. Goddamn it.

"Errr …" Heather slipped her arm free of mine. "I have to return The Biceps's car to him. You two just … go have … yeah, you know what you two want to have."

Her playful innuendo should have set my cheeks on fire. It didn't. Instead, it made my pulse race and my inner thighs constrict. Or maybe that was due to the way Raph was studying me. The way he drew closer to me, just looking at me.

Just me.

If Heather said anything else before taking her leave of us, I didn't hear it. All I could do was gaze up at Raph.

"You're not having lunch with Osmond?" he asked, the low question playing havoc with my sanity.

Christ, he was gorgeous. Have I mentioned that yet? How gorgeous he was? Heart-clenchingly gorgeous.

I shook my head. I was sure at some point I'd recover the higher brain function to form words, but at that moment in time, all my higher brain function was occupied being in awe of how gorgeous and wonderful and sexy and there, right there, Raph was.

Four days, Rowling. The thought whispered through my roaring head. *Only four days.*

Now so close his knees brushed mine, Raph touched the line of my jaw with the back of his knuckles. "Lunch with me instead?"

I swallowed. Words still failed me.

Nervous doubt flared in his eyes. "Please?"

I don't know if it was his uncertainty that helped me find my tongue, the fact it was obvious he wanted to be with me but feared I was going to deny him, or the way the distinct scent of him threaded into my very breath. All I knew for certain was that I wanted to spend every minute I had in Sydney with him.

"Lunch would be wonderful," I said, my voice husky.

The smile that spread across his face sent a shard of wet, tight, delicious heat straight through me. Oh boy.

"Excellent. I know just the place."

He took my hand in his, his palm warm and slightly rough. It reminded me he'd grown up on a cattle ranch, and that reminded me I was heading to the farm in four days, and *that* reminded me I wasn't going to see him anymore after I left Sydney.

My chest clenched at the thought and, nerve endings thrumming with an elemental need I didn't want to name, I tightened my grip on his hand.

Four days. I could live a lifetime in four days. I could.

We walked together through the university grounds, our conversation relaxed. Neither of us brought up our previous tension, it didn't need to be addressed. The simple fact I was here with Raph now was the only thing that mattered.

By the time we got to his ute, we were both laughing. *And* ignoring the people we passed photographing us with their smartphones.

Screw it. If they wanted to experience fame by some tenuous thread of association—a *Hey, I saw Raphael Jones and the American chick he's banging* kind of thing— then let them. As Heather had pointed out, tomorrow something new would be trending on Twitter. Who knows, maybe Miley Cyrus and Liam Hemsworth would be engaged again?

As we approached his dusty, mud-caked ute, Raph waved his hand about in an elaborate flourish. "Your chariot, my lady."

He pulled the door open, revealing the same chaos that I'd encountered yesterday morning. More Red Bull cans were scattered across the passenger-side floor, along with a crumpled McDonald's bag I assumed must have contained yesterday's lunch or dinner. I cocked an eyebrow at him.

He let out a rueful chuckle and shrugged. "What can I say?"

I laughed and made a move to deposit myself on the passenger seat. I stopped when I saw a pile of books. Heart thumping fast, I stared at the titles.

The Parkinson's Disease Treatment Book.

Parkinson's Disease: Top Tips to Optimize Function.

Understanding Parkinson's Disease: A guide for Family and Loved Ones of Sufferers.

Parkinson's Disease for Dummies.

Living with Someone with Parkinson's.

"Fuck."

At Raph's low mutter, I turned from the books and stared up at him, silent. Inside, I was a churning, conflicted, angry, sad, ecstatic, confused mess. It was one thing to commit yourself to a four-day *adventure* with a guy you really, really, really liked. A guy who turned you on more than it was probably socially acceptable to admit. It was another to discover said guy was researching the disease that would ultimately end your life. It told me he was interested in every part of who I was, not just the healthy parts, the squishy, warm parts that fit together so well with his warm, not-so-squishy parts. It told me he was thinking about my life, my future.

It changed the playing field somehow.

"I only ..." he began, frustration etching his face before he dropped his gaze to the incriminating books on the passenger seat. A rough breath left him. He raked a hand though his hair. "I know you don't want to talk about it, but just let me read about it, okay?" He looked back at me. "I just ... it's what I do when I don't understand something. I read about it."

I drew a deep breath. I truly had no idea how I felt about that. Hell, I'd only just decided how I felt about *him*, and here he was, doing *this*.

I stared at the book sitting on the top of the pile. Its title tickled a funny bone I didn't think I had anymore.

Turning back to Raph, I arched my eyebrow. "*Living with Someone with Parkinson's?* Really? You got plans we haven't discussed yet? I mean, I know we've made out and all, but I'm not sure I'm ready to move in with—"

He shut me up with a kiss. He swept his tongue into my mouth, grabbed my butt and, with a chuckle, pulled me close to his body and ground his hips to mine.

Instantly and immediately, I was horny. Horny and happy. Deliriously happy. Who knew?

At the sound of approaching voices, Raph broke our kiss. I *did* groan in protest, I'm afraid.

"We'll continue this later," he murmured with a grin before nudging his head toward the ute. "But for now, you need to get your arse in there, American girl. Before Horn finds me."

"Oh, you being naughty?" I asked as I removed the books —*Parkinson's Disease for Dummies?* Seriously?—from the seat and lowered myself into the car.

"Not yet." Raph leaned into the interior, his eyes dancing. "But I plan to later."

He winked and, as heat flooded my cheeks, he closed the door.

Twenty chat-filled minutes later, we arrived at our destination. Pulling his ute into the valet parking section, Raph released his seat belt and gave me a wide smile. "Ready?"

I looked out the window, the obviously luxurious hotel on

the other side taking me by surprise. "Is this where we're having lunch?"

He laughed. "Yep."

Without further explanation, he climbed from the car, handed his keys to the hovering valet and walked around to my side. He extended a hand to me as I began to climb out. I didn't know if he was just being chivalrous, but the significance of the books now piled on the ute's floor still played with my state of mind.

Raph rolled his eyes. "Bloody hell, woman." With a laugh, he snared my wrist and yanked me completely out of his car, catching my lips with a quick kiss as I bumped into his tall, hard body.

Before I could comprehend the wonderful sensation of his playfulness, his lips left mine. "Let's go," he said, once more taking my hand in his.

We walked into the hotel, and for a brief second, the sheer opulence of the place stole my breath. "I really don't think I'm dressed for this," I whispered.

Raph nudged me with his shoulder. "Shush. Just enjoy yourself, will you? I pulled a lot of strings to set this up."

My eyebrows shot up and I gaped up at him. "Really?"

He laughed. "Nope. I just made a phone call. Sometimes it helps to be a celebrity."

Lucky for Raph, a well-dressed man approached us just as I was about to poke him in the ribs with my elbow.

"Mr. Jones," the man I'm guessing was the concierge said, holding out his hand to Raph. "The dining room you requested is ready. If you will follow me?"

He turned and proceeded to walk toward a bank of elevators on the other side of the lobby. I cast Raph a curious sideways look. He just winked and followed the man in the suit. Body thrumming—yes, I was excited—I followed Raph.

The three of us rode the elevator to the sixth floor. A soft chime filled the small space as the elevator came to a stop, and our suited companion swiped a keycard through a slot and the door slid open. My mouth did the same.

"Your waiter will be with you shortly."

"Thanks," Raph said as he placed his warm, firm hand on the small of my back and strode out of the elevator.

Astonished, I stared at the beautiful private dining room we'd entered and the stunning view of Sydney Harbor and the Opera House beyond its floor-to-ceiling windows. "Wow," I breathed. "I *really* think I'm not dressed for this place."

Raph threaded his fingers through mine and led me to the round table situated beside the window. "I didn't want to share you with anyone," he said as he pulled out an ornate chair and urged me to sit.

Overwhelmed, I gazed up at him. "What if I'd said no to lunch?"

He shrugged. "Then Heather would be getting the surprise of her life."

I burst out laughing and Raph grinned, obviously proud of himself. He pulled out his own chair and sat.

A second later, an immaculately dressed man appeared at our side. White napkins were gently placed across our laps, water glasses filled, and menus provided. All without a word.

Damn near quivering from excitement, I studied the items printed in dark script on the matte gold paper.

"There're no prices," I whispered, peeking at Raph around the side of the menu.

"I know. How dangerous."

With a roll of my eyes, I let out an exasperated sigh and returned my attention to the menu.

To be honest, I didn't understand or recognize ninety

percent of what was written. What the hell is *jus? Mousselin? Agri-doux?*

It didn't matter. I was on a high like I'd never been before and it had nothing to do with the fancy setting and ridiculous menu, and everything to do with the guy sitting opposite me and the adventure I was sharing with him. I could have been standing in line at a Subway and I'd still feel the same.

I felt wonderful.

Alive.

Happy.

Picking the fourth item from the top with random abandon—grilled Northern Territory crocodile with asparagus tips and red-wine *jus*—I lowered my menu and fixed Raph with a level gaze. "Speaking of dangerous," I said, watching him study his menu, "where *is* your bodyguard?"

He pulled a face. "I've given him the day off. In fact, if I had my way, he'd be gone for good. He doesn't know where we are and my phone is off."

"So you *are* being naughty?" I pointed out, delighted. I didn't like Horn. Just in case you hadn't picked up on that little fact by now.

Raph laughed, the sound low and relaxed and so goddamn yummy. "I told you, being naughty comes later."

My body throbbed and pulsed and generally reacted like an impatient freaking sex-fiend's at his words. *And* the open hunger in his eyes as he raised his head and looked at me.

Oh boy.

I wanted to say something pithy and flirty but our waiter arrived before I could. Which was probably a good thing, given I had no clue what pithy and sexy thing to say. *Take me right here on the table, Raph?* Probably not, even if it *was* what I was thinking.

Boy, was I thinking it.

The next fifteen minutes were spent talking movies, American life versus Australian life, farm life versus city life. The topics were inconsequential. The real conversation was taking place with our eyes. Yes, I know that sounds corny, but it was true. While words like *Iron Man* and *Katniss* and *drought* and *rush-hour traffic* passed our lips, our eyes had a completely different conversation.

I was damn near squirming on my seat by the time our food arrived, the junction of my thighs thick with want and impatient need, my nipples hard with the same.

We ate. The food diffused the crushing sexual tension for a while. Long enough for us to laugh about our meals, comment on their elaborate presentations and finally share a few forkfuls of each other's dishes.

That was where we went wrong. Why was watching someone eating from your fork so goddamn arousing? Was it a trust thing? A sharing thing?

Whatever it was, watching Raph slip crocodile from the end of my fork made me want to jump his bones.

When he offered me a taste of his lunch—roasted quail with some fancy stuffing neither of us could translate—I couldn't help but shiver with anticipation as I leaned slightly across the table and parted my lips. Our eyes met. He slowly placed the tip of his fork speared with a small morsel of quail into my mouth.

Onto my tongue.

The sublime flavors caressed my taste buds, more delicious than anything I'd eaten. But it wasn't the food that turned my breath to a ragged moan. It was the way Raph was looking at me. The open, urgent desire in his eyes.

I swallowed the quail, my hands shaking from impatient, nervous need and excitement.

"Th-that's delicious," I rasped, tracing my finger over my

bottom lip. I really needed to rein in my lust. I was going to embarrass myself soon.

Raph regarded me silently.

Christ, I could barely draw breath.

"Maci ..." he said.

The arrival of our waiter prevented him from finishing.

"Dessert?" the man queried.

I shook my head, rising instead to my feet. "If you'll excuse me, I think I need to visit the bathroom."

I didn't miss the devilish light in Raph's eyes as our waiter inclined his head. "Of course, ma'am."

If I wasn't so hyped on sexual need, I'd have laughed. Ma'am. That was a first.

I hurried to the bathroom. I didn't need to pee. I *did* need to calm myself.

Staring at my reflection in the mirror, I drew five deep breaths, held each one and let them out in slow, steady streams through my lips.

I reminded myself we were in a restaurant. True, it was a private dining room, but still, it wasn't like we were going to start making out like rabbits right there.

Of course, then I remembered we did have a tradition of making out like rabbits in public restrooms and the fluttering need in the junction of my thighs grew damp.

God help me, if Raph walked through the door into the ladies' bathroom, I'd probably come before the door could swing closed behind him.

Yes, I was *that* horny.

Raph didn't stride through the door, however, and by the time I finished washing my hands and staring hard at myself in the mirror—a good five minutes later—I'd regained some semblance of control over my feverish libido.

I would walk back out there, smile with relaxed good

humor, settle back into my seat and sip ice water as we continued our conversation about TV shows, ask him what he thought of *The Walking Dead.* Did he think they would ever say the word zombies? That's what I was going to do.

Shaking out my hair, loosening up my shoulders and wriggling my slightly trembling fingers, I pulled open the door and walked back into our private dining room.

The table had been cleared, replaced with a bottle of champagne in a silver ice bucket and two champagne flutes.

Raph stood at the window, one arm resting on the glass above his head, his other hand deep in his pocket, his back to me.

I paused for a moment, sliding a long, lingering gaze over his body. His ass was exquisite in his jeans, his shoulders broad and strong and muscular. He was sublime.

"Are you going to just stare at me or do you think you might want to come over here?"

I jumped a little at his question.

"Busted," I said, tucking my hair behind my ear as I walked over to where he stood. "You okay with me reducing you to a piece of meat I can drool—"

The word *over* didn't get a chance to pass my lips.

The second I drew close to his side, Raph turned, fisted a hand in the hair at my nape and crushed my lips with his.

He slammed me against the glass, hips to hips, his cock thick and hard as it rubbed my belly through our clothes.

I made a hitching sound, totally undone by the concentrated pleasure rushing through me.

Holy fuck.

He lashed my tongue with his, his hands roaming my shoulders, my breasts, my hips, before catching my wrists and pinning them against the window above my head.

Again, I say holy fuck.

I ground my pelvis into the rigid pole of his erection. He deepened the kiss, his plundering tongue sending hot licks of liquid electricity straight to my core, as did his firm grip on my wrists. I was his prisoner, caught between him, the window, and our explosive desire—and I never wanted to escape.

He made love to my mouth until I could barely stand. With every swipe of his tongue, with every nip of his teeth, I grew more enslaved by the potency of his kiss. Pleasure pooled in the pit of my belly, radiated out through my limbs. By the time he released my wrists and smoothed his hands down my arms to cup my breasts, I could barely *breathe*, let alone remain on my feet.

When he dragged his lips over my chin and down my throat, kneading my breasts the whole time, I couldn't control my raw "Oh yeah." I tangled my fingers in his hair, pushing my hips forward. I'd be lying if I said I didn't want him inside me. Now. Right now.

In response to my husky cry, Raph pinched my nipples through the cotton of my shirt. A shudder racked my body, deep and bone melting. I arched into his touch, on fire. Aching for more. "Yeah," I repeated, the word nothing more than a sigh.

With his own raw groan of pleasure, he buried his head into the side of my neck and sucked on my skin.

I gasped, the painful pressure making me throb with wicked hunger. I rubbed the curve of my sex to the hard ridge of his erection, wanting to feel it bruise my skin.

He moaned, his hands on my breasts growing fierce. "I want to be inside you, American girl. Tell me you want that too," he ordered, his breath hot on my neck.

"I want you inside me, Raph," I declared, incapable of anything else. "Here. Against the window. But what if ... people see ... down on the street ..."

"The glass is tinted," he rasped against my skin. "No one can see in from the outside. And the waiters have been dismissed."

I let out a low chuckle. "Then strip me naked and—"

He captured my lips with his, as he undid each button on my shirt with feverish haste. My gasp filled the room, loud and hoarse. And then Raph was releasing the front clasp of my bra and sliding the lace cups from my flesh.

The cool air of the private dining room kissed my newly exposed skin, sending a shiver through me. My nipples puckered into tighter points. My lips parted.

"Oh, Maci," Raph murmured, skimming his thumbs over the swells of my breasts, his nostrils flaring. "You are so beautiful."

I turned my head to the side, suddenly shy. "I twitch too much to be beautiful," I whispered, my throat thick.

"Look at me, American girl." He pressed a finger to my chin, drawing my face back to his. "You are the most beautiful woman I have ever known," he said, tracing his thumb along the line of my bottom lip. "And if I hear you putting yourself down again, I will be forced to spank you."

I burst out laughing at his unexpected tease.

He laughed too, the sound devilish and wonderful.

Smiling up at him, I smoothed my hands over the firm expanse of his chest, his throat, to the thick strands of his hair at the back of his head. "In that case," I said, "I'm a shaky, twitchy, ticky, trembly—"

He silenced me with a kiss as he pulled me harder to his body and grabbed my ass cheeks in a punishingly firm grip.

I giggled into his mouth, the playful noise quickly turning into a groan of raw delight as he dragged his palms over my hips, up my ribs to my breasts again. He stroked each nipple, rolled them between thumb and finger, pinched them until I squirmed against him. Only then did he remove a hand from my breast, but before I could protest, he replaced his fingers with his lips.

Oh boy. Oh fuck. Oh boy.

He drew my nipple deep into his mouth, massaging my other breast as he did so.

I threw back my head, eyes closing, head swimming with exquisite pleasure.

Raph feasted on my flesh, first one breast and then the other, sucking my nipple, nibbling it, laving it with his tongue. With every second that passed, I grew closer to eruption.

When he pulled away from me, releasing my left nipple with a wet pop, I cried out.

Breath ragged, he stared down at me, planting his palms on either side of my head on the glass. "Tell me again," he ground out. "Before it's too late, tell me again."

I knew what he wanted. What he sought. After the madness of our relationship so far, he needed my unequivocal permission.

I gave it to him.

"I want you inside me, Raphael Jones," I said, holding his gaze. "Now."

He captured my lips in a searing kiss and shoved his hands between the material of my skirt and the curve of my hips, grabbing my ass. I matched his ferocity with my own, tugging on his belt and fly with greedy impatience. For once, my fingers didn't betray me. They did what I wanted them to do and did it well. In less than a heartbeat, Raph's engorged length was jutting through the gaping opening of his jeans, thick and hot and erect.

I wrapped my hand around it and squeezed. He bucked, driving his hips forward as he threw back his head and hissed.

I pumped his length, the feel of his arousal in my hand

the most powerful, *steadying* sensation of my life. It was as if the life I'd denied myself since my diagnosis, the refusal to acknowledge there was more to existing than breathing, flowed through me from Raph's flesh, from his body. I know that makes no sense, but I don't know how else to explain it. By holding him, holding his pleasure in my hand, I knew life.

And it was addictive.

And fucking potent.

With a moan, I shoved his jeans down over his hips and reached for his balls with my other hand.

He groaned into my mouth and then tore his lips from mine, cupping my right breast in a mauling caress before sucking my nipple into his mouth again.

We burned in that moment for an eternity—me working his erection with my hand, him worshipping my breasts with his mouth. Fire licked through my veins, the heat of pleasure beyond comprehension. I knew I'd reached the point of incineration when the only thing that would satisfy the lust in me was the feel of his erection on my tongue.

I dropped to my knees, mindless of anything else but tasting him. Possessing him.

I took him into my mouth. Oral sex had never been high on my list of favorite sex acts, but goddamn, did Raph's length filling my mouth flood me with carnal joy. I slid down his erection, taking him as deep in my mouth as I could.

Deeper.

It was his strangled groan that damn near pushed me over the edge. And the way he knotted his hands in my hair and tugged me back to my feet.

"I don't want to come in your mouth, Maci," he rasped, his eyes ablaze. "I want my first time with you to be ..."

"Romantic?" I laughed out the word on a soft breath.

"Perfect," he answered, before lowering himself to *his* knees and smoothing my skirt up my thighs.

Heart racing, I pressed my palms to the window and stared down at him. He roamed his lips over my knees, my inner thighs. He journeyed higher, nipping a path to the very heart of my core.

I hitched in a breath, frozen with agonizing need and anticipation.

He stroked his tongue over the seam of my sex through the cotton of my panties. Panties that were tugged aside with sure fingers before I could gasp.

He flicked his tongue over the button of sensitive flesh in my folds and I cried out. "Oh God, Raph."

Fingers squeezing my ass cheeks, he licked my clit again. I slammed my hips forward, an involuntary action brought about by the sheer and absolute pleasure wrought upon my body. In response, he pressed his mouth to my most intimate flesh and sucked on my clit.

To say my resulting moan was loud and raw was an understatement. I don't know how long he kept me dangling there, on the cusp of an orgasm unlike any I'd experienced before. Five minutes, five hours, five centuries. Time ceased to exist. Every throbbing pulse that claimed my core, that propelled me closer to the point of eruption, robbed me of my ability to exist in reality. There was only the pleasure of Raph's tongue.

I made noises I've never made before, raw noises, horny noises, as I clawed at the window, every muscle in my body trembling. I didn't care why. It didn't matter. Not when I felt so ... so ... holy shit, so alive. So worshipped.

So desired.

When I didn't think I could take any more, when the building pressure at the base of my spine and deep within my center turned to a constricting heat, I raked my nails through his hair and yanked his head away from my sex.

He stared up at me, his lips glistening, concentrated need in his eyes. "You taste like heaven," he murmured.

I feathered my fingers over his bottom lip. "You make me feel like I'm *in* heaven."

It was true. And yet, I needed more.

And it seemed, so did Raph.

With a low growl, he rose to his feet. Sliding his body up mine as he straightened, he grabbed the back of my right thigh and drew my knee up to my chest.

The tip of his erection nudged the lips of my sex. Parted them.

We stared into each other's eyes, hanging on the moment, the contact. The most personal of invasions.

His chest heaved. "I'm not wearing a condom."

I touched his lips, his cheek. "I have an IUD."

A frown pulled at his eyebrows.

"I'm safe," I whispered. "I won't get pregnant. I promise."

"You're not worried about ..."

"I'm clean. And I trust you are too."

He sucked a deep breath in and nodded.

I swallowed. "Then please hurry up. I want you to fuck me so much I think I'll go mad if you don't hurry—"

He penetrated me with one single, powerful upward thrust, pulling me down into his stroke at the same time.

I cried out. Loud. He stretched me wide. He was so much bigger than my previous boyfriends, and it had been so long for me.

I clung to him, waves of pleasure and pain rushing over me.

"Oh God, Maci." He buried his face into the side of my

neck even as he withdrew and slammed back into me again. "You are so tight, so perfect, so mine ... so mine ..."

The words, falling from him in a tumble of panted moans, sent fresh heat and rapture through me. I closed my eyes, undone by his touch, his declaration, undone by him.

It was everything I'd imagined and so much more. So much more.

He moved inside me, in and out, in and out, each thrust deeper, more forceful, more demanding. Each stroke driving me back to that edge, that perilous precipice, that place like the burning edge of a blade, where life and pleasure and reality and fantasy merged, and you've lost yourself to the sensations consuming your body and found yourself in the pleasures of them.

That edge of existence.

"Maci ..." he panted, his thrusts growing faster, more erratic. "Maci, look at me, please? I want to see your eyes when you ... when we ..."

I opened my eyes and gazed into his, just as he squeezed my butt and slammed his length deeper inside me.

My orgasm detonated like an eruption of heat and indescribable perfection. I raked my nails across his back and cried his name. Over and over.

And as my voice began to break, as my cries became ragged breaths, Raph came as well.

I felt him. I felt it. Felt his release pump from him in thick ropes.

Felt him fill me with his pleasure.

And all the while, we gazed at each other. And in his eyes, I saw a future I wanted more than life itself.

An eternity later, we slumped against each other, my cheek against his shoulder, Raph's holding me to him as he turned us around to press his back against the window. Our shallow pants seemed deafening in the private dining room, a rapid, ragged accompaniment to the soft piano music wafting in the air from hidden speakers. The contrast tickled my highly quirky sense of humor and, unable to stop myself, I let out a giggle.

"What's so funny?" Raph's deep voice rumbled in his chest, vibrating through my body. Melding with the tremors already at home in my limbs.

I raised my head and smiled at him. It occurred to me he was still deeply buried inside me. I liked it. I liked him being there. A lot. "How absolutely determined I was to keep you out of my life."

He flashed his dimple at me. "As if that was ever going to happen."

He smoothed his hands over my back, my hip, my thigh. With gentle ease, he lowered my leg, his spent erection slipping from me, skimming his fingers over my skin as my foot returned to the floor. For a second, a wave of unstable shakes hit me and I held on to him tighter.

Our eyes connected again, a question in his. A concern.

I stopped him vocalizing it with a brush of my lips on his. "As if," I whispered, letting him feel my smile.

We both laughed again, a shared, secretive laugh that quickly became a long, languid, thoroughly passionate kiss.

Damn, I was really into this guy. So freaking much.

"I guess," he said when the kiss finally came to an end, "I should let our waiter know he can give us the bill now."

I grinned. "Maybe you should pull up your jeans first?"

He pulled a comically quizzical face. "You think?"

Before I could kiss him again—and really, why wouldn't I? —the only door leading into our dining room swung open.

"Ill-advised, Mr. Jones."

Cold distaste flooded through me at the sound of Horn's flat voice.

Raph tensed as he pulled me closer and glared at his bodyguard. "What the fuck, Horn? How did you find us?"

"I am not going to reveal that, Mr. Jones." The man had the decency to keep his attention on Raph. Or maybe not acknowledging my existence was an attempt at insulting me. If the latter was the case, it didn't work. I'd decided to ignore *his* existence the second he'd offered me the multi-zeroed *encouragement* not to have anything to do with Raph. "You are aware what the family expects of you. This ... adventure you have undertaken is unwise. As well as exposing you to personal danger."

Raph's arms tightened around me. "My stalker, you mean? I'm beginning to suspect there's no such threat. It's just a way to keep tabs on me. I'm not interested in being a part of the family. I'm not interested in anyone *from* the family, no matter what they want to believe. You can tell their royal pains in my arse that my *sister* married into the *family*, not me. I'm done with this. All of it."

Horn regarded him with expressionless eyes. The bulge under his armpit told me loud and clear he was carrying his gun.

"Did you hear me?" Anger turned Raph's question into a menacing growl. "Leave us alone."

Horn regarded me with an emotionless stare. I sucked in a swift breath. I didn't want to, but damn, the guy was intimidating. Nothing in my life had prepared me for this kind of confrontation.

"Now," Raph snarled, drawing me still closer to his chest.

I have to admit, I was completely and utterly undone by his protective rage and how wonderful it felt.

Oh boy, I was not going to fall in love with the guy. I wasn't.

Horn returned his attention to Raph. His eyes narrowed as he adjusted his jacket's lapel and, with an almost inaudible grunt, turned and left.

My breath left me in a massive gush. Who knew I'd been holding it all that time? My head swam as black waves of dizziness filled my vision. I felt my inside shake—*really* shake.

And then Raph let out his own ragged breath as the tension deserted his body and he laughed. "Well, that's one way to kill the mood, I guess."

Four Days and Counting. Damn it.

We returned to Mackellar House, and I had a shower and changed my clothes before heading to class. Believe it or not, I hadn't actually had the chance to shower since the previous morning. Kind of gross, when you think about it. Thank God for Listerine Pocketpaks and panty liners.

Raph walked me to lecture hall one for Environmental Degradation 101. We didn't get harassed by the media or the paparazzi. I suspect that was in part due to the campus security cars cruising the area and the security guys strutting about. The fact Raph stuck a baseball cap on his head and dark sunglasses on his face also helped. As did my decision to do the same. Borrowing a hat from Heather (a big floppy thing that dangled in my eyes and hid half my face), I did everything I could to disguise my identity.

To be honest, it was fun. Like I was suddenly Angelina Jolie.

When we arrived at my afternoon class, Raph tipped my chin up with a soft tap of his finger, flashed his dimple at me and kissed my lips. "Thanks for lunch, American girl."

My heart leapt and I gave a nervous giggle. I knew it was

stupid to get all shy and coy after what we'd done—hello? Hot, wild monkey sex in a restaurant where anyone could walk in. Shy and coy should be a thing of the past, right? But even here, in the hallway outside a lecture room with fellow students jostling past us, all I could think about was how incredible our lunch had been. Not just the sex—incredible doesn't even come close to describing that—but the whole thing. All I could think about was how much I liked this guy, this guarded, sometimes unpredictable Australian guy who made me laugh and feel special.

He smiled at me again, kissed me one more time and then left for his own class.

Oh boy, I could fall in love with him so goddamn easy.

I think I spent the entire lecture gazing out the window like a doofus, drawing flowers and love hearts and stars and koalas on horses in my notebook. At some point, I think I even let out a sigh or two.

Raph met me at the door when class finished and, disguises firmly in place, we spent the thirty minutes before our next lectures relaxing on a grassy knoll in the sun, my head in his lap, his fingers dancing tiny patterns over my shoulders as we talked about anything and everything.

No one bothered us.

It was glorious.

Afternoon lectures passed way too slowly. Mine went longer than Raph's and it was Heather who met me outside Mackellar House four hours later, a delightfully curious expression on her face.

"So?" She barred my entry into the house with her body. "Details?"

I smiled. "A good girl doesn't kiss and tell."

"Oh!" she exclaimed. "I knew it. I *knew* it."

"Knew what?" Raph appeared in the doorway behind her, his smile relaxed.

Heather threw him a wicked smirk. "How big your—"

"Ego is," I finished, grinning at her. "And I said, what ego?"

"You don't remember my ego? Man, I need to try harder." He snaked a strong arm around my waist and pulled me to his body with such force, Heather's floppy hat tumbled from my head. "Think I better take you up to my room right now to show you my *ego* again."

And with that, he led me, laughing, away from an equally amused Heather.

To his room.

Where he did, indeed, show me his *ego*. Four times, in fact.

Somewhere around nine pm we realized food was needed and decided to order takeout. I told Raph I was going for another shower and would happily eat whatever he ordered.

I was only in the communal bathroom for five minutes, however, when Raph strode in, towel over his shoulder, naked from the waist up. He looked at me just as I was about to walk into the shower bay where I'd deposited my own towel and clothes. He kicked the main door shut behind him, leaned his back against it and beckoned me over with a slow jerk of his head.

We continued our tradition of making out in public bathrooms there and then. This time, however, we weren't interrupted by anyone. Not even by a single knock on the door.

I finally returned to my room and my own bed a little past four-thirty in the morning. I figured Raph needed to have some time to himself and I was feeling the shakes starting in my hand. Too much sex, perhaps? Was that even possible?

I'd just lowered my head on my pillow when a soft knock

sounded at the door. Followed by a low, deep voice saying, "Get your arse back in my bed now, woman."

I did. Hey, who was I to argue?

We made love again and then curled up in each other's arms, naked, our hearts beating together, our legs entwined, discovering everything about each other in our murmured words and shared laughter.

The one thing I didn't tell him, however, was that I was leaving Sydney at the end of the week. I wanted to. I really did. I wanted to tell him so we could make plans to keep in touch while I was there. I wanted to tell him so we could decide who was going to travel to where on weekends. I wanted to tell him it was all going to be okay, that long-distance relationships were completely doable.

I wanted to tell him all those things but didn't.

There *was* no happy-ever-after on the horizon for us, there couldn't be. So the fact I was going sooner was a moot point. Besides, I didn't want to dampen the fun we were having by putting a ticking clock on it. Instead, I decided to do what my mom told me to do. Live my life.

As the sun broke the eastern horizon, casting Raph's room in a pale-golden light, I kissed him and said the words I never ever thought I'd say to anyone. "I really enjoy being with you. Want to do it again sometime?"

He laughed, flipped me onto my back and proceeded to show me just how much he did, indeed, want to do it again.

I barely made it back to my room before Brendon banged on my door, telling me to get up. "Twenty-four hours is enough time to be a pathetic layabout," he called through the wood. "Just because you're famous doesn't mean you can slacken off, you hear?"

Suffice to say, I wasn't my best at the gym that morning.

For the next three days, I immersed myself in my Sydney experience and allowed myself the joy of doing so. Every morning, Brendon dragged me out of bed for our pre-breakfast workout. He never said anything about Raph. I knew he still disapproved of the situation—the way they both puffed up and engaged in those chest-thumping staring wars whenever they came face to face in my company told me as much. But he didn't cast dispersions or make any snippy comments either.

Okay, he *might* have rolled his eyes the morning after my lunch with Raph and muttered something that sounded like, "Bastard better let you sleep sometime." And he *might* have ordered that I at least have a nap that afternoon before I bonked the night away, but he did it with a smile, and as I left, the hug he gave me was completely platonic.

I didn't nap, by the way, despite his instruction. I had limited days left. I wasn't going to waste them doing something as inane as sleeping, was I?

So I worked out each morning with a guy who was well and truly on his way to being the best brother I'd never had, meditated afterwards in the quiet of my room in preparation for the day to follow, popped my meds when I was meant to, went to class, worked on my thesis and spent every second between all those things with Raph.

It was bliss.

Wonderful, funny, relaxed bliss.

Horn was nowhere to be seen. I don't know if he was fired or just lurking out of sight. I asked Raph once and the answer I got was a shrug and, "As long as he's nowhere near us, I don't care."

It was a sound philosophy. One I adopted with relish.

The only thing that soured those days was the growing pile of books on Parkinson's I kept finding in Raph's room. On his desk. In his car. How many of the damn things was he reading? To what end?

I didn't want him to be focused on that. I wanted him to be focused on me, Maci Rowling, hot American girl he was having an incredible time with, not Maci Rowling, PD sufferer. I know it sounds stupid I was so intent on keeping these two facets of my life separate, but no matter how many pep talks and lectures I gave myself about letting Raph see the Parkinson's side of my life, I couldn't.

I didn't mention them, even if they were irritating me. Nor did I comment on the times Raph undid his own buttons and fly as we were making out, or the times he would pick up the water bottle I'd purchased at the university cafeteria and twist the lid off as we talked. I knew what he was doing. I'd tried to convince myself he was just being nice, but I'd watched Dad do the same thing to Mom—helping when help wasn't really needed—and recognized it for what it was.

Raph's determination to help me was a faint taint on an otherwise perfect adventure (yes, I'd truly grabbed on to that word), an itch I knew needed scratching but one I ignored because I was too busy having fun.

On my last day in Sydney I woke—as I had every day since our private lunch—in Raph's arms.

The early morning sun was streaming through the window into his room, and for a long moment, I just lay there, curled on my side, his long, hard body spooning my back and thighs, the hard length of his erection nestled against the crevice of my butt cheeks. I watched the dust motes dance on the air, picked out by the golden light of dawn, using the moment as an impromptu meditation session.

In twenty-four hours, I would be at the train station, ready to board the train that would take me to a town called Tamworth, from which I would then catch a bus to a smaller town called Gunnedah, where someone from my host family would collect me. Then it was a ninety-minute drive to their ranch where I would begin my fieldwork on koalas.

Today was my last day with Raph.

Ever.

A cold grief tore at my heart, and I closed my eyes.

I didn't want to go. I wanted to stay here with Raph. Not just in his bed, not just in his arms, but with him. I wanted to continue existing with him, sharing my life with him. He made me feel whole. And he made me feel stable.

When I was with him, I didn't fear the future in front of me. I rarely even *thought* about the future in front of me, with its bleak loss of muscle control and even bleaker degradation of my mind. When I was with Raph, I lived in the moment and loved those moments. They were full of life and laughter and pleasure and desire and ... and ...

Oh God. Oh God, no.

It had happened. I'd done the unimaginable. The stupid, the downright idiotic. I'd done what I promised myself I'd never do.

I'd fallen in love with the guy.

Oh God, this sucked.

Big time.

Drawing in a slow breath, I held it for a count of ten and let it go, opening my eyes as I did so and focusing on the dancing dust motes again.

Jesus, I'd let myself fall in love with Raphael Jones. What was I thinking?

At my back, Raph mumbled something. His arm draped over my waist and, mumbling again, he tucked me closer to his body.

I twisted a little on the bed, looking at him over my shoulder. His eyes were still closed, his breathing deep and regular. He was asleep.

The knot in my tummy rolled over on itself. I returned to my side, the undeniable presence of his body pressed to mine a torture I didn't know what to do with.

"Fuck."

At my whispered curse, Raph mumbled something else and curled his arms tighter around me.

God, it was incredible. And perfect. Without thinking about it, I raised my hand and trailed my fingers up the length of his forearm.

I stopped when I noticed how much my fingers—my whole hand—was trembling.

I swallowed, my throat dry, and stared at my fingers. They shook. Like they always did when I was stressed. Like they always would as the days and months and years passed. Even when stress had nothing to do with it, my fingers, my hand, my whole fucking body would, one day, just shake for no other reason than because I had fucking Parkinson's disease. It was going to destroy everything I knew in my life and there was nothing I could fucking do about it.

Scrunching my eyes closed, I squeezed my fingers as hard as I could into a cruel fist. Pain shot through my palm, lancing up my arm.

I squeezed harder, punishing the unpunishable. Hating my hand, my fingers, hating the way they shook. Hating them.

If they didn't shake, if *I* didn't shake, I could have the life I so wanted to have. I could ... I could ... God, I could tell Raph I was going and maybe, just maybe ask if he'd like to come visit me in the States. I could ask him how he felt about long-distance relationships. Or maybe I could transfer to Sydney University next year to complete my studies. If it wasn't for the way my whole fucking body shook and twitched and betrayed me, we could ... he and I could ... maybe ...

Cold grief shot through me. Equal to the pain I was causing in my hand. Grief and hate and contempt and—

"Hey, American girl." Raph's sleepy voice at my shoulder made me jump. As did the feel of his warm lips on my skin. "You okay?"

I opened my mouth. Closed it again.

He ran a slow hand up my arm, kissing my shoulder again. "You feel tense."

I tried to calm the turbulence in my stomach. I did not want to concern him.

Not today.

Today, I just wanted him to be the relaxed Raph. The one I was going to miss like hell tomorrow. And for the rest of my short, shaky life.

Damn it.

"I'm okay," I murmured, every fiber in my body aching. Christ, why did I have to fall in love with him? "Just slept funny, I think."

He *hmm'd* against the back of my neck, snuggling me closer to him with a firm arm. "That's okay, then." He nipped a path of soft kisses down to my shoulder, smoothing his palm down my belly to the junction of my thighs. "For a moment there, I thought you were about to do a runner, and there's no way I'm ready for you to leave this bed yet."

He brushed his fingertips over the curve of my sex to emphasize his point, finding the tiny nub of my clit with his index and stroking it.

I moaned. I couldn't do this. Not now. I had to ... I had to get my head around the situation. Jesus, I'd fallen in love with him and tomorrow ...

With a forced laughed, I shifted on the bed. "I *am* going to do a runner," I said, inching away from him. "At least, I'm going to go brush my teeth."

Yeah, brushing my teeth. That would give me *all* the time I needed.

Fuck.

Before I could get free of Raph's arms, however, he hooked a thick, muscular thigh over my hip and pressed me back to the mattress. "I don't care about your teeth, American girl," he murmured, covering me completely with his body, his palms smoothing the length of my arms to capture my wrists in a firm grip as his cock nudged between my thighs. "I care about you. And this."

He lowered his head to mine and kissed me.

Oh God, I wished he hadn't. Because it was so good, so perfect, so wonderful, any hope I had of fleeing shattered.

His tongue found mine with coaxing strokes. I moaned, already lost to the pleasure of his touch. He nipped at my lips, gentle little bites he immediately kissed better. I closed my eyes and gave myself over completely to this one last moment of perfection.

I had no other choice.

I was going to cling to this for the rest of my life.

Closing my eyes, I arched beneath him, wanting him inside me already. I was ready. I could feel the moisture of my arousal on my inner thighs.

Raph had other ideas.

With a chuckle—Christ, I would miss that raw, naughty sound—he scored a path down my chin and throat to my collarbone.

I hissed as he grazed his teeth over the ridge and then groaned as he ran his tongue across the same line. A shudder rocked through me. My nipples pinched tight. Real tight. I let out a ragged breath, aching for the feel of his mouth on them.

Raph delivered.

Just as I was about to start begging, he explored my right breast with his mouth and then captured my nipple and sucked it.

"Yes," I rasped, thrusting my hips upward. "Yes."

He feasted on my nipple, drawing it deep into his mouth, rolling it between his teeth, flicking his tongue over its very tip. All the while, he held my wrists to the bed. If he felt the trembles in my limbs, he didn't let me know. Instead, he nudged my thighs wide with a firm knee and moved his mouth to my other breast.

I gasped, loving the sensation of his lips and tongue on my nipple. He hummed around the point of flesh, sending wicked pleasure through my body. Tight heat unfurled in my core, threading through the very fabric of my life.

A soft whimper fell from me and I rolled my head. Releasing one of my wrists, Raph smoothed his hand down my arm to my breast. As he worshipped one nipple with his mouth, he kneaded, pinched and squeezed the other. Hot pleasure crashed over me. I arched again, fresh heat pooling in my sex.

"I love the feel of your breasts, Maci," he murmured, rasping his lips against my nipple. "As much as I love the way you respond when I suck them."

To prove his point, he drew my nipple back into his mouth with fierce suction.

I cried out, wrapping my thigh around his hip in an attempt to bring his rigid length closer. The need to have him inside me was tantamount to my need to breathe. More so. I felt certain I would die soon if he didn't bury himself inside me. I could survive without air for at least six minutes. There was no way I'd survive that long without Raph penetrating me.

There wasn't.

"Please," I moaned, scraping my nails over his bare shoulders. "Please fuck me."

He raised his head from my breast and gave me one of those filthy laughs. "Not yet, babe. Not until I make you come with my mouth first."

Carnal lust poured through me. Raph loved going down on me. I'd lost count how many orgasms he'd given me over the last four days with just his mouth and tongue.

Dimple flashing, he lowered his head back to my breast and continued his worship. I swear, I almost came numerous times as he feasted on my nipples. I'd moan and writhe and plead for more, plead for mercy, and Raph would give me everything and nothing. I can't fathom how many minutes passed while he drove me wilder and wilder just by sucking and biting my breasts alone. I was so wet for him. So ready. My pussy prickled with hot need and pleasure. Every time he raised his head, my breath caught. Hope that he would thrust into me warred with hope he wouldn't.

When he finally moved lower down my torso, his lips journeying with slow intent over the curve of my rib cage to the dip of my belly button, it was all I could do not to cry out with frustrated rapture.

He explored my navel with a series of little tongue flicks and nips, his chest pressed to the curve of my sex, roaming his hands over my thighs. I whimpered on each one. My pussy throbbed, eager and impatient for what was to come.

Raph, however, was in no hurry. He tormented me with his lips, raining a slew of nips all over my belly, my hips, even high inside my thighs. I groaned, aching for him. Aching for his tongue on my most intimate of places.

And finally, after he'd kissed his way down to the toes of my right foot, back up to my belly button, down to the toes of my left foot and back up again, he *finally* stroked his tongue over my sex.

I threw back my head and cried out, bunching my fists in the sheets.

Oh God. Oh God, oh God, oh God, oh God!

With each stroke and lap and lick, he propelled me closer and closer to release. Closer to eruption. I thrust my hips upward, grinding my flesh to his mouth. I tossed my head from side to side. I did all those cliché things you see in the movies and couldn't stop. My body, always ready to do whatever it damn well wanted, had completely surrendered to the pleasure Raph was giving me. I'd become a cliché and I didn't care.

It was too good. Too good. Too—

I orgasmed, biting my lip to silence the cry I knew would wake the rest of Mackellar House.

Holy fuck, I came.

And then, and *only* then, as my sex contracted and throbbed and pulsed, did Raph slide up my body and bury his length inside me.

I lost control of my cry. It reverberated around his room, loud and raw and undeniably torn with pleasure. There was no denying the reason for that cry.

I should have been mortified. Instead, I was drowning in pleasure. Drowning in the sensations Raph awoke in my body. Drowning in love.

We moved together, Raph supporting his weight with an elbow, his other hand gripping the back of my thigh. We moved as one, in perfect rhythm. He kissed my lips, my chin, my jaw. He thrust deep inside me and explored my ear with his tongue and sucked on the side of my throat and we moved as one.

A lifetime, a few moments. I don't know. Don't care.

We moved as one, in harmony.

And when I came again, Raph came. A shudder racked his body, his thrusts grew faster, wilder and, gaze holding mine, my name falling from his lips over and over, he pumped into me.

Oh God, it was perfect.

So perfect.

And so goddamn heartbreaking.

So wretched, knowing I was going to deny myself this.

He slumped on me a few heartbeats later. I hugged him, willing every molecule of my existence to remember this. To absorb his essence. I would hold on to this moment for the rest of my life.

I would draw strength from it when I had none left.

I loved him.

Damn it, I loved him.

"Shit, woman," he muttered against my shoulder. "I didn't think it could get any better, but ..." He lifted his head and shook his head, his smile wide, his breaths shallow. "But that was incredible."

I closed my eyes and drew in his scent. "It was."

He kissed the tip of my nose. "Good thing we've got classes all day today or I think we'd never get out of this bed."

I laughed. I'm sure it sounded weak. I was both exhausted and dying inside.

"However," he said, shifting just enough for his length to slide out of me, "what do you reckon we take a break from all this debauchery for a few hours tomorrow and head to Wet'n'Wild. Will you spend the morning at a water park with me, American girl?"

An image flashed through my head—Raph and I laughing together as we splashed each other in a pool. The joy on our faces was clear. As was the love in my eyes.

My heart clenched, a painful vise. The image was perfect. So perfect it stole my breath and made me insane with longing. And then clarity crashed into me, reality, and I opened my eyes to look up at him.

"I won't be here tomorrow, Raph," I said, my voice steady. Level.

He frowned. "And where will you be, American girl? You and Heather got plans? I'm thinking you need to change those—"

"I'm leaving for Gunnedah tomorrow morning," I cut him off. "For the fieldwork part of my scholarship."

He stared at me. "What?"

Had I thought I was dying inside only a few moments ago? That was nothing compared to the cold grief and pain I felt now. "I'm catching the train at Central Station at six forty-five," I said, forcing my voice to stay composed. It was hard, what with the shocked way Raph looked at me. "Heather's taking me there. I'm spending the next six weeks on a ranch ... I mean a farm, or a property, or whatever you guys call it, and when that's finished, I'm returning straight to Plenty."

He continued to stare at me, the confusion in his face morphing into something else. Disbelief. Followed by anger. "You didn't think you should have told me this, oh, I don't know, at the beginning of the week?"

My stomach rolled.

With greater effort than I thought it would take, I planted my palms to his chest and pushed him off me. I couldn't have this conversation while we were both naked and he was still nestled between my thighs.

He grunted but rolled away. I'm under no delusions it was my brute strength that shifted him. Scrambling from the bed, I snatched up my shirt from the floor and tugged it over my head. Without looking at him, I searched for the rest of my clothes. They had to be here somewhere.

"Maci?"

I tried not to flinch at the anger in his voice.

"Care to explain?"

Finding my shorts near his desk, I pulled them on. "I thought you knew," I said, pretending to still search for my underwear. I didn't give a rat's ass about my underwear, but I couldn't bring myself to look at Raph either. "I thought Heather had told everyone. What did you think was going on here between us anyway?"

"I don't know," he answered. I could tell he was staring at me by the prickling heat razing my back. "Something fucking amazing and incredible comes to mind."

I shook my head, still continuing my underwear-seeking charade. Amazing and incredible were exactly the words I would have used as well, but if I agreed with him, he'd only want to continue what I knew couldn't. "It was just some fun. Some good sex and laughs before I move on."

I heard him climb from the bed a second before he spun me around to face him. "Before you move on?"

The anger, the stunned hurt in his eyes, ripped my heart apart. I wanted to tell him I was sorry. I wanted to say I was stupid. Instead, I shrugged.

He dragged his hands through his hair. "I don't believe you."

I didn't answer. Turning my face away from his intense scrutiny, I pretended to study the world beyond the window.

"No."

The single, flat response made me turn back. It was so full of adamant conviction.

He shook his head, eyes locked on my face. "This is bullshit," he growled.

Yes, it was a growl. He was angry. Really angry.

"Bullshit," he repeated. "What we have ... you can't just shrug that off. I won't let you."

I arched an eyebrow at him, conveying an attitude that screamed *bitch* and God, did I wish I wasn't. But I had to. There was no future for us. There was no future for me. I didn't have a normal life sprawling ahead of me, I had a crappy one. One he didn't deserve to be burdened with.

"Won't let me?" I echoed.

Raph narrowed his eyes. "I won't let you. I can't believe after what we've shared ... how much ..." He shook his head, scoring his fingers over his scalp. "Christ, woman, I trust you. Don't you get the significance of that? I don't trust anyone and yet I trust *you*."

I stared at him, forcing myself not to respond. And then he said the words I didn't want to hear.

"Fuck, Maci, I've fallen in love with you."

I went cold. The pit of my belly fluttered with nervous joy and excitement before reality smothered the deluded reaction. I looked at him, hating myself.

"I didn't ask you to," I said. Damn, I should have been a drama major with how well I was pulling off coldhearted bitch. "I don't want you to."

Before he could respond, I turned to his desk and plucked the top book from the pile. "Just like I didn't ask you to read these," I continued, showing him the cover. *Living With Parkinson's Disease.* "Holy crap, Raph, you're reading books about Parkinson's disease. About how to cope with a loved one who has Parkinson's disease, about living with it. Don't you get how wrong that is?"

His jaw bunched. "It's wrong to care about someone?"

The lump in my throat grew thicker, making it difficult to breath. *Cared* about me. *Loved* me. Everything I'd wanted since meeting him. And my worst nightmare. "Please put on some pants," I beseeched, turning away from him again. I dumped the book back on his desk.

The sudden jolt woke his laptop, the screen filling with a Google page on Parkinson's disease.

I wanted to sob. I wanted to hit him. Just as much as I wanted to hug him.

Life was so unfair. So fucking unfair.

"Is it wrong to want to understand what the person you've fallen in love with has got?" he demanded. I could hear the rustle and snap of denim followed by the distinct sound of a zipper being yanked up. "Wrong to want to know how to help them?"

Knowing it was safe for my sanity to turn around, I faced him again. He was indeed wearing jeans now. Just jeans. Somehow, that made it worse. His naked chest rose and fell with each ragged breath. His stomach—with its exquisite six-pack and sexy-as-sin trail of hair leading down from his navel—hitched.

The dizzy memory of the night before lashed at me. The memory of me licking a path from his navel over that thin line of hair down to his arousal.

Shutting that memory off, I rammed my fists to my hips. It was hard-truth time. I'd been a bitch, now it was time for a reality check. "What I've got? This thing? Parkinson's? It's never going away, Raph. I'm not going to grow out of it. I can't take a magic pill and be cured. It is going to slowly devour everything that makes me *me*, take away every ounce of pride I have, every shred of dignity, and there's nothing you can do to stop that. No matter how many books you read, no matter how many bottles of water you open for me or door handles you turn."

He looked away. "I didn't think you'd noticed."

"I did. You buttoned my shirt yesterday, Raph. Sure, my hands were trembling a little, but I could have done it up myself." I couldn't stop the disappointment in my voice. "If you're doing that now, what are you going to feel you have to do in two weeks? Wipe my ass?"

His dark gaze snapped to mine. "That's not fair."

"None of this is fair, Raph." I drew in a slow breath and released it. "And none of your research and googling for alternative treatments and support groups will cure me."

The muscle in his jaw ticked. "What if I know that? What if it doesn't matter to me?"

I raised my chin. "It *should* matter to you. You're not even twenty-five. You have a whole life ahead of you. I don't. And if you can't see that, then you're a moron."

Cold fury flickered in his eyes again. Chips of dark rage and deep grief. "So you're saying you don't love me? You don't have feelings for me at all?"

My pulse pounding in my ears, I shook my head. "I don't love you."

His Adam's apple jerked up and down. "And what we've been doing was just some no-strings sex?"

I forced out a sarcastic snort. "I'm a college girl from another country, Raph. Of course it's no-strings sex."

Man, I was being a bitch. I knew that. But when you *know* what's ahead of you, when you've witnessed it firsthand —a lifetime of the tremors, of choking on your own spit, of falling over and drooling, of burdening the people who love you no matter how much you try not to—you realize *no one* is going to want to have to deal with that.

Even if Raph thought he did. Even if I desperately wanted him to.

He sucked in a slow breath. His nostrils were white with livid rage. Fury radiated from him. "Well, thanks for finally filling me in then, Maci. You've saved me making a big mistake. And stopped me wasting any more of my time. Fuck knows, I've wasted enough of it on you already."

The words sliced through my heart. I wanted to cry. God, I was dying inside. "You're welcome," I said instead, sick to the stomach. At my hip, my hand shook like a goddamn vibrator on full speed. "Now if you'll excuse me, I have to pack."

Christ, I didn't want to do this. I so didn't. I wanted to go back to him and say sorry. But I couldn't face an almost certain day in the future where he would make excuses to end the relationship, knowing my Parkinson's was the *real* reason. And I knew I didn't have the strength to pretend to believe him when that day came.

It was easier this way. Horrible, yes. Bitchy, definitely. But easier. For both of us.

I turned and walked to his door, pausing for a second as I wrapped my hand—the right one, shaking, but not as bad as my left—around the door knob. "If you find my bra and panties just throw them in the trash. They're not important to me."

Before he could utter a word, and let's be honest, there wasn't much left to be said, I pulled open the door and hurried through it.

Straight into Brendon. "Hey, Plenty, Ohio," he said, catching me with a firm grip around my upper arm as I stumbled backward across the threshold of Raph's room. "I was just coming to get you for—"

"Get me out of here, Brendon," I snarled. Yeah, I snarled it. "Take me back to your apartment. Now."

I didn't look back as I shrugged off Brendon's hands and stormed away from Raph's room.

I didn't pause as I hurried down the stairs. I kept walking. Until I was outside. Until I was at Brendon's car.

Then, only then, did I allow myself the luxury of collapsing to the ground, clutching my hands to my face and holding back the tears, the hot, damning, self-hating tears.

Holding them back. Holding them back.

And then failing.

Brendon found me that way a minute later. Whatever had delayed him, whatever had passed between him and Raph, he didn't say. He crouched down beside me, wrapped a strong arm around my back and helped me to my feet.

"C'mon, Maci," he murmured against my temple. "Let's get you cleaned up. You look an absolute mess with all the tears and streaked mascara and snot."

My answering laugh was tortured and weak. But it was a laugh.

It was the only one I had for the rest of the day.

Heather came and collected me from Brendon's apartment an hour later. In that time I'd showered, washed my hair, removed any signs of tears from my face, and removed any remnants of Raph from my body.

I sat on Brendon's sofa, staring at the exercise bike positioned between me and the television. I heard Brendon and Heather talking in low murmurs in the kitchen, but I didn't care about what was being said.

I had gone into full-on Parkinson's meltdown. My brain had turned the world gray and bleak and miserable and I was drowning in it.

And it was all my fault. All of it.

At some point, Heather took me back to Mackellar House. I needed to pack, after all. Gather up my things and get ready to move on.

That's what I was doing—moving on. There was no point in staying here, even if my heart was telling me I should.

We walked through the building with its noisy floorboards and noisier occupants that had been my home since I'd arrived in Australia. The smells were familiar to me, the faces the same. As confusing and conflicting as my time here had been, I realized as I climbed the stairs that I loved it here at Mackellar House.

I was going to miss it.

I was going to miss it all.

My gut flip-flopped at the thought of leaving.

My mind—fuzzy and tormented—told me it wasn't just the house I was going to miss. Stupid mind. Of course I was going to miss Heather and Brendon. And Raph ...

Was he going to hate me forever, I wondered? After what I'd done to him? Was he going to ... I don't know, miss me?

I shut down that thought. It was too raw and messed-up. I didn't want Raph to miss me. Wanting him to miss me meant I wanted him to think about me and I didn't want that either. He needed to move on.

Huh. Moving on. Yeah, I was beginning to think moving on was a sucky term that didn't come close to conveying how horrible and miserable and wretched the reality was.

We were two steps away from my room, Heather being her normal chatty self, in an effort to cheer me up, no doubt—when the door to Raph's room opened.

I froze. My heart didn't just leap into my throat—it lodged there and damn near suffocated me. I stared into the dim interior.

And sucked in a breath as Shelly White, she of bikini-modeling fame and Twitter infamy, floated across the threshold, hair a wild mess, lipstick smeared.

"Errr ..." Heather uttered beside me.

Shelly smiled at us and then, with a toss of her artfully wild hair, turned back to Raph's open door and wriggled her fingers in a cutesy wave that made me want to throw up.

Or maybe it was the sight of Raph standing in the doorway that made me want to throw up. Raph, who was still naked except for his jeans. Jeans that were hanging low on his hips thanks to an undone fly.

Raph's eyes found mine for a split second before he swung the door shut.

I scrunched up my face and turned to my door. If Shelly said anything to me and Heather, I didn't hear her. She probably did. It was probably for the best I was in a semi-fugue state, or else I might have snapped and done something I'd regret later.

Which was stupid really, because I had no claim over Raph. I'd thrown that claim back in his face but a few hours ago. He could fuck whoever he wanted now.

And apparently he was.

Yay. Awesome. How freaking fantabulous.

Not.

God, could I be any more fucked-up?

No. Probably not.

CHAPTER 7

***Give Me a Home Among the Gum Trees.
But Please, Leave a Canoe***

Three weeks into my fieldwork a flood hit. Biblical in proportion.

I'd spent the last three weeks living with the nicest family in the world. The Scotts—Reginald, Mary and their eldest son, Robbie—ran the second-largest cattle ranch in Gunnedah. Well, outside of Gunnedah.

Gunnedah, I discovered very quickly, was a small country town with only one set of traffic lights, six bars, AKA pubs, and a lot of utes. The Scotts lived on a ranch twenty miles northwest of that. Sorry, a *property*. I was never going to get used to the jargon. They welcomed me, their American intruder, into their family with open arms. They were warm and friendly and laughed often, and didn't try to force me to eat Vegemite, and had a ready supply of Tim Tams in the cupboard.

Robbie helped me with my research. And by helping, I

mean he would drive me out to the large koala colony every morning in his ute, which looked so much like Raph's I wanted to cry every time I climbed into it. He'd leave me there with a picnic basket full of food Mary Scott had prepared for me, and a walkie-talkie to communicate with them. There was no cell phone service this far out whoop whoop—whoop whoop being the Australian term for way out in the country, apparently.

They warned me to watch out for brown snakes. I wanted to point out the grass where I was camping each day was brown and long and how the hell did I have a hope of spotting a brown snake in it, but I never did. Robbie was too nice, and too busy for me to make him waste time dealing with an American's anxiety about snakes.

I'd settled without any hassles in the three weeks since leaving Sydney. My research was going well. Koalas reacted to daily temperature changes in both speed and distance traveled, it seemed. I spoke daily to Heather via Skype and Brendon every second day—where I assured him I was still doing my exercises, and, no, I wasn't forgetting to take my meds.

I *was* keeping up with my meds, and there was nothing like the Australian outback for meditation. I found myself meditating often during the day, especially when the sun was turning the sky pink as it sank toward the western horizon, the wind rustling the gum leaves and the scent of eucalyptus hanging heavy in the air.

I would sit cross-legged on a folding stool—where the brown snakes couldn't get me—eyes closed, focusing on my calm.

I was *not*, in all those twenty-one days, dwelling on Raph. Nope. I wasn't. Nor was I feeling miserable he hadn't tried to contact me. No way. I *wasn't* lying in the comfy single bed in the Scotts' spare room every night, imagining a life without Parkinson's, a life with Raph, torturing myself with the impossible before rolling over and shoving my face into the pillow to muffle my pathetic sobs. And I sure as hell *wasn't* fixated on the memory of Shelly White leaving his room as he stood in the doorway with his jeans undone. Definitely not.

Not at all.

Nuh-uh.

Three weeks of moving on. That's what I was doing. Attempting to put Raph behind me, focusing on my studies, existing.

Just existing.

Yeah, right.

And then the flood hit.

Australia, in case you haven't figured it out by the ridiculous number of memes on the net, is a country of extremes. It's no joke when they say just about every animal here can kill you. The most deadly spider on the planet lives here. So does the most deadly snake, jellyfish, octopus and shark. Thankfully I was staying over six hundred kilometers— roughly 374 miles—from most of them.

But that wasn't the half of it. The weather here was insane. If it wasn't bushfires destroying almost whole states, it was drought killing damn near everything half a day's drive inland from the coast. If it wasn't drought, it was rain. Flooding rain. When it decided to rain in Australia, *really* rain, you were in trouble. Whole towns could be washed away. I kid you not.

On the twenty-second day of my stay with the Scotts, it began to rain. I had driven Robbie's ute into Gunnedah on a supply run, and that was when the heavens opened. Yes, I was driving in Australia. Scary as shit. They drive on the left side of the road, which is the *wrong* side of the road. Oh man, did I have some close calls my first few times behind the wheel. Driving in the rain on the left side of the road was holy-shit petrifying.

By four o'clock that afternoon, the only road leading to the Scotts' property was cut off by a torrential river that hadn't been there a mere three hours previously.

I could get to my koalas via the long route (if they weren't floating away), but I couldn't get to the Scotts'.

Twenty-four hours later, after a night in one of Gunnedah's hotels and no meds, I still couldn't get to the Scotts', and the water was rising.

Whoa.

Unsure of what to do, I rang Sydney University's Dean of Science. We hadn't spoken since he'd informed me I was being shipped off to Gunnedah early. When I told him of my situation—a situation he already knew about, thanks to a worried call from Mary Scott—he told me I was going to be collected by the *backup* host family.

"You will still be able to access the koala population from their property," he said, his tone as condescending and self-righteous as it had been during our last conversation. "I've arranged for your things to be collected from the Scotts via helicopter and delivered to Kangaroo Creek Station. Someone will be picking you up from your current location within the next twelve hours."

And with that, our conversation was finished.

Excellent.

Huddling under the awning of the Plains Hotel, watching the rain pour off it like a continuous sheet of water, I stared at the empty road. Who in their right mind would travel in weather like this? The road itself—one of the two main streets that dissected Gunnedah—could have been a river, there was that much water on it.

I waited.

Wondered if it was raining in Sydney.

Wondered if Raph was getting wet moving between lectures and Mackellar House. I pictured his dark hair tousled and damp, that hint of a dimple flashing at me as I rubbed said damp hair with a towel.

A sharp pang of misery and longing stabbed my chest and, before I could stop myself, I pulled my cell from my backpack, swiped my thumb over the screen and found Raph in my list of contacts.

I wasn't going to talk to him. I really wasn't. I just wanted to hear his voice. Hear his Australian accent. Yes, I know I was surrounded by Australian accents, but that was not the point, okay?

Heart pounding, I held my thumb over the little phone icon, staring at the small image of him at the top of the screen.

I missed him. So freaking much I could hardly breathe.

So much I'd risk the humiliation and embarrassment the call would no doubt cause me just to hear him say my name. Or maybe, if I was lucky, he'd call me *American girl* like he used to, and for one brief, deluded moment I could pretend we were still—

"You the American girl?" a deep male voice with a distinct Australian accent rumbled in front of me.

I let out a startled squeak and almost dropped my phone.

A man stood under the awning in front of me. He studied me with dark eyes, the seams and wrinkles on his sun-leathered face like a map of a life lived hard, the worn cowboy hat on his head dripping with water. "Maci Rowling?"

I stuttered out a nod. Whoa, I was obviously missing Raph more than I realized, although I would have said that was impossible. The guy waiting for me to speak looked like him. Just forty years older.

He narrowed his eyes at me in a puzzled squint. "You okay? Did I scare you?"

I shook my head this time.

He frowned. "Are you ... able to talk?"

"N-no," I blurted, my cheeks growing hot. "I mean, yes, yes, I can. Sorry, you *did* startle me, but that was my fault."

He chuckled. God, he even *sounded* like Raph. Christ, was I going mental?

"No worries. My fault. Shoulda waited until you stopped looking at your phone. You were off with the fairies."

I frowned. Off with the fairies? What the—

The stranger who knew my name suddenly whipped his hat from his head, revealing a shock of salt-and-pepper hair. He wiped his right hand on his thigh and then extended it to me. "Sorry, should introduce myself. I'm Wayne Patterson, owner of Kangaroo Creek Station." He gave me a smile. A reserved smile but still a warm one. "You're staying with us due to the Scotts being flooded out."

Without delay, I stepped forward to take his hand. "Oh God, thank you. Thank you so much for taking me in. I can't tell you enough how grateful I am for this."

He pulled a face at my gushing gratitude. "No worries. We've got plenty of room, what with the kids long gone. I left the missus cleaning out the guesthouse for you. Not much else we can do in this bloody weather. Crikey, it's been donkeys' ages since we've had this kind of dump."

I suppressed a giggle. Crikey? Did he just say *crikey*?

Releasing my hand, he plonked his hat back on his head and half-turned towards the road. The rain was still pouring down. In fact, it might have grown heavier during our brief conversation. I could barely make out anything beyond the gutter. "The ute's unlocked," Wayne Patterson said, glancing at me over his shoulder. He was wearing a brown leather-type rain jacket that seemed to swim on him. "When you hear me honk, just come running. I'll fling the door open for you so you don't get too drenched."

And with that, he grabbed the two bags at my feet filled with the supplies I'd bought for the Scotts yesterday, and strode out from under the awning to damn near disappear in the sheets of water falling from the sky. Strode. Not ran. Strode. As if it was a sunny day. It was, to be honest, both awe-inspiring and crazy.

A second or two later, I heard a car horn sound. I could only assume it came from the pickup-shaped blob parked out in the rain.

Drawing a deep breath, I shoved my phone into my backpack and ran into the rain. Correction. Into the deluge.

Suffice to say, I was saturated by the time I buckled myself into the passenger seat of Mr. Patterson's ute.

He gave a lazy laugh. "Bit heavy, isn't it?" And then, without another word, he gunned the engine and we took off, a wave of muddy water fanning up from the front wheels.

It took us over ninety minutes to get to Kangaroo Creek Station. I discovered in that time that Mr. Patterson was a man of few words. He asked me how my studies were going, listened when I answered, told me his wife—or, as he called her, the missus—was named Helen, but I was welcome to call her Helly, 'cause she was, and said I was to think of Kangaroo Creek as my home until I returned to the States.

I thanked him. He waved off my thanks with a, "No worries, love," and that was it. After that, he didn't initiate any conversation.

I didn't feel uncomfortable. In fact, I took the time to do what I'd done for most of my downtime during the last three weeks—think about Raph and wonder how he was doing.

Apparently self-torture was becoming one of my favorite pastimes.

At the end of a quiet ninety minutes, after Mr. Patterson crossed what must have been the twenty-millionth cattle guard, we pulled to a halt under a corrugated iron awning next to what looked like a small cottage made of the same thing.

"Here we are," Mr. Patterson said, killing the engine. "Helly will no doubt be in there waiting for you."

I looked at the cottage on the other side of the rain-and-mud splattered window.

"I know it don't look like much, but it's nice inside. And it gives you your own space," Patterson continued. "Unless you want to be in the main house with us? Reckon Helly would dust off the daughter's old room and make up the bed if you want?"

I shook my head, turning back to Mr. Patterson. "The guesthouse is awesome," I answered. "It's been a while since I've had my own space." I thought of my room in Mom's small home back in Plenty, situated right beside hers. I thought of my crowded college dorm room with my loud and messy music major roommate. I thought of Mackellar House and its communal bathroom. I thought of Raph.

"A *long* while," I finished.

Patterson nodded. "Good."

He opened his door and climbed out into the deafening roar of the torrential rain on the iron roof.

Unable to stop myself, I imagined Raph there with me. A heartbeat before I squashed the ridiculous fantasy.

I had to stop it. Had to.

Scooping up my backpack and supplies—thank God I'd splurged while in Gunnedah and bought myself a new toothbrush—I followed Mr. Patterson into what was to be my home for the next twenty-one days, the remainder of my time in Australia.

Mrs. Patterson met me at the front door. She was a tall, willowy woman with a stern face, high cheekbones and direct blue eyes. She wore no makeup and her hair—dark brown and straight—was scraped back from her face in a plaited ponytail. Faded jeans and a chambray shirt added to the image of a woman who didn't have a need for finery, as did the muddy splashes staining the ankles and shins of her jeans.

As I climbed the three stairs leading to the covered porch and door, she smiled. Like her husband's, it was warm but reserved. "Maci Rowling?" Her voice was friendly, if somewhat hard to hear over the drumming rain. "I'm Helen. Welcome to Kangaroo Creek. I suspect Wayne has already told you to call me Helly?"

I nodded, starting a little as Mr. Patterson took my backpack and bags from me and disappeared through the open door.

Her eyes twinkled. Despite being blue, they were … familiar. It was impossible, I know, but I felt like I'd met her before. "Did he make the joke about why he calls me that?" she asked, twin dimples creasing her cheeks as her smile grew wider.

"He did, I'm afraid." I liked her already. Not quite sure why, but I did. Perhaps it was the mom factor? I was missing mine like hell, after all.

Hell. Get it?

She rolled her eyes. "He always does. Thinks he's funny." With a graceful half-pirouette, she invited me into the cottage with her hand. "Come in, please. I hope everything will be okay for you."

I gave her my warmest smile. "Everything will be fine."

And it was. I entered the cottage and into heaven.

It was small, warm, homey and surprisingly well fitted

out. There was a forty-inch flat-screen television mounted on the main wall of the living area above an open fireplace, currently filled with logs and puffy little yellow flowers. Flowers I assumed were responsible for the most delicate and sweet perfume filling my every breath. A wooden desk sat under one of three large windows, where Mr. Patterson had placed my laptop bag.

The twin paisley sofas looked soft, as did the cushions of various colors and patterns scattered over them. A coffee table was placed between, with a vase overflowing with more of the same tiny yellow flowers in the middle, a bowl of red and green apples.

Beyond the living area was the kitchen, which looked like it could have featured in an article about how to make old wood, iron and granite work perfectly together. There was a state-of-the-art fridge, complete with water and ice dispenser, a single-shelf wall oven, a microwave, and one of those funky taps you see in fancy New York apartments that are on a springy thing that goes up and down in an arch.

To the right of the kitchen and living area was the bedroom. Not a room as such, rather a section of the cottage dedicated to a bed. And what a bed. Seriously. A massive, wrought iron, four-poster bed with a white gauzy net that would encase it completely, but for the four silken ropes tying it open.

"Wow."

"You like it?"

I nodded at Mrs. Patterson. "It's lovely."

"Our daughter decorated it before she left. As a parting gift, I think. She and her husband stay here whenever they come to visit, which isn't as often as I'd like."

I turned to her, the affection in her voice making me like

her even more. "It really is beautiful. I can't tell you how much I appreciate—"

Like her husband, she brushed off my thanks. "No more. We're glad to help. I must point out though, we're not much for talking, Wayne and I. And it's rare to see us before sundown each night, but we would love you to join us for dinner whenever you want. I've made sure the cupboards in here are stocked well though, in case you prefer to be alone or don't want to interrupt your studies on global warming and koalas." She cast Mr. Patterson a smile. "Isn't that right, dear?"

Mr. Patterson adjusted his hat. "Yep." And without another word, he nodded in my direction and exited the cottage.

Helly turned her twinkling eyes on me again. "He doesn't believe in global warming," she whispered, leaning towards me. "I've had more than one fight with him about it."

I laughed, surprised by her candour.

She smiled a little and then ran her hands over the backside of her jeans. "Now, if you'll excuse me, I have to get back to work. You'll find all your stuff from the Scotts' either beside the bed or tucked under the desk. Dinner is normally around nine pm, but with this rain, we'll most likely eat at seven tonight."

She left as abruptly as her husband.

I blinked and watched the door close behind her. And then, with a happy little laugh, dropped onto the sofa nearest to me.

It was, indeed, as comfy as I suspected.

***

Five days later, I realized I was completely and utterly at home with my new host family. Sure, they weren't a talkative pair. True, they held their emotions in check, but underneath it all, I could see a deep love for each other. It was wonderful. It reminded me of the way my dad loved my mom, unconditionally and yet restrained. Perhaps it was an Australian thing?

Regardless, they made me feel welcome at their dinner table from the first night, and were completely understanding when, on the fourth night, I chose to remain in my cottage to work on the day's research data.

I cooked myself toast and fried eggs and bacon—there was still a feather on the egg when I took it from the fridge. A small, downy feather. Can you believe it? I ignored the ubiquitous jar of Vegemite I found in the cupboard next to the bread bin. The kitchen had a Nespresso machine (it really was well-stocked) and I helped myself to that as well.

Settling down on the sofa opposite the TV, I balanced my dinner on my knee, grabbed the remote from the coffee table, and searched for something to have playing in the background while I ate and made notes in my field books.

I woke up the next morning with my half-eaten dinner on the coffee table, an episode of *Modern Family* playing on the television, and the memory of a dream involving me and Raph and a thunderstorm playing with my sanity.

And so began my fifth day with the Pattersons.

Sometime through the night, the rain had let up. Not much, but enough to make traveling out to my koala population easier. Mr. Patterson gave me the keys to the ute and, appreciating the trust they placed in me, I found myself enjoying the freedom of driving through the Australian bush on my own.

I spent the morning making notes on the koala mother and baby I'd been tracking since the beginning of my fieldwork, as well as two male koalas that seemed on the verge of a territorial battle.

When the rain turned the surrounding area into a gray, washed-out wall of water, I decided to call it quits for the day.

I was halfway back to the cottage when the walkie-talkie Mrs. Patterson contacted me with crackled to life. "Maci, is there any chance the weather has defeated your studies today? Over."

Laughing, I picked up the communication device from the front passenger seat and depressed the com button. "There is, Mrs. P." I couldn't bring myself to call her Helly. She was too nice. Reserved, but nice. "What can I help you with? Do you want me to come to the main house?" I released the button. And then pressed it again with a quick grunt. "Over."

"Is it possible for you to drive into town? Wayne's arthritis medication is running low and I want to be sure we have enough to last at least another fortnight, in case the rain doesn't let up and we get cut off like the Scotts. Over."

I depressed the com button straight away. I definitely could understand her fear. "I can do that, Mrs. P. Easy-peasy. Over."

Yay, I remembered that time. Go me.

"Oh, and while you're in town, is there a chance you could collect our son from the bus shelter? I think his bus arrives in three hours. You won't be able to miss him. He'll be the one who looks like Wayne, just with darker hair. Over."

A sudden beat throbbed hard in my temple. For some stupid reason, I immediately thought of Raph.

Raph, who I'd damn near erased from my mind since arriving here at Kangaroo Creek. Sort of. Well, I hadn't thought about him since I woke up. That was progress, right?

Rubbing at my face in a futile attempt to wipe away the

memory of the guy, I let out a ragged sigh and then depressed the com button again. "I can do that, Mrs. P. Want me to get anything else while I'm in town? Over."

"Not a thing," came the reply. "Drive safely. Over."

Before I could answer, my walkie-talkie crackled to life again. "Oh, and don't let him pull the wool over your eyes, dear. He may come across as an arrogant, condescending so-and-so, but he's actually a nice young man. Once you get past all the scowling. Over."

I laughed, tossed the walkie-talkie on the passenger seat and directed the ute toward the track that would lead me to the dirt road—mud road, at this point—that would take me to Gunnedah.

I was both excited and curious to meet the Pattersons' only son. They didn't talk much about their absent children, probably because they didn't talk much at all. I got the sense Mr. Patterson wasn't altogether pleased with who their daughter had married. "Bunch of uptight, toffee-nosed snobs who think they're too good for us," was all he said when I asked about his in-laws on the first night, and something told me his relationship with his son wasn't smooth either. "Forgets he has parents, with how little he calls home."

I was just about to cross the Kangaroo Creek boundary when the walkie-talkie burst into life again. "Maci." Mrs. Patterson's voice scratched at the speaker, the device almost out of range. "I forgot. Can you remind my son if he doesn't have a peace offering for his father, to get him a bottle of Chivas from the bottle-o? Over."

"A peace offering?" I asked. "Over."

"Yes. Raph was away for Wayne's birthday. If he walks into the house today without something, there'll be blood. Over."

My blood drained from my face. Raph?

Did she say *Raph?*

Surely she didn't say Raph? Did she?

Heart thumping, I raised the walkie-talkie to my lips and depressed the com button. "Did you say Raph? Over."

I released the button and waited.

All I got was silence.

"Mrs. P? Over."

Silence. Still.

Damn it, I was out of range.

Head roaring, I placed the walkie-talkie back on the passenger seat, fixed my eyes on the rain-soaked world outside the ute, gripped the steering wheel to keep my hands from shaking off my goddamn arms, and drove.

I had to have heard wrong. For starters, Raph's last name was Jones.

Secondly, surely they would have mentioned that their son was at the same university I had been. Right? Hell, living in the same student dorm even.

Right?

But then, had I ever told them where I'd been living while in Sydney? No, I hadn't. And Sydney Uni was a huge place. The biggest university in Australia. What were the odds of getting to know someone who wasn't studying the same thing as you? And as I may have already pointed out, the Pattersons weren't ones for wasting words on idle chitchat.

I drove for over an hour, adamant I was *not* going to find Raph at the bus stop. Sixty minutes of convincing myself Mrs. P had said Jase, or Chase, and I'd heard Raph because I was way too hung up on the guy for my own sanity.

Sixty minutes navigating the wild weather and trying to steady my wild heart.

Just as I was approaching the *Welcome to Gunnedah* sign,

with its larger-than-life billboard featuring Gunnedah's own Miranda Kerr hugging a koala, a terrifying thought struck me.

What if I *had* heard correctly and was about to find Raph at the bus stop?

What did I do then?

I lost control of the ute for a second. Thankfully, I was alone on the road.

I gripped the wheel tighter, my knuckles turning white. If Raph was Mr. and Mrs. P's son ... if he was coming back to Kangaroo Creek station ... if I had to see him ... be in the ute with him ... breathe the same air as him ...

A wave of dizziness washed over me.

I yanked the ute to the side of the road, cut the engine and pressed my forehead to the steering wheel. My heart was attempting to prison break its way out of my chest and my pulse was mimicking a marching band's drum line.

All in all, I was a mess. Because I knew the truth.

I was going to see Raph. I hadn't misheard Mrs. P. All the clues pointed toward the obvious. Mr. P's chuckle that sounded like Raph's, his similar body type—tall and lean with broad shoulders. Mrs. P's eyes that were the same as Raph's, the dimples, the aloof manner that hid a deep passion. The daughter overseas with her husband, whose family was *snobby*. If my interaction with the Delvanian royal family via Horn was anything to go by, *snobby* was an understatement.

The fact I was out on a working cattle ranch in the country, the very place Raph had told me he'd grown up, and was going to return to when he finished his studies ...

All the clues pointed to one thing—I was going to be picking up Raphael Jones from the bus stop. Raph. The guy I'd fallen in love with. The guy who'd declared he'd fallen in love with me, only to screw Shelly White a few hours later.

Did he know I was here? Staying in his parents' guesthouse? Was he coming to see his mom and dad for the weekend? Or for *me*?

Cold anger and exasperation shot through my disbelief. Eventually recovering myself, I raised my head from the steering wheel, restarted the engine and pulled out onto the road.

Too bad if he was coming for me. We'd done our thing and our thing was over. Our thing was always going to have a limited shelf life, and the use-by date had expired over three and a half weeks ago. Just in the same way my life of normality would expire when my Parkinson's became too much to handle.

Raph obviously hadn't wasted time moving on, and I was going to show him I hadn't given him a second thought since leaving Sydney. I would treat him as if we were just passing acquaintances, barely look at him. Barely talk to him. Blasé.

Easy.

A perfect plan.

Bravo, me.

I kept hold of that resolve for the remainder of the drive into Gunnedah. I clung to it with a fierce grip as I collected Mr. P's arthritis medication from the drugstore. I damn near strangled it as I bought the nicest, sexiest bra and panties set I could find from the town's one and only department store (a Target, and man, was it small). I felt it slipping away as I sat in the ute across from the empty bus shelter, the bra and panties in its plastic bag shoved in the space behind the driver's seat.

Bra and panties? Why the fuck had I bought a brand new bra and panties set? What was I thinking?

A groan escaped me. My hand shook. Ah, this was going to be bad.

Really bad.

I couldn't do it. I had to get out of—

Before I could start the engine and speed away—to where, you ask? I had no freaking clue—a mud-covered Greyhound bus pulled to a halt at the bus stop, the squeal of its brakes slicing through the constant drumming of the rain.

Whoops. There went the blood in my face again. Damn it.

I didn't move. Couldn't. I was literally trapped by my own body and brain in the car. It had nothing to do with my Parkinson's and everything to do with my fear of seeing Raph.

A thousand heartbeats later, the bus pulled away.

And there he was. Oh fuck, there he was.

Standing under the small shelter, as gorgeous and stunning and handsome and sexy as ever.

He was wearing a pair of black jeans, a blue polo shirt and his baseball cap. Hanging from his right shoulder was a backpack. In his left hand was a bunch of wilted flowers. Roses.

I stared at him through the mud-and-water-streaked window and let out a ragged sigh.

This was going to hurt. A lot.

He saw the ute before I opened the door. A smile pulled at his lips, lips I remembered all too well, and without hesitation or care for the rain, he strode across the road.

Straight for me.

Well, straight for the ute. I suspect *he* suspected it was his mom behind the wheel. Not the American girl who broke his—

He yanked open the door and bent to lean inside, rain trickling from his shoulders. "Hey, Mu—"

His smile faded.

My heart exploded. "Hi, Raph," I croaked.

Yeah, so much for being blasé.

Unreadable blue eyes regarded me. "I wasn't expecting to see you."

My heart imploded this time. At least that cleared up any confusion he'd come to Gunnedah to see—

"I mean," he went on, voice cut with frustration, "I *was* expecting to see you. You're why I'm here. I came here to see you. But I thought Mum would—" Shaking his head, he held up a hand. 'Wait a sec.' Then he closed the door again.

I sat frozen in my seat. He'd come here to see *me*? Had he really just said …

I felt the ute shift as he dumped his pack in the back. I strained to see him in the rearview mirror but the mud-splattered back window and increasing rain made it impossible. God, how long did it take to re-hook the cover over the back?

And while I was asking ridiculous questions, was I *seriously* anxious and impatient for him to climb into the car with me? Was I?

Was I?

The passenger door opened before I got a chance to ponder the answer.

Raph dumped himself—dripping wet—onto the seat, slammed the door and fixed me with a level stare. "Maci …" he murmured, a second before he captured my face in his damp hands and crushed my lips with his.

The kiss was greedy. Hungry. Crazy.

It took me completely by surprise. I stiffened, every fiber in my body on fire. He was kissing me. He'd come to Gunnedah to see me and he was kissing me.

He was kissing me.

So I kissed him back. It was insanity. It was lunacy. It was self-torture. But I kissed him back.

Holy crap, did I kiss him back.

There wasn't any chance of me doing anything else but.

We made love to each other with our tongues. Raph sucked mine into his mouth for a tantalizing moment before nibbling on my bottom lip and plundering my mouth again. His hands buried in my hair. He moaned.

I scrambled for the collar of his shirt, needing to feel his flesh under my palms. I smoothed my hands up the strong column of his neck, raking them in the damp strands of his hair at his nape. He moaned again, a raw, desperate sound I echoed.

When he moved his hands to the front of my shirt, when he popped my buttons, I surrendered completely to the moment. When he dragged his mouth down my throat, over my collarbone to claim my left nipple with his lips through the lace of my bra, I died in the pleasure he awoke in me.

I rolled my head back, tightened my fist in his hair and groaned his name, undone by the sheer urgency of his mouth worshipping my nipple.

Right there. In the ute. On the street. In Gunnedah.

It was perfect.

So perfect.

I never wanted it to end.

But it did. I don't know how long later, but it did. Raph raised his head from my breasts, plundered my mouth again, breathed my name against my lips and then pressed his forehead to mine.

"I'm sorry," he whispered. "That was ... Fuck, American girl, I've missed you."

I gurgled out a weak laugh. "The feeling is mutual."

We sat that way for another indeterminate length of time. It wasn't until our breathing settled somewhat that I opened my eyes and straightened in my seat.

He looked at me, an unreadable emotion burning in his dark eyes.

The inside windows of the ute were fogged up. A little part of me, the part that still wanted to be young and carefree, ached to lift my finger and draw something on the glass. Maybe a heart with an RJ and MR inside it.

Instead, I met Raph's gaze and drew in a steadying breath. "How did you know I was here, Raph? Why are *you* here? And more to the point, why isn't your last name Patterson?"

CHAPTER 8

Shakes Be Damned

"I'm here for *you*, Maci," he answered, tracing my bottom lip with the pad of his thumb. "I'm here because I love you, because the last three and a half weeks have been fucking hell and I can't stand to be away from you.

"I'm here because when I was talking to Mum last night and she told me an American environmentalist was staying with them, I knew it was fate giving us a second chance.

"I'm here because Osmond told me I was being a stupid fuckwit letting you walk away from me, and for the first time since I've known the bastard, I had to agree with him.

"I'm here because no matter what you say, I don't care that you have Parkinson's disease. I don't care that you don't want anyone to look after you. I *want* to look after you. I want to be with you, Maci. I want to see where the road takes us together, and I want to hold your fucking hand, whether it's shaking or not. Do you understand?"

I stared at him. Every word he'd just said, every syllable he'd uttered, stroked my senses.

What could I say? What could I do?

I opened my lips, willing my brain to come to the party. "What about Shelly White?" I asked on a strangled breath.

Oh great. Way to go, Rowling. You idiot.

Disgust etched Raph's face and he shook his head. "I didn't do anything with her. When you saw her leaving my room, I swear I didn't ... God, I couldn't. I love you, Maci. No matter how angry you'd made me, I wouldn't just hop into bed with the first girl who threw herself at me."

"But she did throw herself at you?" Why was I torturing myself?

"She did. And I told her to fuck off. When she tried to shove her hand down my jeans I told her to get out or I'd call Horn."

I studied his face, aching for him to be telling me the truth. A mental image of Shelly sliding her expertly manicured fingers down Raph's jeans tormented me. "So Horn's still around?" I asked. It was the least important thing to grab on to in his declaration, but it was also the least painful.

Raph nodded. "He is. And last night he told me about the bribe the royal family offered you."

I made a disgusted noise in the back of my throat.

Raph traced my bottom lip again, his eyes following the slow path of his thumb. "And he *also* told me I was being a moron for letting you get away. Apparently he tendered his resignation two days ago after a request from the royal family he didn't approve of. He's got a week left with them, guarding the crown princess."

"What was the request?" My voice left me on a scratchy whisper. I didn't know what to do, what to say ... it was all happening so fast ...

Raph gave a wry chuckle. "No idea. He wouldn't say. Just told me to get my arse to wherever you were and to take a bunch of flowers. Who would have thought he was such a nice guy, 'eh?" He held up his finger again. "Speaking of which ..."

With a grunt, he bent to grab something at his feet and straightened to a sitting position again, the bunch of wilted roses in his hand. "These are for you."

I gaped at them. The petals were creased and browning, the stems drooping, the leaves curling. They were the most tragic bunch of roses I'd ever seen, and I loved them.

God, did I love them.

Hot tears prickled at my eyes. I held them in, wishing to God they'd go away. After everything I'd put Raph through, he didn't need to see me cry. I'd been a bitch to him. I'd hurt him when I shouldn't have. And he'd still come for me. The last thing he needed to see was my tears.

"I know you're going to argue with me about all this, American girl," Raph went on. "I know you're going to tell me to sod off, that you don't want a relationship, but I've got two days, not including today, to prove to you that you don't mean it. Two days. This weekend. You're not allowed to work while I'm here. All you're allowed to do is let me love you. And if at the end of the two days, before I go back to uni, you still insist on denying we're meant to be together ..." He shrugged. "Then I'll just have to come back next weekend."

I couldn't help myself. I burst out laughing. "And if I *still* haven't changed my mind? About thinking you're too incredible and wonderful and amazing to *not* be with by the time I go back to Plenty?"

He grinned, sheer joy in his face. "I've got a passport. And lots of frequent flyer miles."

I laughed. Or maybe I sobbed. I wasn't sure. Whatever it was, Raph took it as his cue to kiss me again.

And he did. Whoa.

By the time we stopped, so had the rain. If I was a suspicious person, or one who believed in higher powers, I'd suspect someone up *there* was tampering with the weather just to manipulate my life. Instead, I wiped my palm over the steamy windscreen and studied the rainbow arcing across the sky in front of us.

"Let's hurry up and get to Kangaroo Creek," Raph said, buckling his seat belt.

I raised an eyebrow. "Impatient to get me into bed?"

He pulled a face of wounded indignation. "No. We need to get these flowers into some water. Stat."

I threw back my head and laughed. Damn, I hadn't felt so good in weeks. It wasn't just because Raph was here. It was because he *knew* how I felt about him. Even though I'd been a bitch to him back at Mackellar House, he *knew*. And he was prepared to fight for me, despite everything I'd done to convince him to do otherwise.

It was incredible. Like him.

Turning the key in the ignition, I started the ute and pulled away from the curb.

It took us close to three hours to get back to Kangaroo Creek. The weather had nothing to do with it. Nor did waiting in line at the bottle shop so Raph could buy his father the Chivas. We stopped three times. Once because Raph wouldn't stop feeling me up while I was driving and I was worried we'd crash when I was overcome with giddy delight. Once because I had to tell him I was sorry for hurting him so much. And the last time because I *needed* to straddle his hips and feel the hard length of him buried deep inside me, and I couldn't really do that while driving, could I?

We'd just pulled back onto the road when a thought occurred to me. "What about the name? Why are you Jones, not Patterson?"

He grinned. "Mum and Dad aren't married. Jones is Mum's surname. She was angry with Dad when it was time to put the paperwork in for my birth certificate so she decided to punish him by giving me *her* name rather than his. My sister's a Patterson. Well, now a Sorensen, thanks to marrying the Crown Prince of Delvania. I'm a Jones."

"Why was she angry at him?" I asked, picturing the reserved, contained woman I'd met three days ago.

Raph let out a short laugh. "He went off to the Gunnedah cattle auctions that day and bought a new bull rather than come visit her at the hospital. Mum knows how to do revenge well."

"You're not kidding."

We drove for a while before another thought hit me. "So if she's not a Patterson, why does she let me call her Mrs. P?"

Raph's eyebrows shot up. "She does?"

I nodded.

He let out a low whistle. "Man, she must really like you."

I couldn't help but smile. "I'm very likeable."

He slid his palm up my inner thigh. "And also very fu—"

The walkie-talkie crackled to life, cutting him short. "Maci." Raph's mom's voice sounded from the small speaker. "Are you there? Over."

Raph scooped up the walkie-talkie and depressed the com button. "Hey, Mum."

The rest of the trip—thirty minutes worth—was me listening to Raph and his mother talking. It wasn't hard to tell Mrs. P—or should that be Mrs. J?—was overjoyed to have her son home for the weekend, despite her not saying she'd missed him. There was a delighted tone to her normally reserved voice I hadn't heard before. Subtle, but there all the same.

It made me smile. *And* miss my mom that much more as well.

"Okay, Mum," Raph said into the walkie-talkie as I turned the bend leading to the Kangaroo Creek homestead. "We're at the gate. See you for dinner. Nine okay? Over."

Frowning, I glanced at my watch. It was only 4:47. What was he planning to do for the next four hours?

Returning the walkie-talkie to the center console, he gave me a steady gaze. "Head for the guesthouse."

My heart kicked up a notch. I pictured the bed in my temporary home, with its four posts and romantic gauzy curtains.

As if reading my mind, Raph slid his palm higher up my thigh, his fingertips brushing the junction of my legs where I was the most sensitive. So sensitive I gasped at the touch, even through the denim of my shorts. "Is the four-poster bed still in the guesthouse?" he murmured, drawing close enough to me to nibble on the curve of my shoulder.

I nodded. Inside, I'd begun to tremble. The good kind of tremble. The hot-and-horny kind of tremble.

He hummed an appreciative murmur against my skin. "Excellent. Tell me, how do you feel about being tied up?"

How *did* I feel about being tied up? I'd never been tied up before. If the way my body was responding to his query—all flustered and excited and squirmy in all the right places—I think the answer was, "I feel good about it. Very good indeed."

Slowly turning my head to face him, I moved my lips close to his. "You'll have to catch me first," I murmured.

And with a squeal of delight, I flung open my door, scrambled from the ute and ran up the stairs into the guesthouse.

Raph caught me before I even had a chance to pass the

first sofa in the living area. With a growl and a laugh, he wrapped his arms around my waist and pulled me back to his hard body.

I squealed again, on fire with sheer joy and aroused anticipation, and wriggled in his hold, trying to escape just as much as I was trying to drive him wild by rubbing my ass against his groin.

It worked. At least, I assume it did, given he let out another growl, buried one hand between my thighs and captured one of my breasts with the other. "Right," he rasped in my ear, the thick pole of his erection nudging the crevice of my butt cheeks. "That's it. You're going to get it now."

"Oh," I mocked, rubbing my ass harder to his stiff cock. "Idle threats don't scare—"

But Raph had lifted me off the ground, flung me over his shoulder, and was now carrying me to the bed.

He tossed me onto the mattress, stood at the end, threw back his head and, with an animalistic cry, beat his chest with his fist and tossed his head about.

I burst out laughing and then squealed once more as he launched himself at me. It occurred to me, while he was pinning me to the bed with his lower body, we'd never had the chance to really let our desire and pleasure run amuck back in Mackellar House. There were always people in the nearby rooms who would be able to hear us. Always paparazzi lurking whenever we stepped outside campus.

This was the first time there was no chance of anyone hearing us or interrupting us. No fellow housemates, no media, no bodyguard.

Just Raph and me and a four-poster bed.

My head swam with the exquisite thought. A second before Raph snared my wrists and pinned them to the mattress above my head.

He gazed down into my face, his groin nestled to mine, his desire *very* evident as it pushed against the soft heat of my sex. "I've caught you," he murmured, his nostrils flaring, his voice husky. "Now I get to tie you up."

Mouth dry, pussy damp, I nodded. "You do."

He grew still. "You trust me?"

A smile curled my lips as I realized he expected me to bail on the whole bondage-lite thing. "I trust you," I answered. "More than you could ever—"

He silenced me with a slow, deep, thoroughly thorough kiss.

I didn't mind. Not at all.

The kiss turned hot. Hot enough that I was moaning and arching beneath him, aching in all the right places.

He rolled his hips, the solid length of his erection rubbing against my pussy. The contact sent shards of wet need through me and, tearing my lips from his, I stared up into his eyes. "Raph ..."

I wanted to tell him again I was sorry for what I'd done back at Mackellar House. I wanted to tell him I needed him inside me so bad it hurt. All I could say was his name. God, I didn't just want him, I really *did* love him. Despite all my efforts to keep him from my heart, from my life, I loved him and wanted him there. "Raph, please ..."

"Tell me what you want, American girl," he whispered, his fingers around my wrists loose but still there. "Tell me what you feel."

I knew what he needed to hear. I had never uttered the words. "I want you."

He shook his head, an urgent fire in his dark eyes. "That's not enough, Maci." His voice was strained. Hoarse. "Tell me ..."

I swallowed. My heart hammered. Could I say it? And if I

did, what did that mean for us? For our future? For his? Could I really do that to him?

Raw anxiety etched his face. He watched me. Waited. Between my spread thighs, his hard heat radiated into my core.

Agony seared through me, the agony of knowing and not knowing. The fear of what might happen ...

Pulling a deep breath, I gazed into his eyes. "I love you, Raphael Jones."

The sun came out. That was the only way I could describe the emotion that filled Raph's face. The sun came out and the world was perfect. He took possession of my lips once more. There was no holding back. He made love to my mouth and I made love to his. When I shifted beneath him, when I hooked my leg around his hip and ground my pelvis to his, he let out a groan that was both tortured and arrogant.

With a growl, he dragged his lips up to my ear. "I love you, Maci. And to prove it, I'm going to climb off this bed and watch you strip yourself naked."

Joy and delight threaded through the heady lust heating my veins. We both understood the significance of his state-ment. Raph was letting *me* undress. He was proving he knew I didn't need him to undo my buttons. He was telling me that he understood my fears.

I couldn't stop my smile. Nor my laugh. "And if my hands shake? If my fingers fumble?"

A dark glint filled his eyes. "Then tear your shirt. I know you're strong enough to do it."

If it was possible, I loved him even more at that point.

He crawled backward, smoothing his palms down the length of my body as he did so, over my breasts, my belly, my hips, my thighs, until he straightened to his feet at the end of the bed.

I pushed myself up onto my elbows and studied him. My hands were shaking. I could feel the trembles claiming my muscles. But there was no way I was going to let them defeat me. Not now. Not ever. With Raph loving me, I could conquer the fucking world.

Pushing myself up to a sitting position, I crossed my legs and, giving him the naughtiest smile I could, I popped open my top button.

Raph's gaze lingered on the parted neckline of my shirt.

I popped the next button and, sucking in a deep breath, opened my shirt some more, revealing a hint of bra and boob.

Raph's responding groan filled the room. His chest swelled as he pulled in his own slow breath.

Watching him watch *me*, I released the next button, the one positioned beneath my breasts.

"Fuck, Maci," Raph moaned. He stared at what I'd revealed.

With a soft giggle, I trailed my fingertips over the inner swell of my right boob, following the lacy edge of my bra. "How am I doing?"

He sucked in a breath and raised his gaze to mine. "Should I take off my jeans and show you?"

I laughed. "It might help."

He was unzipping his fly and shoving his jeans down his hips before I could finish the sentence.

His cock tented his boxers, jutting against the black fabric with stiff need. My pulse kicked up a notch at the sight. It wasn't the first time I'd seen it in such a state, but it *was* the first time since I'd finally, irrevocably, told him I loved him.

Which made it different somehow. More ... important. More profound.

Lifting my gaze to his face again, I caught my bottom lip with my tongue. He stared back at me, silent.

Without a word, fingers trembling, I undid the rest of my buttons and slipped my shirt from my shoulders.

At the end of the bed, Raph hooked his hands into the hemline of his polo and tugged it over his head.

God, he was gorgeous.

Once again, our gazes clashed. Held each other prisoner.

I unzipped my shorts and, with a rather clumsy and altogether unsexy jiggle, repositioned myself to my knees.

Raph's stare dropped to the tiny triangle of my lower belly now revealed by my opened fly. His chest rose and fell again.

Heart pounding, sex throbbing, I slipped my hands between my hips and my shorts and shoved them, my shorts, not my hips, down.

"Oh, Maci," he murmured.

The undeniable desire in his voice filled me with joy. And hungry, impatient need.

Unable to wait any longer, I dropped to my butt and kicked my shorts away. Yeah, so not a sexy move, I know, but I was beyond seduction now. I just wanted to feel Raph's body moving over mine. Moving *in* mine. I just wanted to feel his heat seep into my bones as he held me and we made love.

Love. Not just sex, but love.

Because that's what it was. And it was wonderful.

Moving my hands to the side strings of my panties, I smiled up at him and then frowned when he shook his head.

"*I* want to take those off you," he said. "I *need* to take those off you. And your bra. I think if I watch you do it, I'll fucking blow my load in my boxers."

I laughed. "Then take your boxers off and get over—"

He shoved his boxer shorts down his hips and was on the bed before I could finish. Again.

With a rumbly growl, he captured my lips in a hungry kiss and pressed me back to the mattress. He roamed his hands over my body. He knelt between my thighs, unclipping my bra with dexterous skill even as he kissed me crazy. When he moved his hands to my panties, I let out a hitching breath and arched beneath him.

Two seconds later, I was naked. Completely.

A heartbeat later, I was moaning loudly as he swept his tongue over my folds. A heartbeat after *that*, I was fisting the duvet as he sucked the tiny nub of my clit into his mouth.

Oh God, could it get any better?

It did.

Because after he made me come with his mouth, he tied my wrists to the posts at the head of the bed—utilizing his discarded belt and his socks. Necessity is the mother of all invention, after all—and made me come two more times.

With slow, powerful, deep thrusts, he buried himself in my wet heat, stretching me, filling me completely. Moving inside me. Moving with me.

And when he came, when his orgasm took him in the same way mine took me, he called my name and told me he loved me over and over again.

Suffice to say, we only just made it to the main house for dinner at 9:06.

Life *Is* Good

Raph's mother took one look at us and raised an eyebrow. "Am I to assume you two know each other?"

Raph ducked his head. Seeing him this way, like a little boy, was an experience. He was so goddamn endearing. "Maci was in Mackellar House before coming to Gunnedah, Mum."

Mrs. P cast me a long look. "Hmmm."

I frowned. First at her and then at Raph.

I had no idea what *hmmm* meant, and I'm afraid to say I didn't have the courage to ask.

Raph didn't ask either. Instead, he dropped into the closest armchair and let out a sigh that could have been contented, but could also have been exasperated. "And I'm home," he murmured. Or muttered. Again, I wasn't really sure.

I stood still, moving my stare from him to his mother and back to him again. He smiled at me, indicating I join him with a pat of his hand on his thigh.

Surely he couldn't be serious? He wanted me to sit on his lap in front of his mom?

"Are you going to sell your story to the media, Maci?" Mrs. P asked.

I swung back to her. "Am I *what*?"

"Jesus, Mum," Raph growled, throwing himself from the armchair. "I know you don't read the gossip in the papers, and if you were *that* worried about me and my poor fragile heart, you would have been on the phone the second the news of Maci and I being in a ménage relationship with Osmond hit."

Mrs. P regarded her son with a slight frown. "A what? With who?"

Raph grunted. "Yeah, that's what I thought."

"Who's in a ménage relationship?" Mr. Patterson asked, striding into the dining room. To be honest, his sudden appearance made me jump.

"Your son." Mrs. P arched an eyebrow at Raph. "With Maci and someone called Osmond."

Mr. Patterson grunted, a sound freakishly identical to Raph's. "Good for him. Where's dinner?"

If it wasn't for the small twitching of Helen Patterson's lips, I think I may have run from the room, cheeks on fire. I know it was really Helen *Jones's* lips, but that name just didn't want to stick in my head.

Dinner was ... interesting. I learned very quickly why his

parents didn't know who I was. They genuinely didn't seem to bother themselves with what the media was saying about their children. "I'm too busy to worry about drivel like that," Mr. Patterson declared when, unable to hold my tongue any longer, I asked what they thought of their son being an Australian celebrity. "He's a big boy. He can look after himself."

I shot Raph a curious glance. Did they know about Horn? Did they care?

Raph pulled a face. "Thanks, Dad. Gotta love the support."

Mr. Patterson raised his attention from his dinner—roast beef and a pile of vegetables—and gave his son a long, level gaze. A heavy tension fell over the room.

Finally, with another grunt—the patented Patterson grunt, I was beginning to think of it as—he returned his attention to his dinner plate. "You know it's there for you when you really need it, son."

And that was the end of the topic. The conversation moved to the weather, the health of the Kangaroo Creek cattle, the Scotts, who, Mrs. P. informed us, had finally made it through the overflowing river today, and then to Australian politics.

"We're out of here," Raph declared at that point, threading his fingers through mine and tugging me out of my seat. He dropped a quick kiss on Mrs. P's cheek. "Thanks for dinner, Mum. We'll see you sometime over the weekend."

"You're staying with Maci?"

Raph smoothed his arm around my back and smiled down at me. "Absolutely," he murmured.

The weight of the word, the open emotion in his eyes stole my breath away. I knew he wasn't talking about just the weekend.

"Use protection," Mr. Patterson muttered.

God help me, my cheeks flooded with heat.

"Thanks for the advice, Dad," Raph threw over his shoulder as we exited the dining room.

It was, I have to admit, the most surreal meal I'd ever had. And remember, I'd eaten in a cafe with naked people sitting on pedestals.

We walked back to the guesthouse hand in hand. Neither of us spoke for a while. The silence was relaxed and wonderful. In fact, the whole thing was wonderful—Raph's hand holding mine, his tall presence beside me, that distinctly sweet, fresh scent the air gets after rain ... it was perfect.

Raph pulled me to a halt twice. Both times to kiss me. Tender, lingering kisses that filled me with more happiness and joy than I thought was possible.

We checked out the stars, and boy, were there a lot of them. This far away from the bright lights of civilization, the Milky Way looked like a blanket of twinkling diamonds in the black sky. Raph held me close, spooning me from behind as he pointed out various constellations. He knew the stories behind them all, and I listened, rapt, as he recounted the different Aboriginal legends behind each one.

By the time we made it back to the guesthouse, I was damn near floating. I didn't think I'd ever been this happy. Ever.

We showered together, making love under the water before moving to the bed. Once again, Raph tied me up. I have to tell you, there is something utterly addictive about being bound to the bed while your lover explores your body with his hands and tongue and lips. This time, Raph blindfolded me, and holy shit, did it make me hot. Who knew I was so kinky?

Afterwards, I took my meds—there was no way I was

going to forget them—and we settled down to watch some television as we caught our breath.

Somewhere around one am, we made love again, but this time *I* was the one who tied Raph up.

Trust me, if you ever get the chance to do that—tie up your partner—do so. That's all I'm saying.

⁂

The sun was high when I woke the next morning. I lay in Raph's arms for a long moment, pondering my situation, my life.

Only twenty-four hours ago, I was determined to forget about Raph altogether. I was hell bent on erasing him from my memory, even as I accepted it was impossible. I was adamant that cutting him from my life was the right thing to do, the only thing to do, and yet here I was now, blissfully happy in his arms.

What was I to do about that?

It had always been about my future. From the second the doctor told me I had Parkinson's disease, I had known what was going to happen in my life. I knew what to expect as the years unfolded before me. I knew what my ultimate fate was going to be.

And then, along comes this guy, this Australian guy with his emotionally detached upbringing, his celebrity status, his stubborn refusal to let me wallow in my own pity, and *bam*, I was in love and contemplating a future with him in it.

I'd done my best to paint the most horrific image of the life ahead of me in an attempt to scare him off, and it hadn't worked.

What do *we* do now? Given I was returning to Plenty, Ohio, in three weeks? How would it work?

Could it?

"What are you thinking?"

I wriggled in Raph's arms at his sleepy mumble. "Do penguins have knees?"

He laughed softly at my question, tugged me closer to his body and nuzzled a line of kisses along my shoulder and up the back of my neck. "What I want to know is, which armrest is yours at a movie theater?"

I closed my eyes, the soft pressure of his lips on my skin sending a shiver of delight into the center of my being. I'd never get tired of his touch. Ever.

God, what would I do if *he* ever got tired of touching *me*?

What would I do when, in years to come, he got fed up with the way I shook in my sleep? Or when my meds started to impact my sex drive? I'd heard Mom tell Dad once that they did, that they not only reduced her tremors but her libido. What would Raph do when that happened? What would I do?

Hot tears pricked the backs of my eyes, taking me by surprise. I bit back a sob, cursing my stupid brain. The moment was too perfect. How could I be ruining it with stupid, horrible, bleak thoughts?

What the hell was wrong with me?

"Hey." Raph lifted his head from the back of my neck. He gently rolled me onto my back and frowned down at me. "What's going on, American girl?"

The concern in his voice knotted my stomach. I tried to look away. I didn't want him to see me like this.

But he wouldn't let me. Tucking his finger under my chin, he drew my face back to his, his eyes swimming with worry. "Talk to me, Maci," he said. "I can't take away your fear if you don't tell me what it is."

"I didn't want to fall in love with you," I confessed. "It was easier when I knew I'd never have to worry about being a burden to anyone. Now ..." I shrugged. "What happens if you realize you can't deal with what I've got? What happens to my stupid heart then?"

He regarded me with a silent gaze for a long moment. He didn't pull away from me. "There's a word in the dictionary you might be familiar with," he finally said, brushing his thumb along my lower lip.

"What's that?" I asked in a husky whisper.

He smiled. "Unconditional." And then, eyes twinkling, he started singing the Katy Perry song, his voice awful, his enthusiasm awesome, and all thoughts of being miserable and scared and worried left me.

I knew the subject needed to be addressed at some point before the weekend was over, it really did, but for now I was willing to lose myself in the pleasure and happiness of this moment, this reality with Raph.

Sometime later, after more ... y'know ... Raph decided to make breakfast.

"I should warn you," he said, cracking what I think was the sixth egg into a large bowl, "I'm not the best cook in the world."

I sniggered. "Can't be any worse than me. Mom tells me I burn water."

He chuckled. "So it's a life of eating take-away and going out for dinner for us then? Excellent. I've never been a fan of doing the dishes."

Pushing myself from the bed, I crossed to where he stood at the kitchen counter, slid my arms around his waist and rested my cheek against his broad back. "Then I hope you plan on making lots of money," I mumbled, letting my hands roam the six-pack of his stomach, "'cause this tree-hugging greenie with a pending degree in environmental sciences isn't likely to make any."

Damn, I loved the feel of his hard body pressed to mine. It helped that both of us were semi-naked. The warmth from his muscular back seeping into my chest and belly was so perfect it made me a little giddy.

"Hey—" He turned his head and dropped a quick kiss to the tip of my nose, "—I plan on being ridiculously rich. Of course, I also plan on being a world famous artist as well, so it's probably best you don't hold your breath."

I laughed, enjoying the moment.

"I also plan on being an astronaut," he continued, whisking the eggs with reckless abandon. "Just so you know."

"Oh, in that case—" I trailed my fingers over his navel and along the downy line of hair beneath it leading to his groin, "—can I be a life-drawing model? Like the kind we saw at Triptych?"

"No bloody way. I'm not letting weirdos stare at my woman naked, thank you very much."

A tight thrill of excitement shot through me at the possessive tone I heard in his response.

"But if we're eating out all the time ..." I teased, slipping my fingers beneath the elastic band of his boxers. "Or ordering in ..."

"I'll work a double shift at NASA ... *ah*, fuck me, Maci, that feels good."

I squeezed his cock again, giggling into his shoulder at the way he turned the title of America's space agency into a raw groan of pleasure.

We *did* eat our eggs. An hour later. And they weren't exactly ... good. But due to the fact Raph made them for me, with buttered toast that he did very well, and a mug of steaming coffee, they were the most delicious eggs I'd ever had.

Okay, not really. They *were* kind of gross, but the sentiment behind them was romantic and wonderful so I didn't care at all.

We were doing the dishes a short time later when he leaned his ass on the kitchen counter and gave me a contemplative inspection. "The last time we woke up together, I asked you to go to Wet'n'Wild with me."

I nodded, passing him a plate to be dried. At the horrible memory of what had come after that invitation, I pulled a face. Damn, that morning. "You did."

He took the plate and swirled the dishtowel over it. "And we didn't get there."

"We didn't."

"So I was thinking ..." He raised his focus from the plate, a grin I could only describe as devilish playing with his lips. "We could go today."

I raised my eyebrows. "To Sydney?"

He laughed. "I was thinking of the Kangaroo Creek version."

"The what?"

He took the last plate from my hand and winked. "Wait and see. You brought your swimmers, right?"

Thank God I'd spent over two weeks listening to Heather call her bathing suit swimmers, otherwise I'd be more puzzled. I nodded.

With another grin, he whipped the dishtowel over the plate, placed both on the counter and then snared my hips with his hands. "Go get dressed in them. No work today. The koalas can take a break from being studied while they sleep."

I pulled an indignant face, even as I wriggled the lower

half of my belly harder against his groin. "Hey, that's my thesis you're dissing."

He chuckled, stole a kiss and then slapped me on the ass. "And it's brilliant. I stole a peek last night while you were showering. Even I might be convinced there is such a thing as global warming when you're done. Maybe."

I shoved him away with a laugh. "Douche bag."

Nimble as always, he bounced away from me. "Hurry up. We want to hit the slides before the crowds."

Still completely puzzled by the whole situation and more than a little excited, I crossed to the tallboy near the bed and withdrew my bikini from the top drawer.

Twenty minutes later, we pulled to a halt beside the most picturesque billabong I'd ever seen. In fact, the only billabong I'd ever seen.

Damn, it was pretty.

Okay, cultural lesson number 642 about Australia: A billabong is a body of water that forms from an offshoot of a river, usually branching out from the main flow during or after an extended period of rain. Essentially, it's like a pond that appears when there's been lots of rain and then, when it's really dry, it disappears.

Raph had brought me to the main billabong on Kangaroo Creek Station. And we were going to swim in it.

Not just swim in it. Slide into it. Because, yep, right beside the billabong was a sloped stretch of grass-covered land that, with a little bit of splashing and a lot of courage, would make a perfect slide.

Wet. And wild.

We spent the morning there, swimming, engaging in fierce water fights, making out. Lots of making out. But also lots of talking. I think we lay stretched out on our towels with the sun seeping into our wet bodies, drying our skin, for at least an hour, doing nothing else but talking about stuff. Not important stuff, just stuff. The kind of stuff that makes up a life between couples. The kind of stuff my mom and dad used to talk about. "Just shootin' the breeze, honey," Mom would say when I asked her what she and Dad were doing when I'd find them sitting in the front porch swing, iced tea in hand.

Getting-to-know-you stuff. Which I guess is, when it comes down to it, really quite important after all.

And through it all, the splashing, the kissing, the talking, the comfortable silences, I fell deeper and deeper in love with him. And I came to the realization that no matter what my future held, I wanted him in it.

It was that simple.

Rolling onto my side, I draped my leg over his thigh and rested my head in my hand. "Raph?" I said, heart beating fast. It wasn't often a girl admitted she was wrong. I *never* admitted I was wrong. Like, ever. This was a momentous event.

Raph turned his head and gave me a lazy grin. "American girl?"

I looked at him, really looked at him. Burned every feature, every line, every freckle and bit of beard stubble into my brain. In the years to come, I wanted to remember *this* moment. "I was wrong," I said.

He studied me. A slight frown pulled at his eyebrows. "About what?"

"About telling you I didn't want you to care for me, back in Mackellar House when we had our ... fight." I paused, touching my fingers to his chest, above where his heart would be. "I know my life is going to get pretty crappy at some point. Yes, there are medical breakthroughs all the time, and the work Michael J. Fox's foundation is doing is incredible. And I know here in Australia your doctors are making serious headways into treatments. But at the moment, all those treatments are just that—treatments. A way of managing the condition. No one has developed a cure for it, and they may never do so in my lifetime. I *know* all that, and it makes my future worrisome. I've watched Mom and Dad go through it, I've seen the crap of it all and I never wanted to put someone in that situation."

The frown knitting his eyebrows grew deeper. "Your mum and dad?"

I nodded. Oh man, did I feel nervous. "Mom has Parkinson's as well. She was diagnosed over ten years ago. She's ... she's in an advanced state. I've spent so many mealtimes waiting to see if she's going to choke on her soup because her throat decides mid-swallow to stop working. I've spent days at school, at college, wondering if she's fallen over and hurt herself, maybe hit her head and is unconscious, or bleeding out ... It's not ... well, it's not fun."

"Jesus, Maci," Raph breathed. "I didn't ... why didn't you tell me?"

"Pride. Stubborn pride," I answered honestly. "And embarrassment. Humiliation. I didn't want anyone to think of me as broken, or to look at me with pity. I hate that. But you've made me realize ..." I let out a sigh, closing my eyes for a moment as a wave of something profound and significant rolled through me. "I've come to realize the one person I don't want to be stubborn with, the one person who makes me not afraid, who makes me not care about humiliation, is you."

He looked at me, silent.

"I was wrong to say I didn't want you to care about me," I continued, my throat tight. "I kinda like that you do, a lot."

He drew a deep breath. And then, without a word, rolled over until we faced each other, knees to knees, chest to chest, heart to heart. "Do you remember that word I said this morning?"

I nodded.

He touched my bottom lip with his thumb. "What was it again? Say it for me?"

"Unconditional," I whispered. Christ, I felt like every fiber in my body was thrumming.

The corners of his lips twitched. "Sorry? I didn't hear that. What was it again?"

"Unconditional," I repeated, a bit louder this time.

He grinned. "What? I still can't hear you."

"*Unconditional!*" I sang the word in my best Katy Perry voice, which was, to be fair, goddamn awful.

But then, so were Raph's scrambled eggs that morning and I'd loved every bite.

"You better fucking believe it, baby," he growled, eyes dancing with joy as he flattened me to my back and proceeded to make love to me. So many times I lost count of how many orgasms I had.

Whoa.

The next afternoon, Sunday, he left.

I drove him to the bus station, my heart a messed-up mix of grief and rapture. He had to get back to his classes at the university and I had to get back to my fieldwork and thesis. Life was interrupting our heaven. Damn it. But boy, was our heaven wonderful.

We stood under the bus shelter holding each other, refusing to look away. I know it sounds ridiculous and melo-dramatic, but that's what love is, right? Everything's in hyper color when you're in love. Everything's on full volume. Nothing is diluted or filtered.

"I'll be back next Friday," he promised, doing that strokey thing on my bottom lip with his thumb I loved so much. "I'll drive this time. Takes too bloody long on the bus and train. Also means I don't have to leave until late Sunday night."

I forced a smile. I was going to miss him. "Watch out for Shelly," I said, trying to sound witty and failing miserably.

"Who?"

The damn Greyhound bus pulled to a halt beside the curb before I could think of something equally not-witty to respond with.

"Fuck," he muttered, pulling me closer to him. "Fuck, fuck, fuck."

With another forced laugh, I shoved him away from me. "Get out of here, Jones," I ordered. "You're bothering me."

He snared my wrist with impressive reflexes, yanked me back to his body and kissed me, a hard, fast, mind-spinning kiss. "Love you," he whispered against my lips before he let me go and ran for the bus's open door.

"Love you too," I yelled back, grinning.

Yes, I was shaking. I knew it and so did Raph. Probably one of the reasons he didn't want to climb on the bus now.

But he had to. And he did. Which sucked. Big time. But it was easier to deal with because I knew he was coming back. I knew he loved me and I *knew* we were going to work it all out, including the whole Australia-American-geographical-impediment thing.

I knew all those things, so I didn't break down into a sobbing mass of heartbroken misery.

I *knew* those things.

Unfortunately, I was wrong.

And I never saw Raph in Kangaroo Creek again.

Or Sydney, for that matter.

The Royal Family, Photographs and Getting the Fuck out of Dodge—AKA Australia

Bet you thought I was going to say something terrible like Raph's bus crashed on the way to Tamworth or the train to Sydney had an accident and there were no survivors? Nope. Nothing like that.

Raph made it back to Sydney, back to Mackellar House, and we threw ourselves into a highly erotic, thoroughly debauched long-distance relationship.

For four days, we flirted via text, Skype and—when we really wanted to tease the world with the awesomeness of our love—Facebook. We had Skype sex, cybersex, text sex. Yeah, it was as comical as it sounds. And boy, does that guy know how to text dirty. More than once, we even went the retro route and had phone sex. Four days of being with each other when we couldn't *be* with each other.

It was awesome. We laughed, got schmaltzy often, shared our days' highlights and existed together. When I described in great detail the diarrhea of one of my koala subjects, he didn't stop me. In fact, he asked questions that made me think in ways I hadn't before, which in turn opened up a whole new direction of research for my thesis.

Four days of goofy, elated, euphoric bliss. It seemed there was a magical element to that number with Raph and me. Four days in Mackellar House and four days now.

Which meant I shouldn't have been surprised when those four days of joy ended with a jarring, cruel blow.

Returning to the guesthouse after a particularly devastating morning on the fifth day of fieldwork, I shuffled up the front porch steps, spirits low. A feral cat had attacked the koala colony during the night and I'd arrived at the site to find the gutted remains of a mother koala and her baby on the ground beneath her primary tree. I'd been researching them since the beginning; it was heart-wrenching to discover and even more heart-wrenching to document. The photos now in my smartphone's Koala album would haunt me for a long time to come.

Dropping my backpack onto the desk under the window, I crossed the living area to the bathroom, desperate not only to wash up, but to find some way to revive my mood. Perhaps I'd ring Raph after a shower. If nothing else, the sound of his voice would soothe my frazzled nerves.

I took a long shower. Well, long for Kangaroo Creek, which meant I was under there for about seven minutes. Afterwards, I grabbed a towel and walked from the bathroom, drying myself off.

I froze when I found a petite, impeccably dressed, beautiful young woman perched on the edge of one of the sofas in the living room, looking at me.

Actually, the more accurate account of what I did was froze, let out a squeal and staggered back a step, flailing with the damp towel in an effort to cover my naked body.

The young woman—surely no older than eighteen—watched me the whole time, expression bored. "Good morning, Miss Rowling."

She had an accent. A weird one. The kind the villains in those cheesy eighties' spy movies have.

"Who the hell are you?" I demanded with a glare over my shoulder, showing her my back as I knotted the towel around my body.

With a delicate sniff, she rose to her feet. Wow, did she move with graceful poise. "I am Natasha Sorensen. The Crown Princess of Delvania."

I blinked. Gaped at her. Blinked again. My brain refused to process what she'd just said.

"You're who?"

A faint smile curled her lips, one that said she thought I was a poor, pitiful child. Which would have been funny given that she was obviously younger than me, if the situation wasn't so ... unbelievable. And surreal.

"Her Royal Highness, Natasha Sorensen, the Crown Princess of Delvania. But you may call me Your Highness."

My eyebrows shot up my forehead. "My what?"

The situation was starting to sink into my blindsided-brain. Raph's sister's sister-in-law was here. A female member of the royal family who'd tried to pay me off. A hot beat of anger throbbed in my temples. My gut clenched. So did my jaw.

"Your Highness," she supplied, plucking at what I assumed was an inconvenient piece of Australian fluff that had the audacity to attach itself to her sleeve. "You may call me Your Highness."

Narrowing my eyes, I straightened my shoulders and studied her. "How about I don't, and you can say I did?"

The condescending smile on her lips faded. "I see. You are one of *those* girls, are you?"

"If by one of *those* girls," I said, "you mean I'm not going to kowtow and grovel at the feet of some obscure European royal person who walks into my home unannounced and uninvited, or accept their degrading, reprehensible bribe, then yes, I *am* one of those girls."

The princess wrinkled her perfect nose in another sniff. She flicked a quick glance over her shoulder, and for the first time I noticed she hadn't come alone. Horn stood motionless just inside the front door, his expression dour, the bulge near his armpit obvious.

My stomach didn't just clench at the sight of him, it cramped. "Guess I know now why you didn't help me with the paparazzi, right?" I said, forcing my voice to be calm.

He didn't look at me. Didn't even move. He just stood there and oozed threatening menace.

Jesus, this just got ... scary.

Flinty eyes returned to me, the princess raking me over from top to toe, and back to top again, with disdain. "I should have expected this from an American."

Oh boy. She did not just say that, did she?

Grinding my teeth, I folded my arms over my chest and fixed her with a level glare. "Excuse me, Tash—" the look on her face when I called her Tash was priceless, "—but do you mind telling me why you're here? Insulting me?"

The princess plucked at the cursed Australian fluff on her sleeve again. "I am here to clear up a matter of importance before you get hurt, *Maci*."

"Oh, you're here for me?" I poured every ounce of mocking sarcasm into my voice. "Golly, I don't know what to say? How's *go away* sound?"

With another sniff, the princess turned to Horn and clicked her fingers.

He moved. Fast. One second he was a statue at the door, the next he was beside her, dominating the room, flat eyes empty as they zeroed in on me.

I swallowed and took an involuntary step back. Damn it.

But he didn't proceed farther than the princess's side. Instead of coming for me, he offered her royal pain in the ass an iPad.

Without a word, she took it from his hand.

He gave a slight bow and returned to the door. Silent. I'd never seen the guy so scary.

Which probably explained why my heart was hammering

and, goddamn it, my hand was shaking. Balling my fingers into a tight fist, I refused to break eye contact with the princess. Nor did I move to her when she hooked her index finger at me and ordered, "Come here."

"Why don't you come here?" I suggested.

She let out a sigh that clearly suggested I was the biggest inconvenience of her life, and crossed the room to where I stood. "I think you should see this," she said, her accent thick. She really did sound like a Bond villain. She looked like she'd stepped from the pages of *Vogue* but sounded like a Bond villain. It messed with my head.

But no more than the image I saw on the iPad when she presented it to me. "Do you recognize the man in this photo?"

Raph stood on a lush green lawn dressed in the most exquisite tux I've ever seen, his dark hair slicked away from his face, his forehead nearly touching that of the breathtakingly gorgeous, willowy blonde who clung to his biceps, her eyes making love to his as she gazed up at him.

It was an image of two people perfectly matched in looks and sexual allure. Raph, and the very princess currently standing not a foot away from me.

"Perhaps this one?" the princess murmured, swiping her finger tipped with a blood-red nail over the screen to reveal another image of Raph with her. In this one, his hand was resting on the small of her back, his dimple flashing as he smiled at someone offscreen. The princess was pressing her body to his side. Like the previous image, she gazed up at him with open desire.

I swallowed. My mouth was dry. My gut churned.

"Or this one?" She gave another swipe of that blood-red-tipped finger, and there was another image of Raph with the princess, who looked more exquisite and fairytale-ish in every image. This time, however, Raph was wearing a pair of black board shorts that revealed his incredible body, as he stood beside a pool like those found only in the homes of gazillionaires. Or royalty.

The princess was nearby, delicately perched on the edge of the pool, looking back at him over her shoulder as he spoke to another man dressed in swimming attire. She wore a tiny white and blue bikini that showed off her perfect waist, perfect hips, perfect thighs and perfect breasts. There wasn't an ounce of fat to be seen. For a surreal moment, I wondered if she was a robot specially designed for royal families to maintain the facade of bloodline supremacy.

And then I blinked and the image became blurred. Damn it, I was not going to cry in front of this little ... girl. I wasn't.

Driving my nails—not blood-red nor manicured—into my palms, I raised my eyes from the iPad and fixed them on the princess. "It's Raph. Your point being?"

She arched an eyebrow. Bitch. That was my attack move. "Raph? How ... cute. My point is Raphael has commitments to the Delvanian royal family, as you can see in these images. He has a *place* in the family. By *my* side, in case you didn't notice that. Raphael and I have a ... relationship."

I refused to blink. I refused to draw breath. Instead, I lifted my own eyebrow. Two could play at that game. "Funny," I said. "*Relationship* is exactly the word I would use to describe what Raph and I have. I'd also use the word love. You don't intimidate me, bitch."

She laughed. The Crown Princess of Delvania actually laughed at me. The most scornful, indulgent laugh I'd ever heard. "Oh, my dear Miss Rowling, I do admire your gumption."

Yes, she truly did use the word gumption.

"But it is sorely wasted. Look at these images again. Look at Raphael. He is where he was meant to be. He may have been born a commoner on the wrong side of the world, but he was meant to be in Delvania. Our people adore his sister, and they already respect and admire him. He has been my consort to more than one official royal event, and each time he appears, his popularity increases. I've already expressed my desire for a future with him, and Mommy and Daddy, *the king and queen*, are more than happy to accommodate my desire."

I laughed, holding her stare. "You call your mom and dad Mommy and Daddy?"

"Mommy and Daddy," she went on, ice forming in her eyes, "are very happy to accommodate my desire to be with Raphael. *As* is Raphael."

"Bullshit."

The single word slipped from me, blunt and flat.

She lifted an immaculately waxed eyebrow. "Do you want *more* evidence?" She returned her attention to the iPad in her hand, and before I could stop myself, so did I. I wish I hadn't.

With swipe after swipe of her finger, a parade of images of her and Raph scrolled across the screen.

Raph in a suit, the crown princess in a stylish gown, as they mounted steps to what appeared to be a castle.

Raph in polo clothes, atop a horse, the crown princess cheering him on from where she sat, ankles crossed on the hood of an expensive-looking SUV.

Raph in a tux, swirling the crown princess around, her ball gown showing off her petite waist and the creamy perfection of her shoulders and neck.

Raph and the crown princess.

Raph and the crown princess.

Raph and the crown princess.

I stared at them all, heart wild, head roaring.

"Do you see?" the princess said. "Do you see where he belongs?"

Drawing a slow breath, I looked up at her. "I see a guy in every frame interacting with those around him, no more and no less than he's interacting with the pouty little peroxided-blonde who seems to have a fixation with lilac." I arched my eyebrow again. Take that, Tashie. "In fact, you almost look—hmmm, how do I put this? You look a little desperate, given he only seemed to be *really* acknowledging your presence in the first photo. And that's because, if I'm not mistaken, you're treading on his foot, yes?"

The princess's lips compressed to a thin line. Her eyes grew cold. "I have plans for Raphael, Miss Rowling," she said, her voice as menacing as her stare. "Plans that don't include looking after a woman who won't be able to even dress herself soon, or go a day without popping pills to keep from drooling and lurching about like she is intoxicated. Or who will lose the ability to show any expression on her face.

"Imagine what that woman's husband would feel like, wondering if his wife is grateful for him being in her life when she never gives him a smile. A woman whose own mother became a burden to those she loved with the very disease that is killing her. Raphael has no place in that life, Miss Rowling. That life is no life at all." A slow smile curled the princess's lips. "Is it?"

I slapped her.

I slapped the Crown Princess of Delvania's royal face. *Hard.*

Horn was at her side in a blur, but I didn't care. I was aching too much.

"Get out," I ordered, my voice low.

The princess regarded me. She didn't raise her hand to her cheek, where a bright-red imprint of my fingers now branded her flesh. I had to give it to her, she knew how to handle her shit.

"Get out," I repeated. "Unless you want me to show you just what this here *American* can do when pissed. And trust me, it doesn't just involve name-calling and hair-pulling."

Horn's nostrils flared. And yep, his hand went to the inside his jacket lapel. What kind of gun was he going to pull on me?

The princess halted him with a wave of her hand. She smiled at me, cold triumph in her eyes. "Do not bother, Nikolaj. I do believe I have achieved what I intended to."

She raked another gaze over me, tearing me apart, and then with a slight dip of her head, she turned and walked to the door. "It was a pleasure meeting you, Miss Rowling," she said as she stood on the threshold, her smile smug. Cruel. "I wish you luck with your future. 'Tis such a shame someone as beautiful as yourself is afflicted with such a humiliating, insidious sickness. I hope you battle it with dignity."

And then she was gone. Through the door, down the steps. Gone.

Horn studied me, silent, that same unreadable expression on his face I'd grown to loathe. And then he too left. Without a word.

Leaving me alone in the guesthouse.

I lasted on my feet for approximately two seconds. Two seconds of stubborn refusal to surrender to the bone-deep tremors fighting to overwhelm me. Two seconds of sheer obstinate refusal to crumple under the weight of the princess's hideous words.

Two seconds.

And then the weight of those hideous words crushed me and I dropped to the floor, tears like acid in my eyes.

Because everything she'd said, every strike she'd landed,

had all driven home a truth I'd been too deliriously happy to accept.

Raph being with me only fucked up *his* future. My future was already set in stone, but *his* wasn't. I had no right to mess up his future. No right to expect him to sacrifice it for me. And he would. I had no doubt about that. He would.

The cold, harsh truth lashed at me and I squeezed my eyes shut. I knew what the princess was doing, I knew she was emotionally manipulating me and I hated her for it. Hated her for the vile tactic.

Hated her even more for ripping from my face the rose-colored glasses I'd been wearing since Raph turned up in Gunnedah six days ago.

My gut churned. My heart—stupid, naïve, deluded organ that it was—broke.

As much as I hated to admit it, Natasha Sorensen, Crown Princess of the Brutal Truth, was correct. Raph *didn't* deserve the life of looking after a burden. Not when he had a different life—the life captured in the images in her iPad—waiting for him. Not when he had a princess waiting for him.

An American with Parkinson's disease, or a real-life European princess more stunning than I could ever hope to be. A life caring for a woman who would one day be incapable of climbing out of a chair without assistance, or a life of minders and nannies and personal cooks and luxury and parties and balls and ... and ...

I bit back a sob. I had to accept it. As much as I wanted to let Raph decide his future with me—a decision he'd already made clear—I had to stop being selfish.

Opening my eyes, I raised my head and ran my tear-stung stare around the guesthouse. Noted all the places Raph and I had made love. Imprinted on my psyche all the moments we'd shared here in two and a half short, glorious days together.

I took it all in, filled my soul with all the memories, all the moments. And then rose to my feet.

I had to get dressed. Then pack, drive up to the main house, and say my farewells to the Pattersons.

But first, I had to ring Qantas and change the return flight date on my ticket home. I had to get out of here. Out of Australia. Away from Raph. Now. Before I doomed him to a life burdened with me.

I loved him too much to curse him with that.

Mrs. P was, to put it mildly, very surprised by my announcement. She frowned at me, worry etched on her normally reserved face.

"I'm not sure I understand what's going on, Maci. Is everything okay? Has my son done something wrong?" Her eyes narrowed. "Or does this have something to do with the Crown Princess of Delvania's unexpected visit? My daughter's sister-in-law seemed quite interested in you, I must say. Asked quite a few questions about your relationship with Raphael." She paused, a pointed expression on her face. "I must *also* say that I don't think much of her."

I shook my head, my smile wan. "No, Mrs. P, it doesn't have anything to do with the princess." Taking her hands in mine, I drew a slow breath, beginning the story I'd settled on during the short drive from the guesthouse to the main house. "My mom is unwell, she has a condition that requires constant care, and I need to return to her. My fieldwork is all but done. I have enough data now to complete my thesis without needing to constantly unsettle the koalas daily."

I could tell my story didn't convince her. The dubious frown she gave me spoke volumes. However, she didn't put up an argument. Perhaps she could see it would serve no purpose.

Smoothing her arms around my shoulders, she hugged me with a gentle pressure. I must admit, I was shocked at the open display of affection. "You are a wonderful young woman, Maci. And good for Raphael. I've never seen him smile so often."

I didn't need to hear that. It didn't help my state of mind at all. "Thank you," I mumbled.

"You're welcome," she said. "I'm sure we will be seeing you again soon."

I had a hard freaking time holding back the damn tears at that. If only she really knew. Instead, I extracted myself from her hug and gave her what I hoped was a cheery, positive smile. "Definitely. I love this country too much to stay away."

Her lips twitched and, for a brief second, I got a glimpse of the twin dimples in her cheeks. "Just this country?"

Before I could do something stupid like burst out in uncontrolled sobs, I dropped a quick kiss on her cheek. "Please say my goodbyes to Mr. Patterson," I said as I bent to collect my backpack. "You have both been incredible. I can't thank you enough."

And that was it. I turned and left the house.

I found one of the workhands in the main barn and, putting on the best damsel-in-distress routine I could muster, asked him if he'd drive me into Gunnedah.

Thankfully, he'd been planning on doing a supply run later that day so I didn't have to feel any guiltier than I already did.

Guilty about abandoning my studies.

Guilty about leaving Kangaroo Creek early.

Guilty about leaving without letting Raph know.

Guilt sucks.

And if right at this moment, you're thinking I'm an idiot, trust me, I was thinking it five times as much. *Fifty* times as much. But you have to remember, I *knew* what was ahead of me. I'd seen it. I'd watched Dad cry when he didn't think anyone could see him. I'd watched him stare at nothing for long moments when Mom was riding the emotional roller-coaster that is PD. I'd watched him take it all on, the helping, the bathing, the feeding … all of it, and I'd *sworn* to myself when I was diagnosed that I'd never put someone through the same thing.

An hour later, we were barreling along the dirt road headed for Gunnedah.

I sat in the passenger seat and watched the world blurring by. I know it was stupid, but I really *was* going to miss this place. It had reached into my soul and grabbed me. If life had dealt me a different hand, I could have seen myself spending the rest of my life here.

Not just because of Raph, but because it was peaceful. Real.

As we approached the Gunnedah town limits, I turned my cell phone off. It was a chicken move, but I did it anyway. It could stay off until I arrived home.

If I heard Raph's voice now, I'd die even more inside.

I spent that night in a hotel in Tamworth, going over all the notes and data and research I'd collected during my stay here in Australia. I refused to let my mind turn to Raph. Every time I caught myself gazing at my phone, I'd give myself a stern talking to. Somewhere around two am, I gave up pretending I was concentrating on my thesis and medi-tated instead.

I'd like to say it helped.

When the sun broke the eastern sky a few hours later, my mind and body were more frazzled and unsettled than ever.

Sleep deprivation will do that to a person, whether they suffer from Parkinson's disease or not.

My train from Tamworth was due to depart for Sydney at ten am, less than five hours' time.

I showered, washed my hair—it would be my last chance until I arrived in Plenty some twenty-nine hours later—packed up my stuff and sat on the edge of the bed.

My stomach churned. Perhaps I should go for a run? Do some tai chi?

Nervous energy charged through me, making me even more twitchy than normal. It wasn't pretty, I can tell you.

I propelled myself from the bed, crossed to the desk, dropped into the chair and snatched up the hotel-supplied pen and notepad.

I stared at the blank sheet, flicking the pen up and down between my thumb and index finger. I had to do something.

Chest tight, I leaned forward and began to write.

Hey Heather, so it's me.

By the time you get this I'll be back in Plenty. I'm sorry for not saying goodbye in person or even by text or phone. As it turns out, I'm a bit of a chicken. Anyways, I wanted to let you know you are one of the best friends I've ever had. I also wanted to let you know I couldn't have survived those first few days in Australia without you. You are the goofiest, funniest, loveliest and every other kind of positive "est" out there. Never change. Not for anyone. Promise me. And thank you. For making me feel so at home at Mackellar House and for being so incredible. If you're ever in the States, I fully expect to see you at my front door, Tim Tams in hand.

By this stage, you've probably found out I left without saying goodbye to Raph as well. I couldn't do it. I couldn't say goodbye to him. Not just because it would have hurt too much, but because he wouldn't have let me do it. He wouldn't have let me go. I love him, Heather. More than I think I could ever express. When you see him, just let him know I never wanted to hurt him, ever, and that's the reason I did what I did. He'll be angry with me, really angry, but one day I know he'llstopbeing angry with me and understand.

Do me a favor though. If you ever see Shelly White leaving his room, slap her for me, okay? Hard.

Oh, and one last thing, tell Brendon I think he's the sexiest non-brother I've ever kissed. And the girl he followed to America doesn't know what she missed out on.

I love you, woman.

Your friend, shakes and all,

M.

xoxo

I tore the top sheet from the pad, folded it and, needing to do something, left my room and walked to the hotel foyer. The woman at the reception desk gave me an envelope and, hand shaking too much—Had I taken my meds? I couldn't remember—I wrote Heather's name and the address for Mackellar House on the front.

Given that it was Saturday and the Australian postal department doesn't operate on the weekends, Heather would receive my note Wednesday.

By that time, I would be back in Plenty, back at my old college, back in my old life.

Damn, that thought made me miserable.

Deciding I couldn't stand sitting in a hotel room any longer, I collected my stuff and caught a cab to the train station.

Ten hours later, I was in Sydney again. Two hours after that, I walked into Sydney International Airport.

Oh boy. I wasn't prepared for what came next.

Not at all.

First, I saw a man I recognized standing near the men's public restroom. The same men's restroom Raph and I had our very first meeting.

What were the freaking odds?

He'd been one of the paparazzi that had hounded Raph at Triptych cafe and the ringleader of the horde of paparazzi that had swarmed us on the Mackellar House front lawn.

The second thing that happened, apart from my mouth going dry and my grip on my suitcase handle growing tight, was that he saw *me*.

Ravenous delight swept over his face. Seriously. The second his gaze fell on me, it was like a hungry pig had just spotted a bucket of swill. A triumphant, greedy spark lit up his eyes and, without a word, he raised the camera hanging around his neck and snapped a photo of me.

I flinched and then, head down, hurried in the opposite direction. Away from the Qantas check-in counters.

"Maci Rowling?"

Damn it. He was chasing me.

I heard feet pounding on the floor. Heard people letting out surprised grunts and displeased, "Hey, watch it, mate." I didn't want to risk looking over my shoulder to see if he was following me, but I did.

And he was.

The second our eyes connected, he took another photo. "Where've you been?" he called, grin wide. "Where's Jones?"

Head spinning, I looked straight ahead again and kept walking. Faster.

I had no idea where I was going. I just couldn't be here.

The paparazzo followed me. Of course. Holston, I think

I'd heard the other pap call him outside Triptych. Apparently, he was quite notorious.

"Maci?" he shouted. "Hey, Maci? Is it true Jones dumped you for the Delvanian Crown Princess?"

Sick disbelief rolled through me. I scanned the crowded airport, desperate for something. Anything.

Spying a female restroom, I ran for it.

The paparazzo laughed. The smug and crude sound rose above the noise of the hundreds of people hurrying about the airport, scraping at my sanity as I rushed into the restroom.

Ignoring the curious glances of the women washing their hands and fixing their makeup, I leaned against the wall and sucked in breath after breath, my chest squeezed tight. Wow. That was horrible.

"You okay, miss?"

I started at the concerned voice to my right. Jerking up my head, I stared at the woman standing beside me. It took a perilous moment before my mind registered she was wearing an airport security uniform. For the duration of that perilous moment, I'd been very close to whacking my backpack into her with as much force as I could.

"Miss?"

Shaking my head, I hugged myself. I had to control the tremors in my hand somehow. "There's a guy outside," I said. Crap, even my voice was shaking. "He thinks I'm someone else. Someone famous. He's trying to take photos of me and he chased me in here."

The guard's eyes narrowed. I couldn't tell if she was trying to decide what famous person I was, or what famous person I looked like. Apparently, she wasn't interested in Raph's celebrity status because no recognition crossed her face. With a serious nod and a stern expression, she placed her hand on my shoulder. "We'll get rid of him, miss."

She plucked the radio on her shoulder from its clip and raised it to her lips. "West, this is East. We've got a possible pap issue in sector four."

West answered with, "Gotcha. On my way."

East returned her radio to its clip, offered me a reassuring smile and patted my shoulder. "West will deal with the man. Do you want me to escort you to where you need to go? Check-in counter?"

I wanted to say no. I wanted to say I was going to be fine. But with the way the tremors were attacking my hand, my arm—hell, my whole body—I knew I wasn't going to be fine. Not for a long time. "That would be wonderful," I said. The smile I gave her was both sad and grateful.

She nodded. "Easy done."

With a quick turn of her head, she activated her radio. "Got him, West?"

"It was that bastard, Holston," West's voice crackled through the speaker. "We've run him off. It's clear now."

East released her radio and, with another smile at me, took my backpack from my shoulder. "Come on, honey. You look like you really need to sit down. Let's get you checked in, okay?"

And that was how I left Australia. Escorted to the check-in counter by three friendly security guards, East carrying my backpack, West carrying my check-in bag and West's companion—God, wouldn't it be awesome if his name was South?—pulling my suitcase along behind his massive frame.

They stayed with me until I went through the exit gates. They waved at me as I passed through the metal detectors without incident. It was surreal and stupidly touching and it filled my eyes with prickly tears that I blinked away with rapid determination.

I waved at them all, my throat thick. "Thank you," I called back at them.

"You're welcome," East called back with a grin. "Take care, Miss Rowling. Tell Raphael Jones I think he's cute in his tux."

And with that—and a wink—East and her smiling companions turned and left.

I stood motionless, heart thumping in my tight, thick throat. She knew?

"Miss Rowling?"

The deep male voice on my right made me squeal. I spun around, staring up at another security guard. "Errr ..."

He laughed. "I'm North. East suggested you might need ... company."

If I wasn't in such an emotionally whacked-out state, I can honestly say I would have reveled in the celebrity treatment. Instead, I stared at my savior. "Are your names really North, South, East and West?"

He grinned. "Nah, we just call ourselves that after the areas we patrol. Be pretty awesome if they were our names though, 'eh? Would you like me to take your backpack?"

Wanting to laugh *and* cry, I nodded like a silent fool and let him take my backpack from my shoulder.

Suffice to say, I would never forget my departure from the country.

Nor would I forget my arrival in Plenty twenty-three hours later.

I climbed out of the taxi in front of Mom's house. She had no clue I was coming. The afternoon winter sun teased me with a weak heat, nothing like the blazing Australian summer sun I'd spent almost nine weeks baking under, if you don't count the three days of biblical rainfall in Gunnedah. I tugged my jacket closer to my neck, the shock of the severe change in temperature taking me by surprise. Man, I hadn't realized how much I'd acclimatized to the weather in Australia until now.

Paying the cab driver—Jeremy Missen, who I'd gone to school with since elementary, until he'd been expelled for trying to grope our math teacher, Mr. Woodson. Ah, Plenty, you small town, you—I cast a gaze over my childhood home. Inside those walls, beyond that familiar front door with its cheery blue paint, was the rest of my life.

I'd spent the flight home planning out my future. I would move back home—did I really need to be at college anyway? I would look after Mom and study online. I could continue my global-warming research via the internet. Perhaps, as a way of staying connected to Raph—even if he didn't know it—I'd look into finishing my degree through Sydney University's online courses. I'd cancel Mom's daily home-visit nurse, take care of her myself and maybe, just maybe, fool around with the notion of writing about my life with Parkinson's disease.

Mom and I would become a part of Plenty's folk history. The two Rowling women who trembled their way through life. We'd spend our nights watching that new Michael J. Fox sitcom, we'd bake, we'd laugh at the amount of flour we spilled while baking, we'd make sure we took our meds, and we'd never be a burden to anyone but each other.

I could live with that. Mom might get angry at me ... okay, she *would* get angry at me for giving up on my future, but at least I wouldn't be hurting anyone else. Right?

And when the time came, when it was just me, alone ...

An icy wind blasted against me, whipping my coat around my knees, making me stumble a little to the right.

Letting out a wry chuckle, I regained my balance, picked up my luggage and began walking to my childhood home.

As a timely metaphor for what my life would be like when it was *just me*, that icy wind was quite apt. Cold and erratic.

I knocked on the door, the contact of wood on my knuckles both sharp and a little painful.

Mom answered a few heartbeats later.

"G'day, Mom," I said with my best Australian accent. Wow, I sounded like Dad.

She gaped at me. "Maci?"

I nodded, smiled and then stepped across the threshold and hugged her. And then, before she could hug me back, I burst into tears.

They had to come eventually, right?

We talked for an hour. I refused to tell her why I was home early, assuring her I was fine, I was safe and not hurt in any way.

The look she gave me when I said that told me she didn't believe me. "Does this have to do with Raphael Jones?" She narrowed her eyes. "Your cousin Nathan keeps sending me links to stories on the web about you. In fact, he sent me one only this morning. Said Jones had dumped you for a princess and you were heartbroken. There was even a photo of you at the Sydney airport, but I didn't believe it. I told him you would have let me know if you were coming home."

Miffed disappointment twisted her normally blank face. Remember, Parkinson's does that to you eventually, robs your face of emotions. To see *any* kind of expression on Mom's face was wonderful, even if it was one directed at my dickhead of a cousin. "Guess I owe the douche an apology."

I laughed, my cheeks still warm from my tears—thank God, they'd finally stopped flowing. "Never apologize to Nathan, Mom. He follows you around at Christmas, shaking his hands and head."

Mom arched her brow—see where I got that skill from?

"Does he now? Hmm, I think I might have a word with Cousin Nathan sometime soon." She leaned forward in her seat and placed her shaking hand against my cheek. "But not now. Now, I just want to enjoy my beautiful, stubborn, secretive daughter being home with me."

I closed my eyes and turned my face to her palm.

Her familiar smells, her touch ... it was all so wonderful. Comforting. So why did I feel so empty? So lost?

"How long are you home for?" she asked when I opened my eyes and smiled at her.

"Think I might stay for good."

She studied me. "Is that so?"

I nodded.

With a low *hmmm*that made me think of Mrs. P, she pushed herself, oh so slowly from her chair and shuffled toward the kitchen. "How about you go have a shower while I make us some afternoon tea? Isn't that what they call it over there?"

Rising to my own feet, I let out a tired laugh. "It is. And I will."

I showered. It felt wrong to make it a long one. I'd spent so many weeks washing myself in under five minutes that it felt indulgent to linger any longer. Shutting off the water, I stepped from the shower and then dragged my feet to my old room, drying myself as I went. Oh man, I was tired.

Jet lagged and exhausted.

I entered my old bedroom, my gaze sweeping over the familiar furniture, posters, books and, unable to stand on my feet any longer, flopped face first onto my bed.

I'd just close my eyes for a second. Just a second. While Mom served up what would no doubt be a batch of her famous cookies and a glass of milk. She was a traditionalist, my mom. Milk and cookies were a staple not to be cast aside.

I lay on my bed, sinking into the soft mattress, growing heavier. Eyes closed, I let myself wonder what Raph was doing. For a tormenting moment, I wondered if he was missing me, thinking about me. Angry at me.

And then I was asleep.

A pale light washing against my eyelids woke me sometime later. I squinted at the sun streaming through a curtained window, utterly disorientated. Where was I? Where was Raph? Why was it so cold?

My brain was fuzzy. Connections weren't being made. I gazed around the room, my vision blurred with groggy sleep.

It wasn't until I saw the *Thor* movie poster pinned to the wall, with its intimidating image of Chris Hemsworth in menacing Asgardian-God pose, that my brain finally recalled where I was.

A cold fist slammed into my belly, an emotional blow so powerful it felt like a physical strike.

I was home. In Plenty. On the other side of the world from Raph. I'd come home yesterday, sobbed in my mom's arms, showered and then collapsed on my old bed.

Pushing myself up into a sitting position, I let my gaze drift around my room, reacquainting myself with its contents as the tight chill in my soul seeped into my heart. I should be happy. I'd made the choice to return, after all. This was my home. A lifetime of happy laughter and love were inside these walls.

Something soft at my elbow caught my attention and I looked down. At some stage during my catatonic slumber, Mom had tucked me into bed and, like she used to when I was a little girl, placed Mr. Sprinkles in my arms.

With a wry sigh, I picked up the purple and green stuffed hippopotamus I'd cuddled in bed since I was four, and pressed my face to its soft side. "Looks like it's just you and me again, Mr. Sprinkles," I murmured against the worn fabric.

I breathed in Mr. Sprinkles' familiar, comforting smell, squeezed my eyes shut and then climbed from the bed.

I was reminded very quickly just how cold Plenty, Ohio, mornings were in mid-April, especially when you were buck naked and still accustomed to Australian weather.

Skin breaking out in gooseflesh, I scanned my room for something to wear. A warm beat of love throbbed in my heart when I discovered Mom had not only unpacked my suitcase while I slept, but laid out fresh clothes for me—Plenty-appropriate clothes, no less—and plugged my iPhone into its charging dock on my desk.

I snatched up my old cheerleading squad sweats waiting for me on the back of my chair—Go Plenty Woodchucks—dressed, and then hovered my hand over my cell.

It was still turned off.

If I turned it on, how many calls from Raph would I find? How many text messages?

What if I found none?

My fingers trembled, telling me loud and clear my meds were long overdue. I stared at the black screen of my cell for a moment and then turned away.

I wasn't ready for what awaited me on it. Not yet. Maybe not ever. Perhaps the first thing I needed to do tomorrow was buy a new phone?

Shaking my head at how pathetic I was, I dragged my fingers through my hair, rubbed at my face with my hands a few times, and walked out of my room.

Low murmurings from the living room told me Mom was either talking to someone or watching the television. Maybe the *Today* show.

I shuffled down the hallway and into the living room, all

too aware I was still exhausted and quite trembly. I needed coffee. Coffee, meds, bacon, maple syrup, some hash browns and more coff—

I froze.

Raphael Jones gazed at me from the sofa.

"What?" I whispered.

"This lovely young man—" Mom beamed at me from Raph's side, a steaming coffee mug in her hand, "—seems to have come a long way to discuss something with you, Bear."

I stared at him. "W-what?" I whispered again. I'd have liked to blame sleep deprivation and jet lag for my sudden inability to say anything but that one word, but as I'd just woken from over twelve hours of sleep, that excuse wasn't going to cut it.

Raph regarded me, his expression unreadable. "Hello, American girl."

At the sound of his voice, at the sound of his accent, every fiber of my body went into meltdown. "Raph?"

"He tells me, Bear," my mom went on, the smile in her voice evident, "that he's deeply in love with you."

I gaped at Raph. How did he get here? God, did his mom call him the *second* I left Kangaroo Creek?

He studied me, not moving, not speaking. Just watching me.

"He also says," Mom continued, "you're incredibly stubborn, obstinate and a ... what did you call her, Raphael?"

Raph's eyes held mine. The corners of his mouth twitched. A little. "A pain in my arse, Mrs. Rowling."

"A pain in his ass," Mom repeated. "Although he says *ass* much sexier than me. In fact, he says it the same way your dad did. Arse."

I gaped some more. At her. At Raph.

"Is that right, Maci?" Mom continued. "*Are* you a stubborn, obstinate pain in his arse?"

The thick lump in my throat didn't dislodge when I swallowed. Nor did my heart stop trying to hammer its way out of my body.

I couldn't stop staring at him.

His hair was a mess, his eyes were bloodshot, his jeans were crumpled, his shirt creased. He looked terrible. As if he hadn't slept for days, nor had a shower or changed his clothes. In fact, he looked wretched. Distressed.

Determined. Dogged.

And here. So here. Like he always said he would be—here with me.

God, he'd followed me to the other side of the world. When I was trying to let him be free of me, he'd left Australia and followed me to the other side of the world.

"Raph?" I rasped, the sound of his name on my lips wonderful. "What are you—"

"Doing here?" he finished for me. "Had no other choice, did I? The woman I love buggered off on me without a word."

He moved then. Without warning, he rose to his feet and was standing in front of me, right there in front of me. So close I could feel his heat seeping into my body. So close I could smell his distinct scent in each shallow breath I pulled. So close our knees brushed.

"Care to explain, Maci?" His deep voice with its sexy accent caressed my senses. Drove me crazy. "Care to give me a reason for leaving Australia like you did?"

I swallowed. "The Crown Princess of Delvania."

Raph's eyebrows shot up. "The who?"

"The Crown Princess of Delvania." I caught my bottom lip with my teeth. The thought of all those images she'd shown me twisted my chest. "I saw ... The princess came to see me at Kangaroo Creek and showed me ... And I know you don't love her. I'm not jealous," I hastened to clarify. I didn't want him to think I didn't trust him. "Honest. But she's a *princess*. And she doesn't ..."

I stopped. The rest of the sentence didn't want to come. Wouldn't come.

Raph placed a finger under my chin and, with that same soft pressure, made me look up at him again. "Have Parkinson's?"

I nodded with a slight dip of my head and closed my eyes.

"The Crown Princess of Delvania is a snobby, pretentious, spoilt little cow with an ego bigger than Ayres Rock. Worse still, she doesn't believe in global warming."

Opening my eyes, I frowned up at him. "*You* don't believe in global warming," I pointed out. "At least, not its effect on koalas."

He chuckled, trailing his thumb over my lip. "But *you* do. And a couple has to have something to argue about into their twilight years, right?"

I shook my head. "You need to think about this, Raph," I said. "You can't be romantic. You need to be realistic. Think about what being with a princess could be like. And now think about what life will be like with—"

"Bloody hell, woman," he murmured, cutting me off. "I just flew halfway 'round the bloody world to make you realize I'm not going anywhere."

I swallowed. "You did."

"Why would I do that?"

"Because you love me?"

He gazed into my eyes, his arms wrapping tightly around me. "And?"

And it was then I realized it was more. He was *never* going to give up on me. I'd shown him my worst. I'd shown him the coward I could be. I'd shown him my deepest fears, and he was here, in Plenty. He was never going to give up on me.

And God, I loved him for that. More than I could ever express.

No, I *could* express it.

I smiled up at him. "I believe in you, Raph. And because of you, I believe in me. I trust you like you trust me. And I know I've probably made you question that trust with the ridiculous way I've been behaving, and you have every right to be furious at me, but I know, I really know, you will never give up on me."

"I won't, Maci," he murmured. "I promise."

Heart thumping fast, I drew a slow breath. "And I promise I will never give up on you. Never ever again."

A soft, lopsided grin pulled at his lips. His dimple flashed at me from his right cheek. "I know you won't." He brushed his thumb over my bottom lip. "Now will you shut up about some boring princess, tell me that you love me and let me kiss you? Or do I have to spank you, right here in front of your—"

I kissed him. It was, after all, the only way to shut him up. And to let him know he was right. He wasn't going anywhere. He was mine and I was his and that's the way it was. I'd even shake on it. See what I did there?

"That's my girl," I heard Mom say behind him with a delighted laugh as Raph wrapped his arms around me and drew me close. "Told you Australian men really know how to make you feel alive."

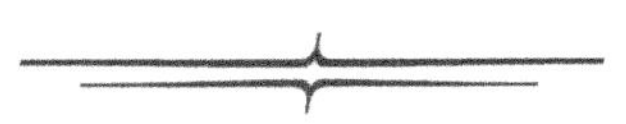

THANK YOU FOR READING

Unconditional is a very personal story for me. As you could probably tell by the book's dedication, Parkinson's disease has very much touched my family. My dad was diagnosed with it when I was only a teenager, followed by my uncle. Then my brother was diagnosed when he was only 47. That absolutely crushed me, and that's when I started working on **Unconditional**. I needed a way to process and understand what was going on for my dad and brother, and my mum and sister-in-law.

While writing **Unconditional**, my dad's little brother (my Uncle Merv) was *also* diagnosed with PD.

And yet, even with all this, my family still finds a way to laugh through it all.

I hope you will join me for the second book in the *Always* series, **Unforgettable**, which finds the eternal optimist, Brendon Osmond, faced with the greatest challenge of his life.

If you enjoyed **Unconditional**, follow me on Bookbub for pre-order, sales, and new-release alerts, sign-up for my newsletter, the Lexxicon. You'll receive a free copy of my (erotic) paranormal short story, **The Cavern**, plus never miss out on exciting announcements and giveaways!

PARKINSON'S DISEASE

More information can be found about Parkinson's disease at:

http://www.parkinsons.org.au (Parkinson's Australia)

http://www.apdaparkinson.org (American Parkinson's Disease Association)

https://www.michaeljfox.org (Michael J. Fox Foundation for Parkinson's Research)

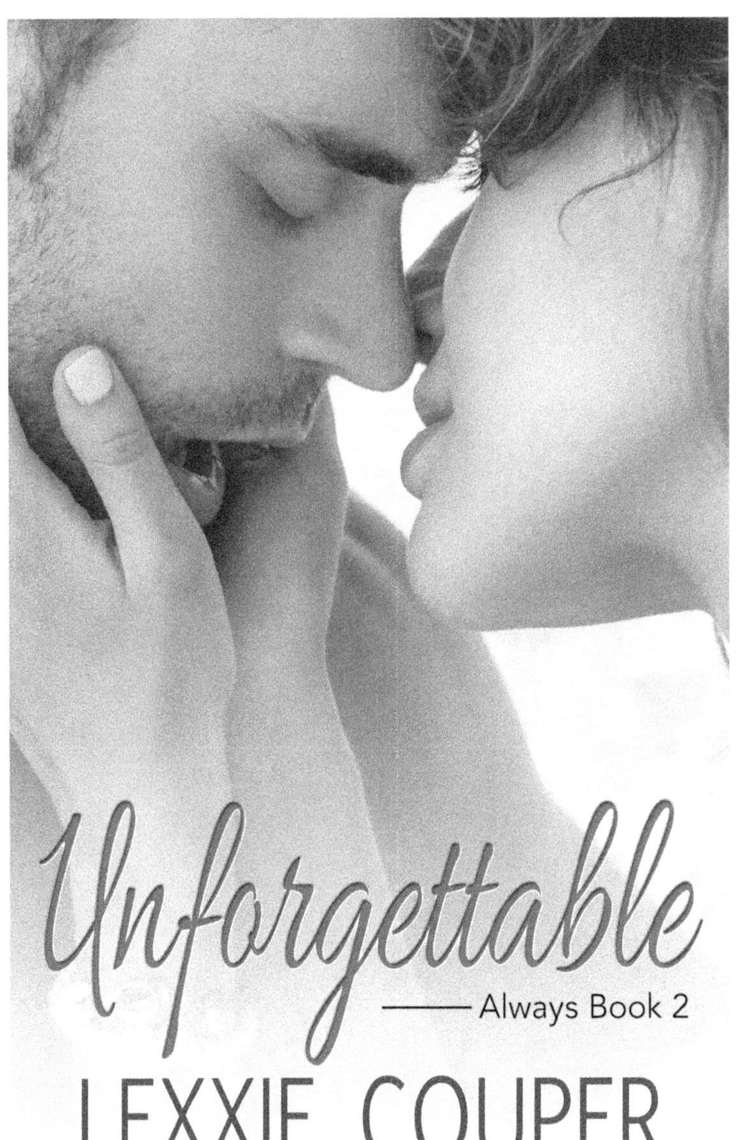

Unforgettable
Always Book 2
LEXXIE COUPER

FIRST CHAPTER PREVIEW:
UNFORGETTABLE

ALWAYS, BOOK TWO

Sometimes being an optimist is hard work.

Unforgettable
(*Always*, Book Two)
Available Here

If you're looking for a tragic, traumatic backstory, I'm going to disappoint you, I'm afraid. I'm not that guy. I laugh easy, joke often, and pretty much see the joy in almost everything around me. I know, unbearable, right? Sorry.

I've been this way forever. Honest, I can't think of a time when I wasn't the "glass is half full" person in the room. When I was a kid most of my friends thought I was weird. Or fake. A lot of them tried their best to drag out the *emo* in me. To mess with me enough to see me snap or crumble. I found out when I was seventeen that my best mate had bet a hundred bucks he'd be able to make me lose my temper enough that I would get suspended from school for a week before we graduated.

He lost.

Can you see what I'm saying? I'm a nice guy. I'm not a prick. I'm not a jerk. I enjoy hanging out with the guys, have a few "friends with benefits" on a semi-regular rotation, take a lot of pride in being healthy and enjoy my job as the Sydney University's gym manager and personal trainer. I've got a Bachelor's degree in Applied Science (Exercise and Sport Science) – those parentheses are important, as is the word *Honors* that goes with it – and six months left before I finish my Master's in Exercise Physiology. I recently bought a betta fish that I call No Direction. I've got plans to open my own personal trainer business one day soon – *Push It P/T* – and spent a total of nine hours last week with a very helpful bank manager discussing loans, long-term business structures, future staff and, eventually, how I could help her lose the excess weight she'd been carrying since the birth of her twins eight months previously.

I can say with all truthfulness that I've only fallen in love twice. The last time I ended up on television and almost in jail after an American student, Maci Rowling became the target of the paparazzi due to the fact she was also involved with one of our local celebrities. (Just to fill you in, she didn't choose me. She went with Raphael Jones. I still give her shit about that.)

The first time I fell in love . . .

Man, I don't really want to talk about the first time. Of course, what we want and what we get isn't always the same thing, right? Hell, I wanted the world to shake when I kissed Maci that time in my living room. I wanted her to say "Raph who?" when questioned by the media. That didn't happen.

What *did* happen was I accepted we weren't meant to be, put my "just friends" hat firmly in place and let it go. Got on with living.

That's what it's all about. Living. Enjoying every minute of every day we have. Not wasting it with second-guessing, regret, hoping in vain, wishful thinking or moping. Yeah, those things aren't really in my vocabulary.

As I've said before, this attitude seems to irritate a lot of people, which I always find puzzling. Why would a happy person with no baggage piss someone off? Is it because I make them feel . . . less in some way? Less successful? Less complete? I don't mean it to. Honest.

Life is about being in the moment. The present. And the present is pretty damn perfect. Except . . .

Okay, I can't skirt around it any more. My brain keeps coming back to something I'd rather it didn't. Actually, not *something*, but *someone*.

That "first" I mentioned earlier. The one that "got away".

Yeah, that's a lot of quotation marks there, isn't it?

I just . . . I don't . . .

Damn it, let's start this again.

G'day. I'm Brendon Osmond. I'm a twenty-five-year-old post-graduate student at Sydney University. Most of my friends call me The Biceps, I suspect because I give Chris Hemsworth in *Thor*-mode a run for his money. I have big plans, big goals and a ridiculously positive outlook on life. Nothing fazes me. Nothing unsettles me.

Until the morning I woke to a text message from someone I didn't expect to hear from again.

Someone. Okay, not just someone . . . *that* one. She of the quotation marks.

It was a simple text but one that shook me a little.

Thinking of you.

That's it. Who sends a text like that after over two and a half years of no contact whatsoever? I mean, I followed this girl to the States, I opened my damn chest, took out my heart and gave it to her, and she gave it back. Told me we had no hope. And now she sends me this text? Without any follow-up? No text to let me know she'd sent that message to the wrong person. No apologies for the utterly random contact. No *LOL Psyche!* complete with a winking smiley face emoticon just to highlight the joke of it all.

Who does that?

Apparently Amanda Sinclair.

Amanda Sinclair, the American girl who made it clear we didn't have a "relationship" because she "wasn't for me". Because she couldn't "be what I wanted". See? More of those damn quotation marks. I don't think I've ever had the need to use quotation marks until Amanda Sinclair entered my life. Amanda Sinclair, the American college student I met almost three years ago during an amateur snowboarding competition down in Thredbo (that's the main ski slopes in Australia, if you don't know) and who I then proceeded to spend the rest of the comp in bed with.

We both lost our respective rounds, but we didn't mind. Not at all. Holy fuck, did we . . . well, fuck. It was the most mind-blowing sex, the most intense, perfect, sublime sex I've ever had.

After the snowboarding competition finished, she followed me back to Sydney and crashed in my one-room apartment. We spent most of the days in bed. Most of the nights as well. We laughed a lot. She had the same approach to life I did: live it, don't dwell on it, regret is just wasted energy, exist for the now. We occasionally went out, caught a movie or two. I once smuggled her into my Biomechanical Analysis of Movement lecture. We sat up the back of the lecture hall, where my professor – who wore glasses with the thickest lenses ever – couldn't see us, and made out. And by make out, I mean Amanda went down on me while I was trying to take notes.

Six weeks after we first met, she realized she'd overstayed her visitor's visa by a week. By that stage I was in love with her. That simple. I have no problems admitting that. If I'm going to spill it all, the whole sordid, woeful story, I may as well go the whole hog and leave nothing out. I was in love with her. And she was in love with me.

Of course, being in love doesn't suddenly change geography. She was from the US and I was Australian. We both had studies to complete, families to think about. So she went back to the States the next day, back to San Diego where she was studying to be a high school English teacher at San Diego State University, and I stayed in Sydney. For three days.

Three days.

Long enough for me to finish my mid-semester thesis (*Carb Depletion and its Impact on Muscle Regeneration*), submit it to my professor, bring the assistant manager up to speed at the university gym, and buy a one-way plane ticket to San Diego.

One week later, I flew back to Australia. Alone.

The crib notes version of that week goes like this:

• I arrive in San Diego.

• Amanda collects me at the airport.

• We spend five incredible days rarely leaving her dorm room.

• I meet her family in the flesh three times.

• I eat with them twice.

• I tell her I love her on the fifth night.

• Amanda tells me on the sixth day she's *bored* with us, that there *is* no *us*.

• I fly back to Sydney on the seventh day.

• Not a word from her since.

That's twenty-seven months and three days of silence (yes, I've kept track, which is pathetic I know) and now this text.

Suffice to say, the guy that's never rattled was feeling . . . shaken. But not rattled. I refuse to be rattled.

I won't lie though. When I finally replied to her text I had to type *Hi* eight times before I got it right.

An hour later, I sent her another one. I tried not to, but I did.

Thinking of you as well.

For the next sixty minutes I checked my phone every minute. Not a single response.

I calculated the time difference between San Diego and Sydney. Seventeen hours. It was almost seven am on Wednesday over there. I downloaded a World Clock app just in case my math skills were as dubious as my math teacher suggested they were back when I was only fifteen.

As it turns out, my math skills were holding steady.

If Amanda was in San Diego – and as I pointed out, it had been over two years since we last spoke, so really I was only guessing that's where she was – she should at least be awake. Maybe eating breakfast somewhere.

Sixty minutes of obsessive-compulsive phone stalking later, I sent off my *third* text.

What's up?

I'd like to say she replied a short time after that. Instead, twenty-four hours passed. Have you ever spent a day, a whole day, waiting on a text? The text tone on my phone is the main chorus from "Eye of the Tiger". I know it's corny but that song from the seventies pumps me up when I'm working out.

I grew to loathe that song in that twenty-four hour period.

Every time I heard Survivor sing that damn chorus my heart went into overdrive, my pulse smashed into my throat and my gut clenched. Every time I looked at my phone and saw the sender wasn't Amanda Sinclair, I wanted to scream.

Go ahead, you can say it. I was rattled.

But that was nothing – the pounding heart, the choking pulse, the churning gut – *nothing*, compared to my body's response when Amanda's reply can through at two am, Friday morning.

I need you.

She didn't answer when I called. That may have been a good thing. To be honest, I'm not sure what I was going to say to her. What she did do was call me an hour later – when I was in the shower, of course, trying to get myself sorted out under a punishing stream of cold water.

I came out to find the *1 New Voicemail message* notification on my screen. Throat tight, I played the message.

"Hi Brendon," Amanda's voice messed with my sanity, her subtle American accent as sexy as ever. "I know . . . I mean . . ." A shaky sigh came through the phone. I don't remember Amanda ever making such a noise before. "This is going to make no sense, and I know I'm asking a lot, but can you come to San Diego ASAP? Please? I'll . . . I'll explain everything when you get here."

The message ended. I played it again. And again. And again. I rang her three times. She didn't answer. Rather than try a fourth time, I opened my laptop and bought a one-way ticket on the first flight I found – Premium Economy. Sydney to LAX. Qantas. 6:40am. My credit card balance was not going to like me, and my bank manager was going to have some kind of conniption, but I didn't care. I'd heard Amanda's voice. I was essentially screwed, but in a good way. Life had presented me something, and I was taking that *something*. Live in the present, remember? The second I bought the ticket, all sense of being rattled and flustered vanished.

Despite the fact it was only 3:45 am on a Friday, I rang Heather Renner.

Now Heather had swooped into my life like a ADHD tornado a few years ago, starting our relationship as just a student who worked out in the uni gym before becoming an acquaintance I enjoyed talking with. We hung out occasionally before the whole Maci/Raph/Brendon situation (or as media called it *The American Love Triangle*), and it was during that time she morphed into one of my closest mates. Heather was Maci's best friend while Maci was in Australia, and she somehow insinuated herself into my daily life after Maci went back to the States. I'm not complaining. Heather – who has only two speeds: on and hyper-on – is funny, infectious and almost impossible to say no to. Once upon a time she had a thing for me. Now she has a thing for her ethics professor, a fact I give her a hard time about constantly. Heather is like the sister I never had, and as such, I had no problem calling her at quarter to four in the morning.

She answered on the second ring. There wasn't a hint of sleep-slurred confusion in her voice.

"I've told you before, Biceps," she chirped, her normal exuberance somehow dialed up to fifty, "I will not go for a jog around Bondi with you."

Heather has tried to convince me more than once she wasn't responsible for the nickname "The Biceps" on campus. One of these days I may believe her.

Gaze fixed on my laptop screen and its ticket-purchase confirmation, I grinned. "Not even if I buy you breakfast at Triptych after?" I asked, completing the telephone conversation routine that had developed between us over the last few months.

She laughed. "Not even then. Now tell me what's wrong. There's no way you'd ring at this time unless there was a problem. Is it Maci? Is she okay? I was only talking to her yesterday and she sounded great. What's happened? Is it Raph? It's not Raph, is it? He was flying back from seeing his mum and dad when I was talking to her. Mid-flight in fact. It's not his plane, is it? Tell me his plane hasn't crashed and there's no sign of the bodies. Jesus, how long will it take us to get to—"

"Heather," I cut her off with a chuckle. See what I mean about only two speeds? "Maci and Raph are fine. At least, I assume they are. I haven't spoken to either of them for a few weeks."

A relieved sigh burst through the phone connection. Followed by an angry grunt. "Then why the hell did you let me think they weren't? That's not nice, Osmond. Not nice at—"

"Heather," I repeated her name, firmer this time. If I'd been in her company I'd have grabbed her by the shoulders to hold her still. At times she was like a wriggling puppy. A wriggling puppy with an IQ of 128. "I need you to feed No Direction for a while."

Silence came from the other end. I couldn't help but lick my index finger and make an invisible stroke in the air. Chalk one up for The Biceps.

"I'm heading to the States," I continued, "and I need you to feed my fish while I'm gone."

Silence. Still.

I frowned. "Heather?"

"You're not going over to try to break up Maci and Raph, are you?"

I burst out laughing.

"I take it that's a no?" Wary confusion filled Heather's voice.

"That's a big no," I answered, pushing myself up from my

desk to make my way to my bedroom. I had a suitcase in the cupboard somewhere, I think. "A friend over there needs my help."

At the word *friend* my chest constricted and my balls tightened. It was an odd sensation. Part nerves, part anticipation. All unfamiliar to me.

"A friend?" Curiosity had replaced Heather's confusion. I could almost see her squirming about on the neon-pink shag-fabric swivel chair that held pride of place in her dorm room. "More details, please. If I'm going to be looking after your cherished pet, I need more than just *a friend*. Is this the *friend* you followed to the US a few years ago?"

"I'll leave the spare key to my apartment in my letterbox," I plowed on as I shoved aside a pile of sweatpants from the bottom of my closet, searching for my suitcase. Nope. Not there. "Just three pieces of food once a day. Don't believe him if he makes out he's still hungry after that."

"Are you really going to the States, Brendon?"

I stopped my hunt for the elusive suitcase. In my chest, my heart was thumping faster than normal. Heather rarely called me Brendon. It meant she was serious. Heather rarely did serious. I owed her an explanation.

"Yes, I'm really going," I said, closing my eyes for a moment. An image of Amanda filled my head straight away. Amanda smiling at me, a promise in her eyes I'd stopped believing in a long time ago. "And yes, it *is* the friend I followed to the States a few years ago. Amanda Sinclair."

"Amanda," Heather repeated, something akin to aggression in her voice. I don't know why. Sometimes I have no clue the whys of the female mind. "That's it. So, she wants to have another go at you, does she?"

The censure in her voice threw me. And the venom.

"I take it you don't approve?"

A soft noise sounded through the connection. "I don't. You may not remember what you were like when you came back from chasing after her the last time, but I do. And since then, you've become *my* friend. And I don't like it when my friends are hurt."

I swallowed. My throat felt thick. Like someone had stuffed it full of sand.

"I'm not going to get hurt, Heather. I've moved on from Amanda. Tried to get Maci in the sack, remember?"

Heather grunted. "Fine. I'll feed your fish. But if you come back all gray and limp and broken and mopey like you did the last time, I'm going to beat the crap out of you and take No Direction away. Do you understand?"

"Deal," I answered.

There was no way I was coming back from the US in that state. I *had* moved on. The only reason I was rushing to see Amanda was because we'd once shared something amazing and she clearly needed my help now. I was happy to give her that help. It didn't mean I was expecting her to give me my heart back while I was there. I wasn't even after *her* heart. She was the past. She wasn't a part of my plan for the future.

Sure, I hear you say, that's why you just maxed out your credit card with a plane fare your bank manager wouldn't approve of.

"Okay." Heather didn't sound convinced. "When's your flight? Do you need a lift to the airport?"

I glanced at the radio alarm clock on my bedside table. "Flight's in three hours."

Peals of laughter followed the statement. "Oh man," Heather cackled. "Yeah, sure, you've moved on."

"For that, you can drive me to the airport," I said, returning to the search for my suitcase. "I'll see you in twenty minutes."

Twenty minutes later, after sending Amanda a text informing her of my flight details and staring at my phone for a reply that never came, I climbed into Heather's beat-up, dubiously reliable hatchback. My passport pressed to my butt as I settled into the front passenger seat. In the boot was my gym bag, crammed full of whatever clean clothes I had at hand. My suitcase, it seemed, was AWOL.

Heather took one look at me and rolled her eyes. "You are so going to get your heart handed to you again, you know that, right?"

"Shut up, Heather." I buckled in, wriggling into the seat – I wasn't built for such a small car – and pointed at the dawn-tainted road ahead of us. "Drive."

She drilled me the whole way. It wasn't until I said, "I don't know" for the umpteenth time that I realized just how out of character I was behaving, how many of my own questions were unanswered. Questions I hadn't been able to ask because I hadn't been able to talk to Amanda.

Holy crap, I was flying to American without actually talking to the person I was heading over to see. What the—

"We're here."

I blinked myself back into the interior of Heather's car. Or rather, the exterior. Huh. Between all the *I don't knows* to Heather's interrogation, we'd arrived at Sydney International.

My heart slammed into my throat, a place it never ventured. The only real time my heart made itself known to me was when I was doing fifty-calorie-burn sprints on the assault bike. Going to see Amanda was nowhere near as grueling as that.

Drawing in a slow breath, I waited for Heather to pull to a halt outside the Departure terminal. "Thanks." Before I could open the door, she grabbed my wrist. Hard. Man, I really needed to reassess her upper-body workouts.

"Listen, Osmond," she said, fixing me with a steady stare. *Heather* and *steady* weren't usually a thing. It was both jarring and oddly sweet. "I know you're this big strong guy who prides himself on rolling with life and not letting anything bring you down, and to be honest, you're pretty much the closest thing I've ever seen to a person living in perfect peace with himself, which is incredible."

I grinned at her compliment.

She didn't grin back. In fact, her grip on my wrist tightened. "But I wasn't kidding when I said I'd beat the crap out of you if you come back broken. I will. If you let Amanda screw you up like she did the last time, I'll kick your arse. Then I'll fly to the States and kick her arse, and you don't want to be responsible for America declaring war on Australia, do you? I mean, you're already on Delvania's watchlist after beating the hell out of their princess's bodyguard, you don't want to be added to the American list for inciting a hyperactive Aussie going thermo on one of their citizens, do you?"

A warm fuzziness bloomed in my chest. The realization you have friends who care about your emotional state and kind of take it personally can blow you away. That kind of friendship is a powerful thing, and for the first time since knowing her I recognized how significant Heather was to me, and me to her. We'd been through some slightly weird stuff together – the whole Maci/Raph/Delvania Royal bodyguard/paparazzi riot just to name one – and come out the other side closer. That she was ready to start an international situation over the state of my heart proved it. I leaned across the center console and kissed her on the cheek.

Two things happened. One, she let out a gasp I could only called surprised. And two, she followed that gasp with a melodramatic *Ewww, gross,* and shoved me away.

I laughed. She did the same, rolling her eyes. "Time for you to get out of my car, Biceps," she ordered with mock command. "Let me know how it's going while you're over there, okay?"

"Will do."

It wasn't until her car turned out of the drop-off bay and disappeared from sight that I realized I had a lump in my throat. When the hell had I become so schmaltzy?

Hitching my gym bag up on my shoulder and patting my butt to make sure my passport was still there, I pivoted on my heel and fixed the automatic doors of the Departure terminal with a steady stare.

You may have gathered by now I don't live life the way it's expected of me. When I decided to apply for a Bachelor of Applied Science my school careers advisor *advised* me I was making a mistake. She told me I should concentrate on a job less *cerebral* in nature. *Laborer* was her suggestion. When I was offered a position playing professional football for the Balmain Tigers at the age of eighteen – complete with a six-figure deal sweeter than any junior football player had ever seen – I turned it down. When I was being threatened by a dick bodyguard bigger than me with a Glock permanently under his arm, I punched him in the face and broke his jaw.

Life is to be lived to the fullest, and I lived it that way. But even I had to admit, standing there on the footpath outside the Sydney International Departure Terminal, that dropping everything to fly to the States to see a girl who'd rejected me almost three years ago, without even speaking to her was . . . well, borderline insane.

So why was I doing it? Because I was still hung up on Amanda? Because she still made me horny? Because I wanted to prove to her – and myself – that she didn't have the power to render me defenseless against her any more, and the moment I saw her in the States I'd know a hundred percent it was over?

No. I was doing it because a person once very important to me had asked me to. There was no other reason than that. And life was to be lived. And experienced. And if I didn't do this, I wasn't experiencing it, was I?

How's that for a reason? And a life philosophy?

I refused to think about it any longer. Actually, refused is the wrong term. I *chose* not to think about it any more. This was one of those situations that didn't require thinking.

I strode into the terminal, checked in, watched my over-stuffed gym bag disappear on the luggage conveyor belt, and then made my way to the appropriate gate.

Halfway there, I stopped at an Australian souvenir shop that charged ridiculous prices for stuff I could have bought at a discount shop for less than five bucks. For reasons I didn't question, or think about – remember, I'd put my brain into neutral – I bought a soft toy koala infused with eucalyptus oil, a soft toy kookaburra that laughed when you squeezed it, and a jar of Vegemite. I don't know why. Amanda's younger sister didn't really like me, and a soft toy wasn't going to change that. I bought them anyway.

It was then I realized I hadn't brought along an on-flight bag. I had a thirteen-hour flight ahead of me, and I hadn't brought anything with me apart from my wallet, iPhone and passport. Not even a book. Or a toothbrush and deodorant.

I wasn't new to traveling (Hello? Previous trip to the US), so the fact I was an hour away from climbing onto a plane bound for the other side of the world, without any of the things that would make that trip bearable, hit me hard.

It took me forty minutes – and further credit card abuse – to procure everything I needed: small backpack, travel tooth-brush, toothpaste, deodorant, new charger for my phone (superfluous and expensive given I already have three at home), new noise-canceling earphones (went the cheap route with those, but still, ouch), and travel pillow (Master's of Exercise Physiology, remember? I know the importance of muscular comfort and posture and there was no way those airline–supplied pillows do anything but give you a stiff neck). I even splashed out and bought a pair of loose, long-legged PJ pants to change into come sleep time. Comfort is your friend on long-haul flights.

I also exchanged every Australian note I had in my wallet for US dollars which gave me a grand total of a hundred and thirteen dollars US.

After logging into my iTunes account on my phone and downloading my music library, along with a biography on Arnold Schwarzenegger in case the inflight movies sucked, I stuffed everything into my new backpack, the soft-toy kookaburra laughing constantly as I did. A part of me wondered if it was trying to tell me something. The rest of me ignored it. What the hell does a soft-toy kookaburra know?

As it turned out, I probably should have listened to it. Sometimes living life in the present takes you by the short-and-curlies and you're left wondering what the hell happened.

The Always Series

Unconditional
Unforgettable
Undeniable

The Outback Skies Series

Bound to You
Breathless for You
Burn for You
Bare for You
Better with You

The Heart of Fame Series

Love's Rhythm
Muscle for Hire
Guarded Desires
Steady Beat
Lead Me On
Blame it on the Bass
Getting Played
Blackthorne

ABOUT LEXXIE COUPER

Lexxie Couper started writing when she was six and hasn't stopped since. She's not a deviant, but she does have a deviant's imagination and a desire to entertain readers with her words. Add the two together and you get erotic romances that can make you laugh, cry, shake with fear or tremble with desire. Sometimes all at once.

When she's not submerged in the worlds she creates, Lexxie's life revolves around her family, a husband who thinks she's insane, an indoor cat who likes to stalk shadows, and her daughters, who both utterly captured her heart and changed her life forever.

Lexxie lives by two simple rules – measure your success not by how much money you have, but by how often you laugh, and always try everything at least once. As a consequence, she's laughed her way through many an eyebrow raising adventure. You can find details of her writing at www.LexxieCouper.com

Lexxie Couper